INTERLUDE

TURNAROUND
BOOKS

Acclaim for Rupert Smith

Praise for *Man's World*

'A funny, poignant and ultimately life-
affirming novel about the fractures and
continuities in gay male life.'
Sarah Waters

'Funny, dirty, deeply romantic, *Man's World* is a
wonderfully evocative novel that hurtles
between now and our recent history in a
wild and emotional waltzer ride.'
Jake Arnott

'A sensational book –
funny, smart and compelling.'
Attitude

'I loved this novel.'
Philip Hensher

Other work by Rupert Smith

As Rupert Smith
I Must Confess
Fly on the Wall
Service Wash
Man's World
Grim

As James Lear
The Low Road
The Palace of Varieties
The Back Passage
Hot Valley
The Secret Tunnel
A Sticky End
The Hardest Thing

As Rupert James
Silk
Stepsisters

Non-fiction includes:
Man Enough to be a Woman (with Jayne County)
Physique: the Life of John S. Barrington
EastEnders: The First 20 Years
A Year at Kew
Strictly Come Dancing
Poets of World War One

INTERLUDE
RUPERT SMITH

TURNAROUND
BOOKS

First published in Great Britain in 2014 by
Turnaround Books
Unit 3 Olympia Trading Estate, Coburg Road, London, N22 6TZ
www.turnaround-uk.com

1 3 5 7 9 10 8 6 4 2

Text copyright © 2014 by Rupert Smith
All rights reserved.
Cover image © Dom Agius
Cover designed by Colourworks

A CIP catalogue record for this book is available from the British Library.

ISBN 13: 9781873262863

Printed and bound in the UK by
CPI Group (UK) Ltd, Croydon, CR0 4YY

For my family,
past, present and future

I
Before

Chapter One: Helen

EVERYONE REMEMBERS the scene at the end of *The Interlude* (1959), when Laurence Olivier takes Jayne Mansfield by the arm as they run down the quayside at Southampton docks, the massive bulk of the *Queen Mary* looming behind them. He looks into her eyes and says, 'Oh Rose, my darling, how can I ever live without you?' She blinks, a tear spills down her face and she says (all together now), 'It was fun, baby, but the show's over. Curtain. The end.' She sashays up the gangway while Olivier trudges back to his waiting wife and child, turning up the collar of his overcoat. The ship's horn sounds and the crowd surges forward to wave to departing loved ones. Olivier does not look back. As he bends down to kiss his daughter, he appears to have aged ten years. The camera zooms out to show the *Queen Mary* moving into open water, and the characters whose lives and loves we have followed for ninety minutes are mere specks on the screen.

'It was fun, baby, but the show's over. Curtain. The end.' It's been quoted, or misquoted, so many times by so many comedians, journalists, politicians, drag queens and drunks that it's up there with 'Frankly my dear, I don't give a damn' and 'Don't let's ask for the moon. We have the stars' in the top ten all-time hackneyed movie lines. I've never understood why. It's not particularly witty or elegant. It was better phrased in the book (1955) on which the film was based: 'We had fun, darling, but it's time to bring the curtain down.

The performance is over.' But there's something about the way that Jayne Mansfield says it – a rare flash of sincerity in an otherwise rather jokey career – and about Olivier's slow, internal death in the reaction shot as the violins soar, that elevates it to a Classic Movie Moment. It's that moment – Mansfield's immaculate mask marred by a single tear, Olivier suddenly showing his age – that forms the basis of my grandfather's reputation, and indeed of my family's wealth. For without the film, I am sure that the novel on which it is based and its author, the once-fashionable Edward Barton, would be entirely forgotten.

I've been thinking about *The Interlude* a lot recently, probably because I've got so much time on my hands. I've been thinking about a lot of things. The children are both at school, and Richard is away from home more and more, seemingly accepting any contract that requires him to work at non-commutable distances from London. We've had our fair share of farewell scenes in the last few months – at railway stations, airports, wherever the exciting world of data analysis takes him – and one of these days I'm going to look into his eyes, blink away a tear and say, 'It was fun, baby, but the show's over. Curtain. The end.' It won't have quite the same impact because I'll be going home to a south London semi full of children's toys, rather than sailing in Cunard style across the Atlantic, and Richard will take it as a joke anyway, but in my heart I wonder if, after all these years, the show actually is over. Curtain. The end. Divorce. Custody. Is it?

This afternoon I lit a fire and settled down with a pot of tea, a packet of biscuits and a brand new DVD of *The Interlude*, fresh from the Amazon warehouse, a long-awaited and timely reissue that will bring yet more money into my grandfather's overflowing coffers, not that he's in any fit state to enjoy it. He's in his nineties now, clinging to life in that great big house in the country, seeing no one, least of all my parents, my father, his son. They have barely been on speaking terms since my teens, for reasons that have never been made clear. Quite suddenly, we stopped visiting Grandad just after Grandma died. I didn't question it at the time – you don't at thirteen, you accept such things as part of the incomprehensible nonsense of adulthood – and when I've probed in more recent years, regretting that my own children have never met their famous forebear, I've been advised in no uncertain terms to let sleeping dogs lie. My family is good at secrets and silences.

But that doesn't stop me wondering, as I put a match to the ripped-up brown cardboard of the Amazon package that is serving as kindling, what exactly caused this great undiscussable family rift. Perhaps the movie will enlighten me. Perhaps the performance of Laurence Olivier as the tormented middle-aged playwright embarking on a passionate-but-doomed affair with an actress half his age will offer some clue to the *casus belli*. The character of Derek Dean, the suave, successful author, an ideal husband and father, has always been interpreted as autobiographical, although Edward Barton himself – the suave, successful author, an ideal husband and father – always denied it. There was no affair, he maintained in interviews, he was faithful to his wife. There was no 'Rose'. It was not autobiography but fiction. Discussion over, curtain, the end, although that never stopped the question from being asked. I suspect that Grandfather Edward was well aware of the publicity value of speculation.

The fire is crackling away nicely now, I've closed the curtains and the matinee begins. Digitally remastered on a wide flat screen, it looks so much better than I remember from previous viewings. I saw it once with my parents when I was about eleven – they must have judged me old enough to watch a melodrama about adultery – gathered around our massive family TV on its walnut veneer corner unit next to the fringed shade of the standard lamp. I saw it again at university, on a little portable telly in a grim rented flat in

Birmingham one afternoon when my flatmate Annette and I bunked off a lecture on Alexander Pope to drink supermarket plonk in our pyjamas. We laughed like drains the whole way through, mocking Olivier's cut-glass accent, his obviously dyed hair and air of repressed aloofness, Mansfield's gushy delivery and overwhelming bosoms. We both sobbed a little at the end – the wine had taken effect, I suppose – and Annette turned to me as the credits rolled and said, 'Based on the novel by Edward Barton, that's funny, I wonder if you're related?' and it took a few moments before I said, 'Actually, he's my grandfather'. She laughed and almost expelled wine through her nostrils before she realised I was serious. That's how deep the family rift had gone: I hadn't even told my best friend that my grandfather was a novelist.

Press play.

First surprise: it's in colour, and I'd always remembered it in black and white. Second surprise, obvious from the lush music and establishing shots of the West End at night, all sparkling lights and fog and women in fur coats getting out of Daimlers: this was a film with a socking great big budget. Third surprise, as Olivier/Derek, looking handsome and urbane in black tie, receives the congratulations of an opening-night party: it's really good. The dialogue zips along, the party scene is a little gem, diamonds and champagne and lipstick and flowers, as good as anything the director, Anthony Asquith (*The Importance of Being Earnest, The VIPs*) ever did. Two minutes in and I'm hooked, breathless, tea and biscuits forgotten. Even Jayne Mansfield, as the hard-boiled American actress who claws her way to stardom in Derek's plays and, by way of thanks, breaks his heart, is brilliant. Overshadowed by her breasts, of course, but still brilliant. Hard to believe that two years later her career was all but over, and a few years later still that beautiful bleached head was smashed or severed, depending who you believe, on a road in the Louisiana swamps.

Edward Barton's career didn't fare much better. In 1959, with a hit film and a string of successful novels under his belt, the world was his oyster – but it went off quickly, as oysters do. He was chronically out of sympathy with the new wave of the late 50s and early 60s, and he didn't help matters by adopting a Crusty Old Man persona, appearing on chat shows and game shows in tweed jackets and cravats, pouring scorn on the welfare state, the unions, unmarried mothers, immigrants, the young in general. By 1967 Edward Barton seemed as out of date as Noël Coward, a kitsch throwback to a bygone age, appreciated, if at all, with affectionate irony. The money kept rolling in – such is the power of television, on which *The Interlude* was regularly shown – but for the last forty years my grandfather has been little more than a footnote to post-war English literature. He has not been 'rediscovered'.

This seems strange, given how good the film is, as pleasing in its way as a beautiful piece of furniture, a well-composed photograph, a perfect English garden. The story unfolds with economy and precision, no line wasted, no effect unplanned. Within five minutes we are right inside Derek Dean's gorgeous life – his beautiful home, his beautiful wife and child, so perfect and happy and bright that it's just asking to be smashed into a thousand pieces. And then along comes the war, and with it the irresistible Rose Morgan, the pushy blonde starlet with an eye on the main chance. The affair develops with a sort of mechanical inevitability, Derek compromises his career and his marriage in order to satisfy her ambition and his passion, and then, when Rose has got what she wants and is ready to return to America as a big star, he throws himself at her feet. 'I know you can never love me,' he says, drunk in her dressing room as she powders her face. 'I know I'm nothing to you – just a shadow that disappears as soon as the lights go on. You've played me like a fiddle, and I should be ashamed of myself, but I don't care. Let me come with you.' Olivier, pale and sweaty, his hair in his eyes, plays the scene painfully well; he looks, for a moment, just like Heathcliff, and if I was Jayne Mansfield I'd have been afraid for my pretty neck. She doesn't turn a bleached hair. 'Go back to your wife and child, Derek,' she says, never taking her eyes off the mirror. 'I have to work.' She gives her nose one final dab of powder, pulls her marabou-trimmed peignoir around her, and walks out, leaving Derek – the author of the play that has made her a star – alone in her dressing room, staring into the mirror, surrounded by telegrams and flowers.

'You've played me like a fiddle.' That's another line that people know, and sometimes say in clipped English accents. Most of them probably don't realise where it comes from. It's time they found out.

By the time the *Queen Mary* has pulled out into the Atlantic, the music is swelling and the credits are rolling, I'm a) crying quite freely and b) determined to restore Edward Barton's reputation as one of the great living post-war English novelists. Obviously there are sound economic reasons for doing so: I don't know the details of my grandfather's will, but some of the money, surely, will go to my father as one of Edward's two children, and I, as an only child, stand to inherit the bulk of my parents' estate in the fullness of time. But that's a long way off: my father's not even sixty yet, he could have another thirty years in him, by which time all the money could have gone on care and taxes. Like any mother I'd like to provide for my children, but – scary thought – they could quite easily have children of their own by the time the residue of the Edward Barton estate comes my way. So no – my interest in grandfather's critical reputation is not primarily financial. Nobody could accuse me of mercenary motives. I just think, if you've got a neglected genius in the family, you ought to do something about it.

But what? Re-read the work for starters; there's a handful of novels, mostly out of print. Ask my parents for information. Set up a meeting with Edward himself, if he's still in possession of his marbles. Find out if there really was a 'Rose' after all; maybe, with my grandmother long since cold in her grave, he's ready to tell the truth. And then, if it all falls into place – what? Write a book? Well, I've always wanted to. Meant to, in fact, but marriage came along, and after marriage, children, and seven years in which day blurred into day in a ceaseless round of feeding, cleaning, bathing, washing, shopping, cooking and, when at all possible, sleeping. Not much time for writing, or thinking, or any of the other things that used to mean so much to me, like sex. For the amount of sex I've had with Richard in the last five years I might as well be single.

Time for a change. Children at school, husband away, opportunities to be seized, and what greater challenge than to explore the big secret at the heart of my family – to reveal the truth, to restore a reputation and, as a kind of by-product, secure the financial future of my children and grandchildren. Suddenly, it seems urgent. I switch off the TV and race upstairs. High up on one of the bookshelves is an old paperback copy of *The Interlude*, signed and presented by my grandfather when I was far too young to read it, unopened for decades.

It is up there, on those rarely dusted shelves, that my project begins.

I'd no sooner blown the dust off the top of the book than Annette arrived with the children. It's her turn to do the afternoon school run this week, which means a cup of tea and a chat while her two and my two roll around in front of the TV. 'Oh, Mrs Bainbridge is such a *pain*,' she said, picking up on a conversation that we were having on Friday, in her house, when I was on the school run. 'She just seems to undermine everything that Holly does.' Holly is her seven-year-old. 'I mean, it's clear that she's a gifted child, but if you listened to what Mrs Bainbridge says you'd think she was, you know' – she lowered her voice to a whisper – 'retarded or something. It's not on. I'm bringing it up at the next PTA.' I switched off, poured tea and sliced cake. Time passed. And then I heard Annette say, 'And Richard. How is Richard?'

'He's fine. At least he was, last time I saw him.'

Her eyebrows came up.

'What do you mean?' She was on the scent of scandal, like a dog after a fox.

'He's away all week, and when he's here he's only interested in the children.'

'You are ... okay, aren't you? You and Richard?'

'Of course we are.' Pause. 'But ...'

'What?'

'Seven-year itch, I suppose.'

She didn't like this, and scowled again. Adultery would be punishable by stoning if Annette had her way; I sometimes wonder if she's secretly Muslim. 'Don't be stupid,' she said.

'I know, I know. I love Richard.'

'Of course you do.'

'And I love the kids.'

'Right.'

'But don't you sometimes wonder ... ?' From the look on her face it was clear that Annette has never wondered, and disapproves of wondering in others. Change the subject. 'I'm thinking of doing a course, now that Lucy's going to school.'

She sounded suspicious. 'What in?'

'Creative writing.'

'Why?'

Because I am bored out of my mind. 'Because I always wanted to write.'

'Didn't we all,' said Annette, 'in those days.' As if writing is like love bites and tongue piercings, best forgotten after the age of 23.

'There's a course at the Milton. Two hours every Tuesday. Starts next week.'

'Why don't you do something useful like cookery or dressmaking?'

'It might be fun. Meet some new people.'

'Have you told Richard?'

I hadn't, but I said, 'Of course, he thinks it's a great idea.'

'I hope you know what you're doing.' She went to collect Holly and Poppy – plant names were in during Annette's pregnancies – leaving me feeling as if I'd just admitted to an affair.

'Give my love to Richard,' she said in a pointed way as she was leaving, shepherding the girls ahead of her.

I joined Ben and Lucy in front of the TV wondering if, after all, Annette was right to be suspicious.

Milton College is predictably shabby, the walls dusty and cobwebby, the parquet in the lobby almost black with dirt. The smell of chalk and disinfectant hits you the moment you walk in. Judging by the people milling around noticeboards, I'm not going to be making a new set of friends here; these are the job seekers, the early retired, the mad and the sad. There's an air of well-intentioned hopelessness about the place. I almost turned straight round and went home.

There were ten of us in the classroom waiting for the tutor to turn up, seated as far as possible from each other. Perhaps in weeks to come we would bond, but for now I had the sinking feeling that this little stab at freedom and self-fulfilment was already doomed. Annette was right, I thought, the future is an endless string of afternoons at her house or mine, the children growing older, the conversations remaining the same, only the names of the teachers changing.

And then he walked into the room. Harry Ross. The prospectus had not prepared me for his black curly hair, tanned skin, bright blue eyes and open-necked denim shirt. He sat on the edge of his desk, strong thighs in jeans just feet away from me. *Double denim, how awful*, said a niggling voice in my mind, quickly silenced; it suited him.

He said, 'Morning all,' the voice deep and humorous with an estuarial tang, possibly fake. 'I'm Harry, and I'll get to know you all over the next few weeks.' He smiled – even white teeth between full pink lips, framed by dark stubble – and the class smiled with him. The temperature in the room seemed to increase. Eight of us were women, and of the two men one looked as if he was not immune to the tutor's charms. The other was primarily there for warmth and shelter.

'I'm not going to embarrass you by asking you who you are, why you're here and what you hope to get out of this course, blah blah blah.' He picked up an A4 file. 'I'm supposed to hand out a load of feedback forms and get you to tick a load of boxes.' Now there seemed to be an Irish lilt to the voice. 'But that can wait. We're here to talk about writing.'

He invested the word with all the longing and frustration that brought us to this shabby room on a gloomy October morning. Writing. A chance to express ourselves, to escape ourselves, to mine the vein of gold beneath the rubble of our daily lives. If anyone could find it, it was Harry Ross. At least nine would-be authors had just cast him as the romantic lead. The tenth was unconscious, huddled into the radiator.

For forty minutes he held us spellbound. He read some of his favourite pieces, which seemed also to be our favourite pieces – from Thomas Hardy, Virginia Woolf, Marian Keyes (to show he wasn't a snob). By coffee time we were putty in his hands. We were garrulous as we queued up for the canteen's brown, burnt-tasting liquid. Oh, that bit from *Tess*! Hands went to bosoms. Oh, Virginia Woolf, haven't read her since college, always loved her. Oh, I always felt a bit guilty about reading Marian Keyes, but since the children came along ...

'You're Helen Barton.'

I'm 'one of those modern women', as my mother calls us, who hasn't taken my husband's name. 'I am.' His hand was on my arm, and he steered me towards a table.

'Granddaughter of the more famous Edward?'

We sat on institutional plastic chairs. 'How on earth could you know that?'

'Hunch.' He smiled – lines appeared in the most attractive places. 'Plus you have a copy of *The Interlude* sticking out of your bag.'

'Quite the detective.'

'What's he like?'

'My grandfather? Old. Kind. Like a grandfather.'

'Do you know him well?'

'Not terribly. He's very reclusive.'

'You don't see him.'

'No. But I should.'

'Too right you should!' The east London lad was back. "E's one of the greats!'

'You really think so?'

'Not fashionable, but' – he ran his fingers through glossy curls – 'who cares about fashion? A good book is a good book, end of.'

'Stuffy, middle class, passé. That's what the critics said.'

'What do critics know?' He pronounced it without the central 't' – *cri'ics*. 'Your grandfather's a writer's writer.' *A wri'er's wri'er.*

I recognised my cue. 'You're a writer, then?'

'Of course.' He glanced round the canteen. 'This pays the bills.'

'Had anything published?'

His face darkened, and he pushed a couple of grains of sugar around the Formica tabletop. 'My agent is sending something out at the moment. I don't expect any of those fools will get it. It's not exactly an easy read.'

I was going to ask what it was about, but stopped myself just in time. Instead, I glanced at my watch – the break was over – and said, 'Well, good luck with that.'

We returned to the classroom, and for the remaining half hour laboured over the various types of novel that we might attempt to write – the novel of ideas, the 'Bildungsroman', phrases and labels I hadn't heard since college. By the end of the session, I had already completed (in my mind) a searing account of the interior life of a woman ground down by the tyranny of motherhood, the first chapter of which I was determined to deliver into Harry's large, tanned hands next week.

'Remember,' he said, as a parting shot, 'make the reader work. Don't give them what they expect. Subvert their expectations.'

Little wonder that he remained unpublished – and yet that dark curly hair, those piercing blue eyes, would look so very right on a book jacket.

In the week that followed I made a big effort to see everything in literary terms. Peeling vegetables became a metaphor – stripping away the outer layers to reveal the truth – although what truth there is in a carrot that's been knocking around the bottom of the crisper drawer for a fortnight I couldn't say. Onions seemed even more exciting – peel away layer after layer, and you're left with – what? Nothing. Perhaps the process of peeling was the 'truth' I was seeking. Harry would like that. I ruined quite a few onions, and ended up with a tasteless stew, but it seemed a small price to pay for a revelation.

As I peeled or chopped or stirred, as I hoovered and wiped, loaded and unloaded appliances, ironed, folded and shopped, I began to think that my life, although profoundly boring on the surface, was quite interesting in literary terms.

A married woman deeply immersed in the process of child-rearing, her inner life submerged but, like an underground river, ready to burst out in a stream – yes, good that, river, stream – of consciousness. A bored housewife, the starting point of novels from *Madame Bovary* onwards. The potential was massive. I was on the brink of something. I could hardly wait to get it all down on paper.

Perhaps I have inherited something of my grandfather's talent: the phrase 'it often skips a generation' popped into my head. *Helen Barton, granddaughter of the great post-war novelist Edward.* What a great angle for magazine features. What a useful calling card when it came to agents and publishers.

Richard is still away, the children are in bed and the TV is switched off. I recline on the sofa, a blanket over my lap, a glass of wine within reach, and open *The Interlude.*

'To my beloved granddaughter Helen,' reads the inscription in flowing blue ink that bleeds slightly into the cheap, absorbent paper of the title page, 'from Edward Barton'. Not 'from Grandad'. No date, and I don't remember receiving it; it has just always been around on bookshelves. I skimmed it some time in my teens, but that's it. Time to discover what makes my grandfather 'one of the greats'.

First published in Great Britain in 1955.
This edition published in 1959, reprinted in 1960 (twice), 1961, 1962 (twice).
© Edward Barton 1955.

The paper has yellowed around the edges, the glue has dried and cracked. It smells musty and dusty, of libraries and second-hand bookshops. Please let me enjoy it. Please don't let it be a disappointment.

There's an epigraph on the page before Chapter One, four lines of verse that I don't remember seeing before.

What came of her? The bitter nights
Destroy the rose and lily,
And souls are lost among the lights
Of painted Piccadilly.

James Elroy Flecker, 'The Ballad of Camden Town'

James Elroy Flecker: Google him tomorrow. Good quote, though. Very atmospheric. I feel a tingle, as if I'm being tugged back in time to a West End of smog and electric light, of tarts with cigarettes clustering around Eros, of men in soft felt hats.

I'm about to turn the page, but suddenly I stop. What came of her? What came of who? *Her* – the mysterious Rose. Rose: of course, there she is – 'the rose and lily'. The clues begin on the very first page, and I must be alert to them, a detective as well as a reader. 'Souls are lost among the lights of painted Piccadilly.' There's a tragedy here.

I shiver, and pull the blanket over my chest, tucking it under me. Wetting the middle finger of my right hand, I turn the page.

Chapter Two: The Interlude

(Bond and Lock, London, 1955)

I WOULD NOT SAY that I left home at the age of eighteen, rather that home left me. My parents' affection, never spontaneous or gladly given, withdrew like the tide throughout the years of my adolescence, leaving us stranded in a silent house, awkward in each other's presence. I went to school, my father went to work, my mother stayed at home, and in the evenings we went our separate ways – I to my bedroom, my father to his study, my mother to what she still called the drawing room. And there we waited out the hours until we could retire. When I think back to that time, I hear above all the slow ticking of the clock.

The second hand delivered me at length to my eighteenth birthday, the giving and receiving of cards at breakfast, and with them one of my father's sporadic displays of interest in my future.

'You will be leaving school soon, Derek.'

'Yes, Father.'

'You will, of course, wish to go to university.'

'Yes, Father.'

'Have you chosen a college?' My father was a Cambridge man, and expected me to follow his example. Caius, preferably, scene of his golden youth before the war, before the long, slow pageant of disappointments that made up his adult life.

'Yes, Father.'

'You have?' He smashed the top of his boiled egg. 'That is a surprise.'

I filled my mouth with toast.

'And may one be permitted to know,' said my father, picking minute fragments of eggshell from his spoon, 'whom you have favoured with your choice?'

I swallowed. 'University College ...'

'Oxford?' His face darkened. 'Well, I must say ...'

'London.'

My mother made a whimpering noise, and dabbed her pale lips with the corner of her napkin. My father slowly, methodically transferred the yolk of his egg to a thin triangle of toast and then, satisfied that the surface was covered evenly, laid down his spoon.

'London?'

'Yes, Father.'

'I should have thought,' he said, 'that you would have consulted me before throwing away your education on – where was it?'

'University College.'

'Quite so.' He picked up knife and fork, cut off a geometrically precise corner of toast and raised it to his lips.

'It's a good college.'

He chewed, swallowed, and sipped his tea. 'I suppose not everyone is university material.'

'It is a university. The University of London.'

'Cambridge rejected you, I take it.'

'I did not apply to Cambridge.'

'Ah.' Another triangle of toast, another sip of tea. 'On the advice of your headmaster, perhaps.'

'No.'

'Then why?'

'Because I want to go to London. I want to be at the heart of things, not stuck in the middle of nowhere.'

'One hears that sort of thing so often from people who could not get in.'

'Cambridge is not the centre of the universe.'

My mother rang for the maid. In her presence further argument would be impossible. My father stood, wiped his hands and folded his napkin. 'Perhaps, under the circumstances, it is for the best. You are not strong, Derek.'

The maid came in. 'You may clear, Margaret.'

'Yes, ma'am.'

My father left the room; in two minutes he would walk up the road, furled umbrella in one hand, briefcase in the other, bowler hat on his head whatever the weather, to the station and thence by train to Marylebone, by underground to the City and his desk. The same every day for twenty years, and then home again in reverse order. The daily routine of a Cambridge man.

You are not strong, Derek. The words I grew up hearing, day after day, year after year, since a bout of polio in early infancy left me with a weakened left leg and a 'delicate' chest. An excuse for keeping me away from other children and rough games, keeping me in bed at the first sign of a cold, alone, with only books for company. No brothers or sisters. My mother, too, was 'delicate'; a second child, it was assumed, would have killed her. I grew up in a sickroom atmosphere, in a state of permanent, chronic invalidity, and it was this as much as anything that made me yearn for the rough and tumble of city life, to exchange silence and closed curtains for the bustle and smoke of London.

That, and a longing to begin.

My life had been an extended hush before the curtain is raised, a breath long held, a prelude. Nothing happened, or was allowed to happen. While Europe laboured through war and revolution, while all around were strikes and elections, massacres and assassinations, I stood apart, connected at best through newspaper headlines and radio broadcasts, through books and films, to the world of cause and effect, of love and hate and blood and bone. I was the eternal onlooker, the spectator, and while even my schoolfellows in a provincial town in the heart of the Home Counties succumbed, occasionally, to a broken arm or a broken heart, I watched and envied and waited for my turn.

And now my turn had come.

I would leave home in October, exchanging the comforts of a large suburban villa for a small cell-like room in Bloomsbury with a gas fire and a narrow metal bedstead, a rickety, ink-stained desk and a hard wooden chair. And it was on that simple set that the curtain would rise, and the first act would commence.

The room was at the top of a dilapidated house in Torrington Place, its fanciful red brick facade encrusted with curlicues and ogees and I know not what, suggesting a more prosperous past. Into those four floors were crammed twelve rooms, getting smaller the higher you climbed up the creaky stairs. The landlady lived in the basement, whence came a constant smell of boiled bacon, and appeared without fail whenever the front door opened. She was short and round and Irish, plentiful grey hair piled up in rolls and buns, a faded blue apron covering heavy woollen skirts. House lore suggested that she had a husband down there, possibly even a child or a grandchild, but these were never seen, and the legend passed from one generation of tenants to the next, embellished a little each time, until that bacon-scented basement became a fabulous realm about which, like Heaven, we could only speculate.

Most of Mrs Flanagan's tenants were undergraduates, and all of us male. The largest of the rooms on the first floor front – the room with the oriel window and commanding views of leafy Torrington Place – was reserved for postgraduates;

the current incumbent, a tall, thin, stooping man with wispy moustache, had been there for three years, researching a doctorate on fourteenth-century monasticism and living even more frugally than his subjects. He brewed endless pots of tea on the gas ring on the landing, using each set of tea leaves three times, drying them out on newspaper in his room, so poor was he. His long, tombstone teeth were stained brown from tannin, his moustache dyed yellow by the matchstick-thin cigarettes he rolled when funds allowed. I saw him, one morning, washing at the sink in the one bathroom we all shared; he looked like a skeleton, ribs and shoulder blades barely covered by the palest of grey skin.

Cold and hunger and dirt did not frighten me, however. Even the climb from the hallway, with its loose black-and-white tiles, up four flights to what must once have been the servants' bedrooms, could not dampen my spirits, although, with my weak chest and leg, it sometimes felt like a very long climb indeed. Forced to make the ascent several times a day, I found my leg growing stronger, my lungs bigger, my breath more sound. I took to walking in Regent's Park every morning before lectures, at first a gentle stroll around the Inner Circle, where the last few roses defied the coming winter, but later around the entire circumference of the Outer Circle, saying good morning to the camels at the zoo, sometimes breaking into a slow trot. For the first time I had colour in my cheeks and muscle on my limbs, my eyes shone and my hair seemed to thicken. I husbanded my coppers and went to the Greek barber's on Euston Road, emerging sleek with Brylcreem, the parting razor sharp, the back of my neck smooth as silk. I no longer looked, or felt, like a child. I was a young man – and I could see, from the glances of female students, that the change had been noticed.

Reading English Literature in a central London college in those years between the wars – in that peaceful interlude between the two great acts of destruction that define our century – was as pleasant a form of lotus-eating as I can now imagine. Bloomsbury still stank of art and letters and tantalising whispers of sexual freedom and for us, the young, it was a religion. We glimpsed the high priests and priestesses walking through fallen leaves in Russell Square and Bedford Square, shabbily dressed, their eyes haunted by dreams and memories, like opium eaters gazing through the fog of consciousness to fantastical visions beyond the brick and smoke of London.

> Weave a circle round him thrice,
> And close your eyes with holy dread,
> For he on honey-dew hath fed,
> And drunk the milk of Paradise.

In tutorials and seminars we discussed Chaucer, Shakespeare, Milton, Dryden and Pope, Wordsworth, Coleridge and Keats. In our bedrooms and in the cafes around Bloomsbury and Fitzrovia we read Orwell and Waugh, Maugham, Woolf and Huxley and (although we barely admitted it to each other) devoured each new Agatha Christie the moment it was published. We studied the sculptures at the Museum, heard poetry declaimed in pubs and, every week, went to cinemas in Camden Town or Leicester Square to see gangster films and horror films, Bette Davis and Charlie Chaplin. For all except the wealthiest, the theatre was beyond our reach.

It was a rich stew, the ingredients thrown in with the carelessness of youth, but there was something missing – the salt, the spice, the one ingredient that would give flavour to the whole. I read about love in Chaucer and Shakespeare, I saw it enacted on the screen by Fred Astaire and Greta Garbo, or on the canvases hanging in the National Gallery. I knew what it looked like, even how it felt – in theory. We talked about it, my friends and I, over those never-ending cups of tea and frugal meals in steamed-up cafes, during walks around the park in which we said that we would never marry for money, we would never let convention stand in the way of passion, that we considered ourselves free from the constraints that hobbled our parents' generation. We were moderns, not Victorians, and we lived, like Tosca, for art and love. But of the practical side of love I knew nothing. There were girls with whom one shared those frugal meals and with whom one might, perhaps, hold hands in the park. Girls who looked at one in a certain way, lips parted in expectation of a kiss that never came, girls who sighed over poetry and paintings, who dreamed of Robert Donat and Clark Gable and, perhaps, of romance closer to home. But I had neither the means nor the inclination to take these girls on dates. And so a year passed, and a long, eventless summer at home, with no knowledge of the passion that inspired the poets. I was free, yes, but what good was freedom without knowledge?

Knowledge was coming, lurking in the future like the serpent in the garden, and with knowledge came love and the bitter sting of regret, the pain of exile from paradise. There was much else I had read about but not known – remorse, jealousy, the ashen taste of sated lust – all of it waiting for me, the sweet and the sour, the joy and the sorrow that would bring me at last to man's estate.

It began, as these things do, unremarkably.

There was at that time a small theatre in University College – not yet the large, fully equipped theatre that would replace it, little more, really, than a room with a raised platform for a stage, curtains hung from a wire that was screwed into crumbling walls, and space enough for sixty chairs packed into tight rows. It was here that the Dramatic Society gave its occasional presentations, or the Light Opera Group delighted us with selections from Gilbert and Sullivan, Offenbach and Lehar. Very occasionally the theatre was leased to visiting companies who served up more advanced fare – Ibsen, Shaw and Masefield, selections from the French and the German and sometimes the Russian, although the college authorities viewed that with suspicion. In the autumn term of my second year, I was one of eight people who attended a production of Ibsen's *Ghosts* by a touring outfit calling themselves The Company, five actors who also sold tickets and programmes, operated the curtains and lights and, in the interval, poured glasses of weak orange squash while still in their costumes and make-up. Five of us returned for the second half – just the same number as were on the stage – and followed the story of jealousy, sickness and incest to its bitter, but unintentionally comic, end. In the closing moments, as Mrs Alving, a large, blowsy woman with dyed red hair and a full bosom, nursed her dying son Osvald, the lights faded on this pitiful scene. 'Mother, mother,' said Osvald, as his brain softened, 'give me the sun ... give me the sun ...' The actor who was operating the lights, and who had appeared earlier as Pastor Manders, gingerly closed the gates around the hot bulb, achieving the twilight effect at considerable risk of burnt fingers. But he appeared to have been refreshing himself with something stronger than orange squash – we had already noted his red nose and a tendency to fumble lines. As Mrs Alving sobbed dramatically into her hands, Pastor Manders stumbled, bringing the lamp down with him, inadvertently flooding the stage with broad artificial sunlight. The actors, one dying, the other grieving, looked up in horrified surprise as their co-stars hastily drew the curtain, leaving only Pastor Manders's feet visible. We hurried out, and contained our laughter as long as we could.

We were reliving the moment over halves of bitter in a pub on Tottenham Court Road when, suddenly, the bar became quiet, and my loud, exaggerated delivery of 'Mother, give me the sun' echoed into absolute silence. A cold draught and sidelong glances told me all I needed to know. I turned and faced the considerable bulk of Mrs Alving, copious red hair pinned up, a fox fur coat pulled tight around her shoulders, and a look on her face that turned the beer to vinegar in my stomach.

'Young man,' she said, when my embarrassment had reached its apex, 'it is unkind to make fun of other people's misfortunes.' For a moment she looked like Lady Macbeth as portrayed by Ellen Terry in the Sargent portrait, all heavy limbs, flashing eyes and cruel scarlet mouth. I shrank as if from a blow. 'Perhaps,' she said, 'you think you can do better.' I looked at the floor. 'But perhaps not.'

My friends, far from leaping to my defence, seemed suddenly interested in their shoes, their fingernails, their beer mats. And then the door opened again, and a tall, distinguished man in a black cape and wide-brimmed hat, sporting a full, well-shaped beard, appeared behind her. We had recently seen him impersonating Jacob Engstrand, Ibsen's hapless carpenter. 'Now now, my dear, there is no need for unpleasantness.' His voice was deep and rounded, very different from the cockney accent he had essayed for the role. 'I'm sure no harm was meant.' He removed his hat, and extended the gesture into a sweeping bow. 'May I present myself. Terence Black.' The hair was combed carefully to conceal a bald patch, and looked dyed. 'And this is my wife, Leonie.'

Unaccustomed to bowing, I inclined stiffly from the waist; one of my friends sniggered. 'Derek Dean.' Black took my hand and pumped it. 'I hope we have not caused offence.'

'Pish! No offence in the world, dear boy, no offence in the world. Nothing that can not be washed away with drink. Give me a bowl of wine, in this I bury all unkindness. Brutus, dear boy, I played him opposite Frank Benson, to no little acclaim, now, come along, let us libate.' He put an arm around my shoulders and steered me to the bar. 'Beer for me, beer! And a whisky to follow. And for the lady, port. Large. Hers being, I feel, the greater grievance.'

I handed my money to the barmaid, leaving myself nothing for food or books. By the time I returned to the table carrying a tray, the Blacks had established themselves in my circle, she in a chair that she occupied like a throne, he perched on the end of the banquette where he could stretch out his long legs. I found a stool, and took up a place on the perimeter, a distant satellite around the burning golden sun that was Leonie Black. Four undergraduates who, just moments ago, had been laughing at her, were now held rapt as anecdotes fell from her full red lips like ripe fruit from the vine.

'And darlings,' she said, 'the time we were in Eastbourne, was it, Terence? Eastbourne or Bournemouth or one of those ghastly coastal graveyards, playing in oh, what was it, something by Maeterlinck, I forget which' – she lowered her voice, as if sharing a joke – 'they're all the same, aren't they?'

'*Pelléas and Mélisande*,' said Terence, wiping his wet whiskers with a pocket handkerchief.

'Oh! Mélisande! Now there was a role! Who writes like that today?' She sighed, and drank half her port. 'Act Three, I am discovered at the castle window combing my blonde tresses. A wig, darlings, because I am naturally *rousse*.' She patted the back of her hair, the colour of which owed something to henna, then set her arms out to declaim. 'My long locks fall foaming to the threshold of the tower, My locks await your coming all along the tower, and so on and so forth, although how her *hair* could await him I never understood, but it's the poetry that matters, the wonderful misty symbolism, don't you think?'

Four heads nodded.

'And then Pelléas enters, the ardent young lover, oh, as handsome as the sun! How the ladies of Eastbourne gasped!'

'Holla, ho ho!' said Terence, shading his eyes with his hand, peering into a misty, symbolic distance.

'Who is there?'

'I, I and I! What art thou doing there at thy window, singing like a bird?'

Eleanora held an arm across her bosom, and turned away. 'I am doing my hair for the night.'

'Is it that I see upon the wall? I thought you had some light!'

'I have opened the window, it is too hot in the tower, it is beautiful tonight.' Her voice dropped from Mélisande's girlish soprano to her own rich mezzo. 'And then I lean out of the window, which was only a hole in a painted plywood flat, with me standing on a stool behind, and he says ...'

'Do not stay in the shadow, Mélisande! Lean forward till I see your unbound hair.'

'I am frightful so,' she piped.

'Lean out, lean out, let me come nearer thee.'

'And then I have to say, "I cannot come nearer thee, I am leaning out as far as I can," which was all too true, darlings, because somehow I had become wedged in the window, which the damn fool carpenter had cut far too small, so there was my head and shoulders and my gorgeous tumbling locks which had so bewitched Pelléas on one side, and the rest of me teetering on a stool on the other, and something had to give.'

'Give me at least thy hand tonight,' said Terence, reaching up.

'Well, my hands were stuck behind the wall, and I say no, no, no, and he says ...'

'Yes, yes, yes!'

'And then I try to wriggle my fingers through just here, by my *poitrine*, and there is the most sickening sensation of falling and breaking, the stool simply flies out from under my feet and for a moment I am suspended in midair, the flat starts to tip forward, there is nothing I can do, I am falling, falling ... Will I break my nose on the stage? Is this how it ends for Leonie Black? Eastbourne holds its breath. I see the stage rushing up to meet me, I am helpless, I scream, and I fall ...'

'Straight into my arms!'

'Ah! He catches me, and for a moment staggers under the weight of the entire castle which has just dropped upon him, but the audience is on its feet, cheering, cheering, I doubt very much whether Monsieur Maeterlinck ever received such an ovation, and by the time we had got to the end of Act Five, when I die reaching out my feeble arms towards the deformed child I have just brought into the world, there isn't a dry eye in the house. Oh, they cheered and cheered, didn't they, Billy?'

'Cheered and cheered, my dear.'

'Bouquets and champagne and oysters. Wonderful, wonderful days.'

They sighed into their drinks.

'And so, you see,' she said, setting down her empty glass in the middle of the table, 'a little mishap such as befell us tonight barely registers on one's consciousness. Live theatre! Alive! Alive!' She raised her arms, looking more like Lady Macbeth than ever, and then, as every eye fixed upon her, threw her head back and laughed, showing all her teeth. 'Don't look so frightened, darlings! I don't bite! Especially,' she said, nodding towards her glass, 'if I am occupied with a drink.'

Throughout this little performance, Terence Black watched me carefully. As the other students clustered around Leonie, begging for more stories, he beckoned me towards him. A thick gold band gleamed on his ring finger.

'A brave woman,' he said.

'Yes.'

'A noble spirit, both on stage and off. Quick to anger, quicker to forgive. And yet such things wound her deeply.'

'I'm sorry.'

'Tonight's little escapade,' he said, 'is, I'm afraid, but one of many. And we shall have to let the old boy go.'

'I see.' I did not know what else to say.

'A great performer once, of course. Worked with Beerbohm Tree, George Du Maurier, all the greats. Hard to believe it now but alas, not the first career undone by drink.'

'How sad.'

'And that leaves us in a rather awkward situation.'

'I suppose it would.'

'A company of four, with parts for five.'

'You might double up.'

'Yes, dear boy, we might as you say double up. Quite possible, and we have done it before. Not for the Ibsen, alas, but I suppose we might suspend the Ibsen for the time being. Do you think the students would mind?'

'Not terribly.'

'No.' He stroked his beard, never taking his eyes off me. 'Not terribly.'

'I mean, it was wonderful, but ... '

'Hardly the draw it once was, hmm? Not the great *succès de scandale* that it was in our fathers' day? No. I suppose to the younger generation Ibsen is *vieux jeu*.'

'Maybe.'

'And yet she loves the part. Mrs Alving. Gives herself to it – almost too much. It exhausts her.'

Leonie's eyes were sparkling, her cheeks flushed, conjuring pictures from the air and drinks from the students.

'So I see.'

'And one must remain above all *connected*, don't you think? To the greater tides of art, and indeed of life itself.'

'Undoubtedly.'

'We have a new piece almost ready to go into the repertoire,' he said. 'I wonder ... '

'And the theatre booked for two more nights.'

'Quite so. Two more nights.' He seemed to be thinking something through, sipping his beer, always watching me. I lit a cigarette to disguise my unease, and offered him one. He took it without comment. 'Yes, I wonder.'

'What do you wonder?' I offered him a match.

'As you were, so to speak, part of the problem, could you perhaps be part of the solution?'

'I don't understand.'

'I will speak frankly.' He inhaled deeply, blew out a long, grey cone of smoke. Gales of laughter broke out from the table; Leonie's audience was growing as more drinkers pulled up their chairs. She was considerably more successful in the saloon bar than she had been in *Ghosts*.

'Do you act?'

'I? Never.'

'Dance?'

'Do I dance?'

'Yes. Dance. Don't worry, dear boy, I am not asking you to join me in a quickstep. I wish to know, simply, whether you can move.'

'Move?'

'Move! Move! It's like addressing a parrot!' He calmed himself with beer; drinks were flowing freely now from bar to table. None came to me. 'I take it that, like most young men of your generation, you go to dances.'

'When I can,' I said, remembering awkward shuffles around crowded floors with the daughters of my parents' friends.

'I knew it. You have a dancer's physique. Stand up.'

'What?'

'Stand! Now!'

I stood.

'Chin up! Shoulders back! Stomach in! Good.' Terence surveyed me. 'How tall are you?'

'Five foot eleven. I had polio as a ...'

He ignored that. 'Good. Good. A forty-inch chest, I suppose, and perhaps a thirty-inch waist. The details I will leave to our wardrobe mistress.'

'The details of what?'

'Oh, dear boy, did I not say? The details of your costume.'

'I don't understand.'

'You are going to perform for me. Tomorrow. In a world premiere of a new dance drama. That means no lines to learn. Just moves. I suppose you can manage that.'

'No! I mean, I've never performed in public before.'

'Come now, this is no time for false modesty. Hold out your arms – so, and so.' He pushed my arms up to the side, at ninety degrees to my body. 'There. Now relax. Let them rest in the air like wings, like wings.' I did the best I could, feeling my arms curving inwards, the hands heavy on my wrists, imagining my fingers to be feathers. 'I see potential, yes, definite potential! Now relax the waist, transfer the weight to the right leg, that's it, let the left knee go, and circle the head from the neck, round, round, that's right!'

I did as I was told, horribly conscious of the display I was making.

'Come and see me tomorrow morning, first thing. First thing, mind you! Ten o'clock!'

'But I have lectures.'

'What can you learn from them that you cannot learn from *me*?' He stood too, as tall as me, his great square beard sticking out like something from the Assyrian room at the museum. 'This is education, boy. This!' He gestured around him – the group held rapt around his wife, the smoke-stained walls of the bar, the haphazard sporting prints and dingy brasses.

'What must I do?'

'Tomorrow night, boy, you will appear in the first performance of a new piece by Terence Black. A dance drama inspired by the poetry and paintings of William Blake. I suppose even you have heard of William Blake.'

'Yes. Even I.'

'It has long been my dream to present my interpretation of the *Songs of Experience*. Have you read them?'

'Some of them.'

His brows lowered. 'Which ones?'

Damn Blake: which were *Songs of Innocence*, which of *Experience*? '"The Tyger",' I said.

'Of course, of course "The Tyger", children read "The Tyger". Another!'

Something about a rose. 'O Rose thou art sick,' I said, unable to remember the title.

'Good!' He clapped his hands, and sat. 'The invisible worm that flies in the night, and so forth. His dark secret love doth thy life destroy.' He sighed. 'Ah, yes. Have you ever known a dark secret love, dear boy?'

'Not yet.'

'Good answer. For you surely will. You surely will. What is your name?'

'Derek Dean.'

'It will do, I suppose, unless you would prefer to be ... Russian. Dimitri Deanovich, or some such?'

'No thank you.'

'Perhaps for the best. Very well, Derek Dean.' We shook hands. 'Tomorrow, at the crack of dawn.' He handed me a soiled card, an address in Kentish Town. 'And now, I must drag my beloved wife away from her admirers before they demand too much of her.'

Several drinks later, they left.

'Your role,' said Terence, striding around the attic room that served as The Company's rehearsal space, 'is that of the bard. Hear the voice of the bard, who present, past and future sees, and so on, tum-te-tum-te-tum, highly metrical, do you hear?' He stamped his foot in time, raising dust from bare floorboards. 'Tum-te-tum-te-tum. I'm sure you can follow that. Whose ears have heard the holy word that walked among the ancient trees. Come on, Derek, walk! Walk! In time! Left and right and left, pause, left and right and left. Good. Now hold this.' He handed me a piece of painted wood cut in the shape of a lyre. 'And strum, strum, strum. Keep walking! Strum and walk, strum and walk, that's it, you can do it, and rest.'

We had about seven hours in which to prepare the world premiere of *Songs of Experience*, a dance drama by Terence Black. I had arrived in Kentish Town punctually at ten o'clock, glancing over my shoulder all the way through Camden lest the college authorities apprehend me for cutting lectures. The Blacks' notion of timekeeping was predictably lax. Leonie came to the door in a dressing gown, her hair loose and a sleepy look on her face. It took a few moments of confused conversation on the doorstep before I could convince her that I was neither a salesman nor a creditor.

'Oh my goodness!' The light dawned, and she beamed, opening her arms. 'The dancer! Why didn't you say? Come in, come in. He's ready for you.'

It took a further half-hour, during which she plied me with tea, before Terence emerged from the back of the house in shirtsleeves, a smear of shaving soap behind his left ear.

'At last, at last,' he said, as if it were I who had kept him waiting. 'Well well, never mind, work to be done. Let us ascend to the upper levels.'

This was not so much rehearsal as an act of creation, insofar as Terence seemed to be making the whole thing up as he went along. As I understood it, he and Leonie would take turns reading selected poems by William Blake while I was required merely to strum my lyre, walk in time to the metre and 'be prepared, dear boy, to be snatched up in the frenzy of the dance'.

'Now,' said Terence, sitting by the window, his long legs crossed at the knee, 'which ones shall we give them?' He flicked through a well-worn copy of Blake's poems. '"The Clod and the Pebble", that's a beauty. Love seeketh not itself to please, nor for itself has any care.' He sighed, and stared out of the window, meditatively smoking. 'How true, how very true. When one is in love, one simply gives, without reckoning the cost.' He turned to me, a great sadness in his eyes. 'Perhaps I will ask my wife to read that one. I feel that I can ...' He waved his arms, as if distributing love, or perhaps leaflets. 'Yes, I can interpret that. It feels right.'

'And what do I do?'

'Patience! Let us first shape the programme. We must of course give them your favourite, "The Tyger", even though it's a terrible old chestnut. Do you think you can muster the spirit of the tiger?'

'On all fours?'

'If necessary.'

'But my trousers ...'

He tutted. 'You won't be wearing *trousers*, my dear, and even if you were what are trousers in a question of artistic interpretation?' He snapped his fingers. '*Rien!*' Further flicking. 'And of course, just for you, "The Sick Rose". I feel certain that Leonie can wilt convincingly. You, of course, are the invisible worm that flies in the night in the howling storm. What a part! What a debut!'

By lunchtime, we had selected some dozen *Songs of Experience*. My duties, apart from strumming, involved crawling as a tiger, burrowing as a worm, flying as an angel and repining as a chimney sweep. It was a rough outline on which to build a performance, and I would be obliged, said Terence, to improvise.

I hoped with all my heart that nobody would come.

'And now,' he said, when Leonie joined us with a plate of ham sandwiches and three bottles of beer, 'to costumes. My wife and I shall be dressed in white shifts. We still have them, don't we, from *The Herne's Egg*? Yeats, dear boy. The most wonderful piece. Leonie and I as druidic priest and priestess, standing quite still, frieze-like, in white robes, with golden staffs in our hands, our heads crowned with garlands of oak. What happened to the staffs and the garlands?'

'The garlands shed their leaves and I put them on the fire. And I grew runner beans up the staffs.'

'And they say that art is useless! Ah, well, as long as the robes are intact. You haven't turned them into tablecloths or tea towels.'

'No, my dear,' said Leonie. 'They had already served their turn as bedsheets.'

'And what will I be wearing?'

'Ah.' Terence stared up through the ceiling. 'I see ... clouds.'

'I thought you might,' said Leonie.

'A length of netting, twisted here' – he touched me on the shoulder – 'and here' – he touched me on the hip. 'The feet bare, of course. And perhaps paint.'

'Certainly paint,' said Leonie.

'What sort of paint?'

'Body paint,' said Terence. 'Don't look like that, dear boy, it's quite wash-offable. Blakean curls and tendrils up the legs and the across the back, over the shoulders, down the chest. Yes ...' He stroked his beard. 'I see the potential. Disrobe.'

'What?'

'Undress. Divest.'

'Now? In front of ... '

'I've seen it all before, dear, don't you worry,' said Leonie. 'One does in the theatre. And besides, I have a son of about your age. Hard to believe, yes, but one was terribly young to be a mother. Don't be shy.'

The attic was none too warm, and the added element of fear set my teeth chattering. Soon I was standing in nothing but underpants and socks.

'Good, good,' said Terence, walking around me as if I were a piece of sculpture. 'Oh yes. Fine. Very fine. Wouldn't you agree, my dear?'

'Very fine indeed,' said Eleanora, joining her husband in his perambulation.

'Excellent proportion. Along classical lines.' He held up a thumb, the better to measure me. 'Shoulders twice as broad as the waist. Legs four times the length of the head. Just so. Anthropometrically perfect. I congratulate you, my boy. Perhaps a slight unevenness in the left leg ...'

'I told you, I had polio.'

'No! But it is the little faults that reveal the greater perfections, a sweet disorder in the dress and so on. I think we shall make an impression.'

They circulated slowly, their eyes wide, dark, like hunters. The room was absolutely quiet but for the soft pad of their feet on the dusty floorboards. My face was hot, my hands and feet cold.

'Please can I get dressed again now?'

'Of course!' said Terence. 'I have seen what I need to see.'

'And so have I,' said Leonie, briefly catching my eye. Did she wink?

The performance that night was – what shall I say? A triumph? A disaster? To my horror, dozens of students filed into the theatre, paying their shillings at the door. Leonie, in her white druidic shift, watched them through a peephole in the backdrop – another set of patched bedsheets, dyed green to suggest a sylvan setting – and counted. 'Twenty ... Forty ... Forty-five ... That's a lot of shillings, Terence.'

Terence knelt at my feet, applying cold wet blue paint to my legs, long curving lines that ended only where my underpants began, and not always then. 'If we are lucky we will take fully five pounds on the door,' he said, a brush clenched between his teeth. One hand rested on my calf. 'You see, Derek? You have star quality.'

I thought it more likely that word had spread among the student body that one of their number would be making a fool of himself in little more than a nappy and some blue paint.

'Now, let me see.' Terence got up slowly, his legs giving him pain, and looked at me, stroking his beard. 'Yes. Like this, I think.' He ran the brush up my back, making me shiver, and branched the lines out over my shoulder blades. 'Good, good. And now ...' He came to the front, swirling the lines down over my chest and stomach, adding curls and squiggles here and there, occasionally rubbing away a drip or a smudge with his fingers. The paint dried quickly, making my skin itch and tingle. 'Don't touch it! And for heaven's sake try not to perspire. You'll run.'

Eight o'clock came around too soon, and there was nothing for it: I had to go on. Either that, or run through the audience in my nappy and paint to escape through the doors. At the last moment, Terence threw his robe over his head.

'Break a leg, darling,' whispered Leonie, her hand resting on my shoulder. 'You look divine.'

And they walked on stage, pushing me before them.

I stood in the light, horribly conscious of the goosepimples that had broken out all over my body. The audience was utterly silent.

'Hear the voice of the bard, who present, past and future sees!' declaimed Terence. My lyre hung useless and unplucked at my side. I could not move.

'Whose ears have heard the holy word that walk'd among the ancient trees!'

A swirl of white, and Leonie pirouetted in front of me, her feet thumping on the floor; she was not a light woman. She stopped, and held her arms out, obscuring me from view. 'For Christ's sake, darling,' she whispered, 'pull yourself together and play your damn banjo.' And then she twirled across to stage left.

I lifted the instrument, which weighed only a few ounces but felt as if it was made of lead, struggled for a moment with a sense of utter mortification and dread, as if every childhood nightmare had suddenly come true – and then, extending one leg and placing my weight on the other as Terence had instructed, began to strum.

And from that point on I remember nothing but the glare of the lights, the swirl of white robes and the occasional fragment of Blake, shining like diamonds.

Fear made me bold. As the tiger I stalked and pounced and roared. I was pitiful as a chimney sweep, noble as an angel, repulsive as a worm. For the finale, all I had to do was stand downstage with my arms raised above my head, flanked by Leonie and Terence with arms outstretched, alternating lines which seemed, at the time, fraught with profound significance.

Terence: The modest rose puts forth a thorn.
Leonie: The humble sheep, a threat'ning horn.
Terence: While the lily white shall in love delight.
Leonie: Nor a thorn nor a threat stain her beauty bright.

They raised their arms until all three of us were, as it were, praying towards the sun – a heavy-looking light that, had it fallen, would have brained me – we held the pose, we stretched, we strained, and then came merciful darkness.

And with it applause. Loud, sustained applause. Not the slow ironic handclap of disdain but genuine enthusiasm. There were cheers and whistles. The lights came back up, we took our bows and left the stage; the applause continued. We went out again. They clapped more. We bowed, they cheered, we left. This went on and on until, at length, Terence judged that we had given enough. We had taken, he told me later, five curtain calls.

'Unprecedented,' said Terence as he wiped the paint off my sweaty body with a damp cloth. 'I knew the idea was good. I knew it. I see great things for this piece, great things. A transfer. Sadler's Wells. The Birmingham Rep. The Abbey. Ah, yes ...'

'I think,' said Leonie, 'that we have a new leading man.' She dropped her robe, unpinned her hair, and, as Terence fussed around my lower person, kissed me on the lips.

Leonie called at my lodgings the following week. It was a Friday evening, and I was sitting at my desk, a blanket round my shoulders and gloves on my hands, poring over *Timon of Athens*, when Mrs Flanagan pounded on my door.

'Yes, Mrs Flanagan?'

'There is a *woman* downstairs to see you.'

'A woman?'

'A woman with *red hair*.'

'Ah. Thank you, Mrs Flanagan.'

'I do not allow lady callers.'

'I am aware of that, Mrs Flanagan.'

'She will not be coming up to your room.'

I tried to look affronted. 'Certainly not. She is ... a friend of my mother's.'

'Hmm.' She stood in the doorway, beefy arms folded across her heaving bosom; the climb to the upper regions of the house was not one she made willingly. 'This must not happen again, Mr Dean.'

'No, Mrs Flanagan.'

I bounded down the stairs, my landlady shuffling and groaning behind me.

Leonie was decked out in her finest: the fox fur, which didn't bear terribly close inspection, a chic felt hat that curled down over her right ear, and some heavy-looking pearls that could not possibly be real. Even on a social call – as I assumed this was – Leonie seemed dressed for the stage. Her face was fully, exaggeratedly made up, her hair aggressively red, perhaps freshly dyed. Little wonder that Mrs Flanagan tutted as she descended to her mythical regions.

'What an extraordinary woman,' said Leonie, in a voice I was quite certain would carry to the basement. 'Like a landlady from a Noël Coward comedy. Too realistic!'

'Well, she is real. A real, live landlady.'

'Life is sometimes so much like the stage,' she said and, holding my shoulders, kissed me on both cheeks. She was wearing a musky, intoxicating perfume. 'I have come to liberate you, Derek. To take you away from all this' – she waved one gloved hand around the dingy hall, the creaky stairs, and I noticed, ungallantly, that her gloves were split at the seams – 'and ask you to be my guest for dinner. Now, now,' she said, putting a finger to my lips. 'I will brook no denial, as my husband would say. Thanks to you, we are rather flush.' She held out an arm, obliging me to take it, as we left the house. 'There is a divine little restaurant on Charlotte Street to which I am taking you. No. Don't say I can't, because I shall.'

'I can't afford dinners in restaurants.' This was true; I was more than usually broke, waiting for a postal order from my parents in order to buy tea and tobacco.

'But I can, thanks to you.' She squeezed my arm, drawing us close; the fox fur collar tickled the side of my face. 'Don't worry, darling, you won't be compromised. I shall discreetly slip the money under the table. One must keep up appearances at all costs.'

'Where is Terence?'

'Terence?' Her voice sounded vague, as if she was having trouble placing the name. 'Why? Would you feel safer if he were here?'

'Don't be silly,' I said, wondering if I was being seduced. I longed to be seduced. I had not expected it to happen with a married woman some years my senior walking down the cigarette-strewn pavements of Goodge Street. Seduction: the word seemed as hot and heavy as the perfume on Leonie's skin, the fur of her coat.

'This is it.' We stopped in front of a tiny shop front on Charlotte Street, a row of electric bulbs haloed by drizzle, illuminating a painted sign of red and gold. Le Relais, *restaurant français*. Tarnished gold lettering in the window promised *plat du jour*, *à la carte*, *bons vins* and *nos desserts*. An obvious-looking Frenchman in a long white apron stood in the doorway. 'The gentleman goes first,' whispered Leonie, 'and asks for a table for two. I don't suppose you can muster a little schoolboy French, can you?'

'Probably best not to try.'

The waiter barely noticed me, showed us straight to a cosy corner table and said, as he laid our napkins on our laps, 'Bonsoir, Madame Black.'

'Bonsoir, Gaston. My usual, please.'

'Madame. And for sir?'

I wondered what her 'usual' was, and tried to think of something suitably worldly to order. My father sometimes indulged in a whisky and soda before dinner, my mother dampened her lips with a little dry sherry, but neither seemed appropriately French.

'I'll have the same,' I said, sounding unbearably gauche, but Gaston nodded approvingly, and disappeared. 'What have I just ordered?'

'A dry martini.'

'Oh. Like in the movies.'

Leonie peeled off her gloves. 'Absolutely like in the movies.' She put one hand over mine, and leaned forward. 'Would you prefer, darling, if I told you what to order? So you can do it properly, you understand.'

I scanned the menu, which was in French, but might as well have been in Greek for all the sense I could get from it. 'Would you mind?'

'Not at all. One should never be ashamed to learn. And I am always happy to teach.' Her hand, warm and heavy, was still on mine. 'That is one of the benefits of experience.'

And so I ate my first real French meal – and even today, after so many meals that followed, some of them taken *en plein air* in the citrus-and-pine-scented groves of Provence, that first one lingers in my memory, a taste of paradise.

We ate *pâté* on tiny pieces of toast. We ate *entrecôte* steaks cooked *à point*, through which our knives glided as if through butter, red bloody juices oozing across the plate towards our *gratin dauphinois*, thick with cream and pungent with garlic. Oh, how my parents would hate this, I thought. The meat would be undercooked, the potatoes 'messed about with', the flavourings too strong, the fear of bad breath overwhelming. We drank red wine from a decanter, potent and bittersweet. Leonie smoked between courses, even during courses, leaving her pillar-box-red lipstick smeared over butts, napkins and glasses. She ate with gusto, talking while chewing, keeping up an enthusiastic interrogation during which she found out all there was to know about my past, and, when that ran out, about my hopes for the future.

'Of course you want to write,' she said, when I divulged what I thought was my deepest, darkest secret. 'Anyone can see you have a talent. Even Terence, who is somewhat blinded by your beauty at this point, knows that there is more to you than mere ... ' She waved a hand in the air, suggesting something unsayable. 'You have talent, you are young, you are *bien élevé*. You will go far. I see it in my crystal ball.'

She fed my starving self-esteem just as surely as she filled my stomach. Her words were intoxicating. No dream was too absurd, no ambition dashed by the cold water of disapproval. My parents thought it vulgar to discuss one's abilities: that, they said, was for others to do. Leonie not only tolerated but reflected my high opinion of myself. By the time we had finished our sorbets and were enjoying a glass of brandy, I was convinced that fame and fortune were just moments away.

I paid the bill – Leonie had, as promised, slipped the money beneath the table, squeezing my knee as she did so

– and we left the restaurant. The drizzle had resolved into steady rain, and neither of us had an umbrella.

'Oh! Bother this weather,' said Leonie, pulling up her collar as we sheltered under the dripping awning of Le Relais. 'To find one's way back to Kentish Town in *this* ... ' She touched her forehead, anguished. 'Not to be thought of.'

'We could get a cup of coffee.' One of the more Bohemian local cafes stayed open all night.

'Oh darling, don't be offended, but really, I've eaten and drunk enough for one evening.'

My castles in the air came tumbling down; over dinner, and with the brandy heating my stomach, I had formed fanciful expectations of how the night might end. I was in no hurry to surrender Leonie to a bus or a taxi.

'That's quite all right,' I said, a young English gentleman once again. 'Thank you for a lovely evening.'

'Don't go all formal on me, darling. Tell me something.' She looked up at me, her eyelashes sparkling with drops of rain that had blown under the awning. 'What time does the dragon landlady retire for the night?'

'I don't know.'

'I mean, if one were to come home at, say' – she glanced at her wristwatch – 'eleven o'clock, would the old gorgon pop out of her cave?'

'I suppose not.'

'And would one encounter one's neighbours on the *escalier*?'

'Unlikely.' Apart from the starving postgraduate, who seemed never to sleep, the rest of the house was silent by ten.

Leonie was quiet, fiddling with her gloves. 'I wonder,' she said at length.

'What?'

'Whether, perhaps, you would like to invite me up to your room for a little *digestif*?'

There was nothing drinkable in my room apart from a half bottle of whisky that I kept for 'emergencies'. I told her as much.

'Well darling, I would say this is just such an emergency. Wouldn't you?'

We made it past the dragon's den and all the way to the top of the house without hindrance. Once inside my room, the door firmly closed and the curtains drawn, all pretence of wanting a *digestif* was dropped. Leonie threw her fur coat over my bed, and herself on top of it, her arms open, drawing me down.

I did not sleep that night. The bed, narrow at the best of times, was not designed for two. At length I gave up and camped coldly on the floor, with only the rug for cover. The steak and brandy lay heavy on my stomach, while my mind and heart raced.

So this, at last, was love.

As the first grey light of a winter morning showed through the thin stuff of the curtains, I looked at Leonie's sleeping bulk rising and falling beneath the blankets, and I felt – I believed, perhaps imagined – that I loved her. And when she woke and, finding herself alone, softly called my name, I returned to her.

A year passed quickly, my youth running like water through my fingers.

There were more shows, just as Terence had predicted. We took *Songs of Experience* on a brief tour, and were gratified to receive notices not only in the local press and *Theatre Arts Monthly*, but also in national newspapers. *The Stage* cited us as 'the very latest in the advanced drama', and even ran a tiny photograph of the final tableau. Terence was overjoyed, and busied himself with plans for larger tours, more ambitious productions, a fully-staged, large-company version of Blake's 'Jerusalem', a masque with music by Handel, Purcell and Byrd, phalanxes of naked, painted youths 'descending like angels from the upper spheres'. It distracted him from what was going on under his very nose, often under his roof, as I became a fixture not only in The Company but also in his wife's bed.

The college authorities noticed that I had ceased attending lectures and, after a short interview with the Dean, I was 'sent down', as my father put it. He was neither angry nor, apparently, displeased. Since my defection to London, he treated me as little more than an acquaintance. My mother worried quietly about my future, and pressed her handkerchief to her lips, wondering what she'd done to deserve such a son, and I said little to comfort her. I was in love, and embarking on life, and I saw my parents down the wrong end of a telescope, small and distant. I left university without a backward glance, believing that I could learn all I needed to know from Terence and Leonie. Terence taught me about the art and practicalities of the theatre. Leonie was my tutor in matters of the heart and the body.

She was a patient and indulgent mistress, and took delight in my eagerness, even in my ineptitude. Was I in love? I was certainly preoccupied with Leonie, and never looked elsewhere. I came to rely on her. When I left the university, it was she who found me accommodation near Mornington Crescent – closer to the house in Kentish Town, in a block of flats where we had complete privacy, and where there was no Mrs Flanagan guarding the door. It was Leonie who provided me with money – my 'wages' as a performer in The Company, supplemented, I was sure, by her generosity. She taught me how to dress, how to behave, how to please with my manners and deportment just as surely as she taught me how to please with my body. Under her tutelage I became an elegant young man, groomed and perfumed – all that my father, with his rolled umbrella and bowler hat, found most disgusting. But, although he worked every day in the City, we took very good care not to see each other.

My days fell into a topsy-turvy routine. I worked at night, never rising before nine – much later if I had spent the night with Leonie, who loved to lie abed drinking tea and making love, 'wasting the best part of the day', my parents might have said, but to me it did not seem like time wasted. Then there were the 'tiresome necessities' to attend to: bills to be paid or, rather, creditors to be fobbed off; arrangements made for transport and accommodation; staff and cast to be hired or fired. Terence left the business side of The Company to his capable wife, preoccupied as he was with artistic decisions, rehearsals, painting scenery, designing costumes and posters. Between them, like Jack Spratt and his wife, they coped with the task of writing, producing and performing a string of shows that were soon much in demand up and down the country. 'You've breathed new life into The Company,' Terence told me one summer evening while arranging my costume (a hessian tabard, open at the sides, under which I wore only a dance belt). 'Youth at the helm! Youth and beauty!' He lifted the front of my tabard in order to fasten the tapes that prevented it from flying up during the turns and revealing even more of me to the burghers of Croydon, where we were booked that night. 'There. And now the boots.'

I was used to Terence's ministrations, and regarded them as part of the job. Each new production required a yet-more-minimal costume, infinite minute adjustments, make-up and body paint in the strangest places, until I was completely inured to being manhandled. Now he knelt at my feet, lacing the calf-length, soft leather boots in which I was required to dance.

'I hope you realise, Derek, that you are becoming, in your way, an attraction.'

'Perhaps.' It was hard to ignore the notes and gifts that were delivered at the stage door, some of them proposing the most generous terms.

'Audiences come to the theatre for a glimpse of beauty, a vision of the ideal.' He smoothed the leather up the length of my calf. 'And that is what we give them, you and I. An ideal.'

'I suppose so.'

'I am very grateful to you, Derek.' He stopped lacing and smoothing, looking up at me with a puzzled expression on his face. His wire-framed spectacles were perched halfway down his nose – he had difficulty with close work – and his blue eyes sparkled under grey brows.

'I know.' He tolerated my friendship with his wife; that, surely, was thanks enough.

'And you,' he said, 'are you grateful? Are you what the French would call *reconnaissant*? Hmm?' He had not let go of my leg.

'Of course I am, Terence. This is a wonderful experience for me.'

'Indeed it is.' He sighed. 'But I wonder ... if you ever think of what you can give in return.'

'I'm working very hard on my performances.'

'Yes ...' His eyes narrowed. 'I don't doubt that.'

'What else can I do?'

He stroked his beard with one hand, while the other ran up my thigh. 'There are so many ways of creating beauty,' he said, and might have expanded on his theme, but at that moment Leonie walked into the dressing room, her hair hanging down her back in a heavy, wet coil. She was fiddling with a large gold clasp on her shoulder, from which hung folds of classical-looking drapery. That night we were giving Croydon our interpretation of *Hero and Leander*, with Leonie and myself in the title roles, four additional dancers appearing as, variously, soldiers, priestesses, birds and fish, while Terence recited chunks of Ovid and Marlowe and operated the gramophone (we did not run to a pianist). At the climax of the piece, while the other dancers manipulated a piece of parachute silk which represented the Hellespont, Terence appeared armed with a trident as a jealous Neptune to snatch me down to a watery grave. This involved removing my tabard. My death among the waves, clad only in that flesh-coloured dance belt, was an extended ballet to Debussy's *La Mer*, during which Neptune shook his trident, Hero tore her hair in grief and I was stranded downstage in a puddle of water, one of the dancers having chucked a bucket over me while concealed by the Hellespont. It was a difficult, embarrassing role, not to mention cold and damp.

Terence got to his feet, knees creaking and popping, and started changing into his robes. Husband and wife exchanged a swift, furious glance that I was not meant to see.

'Derek, darling,' said Leonie, 'fix this bloody thing for me. I'm all fingers and thumbs tonight.'

I was glad of the excuse to stand up; at least in an upright position, the tabard afforded me some coverage. I fastened the clasp, which had started life as part of a brass lampshade, and excused myself. We had ten minutes before curtain up, and I preferred to wait with the *corps de ballet*.

The other dancers – two boys and two girls, although it was difficult to tell which was which – were painting their faces in one shared, smeared mirror. They regarded me with suspicion at best, hostility at worst, and I knew why. They were 'professionals', I a mere amateur who had leapfrogged into the spotlight by the most ignoble means.

'Here he is,' said one of the boys, a creature with suspiciously gilded locks who was drawing thick black lines under his eyes. 'Our star.'

'Has he dressed you, dear?' asked one of the girls, painting huge red dots on either side of her long nose. This was meant to make her eyes appear large and wide set; it looked like a nasty case of conjunctivitis.

'Or *undressed* you, more like,' said the other boy, sitting crosslegged in his Grecian tunic, smoking a cigarette and leafing through *Picturegoer* magazine. 'Funny how long it takes.'

'Terence's a perfectionist,' said his friend, admiring himself in the mirror. 'He likes to handle all the details himself.'

'You're just jealous,' said the second girl, a top-heavy brunette with no obvious dance talent but a large trust fund to work through, 'because he's never handled your details.'

'Oh!' The two boys clutched their chests. 'The very thought!'

'That old goat!'

'Anyway it's not *Terence* you've got to worry about, is it, Derek? You're more of a ladies' man.'

I treated this as good-natured banter, although it was nothing of the sort. But to rise to the bait would have made my position impossible. As it was, the bucket of water seemed to be getting colder every night, thrown with more than necessary force.

'Five minutes, please,' came the voice of the stage manager, rapping on the dressing room door.

'You'd better run along, dear.'

I went back into the corridor. Even from there, with the door closed, I could hear Terence and Leonie's raised voices.

'Oh, don't be ridiculous,' boomed Leonie's rich contralto.

'Ridiculous?' Terence attempted to answer in a low baritone, but broke in the middle, and cleared his throat. 'If I am ridiculous,' he continued in a stage whisper, 'then who has made me so?'

'Darling ...'

'Don't call me that!'

'Very well. If you wish to go over all this once again, let us at least wait until after the show.'

'Oh yes. Sweep it under the carpet. Pretend nothing's wrong. Let them all applaud him and love him and we can carry on as if nothing's happened.'

'Nothing has happened!'

'I'm not blind, Leonie. I have eyes. And I have feelings.'

'Why now, Terence? After all that has passed between us, all these years of contentment and understanding ...'

'Contentment? Hah!' I could imagine the scene behind the dressing room door, Terence's finger trembling, Leonie at bay against the wall, her magnificent eyes flashing fire. 'You are content, I'm sure. But I?'

'Have I ever complained when you have taken a lover?'

'This is different.'

'Have I complained when your behaviour has made me look ridiculous? When it has exposed us to the dangers of the law?'

'Oh, this is ugly, Leonie. Ugly.'

'And who has made it so? With your furtive, insinuating ways ...'

'Ah!'

I thought, for a moment, that one of them had struck the other, so sharp was the cry. What should I do? Clad as I was in the briefest of garments, leather boots up to my knees and full stage make-up, I could only make things worse. Instead I coughed loudly. Silence fell immediately.

The door opened an inch, and Terence's beard appeared.

'Two minutes, Terence,' I said, trying to keep my voice low and even.

'Very well.' He sounded shaken, and closed the door quickly – but not before I had seen the wetness of his eyes.

The performance passed without incident, at least as far as the audience was concerned. They sat quietly throughout my gyrations, listened attentively to Terence's readings, and if there was a certain amount of uneasy shifting during my near-naked final solo I put it down to a keen interest in modern dance. The applause was sincere as we took our bows.

But to me, the entire evening teetered on the brink of disaster. Terence took frequent nips from a bottle of brandy secreted in the folds of his Homeric robes, and when he came on as the angry Sea God his eyes were red, his step unsteady and he was a little too ready with the trident. Leonie retaliated by hogging the stage, blocking her husband from view and spending far longer grieving over my naked body than she was supposed to, brushing my torso with her loosened hair, holding me in wild embraces like a passionate Pieta. The other dancers goggled and giggled and forgot to manipulate the silken waves, which fell limp and lifeless.

'That was a bloody disaster!' stormed Terence as we wiped off our make-up. 'A total humiliation! How dare you? How dare you make me look like an idiot?'

A tap on the dressing room door, and the stage manager put his head round. 'Are we decent? Good. Gentleman to see you, Mr Black.'

'I can see no one.'

'Says he's the manager of the Liverpool Playhouse.'

'What?'

'And he's sent this.' He proffered a large bottle of champagne.

'Ah,' said Terence, mollified as always by admiration, 'in that case, show him in, show him in! Leonie, procure glasses. Derek ...'

I had finished cleaning my face, and was about to pull my shirt over my head. Terence stayed my hand.

'Not yet.' He looked me up and down and then, satisfied, said 'Please, come in.'

By the time our visitor left we had secured a two-week engagement at the Playhouse, at extremely advantageous terms. The manager conducted the negotiations without, I think, taking his eyes from me. When we parted that night, Terence to Kentish Town, Leonie and I to the flat in Mornington Crescent, we were, once again, the best of friends.

And so our lives continued throughout that year, decorative onstage, decorous off, except for occasional flare-ups when

Terence, frustrated or disappointed in his own adventures, sought to remind his wife of the duty she owed him. One day, during a lengthy stopover at Crewe Junction, he accused me of stealing the takings and threatened to dismiss me from the company. On another occasion we went on at the Maddermarket Theatre in Norwich nearly an hour late: Terence had gone AWOL, and by the time one of the dancers found him in a nearby pub he had drunk so much Guinness that he was in no fit state to perform. Leonie was about to announce the sad news to the audience when Terence arrived, eight sheets to the wind, and proceeded to regale the house with unbilled recitations from Shakespearean tragedy, focusing mostly on those speeches dealing with woman's infidelity. We got him off after twenty minutes, and gave a hastily reworked *Songs of Experience*; I don't think Norwich was any the wiser.

But these outbreaks were rare, and for the most part Terence was content to bank the takings and conceive his next production. *Paradise Lost* was in the works, with Leonie and me as Adam and Eve, Terence as God. He was already stitching my fig-leaf girdle.

We might have gone on, up and down the railway lines, in and out of theatres, but for one thing. Even in our rarefied world of art and love, it was impossible to ignore the fact that Europe was sliding into war. We did not read the papers – at least, only the reviews – and so we knew little of the Munich Agreement, the Anschluss, the war in Spain, the deepening crisis that could have only one outcome. Terence regarded the news as a distraction, Leonie dismissed it with a nervous wave of the hand, and the rest of the company seemed genuinely ignorant of anything that did not directly concern them. And I was like Tennyson's Lotos-Eaters, to whom 'the gushing of the wave/Far far away did seem to mourn and rave/On alien shores'. I saw the headlines, heard the anxious chatter in the cafes, but I closed my ears and dreamed of a glorious future. My sights were set on the West End, on fame and glory as an actor, a dancer, a writer perhaps – I knew not which, and did not really care. When war was declared, I was 22 years old, but my outlook was that of a schoolboy.

I was in the flat, breakfasting with Leonie – it was about noon, and I distinctly recall that I was eating an egg, sitting up in bed, a sheet pulled over my chest, a tray on my lap as she dunked bread and butter soldiers into the yolk and fed them to me. 'Well, darling,' she said, wiping her fingers on a towel, 'I suppose things are going to change now, aren't they?'

'I don't see why.'

'Because of the war, silly.'

'There won't be a war.' I must have been the only man in London who still adhered to that ridiculous folly – and in only 48 hours, all doubt would be removed for ever.

'I'm very much afraid, my dear, that there will.'

'It needn't affect us.'

She sighed, and stroked my hair. 'I remember the last war ... just about. It affected us all.'

'But this one will be different. Fought with machines.'

'Let us hope so. But if they introduce conscription ...'

'Which they won't.'

'Then I shall lose you.'

'It won't happen.' I pulled her towards me, and kissed her.

That was on the Friday – the day that Germany invaded Poland. On Sunday, Britain declared war. I sat at home, nervous and unoccupied – all shows were cancelled – and waited for my call-up papers to arrive. My parents had some wild plan of closing up the house and moving to Scotland; they expected bombs to start raining from the sky that very instant. They summoned me home for a final, awkward interview, during which my father offered me the chance to go with them and 'save your skin', as he put it; I think he was relieved when I declined. 'I shall carry on working,' I said.

'If you can call that work.' Old-fashioned in all his opinions, my father regarded the stage as a branch of prostitution.

'And then, I suppose, I shall be called up.'

My mother squeaked, and started clearing plates.

'I very much doubt that, Derek,' said my father. 'You are not strong.'

'Strong enough to be shot, I suppose.' I intended to hurt them, although the thought of military service filled me with cold, sick dread.

I seldom saw my father angry, and was shocked when his face went dark. 'You are a fool, Derek. I am ashamed of you.' As he marched out of the room, I remembered – too late – that he had lost two brothers in the last war – two uncles that I had never known.

I left, and buried my shame in Leonie's comforting bosom. I did not see my parents again for many years.

The early months of the war passed in an eventless haze. Sandbags appeared all over London, air raid shelters sprang up and gasmasks were handed out, we watched the skies day and night until silence made us careless. We navigated through the blackout, making light of the darkness, joking about it. Things were happening elsewhere in the world – in France, in Russia, in the Low Countries – but the war seemed far from home, a conflict that would be fought and won on the battlefields of Europe. I waited every day for the envelope that would summon me to serve my country, and every day I was reprieved. The Company resumed its performance schedule, bringing Terence's visions of beauty to dwindling provincial audiences, but as theatres closed and rationing started to bite, our spectacles became less spectacular. Dancers deserted us, evacuated or drafted. By the beginning of 1940 we were a trio.

One day, when we had no bookings at all, Terence received an official letter informing him that The Company had been chosen 'from amongst many of the smaller-scale companies' to embark on a tour of army training camps around the

UK. Travel and subsistence would be paid for by the Entertainments National Service Association, and we would receive a small stipend, enough to live on, certainly a good deal more than our diminished box office was providing.

'It's undoubtedly a great honour,' said Terence, who immediately started work on a sort of patriotic dance-drama in which Leonie would represent Europe, and I would appear variously as the 'rampaging beast' of Germany, the 'spirit of Albion' and, finally, as 'Reconciliation' in a closing number that got yet more use out of that well-worn dance belt. The idea of performing before audiences of rowdy squaddies filled me with dread, but Terence was adamant. 'Think, dear boy, of how much more terrifying it would be to face the enemy in open battle.'

As if to test this theory, I was summoned to a recruiting station, and reported with somewhat less trepidation than I had imagined. Surely I could serve my country more usefully than by parading my freezing painted flesh in front of men braver than me? A doctor asked me to remove my clothes, and seemed taken aback by the alacrity with which I obeyed; most of his charges, I suppose, were less used to public nudity. He listened to my lungs with a stethoscope, surveyed my limbs, poked and prodded me and scribbled on a clipboard.

'Polio, eh?'

'Yes. How on earth could you know?'

He gave a long, complex reply, full of phrases that sounded like 'defibrillation of the quadriceps major' and 'sussuration of the lower alvioli'.

'Does it matter?'

'I'm afraid it matters very much.' He consulted his clipboard. 'I am unable to pass you.'

'Oh.' I did not know whether to grieve or rejoice. Part of me – the cowardly part – was relieved to stay at home under the wing, however stifling, of Leonie and Terence.

'Many of the young men I have seen today would pay good money for what I'm putting on your discharge form.'

'And what's that?'

He showed me. *Unfit for active service.*

'What does it mean?'

'You can't join the armed forces, in a nutshell.'

'But surely there's something I can do?'

'I suggest you try the Civil Service. They're always on the look out for bright young men.'

And that was that: my card was marked, I was rejected, stamped 'unfit', and obliged to carry my discharge papers with me at all times. I returned to Kentish Town, where we were supposed to be rehearsing *Europe: A Tragedy*, Terence's political dance drama, fully expecting to spend the rest of the day in a state of near nakedness while Terence fussed around with music and bits of material. My father's disgust seemed all too justified. However, when I walked through the front door, the house was in uproar.

'No, no, no!' I heard Terence's voice booming from the first-floor living room. 'A thousand times no!'

'Darling, calm down. It is not the end of the world.'

'That is precisely what it is! The end of the world. Armageddon. The Apocalypse. Oh, I can not bear it. I shall go upstairs and open a vein.'

'See if I care!' Leonie burst on to the landing and saw me. 'Derek! Thank God! Perhaps you can talk some sense into him.'

'What's happened?'

'Orders from the government. He's furious.'

Terence was pacing the worn carpet, waving a very creased piece of paper above his head. His hair was standing on end, as if he'd attempted to tug it out.

'Telling *me* how to put on a show! Telling *me* who to cast! What sort of material is "suitable". Suitable! How would some Whitehall pen pusher know what is suitable? What do they know about the art of the theatre, how we feed the soul with movement and light and poetry?'

'What's happened?'

'Oh, they imagine,' he continued, with deep, tragic vibrato, 'that the soul of the Common Man is satisfied with the kind of trash' – he slapped the letter against this hand, causing it to tear – 'that they give them. With popular songs and – what was it? Comic sketches. How can that possibly nurture the souls of young men who are doomed to die?'

'I'm not sure they would want to be reminded of that.'

'Ridiculous! These young men stand on the edge of the abyss. How dare they blind them with this ... this ... tinsel? We minister to their spiritual needs, their deep hunger for meaning and understanding through beauty and art ...'

Leonie beckoned me out on to the landing, and shut the door softly on her husband's rantings.

'The ENSA people, I suppose,' I said.

'They want him to put on a light-hearted revue with comedy and songs.'

'Is that so bad?'

'Not really. Might make a nice change to get laughs.'

We got plenty of laughs, but not always for the right reasons. 'I suppose he's put his foot down.'

'He has no choice, my dear. If he doesn't do what they ask, they won't pay him. He just needs to get this out of his system.'

'It's not so bad, is it?'

'No, dear. We'll manage. I think the thing that's upset him most is that they're foisting this young woman on us.'

'Who?'

'A singer and variety artiste, according to the letter. Her name is Rose Morgan. She is to be "heavily featured", having already proved herself popular with the troops, apparently.'

The door burst open, and there stood Terence, a threadbare prophet. 'Popular with the troops! Oh yes, we can well imagine how she managed that. Pah!' He balled the letter up and tossed it to the foot of the stairs.

'I suppose this means,' I said, 'that *Europe: A Tragedy* goes on the back burner.'

Terence made an inarticulate noise and repaired to the living room. We did not see him again for the rest of the day. Leonie left sandwiches and a bottle of beer outside the door, and we got the tram into town.

'Will he do it?'

'He has no choice. It won't be so bad. Terry's a great one for making the best of things. In a few weeks he'll have convinced himself that it was all his idea, that light comic revue is the most advanced of all the arts and that Miss Rose Morgan is a genius.'

She squeezed my arm, and said in a lower voice, 'and of course, once he meets the soldiers ... Well, that's a story for another day.'

'But what will we do?'

'Oh, you know the sort of thing. A handful of popular songs. Some amusing skits, topical stuff about the blackout, rationing, Hitler, Churchill.'

'But Terence doesn't know about those things.'

'Of course he doesn't, darling. Honestly, you are being rather dense today.'

'What do you mean?'

'I mean you'll write it.'

'Well, I don't know ... '

'Come on. You're a natural. Clever young chap like you. Just promise me one thing.'

'Yes?'

'Don't make me play old bags all the time. Charladies and grannies and so on. Give me a little bit of glamour once in a while.'

'Don't be daft.' I kissed her as the tram trundled past Euston station, but my mind was racing ahead. Amusing skits. Comic sketches. Topical stuff. Myself and Miss Rose Morgan as a sophisticated double act, England's answer to the Lunts, wowing the boys with our wit and verve. I wondered if I dared dance – perhaps Miss Morgan could teach me. Was she blonde or brunette? Tall or short? Would she like me? I felt certain that she would.

We ate a poor excuse for shepherd's pie in a café off Leicester Square, and spoke very little. I did not realise, as I chewed the last spoonful of something that had been advertised as treacle sponge pudding and custard, that I had not said a word for nearly ten minutes. Leonie lit a cigarette, blew out smoke and patted my hand: a lover's touch no more.

'I suppose these things happen, don't they?'

'What's that, darling?' I was far away, imagining myself and Miss Morgan in gorgeous hotel suites, travelling first class, perhaps crossing the Atlantic.

'When something just ... ends.'

'I'm sorry, I don't quite follow.'

'It's all right, Derek. I understand, and I shall never hold it against you.'

'I don't know what you're talking about,' I said, but I did. Whatever had been between us, nurtured like a rare orchid in the hothouse in which we had dwelt for the last three years, had perished in the cold air of reality.

'By the way, I forgot to ask,' she said, fishing in her purse to pay the waiter – now there was no pretence of passing money under the table – 'how did your interview go today?'

'Perfectly well,' I said, and helped her into her coat. She asked for no further details, and I offered none, absorbed as we both were in our own private musings. I got off at Mornington Crescent.

'Goodnight, darling,' she said, but made no effort to kiss me.

'You won't ... ?'

'Not tonight, I think, do you? No. Not tonight.'

I watched until the tram was swallowed by the darkness, and made my way, carefully, slowly, through the black of night, to my front door.

Chapter Three: Helen

MY PARENTS LIVE IN the house to which they retired in Suffolk – not one of the particularly pretty parts of Suffolk, it has little to offer except a neat garden in which the children cannot play and some nice drives, if you like that sort of thing, which neither I nor the children do. It is not near enough to the coast for a seaside visit, nor sufficiently rural to make it a wilderness adventure. They live in a detached house on a road of other detached houses, the gardens separated by larch lap fencing or living screens of leylandii, the drives gravelled, the windows leaded. I don't see them as often as I should, but even twice a year seems to be more than any of us would like. I've long since stopped taking Ben and Lucy: there's nothing for them to do that doesn't get them into trouble, and they're not good at sitting still listening to grown-up conversation. My parents seem quite satisfied with this arrangement. At first I was hurt by their lack of affection for their grandchildren, but now I'm used to it. Richard's family makes up any shortfall in the affection department.

So on Sunday Richard took the kids to see his mum and dad while I drove up the motorway for what amounted to a duty call – except this time I was going for a reason. I wanted my grandfather's address, and I wanted to know why they were no longer on speaking terms.

Lunch was ready when I arrived, and we had time for a small dry sherry while things kept warm in the hostess trolley. I knew exactly what would be on the menu: a leg of lamb from the farm shop up the road, carrots, boiled potatoes (roast potatoes were out of bounds these days), frozen peas, stewed fruit for dessert. We talked about the garden: falling leaves, fluffy seed heads, a few late roses, increased bird activity. We talked about the weather: unusually mild after a recent cold snap, likely to get chilly again but then it is nearly November, not enough rain but there never is. We were running out of things to say, and the sherry only half drunk, when the elderly cat came to the rescue, scratching half-heartedly at the carpet and thus allowing my parents to go into their regular routine about how she shouldn't be allowed in the room, yes she should, no she shouldn't, etc.

We ate our food in silence, and were starting dessert when I thought the time had come to get the ball rolling.

'Richard sends his best.'

'Oh, good,' said my mother. Neither of them sent their best back.

'And the children send their love.' This was not true.

'Thank you, dear.'

'They're both well.'

'Good.'

'Growing up so fast.'

'Well they do,' said my mother. 'We know that.'

'Ben's seven now.'

'Yes.' They were alert, perhaps guessing my purpose. My parents have a sixth sense that can detect emotion before it's expressed.

'Of course, he's at that age where he asks all sorts of funny questions.'

'More apple?'

'No thank you, Mum. It's okay. You don't have to clear yet. I'll do all that.'

She grabbed my bowl and started clattering around at the sink. That left my father, pinned up against the French doors at the end of the table.

'You'll never guess what he asked me yesterday, Dad,' I said, forcing a note of false jollity into my voice.

'I don't imagine I will.'

You can squirm all you like, but you're not getting away. 'He asked me if my mummy and daddy had a mummy and daddy of their own.'

'Indeed.'

'So I had to explain that everyone has mummies and daddies.'

'Quite so.'

'And then he wanted to know who they were and what they looked like, and so on and so forth.'

'Ah.' The crashing at the sink got louder.

'I told him all I could remember about your parents, which isn't very much. But I realised that I hardly know anything about Mum's mum and dad.'

'David,' said my mother, 'I think there's a litter tray to do on the conservatory.'

My father half rose.

'It'll wait,' I said.

'Please could you do it now, David? You know how that smell lingers, and I've got things hanging on the line out there.'

Damn that cat: I swear they've trained it to crap on cue. My father disappeared.

'Have you got any photos of your parents, Mum?'

Crash! Bang! Wallop! I have never heard such noisy washing up.

'I was just wondering if I could possibly borrow them, so I could copy them and show Ben.'

'I don't know, darling.' Her voice was strained. To the percussion of pots and pans was added the whoosh of cat litter being poured from a sack.

'You must have some, surely.'

'Well, if I do they're probably in the attic.'

Aha! So she did have some. And she knew exactly where they were. My mother knows such things.

'I could pop up and get them.'

'Not today, darling.'

'Please, Mum. Ben really wants to know.' Time for a barefaced lie. 'He told me that he loves you so much that he wants to know everything about you.'

Her hands lay still in the soapy water, and she stared out of the window. 'Well,' she said at last, 'I suppose he has a right.'

'I'll go and get them now.'

She looked at me, and I saw something in her eyes – fear? Vulnerability? – that I was not used to seeing. She wiped her hands.

'I've just remembered. There's a box in the bedroom.'

She was gone longer than necessary. Presumably she was thinking things over, what to reveal, what to conceal. My father asked a few questions about Richard's work – he wasn't too sure what data analysis was, but he liked the cold, scientific sound of it.

At length my mother returned with a small flat cardboard box, the sort of thing that might once have contained a silk scarf or a nightgown, a gift box, the lid covered with a cheerful design of holly and poinsettias from a long-ago Christmas. I had an immediate pang of recognition. Of course! The photo box. I hadn't seen it since I was – what, twelve? Ten? When I used to sit on my mother's knee demanding to see pictures of Mummy and Daddy when they were little, of Grandma and Grandpa, of how things were in the old days, the black and white days.

'Wow,' I said, 'that brings back memories.'

My parents exchanged a look. 'I'll finish off the washing up,' said my father. There were only a few glasses left, but he could spin the job out for hours. 'You go through, and I'll bring some coffee.'

'There you are then.' My mother sat down heavily in her armchair, nodding to the box she'd left on the table. 'Anything you need will be in there.'

'I thought we could go through it together.'

'Not now, Helen. I've got a bit of a headache.'

My mother develops headaches in the same way that the cat knows when to fill its litter tray, as a strategic manoeuvre.

The lid came off with a soft *woomph*, rustling a sheet of white tissue paper that had been carefully folded over the photos, putting them to bed, tucking them away. I opened it, terribly aware that my fingers were damp. My mother concentrated on her crossword, trying not to watch me.

There were perhaps a hundred photographs in the box, some large, some small, some colour, most black and white, some in fancy cardboard folders, some with deckle edges, some blurred, fugitive moments snatched from the past.

'Ah, I remember this one.' A glossy ten-by-eight of my parents on their wedding day, posing against the church wall, her hair set in curls, a little veil exploding from her head like a puff of smoke, he handsome and besuited, already balding, a flower in his buttonhole. On the back, in my father's handwriting, 'Rosemary and David Barton, 1976'. This photo, or a copy, used to hang framed on their bedroom wall, so familiar that I became blind to it; was it still there? I couldn't remember.

My mother's eyes flicked up and quickly down again. She tutted. 'Oh, that!'

'You looked lovely.' Surely any woman would like to be told she looked lovely on her wedding day. Not my mother, apparently.

'Hmmph.'

'Daddy was awfully good-looking, wasn't he?'

'Yes, dear, if you say so.'

I saw an opening, and jumped in. 'I suppose he takes after his father.' Silence. 'Are there any pictures of Grandpa Edward when he was that age?'

'I very much doubt it.'

Why not? No, it was too early to ask the direct question. Besides, it was easy enough to find pictures of Edward Barton on the internet. I had already googled him, and knew what he looked like in his thirties, forties, fifties. Dapper, handsome, his hair brushed back, just as my father wore it on his wedding day.

'Look! That's me! Gosh, I can't have been more than four there. Look, Mum.' I held out the photo, a faded colour snap with rounded corners. The reds had turned to yellow, the greens to brown. I sat on the sand, fat and solid in my anorak, determinedly playing with a bucket and spade. My mother lay beside me, her hair caught up in the wind that whipped along the beach. My father was a half-standing, half-sitting blur, rushing back to catch the self-timer. 'Now, where was that? I can remember the beach. I can even remember those shoes I was wearing, they had little flowers on them.' I held it out again; this time she was more interested, some long-suppressed maternal urge fighting its way to the surface. She took the picture, adjusted her glasses, angled it to the light.

'Oh yes!' Her face flushed. 'That was in Devon, Branscombe Bay. It rained for the whole week but you would insist on going to the beach. I think your father took that photograph to record the fact that the sun almost came out for a minute.'

I went round to the side of her chair. 'Look at your hair! It was very long then.'

'Yes, and didn't you love to pull it. Your little fists used to grab it, and ... ' She stopped and sighed and handed back the photograph. 'Well, then,' she said, and returned to her crossword.

A thick manila envelope presented itself next, containing half a dozen very old black and white photographs, all from the same studio, Reynolds of Regent Street, the name printed on the border of each print. Formal portraits of a man and a woman taken, judging by the clothes, some time before the war. She was a handsome, full-figured woman with heavy hair piled up on top of her head. He was tall, rather gaunt, his neat beard liberally streaked with grey ...

Oh my God. Terence and Leonie. It had to be. Six photographs of them standing and sitting, full length and head and shoulders.

My heart was pounding, and I had to look through them a couple of times before I could compose myself to say, in a light, only-slightly-inquisitive voice, 'So who's this, Mum?'

'Who, darl ... ' She recoiled. 'Oh.' She took her glasses off and rubbed her eyes, looking suddenly very old and frail. 'Those are my grandparents. My father's parents.'

'Aaah!' Heart racing. Deep breath. Control the voice. 'What were their names?'

'William and Eleanora Moody.'

'Moody? But that's not your maiden name.'

'No. My father changed it, for professional reasons, to Hamilton.'

'Any particular reason?'

'I suppose he thought Billy Moody didn't sound good. Although God knows, the name suited him.'

'And Hamilton?'

'His mother's maiden name. It's a better name for an actor. Billy Hamilton. Not that it did him much good.'

'I'd forgotten he was an actor.'

'Well, darling, he didn't really do a great deal. Stunt work sometimes. Going to parties, he was good at that. Hanging around the bars and clubs where actors went. But actual acting? No, not much.'

'And his parents?'

'Well of course they were theatrical. In every sense of the word.'

'I wish I'd known them.'

She took the photograph from me, ran her fingers over its surface as if reading Braille. 'Eleanora died when you were three. Don't you remember her at all?'

'Not really.'

'What a shame. She was quite a woman.' This was promising. And yet – here was my own mother, who barely had anything to do with my children, so little that they would surely forget her ... What a shame you hardly knew her, that you don't remember her, even though she was alive all that time, just up the motorway, but she didn't care much for you, you see ...

'What colour was Eleanora's hair?'

'Dyed red,' said my mother, 'right to the very end of her life.'

'So I suppose,' I said, as if this had only just occurred to me, 'that she was the basis for the character of Leonie in *The Interlude*.'

Her voice changed – hard again, businesslike. 'Possibly. I forget all the ins and outs.'

'But in the book ...'

'Oh, that wretched book! It's caused so much trouble!'

'He has an affair with Leonie right at the beginning. It's quite explicit.'

She turned the corners of her mouth down and wrinkled her nose, as if she could smell the cat litter. 'I'm well aware of that.'

'So is it true?'

'What?'

'Did my grandfather Edward have an affair with your grandmother Eleanora?'

'I have absolutely no idea what went on in that man's mind.'

'What did your father think about it?'

'Not much. He'd gone to America by the time the book came out. It rather passed us by.'

'But the film. Surely he saw the film.'

'I suppose so, darling. Look, do we have to go into all this now?'

'I'm just curious.' Time was running out. 'Your parents and Daddy's parents knew each other, didn't they?'

'Of course they did. Edward worked with my father for a while. They kept in touch. That's how we met, when we were quite young.'

'I wish you'd tell me about it.'

'There's nothing much to tell. Really, Helen, can't this wait for another day?' It was getting dark outside, and she looked at her watch. Soon it would be time for me to go. There was so much I needed to ask.

'Who was Rose?'

A momentary flinch, nothing more. 'Who, darling?'

'Rose. In the book. The actress that he has an affair with.'

'I don't remember. Everyone has an affair with everyone else, as I recall.'

'Jayne Mansfield played her in the film. Blonde woman with big bosoms, remember?'

'I don't think she existed in real life.'

'That's what Edward always said.'

'Well then.'

'But ...' No: tread softly. 'She's a wonderful character.'

'Wonderful? A hard-hearted tart who breaks up his marriage? You have funny ideas sometimes.'

'Thank goodness she didn't really exist, then.'

My mother put her newspaper down with an annoyed little slap. 'There's no good looking in those books for the truth, you know. Edward was always a liar.' Some residue of anger was bubbling up to the surface. 'All that stuff about having polio, and not being able to serve in the army. There was nothing wrong with Edward Barton except he was a habitual liar and he drank too much.'

'You talk about him as if he was dead.'

'Well he might as well be, shut away in that house.'

'What did he and Daddy argue about?'

The door opened, and my father entered with a tray. 'Coffee,' he said, the spoons rattling in the saucers. 'Here we are.'

'I'm going to the loo,' said my mother, hurrying from the room. My father looked out of the window, his back towards me.

'Daddy,' I said, carefully replacing photographs, smoothing out tissue paper.

'Hmm?'

'Where does your father live?'

'What? Oh look, that bloody magpie's back.' He waved his arms, tapped on the glass. 'Shoo! Go on! Bugger off!'

'Dad ...'

'You have to get rid of them. They're vermin.'

'Where does Edward Barton live?'

'Why on earth would you need to know that?' He did not turn round.

'I thought I might get in touch with him.' Silence. 'Write him a letter, or something. I just re-read *The Interlude*, you see, and I thought it was ...'

'Why?' His voice was sharp.

'Why did I read it?'

'Yes.' A note of accusation.

'Because he's my grandfather.' Pause, silence. 'And because it's a great book.'

'There's nothing great about it.'

The sight of his cardiganed back was starting to annoy me, and I snapped, 'Well, you've done very nicely out of it, I should have thought.'

No reply.

'Look, Daddy, I just want to get in touch with him before he, you know ...'

'You won't get any sense out of him.'

'I'd like to have a go.'

'What's the point?' Now he turned round, his face pale. 'He's never been a part of your life.'

'That's not true.'

'That was a long time ago.'

'Why did you argue? What was it about?'

'There was no argument.'

'There must have been.'

'We just ... look, we came to the conclusion that we had very little in common. It was quite mutual I assure you.'

'Daddy ... He's your father.'

'Be that as it may.' He sat down and sighed. 'I suppose it won't do any harm. God knows what sort of state you'll find him in. I don't think he's very well.'

'He's very old.'

'I mean in the ...' He tapped his temple. 'You know.'

'That's sad. But still.'

He could see I was not to be deterred. 'All right. All *right.*' He lowered his voice, perhaps not wanting my mother to overhear. 'I'll give you his address. But promise me something, Helen.'

'What?'

'Don't rake things up.'

'What sort of things?'

My mother was back. 'Oh, that sodding magpie,' said my father, getting up and waving his arms. 'I'll wring its bloody neck.'

I didn't wait for Harry to ask me out for dinner – he has no money, and it would put him in an awkward position if we had to go Dutch. Anyway, I didn't mind paying: I wanted his advice, and it was worth the price of a meal. The fact that on the evening in question Richard was working in Bristol and the kids were having a sleepover at Annette's was just a coincidence.

I hadn't talked to anyone about what my parents told me. I spent some sleepless nights trying to figure out my family tree. I drew it on scraps of paper and even tried something complicated with an Excel spreadsheet, but the facts refused to focus, overlaid every time by the more vivid images of Edward Barton's fiction. He was my grandfather, my father's father, and he had imagined an affair with my great grandmother, my mother's mother's mother – nasty lies, according to my parents, but what would Edward tell me? And what good would it do me – or my children – to know this unsavoury truth? Was I researching a biography, or just going through my family's closet? Was it good for me as a writer? Was there a point to this muckraking?

I knew what Richard and Annette would say, but it was Harry's opinion I wanted. I mentioned it quite casually after class one day – 'could I pick your brains about something?' – and he was on the scent of opportunity straight away. 'About your grandfather?'

I took him to a little place off Charing Cross Road, eight tables, low lighting, a fantastic cellar and the kind of service that's there when you want it, invisible when you don't. No fussy filling of wineglasses, no 'hi guys' or trying to be your new best friend. I've been there maybe ten times, but when we walked in it was Harry they seemed to recognise, Harry who got the smiles and the 'good evenings'. We were shown to our table, candles were lit and drinks ordered.

'This is nice,' he said, putting a hand on mine. 'Thank you.'

'My pleasure.'

'I don't often go to places like this.' He looked around, approving the chalkboards, the gingham tablecloths. 'It's quite a treat.' He'd made an effort for the evening: in place of his usual denim shirts and scruffy fisherman's sweaters he was wearing a jacket and a shirt with a proper collar. Jeans, of course, but neither faded nor ripped. Impossible not to notice how well they fitted. My dress was one of the most expensive pieces in my wardrobe, a little Jasper Conran number in dark plum, but I felt dowdy while Harry was dazzling. His physical beauty seemed too large, too bright for the enclosed surroundings. I wanted to put on shades.

We made small talk about the course, my fellow students, his bosses. We ordered – I went for a safe chicken escalope, he ordered something daring that involved offal. He chose wine with effortless *savoir faire*.

'So,' he said, as we waited for the food, 'you've contacted him.'

'I've written him a letter, yes.'

'What did you ask him?'

'I just said hello, that sort of thing. Said I'd like to get to know him. There's some very interesting family stuff that I want to...'

'You know what?' said Harry, apparently not finding the family stuff as interesting as I did. 'You should ask him about the screen rights.'

'Sorry?'

'To *The Interlude*. It would make a fantastic movie.'

'It already did.'

'But a new version that blows the lid off the crucible of post-War English morality.'

I wasn't sure if crucibles had lids, but let it pass. 'Go on.'

'A good screenwriter could make something amazing out of it.' He touched my hand again, rubbing my thumb with his. 'Ask him.'

'He hasn't heard from me for about a hundred years, Harry. I can hardly say "Hello Mr Barton, it's your long-lost granddaughter here, any chance of an option on *The Interlude*?", can I?'

He withdrew his hand.

'Anyway, I've got no idea whether he'll even reply. Apparently he's a bit doolally.'

'Then we should contact his agent.'

We? 'I don't think he has an agent any more. He's very old.'

'Someone must take care of business for him.'

'Let's take this a bit more slowly, shall we?'

'I'm sorry, Helen. I know I'm running ahead of myself. It's in my nature. Once I get excited by something, I just want to ... You know.' He put his hands behind his head, the muscles bulging in his shirtsleeves. 'Grab it.'

The wine came, he tasted and nodded. It was delicious.

'Anyway,' I said, 'I wanted to ask you something.'

'No such thing as a free meal, right?'

I thought this remark vulgar, but let it pass. 'Do you think ... I mean, as a writer.'

'Of course.' He touched my hand again.

'Can you justify causing pain to other people?'

'That old chestnut.'

'I mean, if you dig up things that people would prefer you not to ...'

'A writer's only duty is to the truth.' Under the table, our legs touched.

It was hard to concentrate. 'But I'm not a writer. I'm a housewife and a mother.'

'You could be.' He looked straight into my eyes, and the meaning I saw there was quite explicit.

'What I mean is – if I find out that what Edward Barton was writing was the truth ...'

'You mean, if he really did have an affair?'

'Mmm.' I took a sip of wine. This wasn't at all what I expected. Was it? 'If I was to write something that hurt my parents ... Or my husband ...'

'Helen.' Harry interrupted me. 'A writer doesn't count the cost. A writer works on instinct.' He turned my hand over, traced the veins on my wrist. 'That's what it means,' he said, 'to be a writer.'

The food arrived. We ate. I tasted nothing. We talked of other things, Harry's literary projects, the novel that was no closer, it seemed, to a deal. He reverted constantly to his wish to write for the screen. He mentioned a forthcoming cull at Milton College, in which his job might cease to be. 'If I was published,' he said, 'they wouldn't dare.' His eyes flashed under dark brows. 'Published or produced.'

I said very little about myself. What could I say, that didn't involve my husband or children? Harry went to the loo while I settled the bill. He reappeared with my coat, and helped me into it, standing close, breathing on my neck. If there was any doubt in my mind about how the evening was going to end, it evaporated at that moment.

We took a taxi. Ruinously expensive – but what price his hand on my leg, his lips on my throat? By the time we were heading south down Whitehall we were kissing with tongues. He tasted of wine and garlic. I pushed thoughts of Richard, far away in Bristol, from my mind. Harry was here and now in the back of a cab.

We crossed the river.

Chapter Four: Helen

I SAT ON THE TRAIN, watching the drab brown countryside flashing past the window, here and there a splash of bright yellow or deep orange on some tree that held on to its leaves, but mostly, as the grey of the city gave way to the country, just wet, cold sludge. Trains don't rock in rhythm any more, but even so I kept hearing the word, in time with the imaginary beat of the wheels, 'Adultery ... Adultery ... Adultery ... ' I felt like Garbo in *Anna Karenina*, Celia Johnson in *Brief Encounter*, or any other gorgeous actress who has had regrets on a train. It was warm in the carriage, and I snuggled into my faux fur coat, savouring the guilt. Since that first hectic night, Harry and I had been together precisely five times in three weeks, and I could still give a blow-by-blow account of each meeting, with a beginning, a middle and an end, interesting subplots, a few red herrings, and an explosive climax. It was a very literary affair.

How easy it had been, with Richard away and the children so much in demand for play dates and sleepovers... How little resistance I encountered, from duty or circumstance or my own conscience. I slipped into a double life quite easily. Nothing happened. No alarms went off. Richard did not denounce me as a vile fornicator, unfit to be the mother of his innocent children. I did not look different or smell different. We still made love, when he was at home, which was mostly at weekends. I was no more or less enthusiastic than before

– nothing gave the game away. I saw the two things – sex with my husband, and sex with my lover – as quite unrelated. Richard was happy, the children were happy, and if they could cope with my infidelity, I was quite sure I could.

Sometimes when falling asleep at night, I saw myself walking along a clifftop like the Fool in the Tarot pack, merrily chasing butterflies on the edge of the abyss – one false step, and down I go ... But those visions didn't last. A few deep breaths slowed my heart and cleared my brain, and I slept, for the most part, calmly. No nightmares. No miserable watches of the night, wrestling with my conscience. What with childcare, home-making, creative writing classes and having an affair, I was too tired for conscience.

I held the letter in my hands. Edward Barton's letter, my grandfather's letter, written with a fountain pen in blue ink on pale blue watermarked paper. Printed at the top of the page in Roman capitals was STONEFIELD, the name of the house.

My dear Helen,

Thank you so much for your kind letter. Of course I would be delighted to see you. As my health prevents me from travelling to town as much as I would like, perhaps you could visit me at home some time? It would be such a pleasure for me. Lunchtime is best, as I find I can no longer stay up as late as I once did. Thank you also for the lovely things you said about *The Interlude*. I haven't read the book for an awfully long time, but seeing it through your eyes is almost enough to make me curious. Please let me know a date that suits, and I will look forward to seeing you then.

Your affectionate grandfather,
Edward

The writing was firm and fluid, not at all what I'd expected. According to my parents, the old man was a raving alcoholic and/or completely demented, surviving from one bottle of Scotch to the next. So who was this charming, gracious correspondent, this 'affectionate grandfather'? I rang to make a date, and spoke to his secretary Samuel, who was efficient and polite and gave me precise directions to the house. Train to Banbury, and then a taxi, if I didn't mind – it was rather an upheaval to get the old man into a car, and he couldn't leave him unattended. Only three miles. Of course I didn't mind. I was thrilled. I didn't tell my parents.

I put the letter away and stared out of the carriage window, seeing nothing, replaying the events of the night before – Harry, of course, the best yet, a full orchestral symphony with choir and organ ... Oh yes, definitely with an organ, and what an organ ... I smiled and closed my eyes and must have dozed for a while, as the next thing I heard was the conductor's voice saying that we would shortly be arriving at Banbury, and to take all my personal belongings with me when I left the train.

I felt drugged by my nap and had no desire to stir from the warm carriage on to the cold, wet platform of a country station. And what an ugly station it was, railings and a car park and what might have been a goods yard, some dilapidated steps leading down to a dispiriting ticket office and then nothing, just tarmac and chainlink fence.

But there were cabs.

I gave directions to Stonefield and we were off, round a Byzantine one-way system, through roadworks and traffic lights and finally into the open countryside, along the side of Edge Hill, the great flat battleground far below us. From motorway to A road to B road, finally to narrow country lanes flanked by hedges, fields flickering bright green through the gaps, rooks overhead, light drizzle on the windscreen.

'Don't suppose you get out of town much,' said the driver, reading me for exactly what I am – a pampered city creature in my faux fur coat and unsuitable footwear. One soft patch of mud and I'd be up to my stockinged ankles.

'No, and it's lovely,' I said, my voice sounding crushingly posh after his soft, flat Midlands murmur.

He didn't speak for the rest of the journey. It did not take long.

We rounded a corner and there, nestling against a copse of trees, was Stonefield, a large, handsome grey house, wet slates shining on the roof, smoke coming from the chimney.

'That's it,' said the driver, swinging into a rutted track with a high ridge of grass in the centre. 'Sure this is the place you want?'

'Absolutely. My grandfather lives here.'

'Well,' he said.

We lost sight of the house as the drive dipped and turned, leading to a dark dead end surrounded by yew trees and laurels. Tall black iron railings to the left, and beyond them a screen of unkempt bushes. The double gates, wide enough to admit a carriage, were open. I was expected. I paid the driver, and off he went. I was alone, far from home, the only sound the gentle drip of wet laurel leaves, the song of a bird.

The front door opened, and a middle-aged black man in a sports jacket and grey slacks stepped out to meet me.

'Helen?' He held out his hand.

'Yes, hello. You must be Samuel.'

'Please come in. He's expecting you.' He took my coat – a butler as well as a secretary, it seemed. 'If you just wait in here for a minute' – he opened a door off the hall – 'I'll go and see if he's ready. Make yourself comfortable. There are drinks, if you need one.' He closed the door softly, and I heard the receding creak of the stairs.

It was a beautiful room, full of old, comfortable furniture, rugs and blankets thrown here and there, cushions and bolsters. Floor-length curtains in William Morris prints hung at the French windows, beyond which a paved terrace led to the lawn. A baby grand was covered in silver-framed photographs of my grandfather with various celebrities, among them Laurence Olivier and Jayne Mansfield. There were prints and paintings on every wall – good stuff, by the look of it. And books, books, books. Shelves everywhere. Piles of books on tables, on the floor. Not strewn, but carefully placed to be in easy reach if, for instance, you chose to recline on the big squashy sofa. A cushion or two behind the head, a rug drawn up to the chest, a cup of tea somewhere nearby, and a pleasant afternoon could slip away ...

'He'll see you now.'

I jumped a little; Samuel moved very quietly.

'Oh good. Thank you.'

We climbed the stairs – more paintings, more photos lined the walls, each one a piece of the puzzle, tempting and teasing me until I seemed to know less, not more, about the man I was about to meet. So many people and places and things, going back so far, before I was born, the past more real in this house than me, the intruder from the present.

The landing was deeply carpeted. Vases of flowers at every window. More stairs leading up to the top floor.

'Here we are. He's up and dressed,' said Samuel in a hushed voice, 'but he does get rather tired, so please don't be offended if he has to ring for me.'

'I understand, of course.'

He tapped on the door. 'Enter!' came a voice from within, higher than I had expected, cracked with age. He's in his nineties, I told myself. Of course he sounds old.

Samuel opened the door. I saw heavy red velvet edged with gold braid, like the curtain at an old-fashioned theatre. Samuel's hand found the opening, and pulled the curtain aside. I stepped into a reddish gloom.

'Helen.'

Click! A light came on, a table lamp, and beside it the silhouette of my grandfather seated in a wing-backed chair.

'Come in, child.'

I stepped forward. Click! Another light on another table beside him, and this time a soft yellow glow lit the old man in his chair, a tartan rug over his knees, a tweed jacket, soft cotton shirt and a plaid tie. His hair, still thick, was soft and white, brushed back from his face. His hands, big and knuckly, lay in his lap. 'Come here, my dear. Let me see you.'

I stepped forward. The room smelt of old leather and pipe tobacco. He laughed softly, a creaky, wheezy sound. 'I'm sorry,' he said, wiping his mouth, 'but I was about to say that you've grown. Which, really, is not surprising.'

I bent down and kissed him on the cheek. His skin was smooth and well shaven.

'You were a child when I saw you last. Thirteen years old, I think.'

'That's right.' He'd remembered. I must have meant something to him. 'When Grandma died.'

'Grandma ...' He took my hand. His was dry and papery, but the grip was strong. 'I'd forgotten that you called her that. Grandma ...' He laughed, a sad, short laugh. 'My Geraldine. Grandma. I don't think she liked that very much.'

'I'm sorry.'

'She hated getting old, but she loved children. Always wanted to be with the children.' He squeezed my hand again. 'Adored you. Her only grandchild. Isn't that funny? You're the only one.'

'And I have two children of my own now.'

'Two?' This was news to him. 'Well. My great-grandchildren.' He let go of my hand.

'I'd love you to meet them.'

'Yes ...' He sounded vague, and I wondered if he was tired already. He sighed deeply. 'Sit down, my dear. Over there.' He indicated a chair by the window, at rightangles to his. 'I'm sorry about the gloom. My eyes aren't much good any more. I save them for reading and writing, what little I can manage.'

I watched his slow, tortoise-like movements as he moved the

rug, fished around beneath himself for a handkerchief, blew his nose, put the handkerchief away, replaced the rug, and finally settled.

'Thank you for letting me come and see you.'

'How is your father?'

'He's fine.'

'And your mother?'

'Yes, fine, thank you.' I wanted to say 'they send their love,' but they didn't.

'I was surprised to get your letter.' His speech betrayed the vowels of a bygone age – 'surpraaahsed'. 'And delighted, of course.'

'It seems so silly, not knowing you.'

'Ah, well.' He was waiting for more.

'And I read *The Interlude*. It's such a wonderful book.'

'Thank you. Was this your father's idea?'

'No.'

'Your mother's?'

'Certainly not. In fact, they weren't keen on my coming at all.'

'Ah!' He raised his hands, palms outward, as if pushing something away. 'You are not their ambassador, then.'

'I'm afraid not.'

'I'm rather glad. That means we can talk about them behind their backs.' He smiled. 'One of the few pleasures that remains as one gets older. I sometimes think that's what friends are for. And family even more so.' He rubbed his hands together. 'To gossip about.'

'I suppose that's where you got a lot of your ideas from. For your novels.'

'Not so fast, not so fast. I want to hear all about David and Rosemary first. Tell me, are you close to your parents?'

'I suppose so. I see them quite regularly.'

'That's not quite what I meant. Would you tell them, for instance, if you had done something wicked?'

That hit home. 'No, I don't think I would.'

'Why not?'

'They wouldn't necessarily understand.'

'Or approve?'

'Probably not.'

'Why do you think that is?'

I had come here to interview him, but he was asking the questions. 'I don't know. They've never been very ...'

'Yes?'

'Warm. Sympathetic.'

'Ah!' He clapped. 'Exactly so. Not very warm or sympathetic. I must be a wicked old man to say this, but I always found my son to be rather a cold fish.'

'Well ...' Some trace of filial loyalty prevented me from agreeing.

'Was he a loving father?'

'When I was little, yes.'

'But not later? In your teens? Your adult life?'

'Not really. He became ... distant.'

'Yes, yes.' He nodded, and closed his eyes, swallowed. 'I suppose fathers often do. And your mother? Rosemary? She was a beautiful child, oh, so beautiful, running around in the Connecticut sun as brown as a berry, her hair almost white. I was very fond of her.'

It was hard to imagine my mother running around, blonde and carefree, in the Connecticut sunshine. Nowadays her hair was brown and set. 'We get along all right.'

'*All right*. Oh well. At least you're all on speaking terms, that's the great thing. So many families aren't, you know, what with divorces and all that complication. I do think that's the saddest thing of all, when families break up.'

I thought of Richard and the children and the danger I was putting us all in. The luxury of regret when I was still sore from last night ...

'I suppose they've told you all sorts of things about me.'

'Well ...'

'That I'm a drunk, for instance.'

'Oh.'

'You can't deny it. That's your mother, I bet. She became such a prude. A couple of glasses of wine with dinner, a brandy or a G and T, and you were a hopeless dipso. Is she still like that? Disapproving?'

'She has a drink sometimes.'

'Don't tell me. A dry sherry.'

'Yes.'

'I knew it! A dry sherry, indeed. What a finicking little drink that is. And what about David? I suppose she's padlocked the drinks cabinet so he can't get anywhere near it.'

'Well ...'

'And my daughter Valerie, she's a dried-up old prune. God! What did I do to be cursed with such puritanical children! What's life for, if not for living? I'd rather bang down the lid of my own coffin than live like that, counting every drop and every crumb. Well, they didn't go through the war, did they? War teaches you to live each second to the full. To grab at life, to take it and squeeze it. Oh, we live in a world of accountants now.' He stopped, a wiped his mouth. 'I'm sorry, my dear. I get on what Samuel calls my rocking horse, and I don't know when to stop.'

'It's all right. I agree with you.'

'You do? Are you a grabber? A squeezer?'

'I suppose I am, rather.'

He leaned forward in his chair. 'Are you married?'

'I have a husband. Richard.'

'Good! Splendid! A very fine fellow, I'm quite sure.'

'Yes, he's a ...'

'Now, what did you want to ask me?'

Time for business, then. 'Well, there are so many things.'

'What springs to mind?' He picked up a little bell, and rang it. 'I shall ask Samuel for drinks, shall I? Now that I've ascertained that you won't disapprove.' Samuel appeared noiselessly at the door; he must have been waiting on the landing. 'Drinks, Samuel. Whisky for me. And let me see, what does one serve one's granddaughter? Orange squash?'

'I'll have a vodka and tonic, if that's okay.'

'Vod and ton. Very good.' Samuel withdrew. 'Now, the floor is yours. Ask, and it shall be given unto you, within reason. You haven't come to touch me for money, have you?'

'No.'

'Just as well. There's precious little left, and I need that. *He* doesn't come cheap.' He nodded towards the door. 'And there's the upkeep of this old ruin, which costs a small fortune.'

'But surely the books and the films still bring in a decent amount?'

'You'd be sorely disappointed if I told you how much. People imagine one is rolling in it. Lousy with it, as we used to say. I don't complain. I've managed to survive for an awfully long time without doing a stroke of work, which is something of an achievement.'

This seemed to invite the question I'd been longing to ask: why no more books after *The Interlude*? In over fifty years, during which he could have capitalised on his fame and success – nothing. I thought for a moment, trying to frame the question in a way that did not sound offensive, and the opportunity passed.

'Of course, I've had a very happy life. A wonderful marriage that ended too soon. Wonderful friends, and a certain measure of success. You liked *The Interlude*, you say?'

'Very much.'

'Doesn't it seem hopelessly old-fashioned?'

'Not at all. In fact I was saying to my ... friend that it seems very up to date. Quite challenging, in its way.'

'Really? Do go on.'

He was lapping it up. 'The treatment of sex, for instance.'

'Oh, the sex. Well, it was regarded as terribly shocking at the time. Nauseating, said some of the critics. Unwholesome. Decadent. All the usual claptrap that you get when you're honest about it.'

'And were you honest?'

'About sex? Yes, within the bounds of decorum. One didn't use four-letter words in those days. The Chatterley Trial was still a little way off, even then. And besides, I never had a taste for vulgarity. I do think there's a difference between honesty and vulgarity. Although, as your parents have probably told you, I can be terribly vulgar in private life, especially after a nip of dry sherry.'

Samuel returned with drinks on a tray: whisky in a cut crystal tumbler for Edward, vod and ton in a highball glass for me, plenty of ice, no lemon.

'That's all, Samuel. When's lunch?'

'Ready whenever you are. Just ring.'

'Off you pop, then.'

The door closed, and we were alone. Edward took a good long gulp of whisky.

'How much,' he said, 'do you know of your ancestry?'

'The basics,' I said. 'You and Geraldine on my father's side.'

'And on your mother's side?'

'Her father was an actor called Billy Hamilton.'

'Ah! You know that.'

'And her mother was American.'

'Her name?'

I racked my brains. Did I ever know my grandmother's name? She who died long, long before I was born. 'I can't remember.'

'Laura Casselden. Daughter of a very wealthy Hollywood producer. I forget his first name. Met him once or twice. Would be easy to find out, if you're genealogically inclined. The wife was from one of those decayed East Coast families, not quite Kennedy but not far off, half of them were barmy and the rest were gold-diggers.'

'Which was she?'

'Definitely not barmy, if that's what you're worried about. No hereditary insanity as far as we know.' He laughed. 'It's not an Ibsen play, thank God.'

'Like *Ghosts*.'

'Good.' He nodded, satisfied that I'd read with proper attention. 'And what have they told you about Billy?'

'That his parents were actors. William and Eleanora Moody.'

'Tick. V. G. Ten out of ten.'

'With whom, I believe, you worked.' I kept my face impassive.

'Worked? I suppose you could call it that.' His eyebrow was cocked, one side of his mouth turned up, and he looked at me, waiting for the question.

Right. Here goes. 'So how much of the early part of *The Interlude* is true, then?'

'All of it, of course.'

'Ah.' I sipped my drink. 'So you and Eleanora ...'

'Were lovers. Yes. Complicated, isn't it? If you worked it out on paper, it would be madly incestuous.'

'Eleanora was Billy's mother ... so she was my great-grandmother.'

'If I was still capable of shame, you'd make me blush. Fortunately, my dear, I don't have enough blood to spare.'

'And what about her husband? Didn't he mind?'

'Well, what do you think?'

'I imagine he was jealous.'

'Good answer. But not jealous in quite the conventional way.'

'He wanted you for himself.'

'Rather.'

'And did he ...'

'I'm afraid poor old William was more of a looker than a doer. It can't have been easy for him, growing up when he did. A child of the Victorian era, the Oscar Wilde scandal and so forth, he didn't have much of a chance. I think they either ran away to Paris in those days, or made a respectable marriage, which is what William did. And then he sublimated it all into his art. Eleanora didn't mind too much. She was a free spirit, and always had some young lover on the go. I wasn't the only one. William gave her a certain degree of security, and, more importantly, allowed her to be on stage – which she adored. Terrible old ham, of course – well, they both were, relics of a bygone age even in the thirties – but they took it ever so seriously. Oh, it was dreadful rubbish, my dear! The fag-end of the art theatre, a scrap of Expressionism here, a bit of Symbolism there, a pinch of Vorticism and Futurism and all those bloody awful isms that flourished between the wars. All it really amounted to was an excuse for William to get attractive young men to parade up and down in their underpants.'

'While he body-painted them.'

'Oh, I'd quite forgotten about that. Ugh!' He shuddered. 'I can still feel that stuff dripping down my back. Silly old sod. Why didn't he just take what he wanted?'

'Would he have got it?'

'Once or twice, maybe. Don't look shocked, child. People did it even then. Not my cup of tea, but where's the harm in making an old man happy? Perhaps some of the other boys did, I don't know. I had my hands full.'

'With Eleanora?'

'Indeed. And quite a handful she was. A very handsome woman, you know.'

'Were you in love with her?'

'Was I in love with her ... ' He sipped his drink. 'I was very young, and she was the first woman I ever went to bed with. Of course I was in love with her – or what I thought was love, anyway. I was overwhelmed by her. One is, isn't one? By one's first.'

I thought of the two boyfriends before Richard; overwhelmed was certainly not the word. Harry, yes. A tsunami.

'And what was she like?'

'Eleanora? Exactly as described in the book. Nothing was changed except the name. I forget what I called her.'

'Leonie Black. Terence and Leonie Black.'

'Good lord. Haven't thought of that for years. I didn't take great pains to disguise her, did I?'

'Haven't you watched the film?'

'No, my dear. It may surprise you to learn that I don't actually like the film very much.'

'Oh, but it's wonderful!'

'So everyone tells me. But I can't view it objectively. All I see is the people it was based on and, for that matter, the people that were in it. All of them dead.' He sighed. 'It wasn't a terribly happy experience for me, making the film. A strange time in my life ...'

We were getting close to the heart of the mystery – the sudden drying up of the wellspring from which had poured, in previous years, so much writing.

'Anyway, enough of that. Ask me more about the book.'

'So if the part about Leonie is true, then ...'

'Ah!' He placed his empty glass carefully back on the tray. 'The sixty-four-thousand-dollar question, as they said on that awful gameshow. Did I have an affair? That's what you're driving at, I take it.'

'Rose.' My heart beat faster, and I had to relax the grip on my glass before it shattered in my hand. 'I did wonder.'

'Everyone wondered, including my wife.'

'I can imagine.'

'There was an actress that I based the character of Rose on. She was real enough.'

'I thought so.'

'Her name was Lily, and she did have an affair with an actor in the company.'

'But not you?'

'Not, alas, me. You see, I met Geraldine, and I settled into what I can only describe as a very contented marriage. Happy ever after, do you see? Which, from a novelist's point of view, is an absolute disaster. I mean, what have you got to write about? No more upheavals and dramas. Happiness is marvellous in real life, but it's a terrible handicap for an artist. So what can one do?'

'You write about your friends.'

'Bingo. Clever girl. You become a sort of vampire. You take a little bit here, a little bit there, and you send yourself off on an adventure.'

'But in fact you were faithful to Geraldine.'

'Well ...' He pressed his fingertips together, and considered something. 'I suppose it won't do any harm now, it's so long ago, and besides, the wench is dead. I wasn't quite the perfect faithful husband that I pretended to be. One was away from home so often, on promotional tours or film sets or whatever. There was the occasional lapse. Actresses, you know, who desperately wanted one to put them in a movie. Or literary ladies in the USA, they were the worst, positively predatory, bagging one as if they were big-game hunters. But there was no great love. Nothing that I would even call an affair, and I certainly didn't feel the need to tell my wife. One didn't in those days.

'Do my parents know about you and Eleanora?'

'I really have no idea. Did you ask?'

'It's not the sort of thing I could discuss with them.'

'No, my dear, I don't suppose it is. Of course, Billy knew – I mean, he could hardly fail to. I was screwing his mother when I met him.' The coarse word sounded strange coming from this frail, white-haired old man. 'I thought he was going to beat me up or something. I don't think he was terribly pleased, as I was only a few years older than he was, but then again I wasn't exactly the first. Anyway, it didn't last for long, and somehow he and I became friends. Which, to cut a very long story short, is how your parents met.'

'Your son married his daughter.'

'Precisely. It was like one of those old-fashioned dynastic marriages.' He sighed. 'All very romantic, of course.'

'So why didn't you write about it?'

'I beg your pardon?'

'You just stopped in the sixties, when you would surely have had a lot more freedom.'

'I'd run out of steam by then. I firmly believe in shutting up when you've got nothing worthwhile to say. There's nothing worse than these writers who churn out book after book, each one a little duller, until nobody can remember why they liked them in the first place.'

'But surely after *The Interlude* you could have written anything you liked.'

'If I'd carried on, it would have just been for the sake of making money – and, at the time, money was not an issue. I was rich enough to be pig-headed about it. My agent was furious of course: I was the goose that laid the golden egg, and he never forgave me for stopping. I see his point now. I could have knocked out a handful of commercial successes, made a couple more big films, and I'd be sitting pretty today. But there it is. I did what seemed right at the time. I don't regret it. The only thing I do regret is that one seems to have been somewhat ... forgotten.'

'That will change.'

'You think so? Not in my lifetime, I'm afraid.'

'But supposing that they did a TV adaptation ...'

He threw his hands in the air. 'Oh, don't start that. I've been round the houses with TV people more times than I care to remember. Nothing ever comes of it.'

'Maybe now the time is right.'

'Maybe.' He closed his eyes, and fell silent. Was this the end of our interview? He rang the bell. 'I wonder if we might go for a little turn around the garden before lunch? It's not absolutely raining, is it?'

I peeped out through the curtain. 'No. It looks quite nice.'

'Samuel will tell me off, and I shall insist. I haven't been outside for days. I like to see what's going on in nature. You don't mind me leaning on you, do you?'

'Of course not.'

Samuel was reluctant to let his employer out into the cold, damp November air, but after twenty minutes of arguing and tying of scarves, Edward and I were walking at a snail's pace along what might once have been well-tended formal flower beds. Huge dahlias lolled here and there, held up by spiders' webs. The terrace was black with berries from the ivy that clad that side of the house, pecked at by pigeons. He pointed things out: a once-magnificent hydrangea, now sadly woody and half dead; a pond that he dug himself, where in happier times goldfish frolicked, now a sort of boggy declivity choked with duckweed.

'I can't tell you how much this has bucked me up,' he said, when we had completed a circuit of the house. There was a broken-down greenhouse, the glass thick with algae, and by it a bench, on to which Edward carefully lowered himself. 'I've always rather dreaded thinking about the past and what might have been, but now, talking about it with you, it isn't really so bad.'

'Bad? You achieved so much!'

'The critics never liked me though. Nothing sets them off like popularity. They find it suspicious.'

'How would you feel,' I asked, 'if someone wrote a book about you?'

'Good luck to them,' he said, gazing into the distance.

'And if someone were to adapt *The Interlude* for television ...'

'Is there something you want to say, Helen? That's the second time you've mentioned it.'

'I have a friend who would love to have a go.'

'And is he very rich and powerful in the world of television, your ... friend?'

'No. But he's a very talented writer.' I still hadn't read any of Harry's work, but he'd told me so often how good it was that I was inclined to believe him. 'I think he'd make a wonderful job of it.'

'Well then, he must give it a shot.'

'Really? Can he?'

'I'm afraid he'll be wasting his time.'

'Are the rights available?'

'Excessively so. I haven't been optioned for many a long year.'

'So can I tell him ...'

'Tell him to do his worst, with my blessing.'

'Thank you.'

'And I have a little favour to ask you in return.'

Some hideous negotiation with my parents?

'Go on.'

'It's a big thing to ask, and I have always intended to ask Samuel – but he's going to have quite enough to deal with when I go, with the house and everything. I need someone to go through all the papers and books and things in there' – he waved towards the house – 'and decide what, if anything, is worth keeping. There's the diaries and notebooks and original manuscripts. And for that matter, there are the books themselves – all of them, apart from *The Interlude*, out of print. I suppose what I'm really asking is ...'

'Yes?'

'Would you like to be my literary executor?'

'Oh.' My stomach flipped over. 'Are you serious?'

'You seem like an intelligent enough young woman. And after all, you are family, aren't you?'

'Yes, but ...'

'Well I'm certainly not going to leave it to my children. Can you imagine? They'd stick it all on the bonfire before I was even cold.'

'I'm sure they wouldn't.'

'You don't know them.' He shook his head and held up his hands. 'Let's not go into all that. Suffice to say that neither David nor Valerie was ever interested in my writing. On the whole I think they were embarrassed by it.'

'I see.'

'I don't really care what happens after I'm dead – I'm not one of those writers like Waugh who become obsessed by reputation and posterity. When I'm dead, I'm dead. But on the other hand, I'm not completely irresponsible. I recognise that my literary estate has potential value – to scholars, if nothing else. And who knows? Someone might make a few bob out of it one day; stranger things have happened. I don't imagine it's going to make you a terribly rich woman, and you'll probably curse the day you agreed to take it on. But if you would just think about it, then I could instruct my solicitor to make a little amendment to my will ...'

'Of course I'll do it.'

'Really?'

'Absolutely. It would be an honour.'

'Well, I must say ... ' Some colour came to his cheeks. 'That's just wonderful. Thank you so much.' He took my hand in both of his. 'And now,' he said, 'if you don't mind, I shall have to trundle back indoors and take a rest. Samuel will give you lunch.'

'I've tired you out.'

'You've done me all the good in the world. Just the old motor needs a rest.' He tapped his chest. 'When you get to my age, you respect the signs.'

He took my arm, and we shuffled back to the house. Samuel ushered me into the dining room, where there was a cold lunch laid out. From the sounds that followed, I think he carried Edward up to bed.

I poured myself a glass of white wine and ate a couple of chicken sandwiches and some grapes. The sun was low in the sky, shining through a break in the clouds straight through the French windows. Now I could see that everything was covered in a film of dust, that the silver of the photograph frames was tarnished, the rugs threadbare and the furniture worn. There were cobwebs around the overhead light and up in the corners of the ceiling, and the windows themselves were filthy. I longed to roll my sleeves up and get busy with a bucket of sudsy water and a tin of beeswax.

Twenty minutes passed in silence. Half an hour. I wondered if I should call a cab and slip away. I was turning on my phone when Samuel materialised in the doorway.

'I'm so sorry to have neglected you. Did you find something edible? He was a bit poorly.'

'Oh dear. I hope it's not my fault.'

'Not at all. He's prone to acid reflux. That's why I try to keep him quiet.'

'I'm sorry. If I'd known ...'

'It wouldn't have made any difference. He's as stubborn as a mule, even now he's in his nineties.'

'Have you been with him for a long time, Samuel?'

'Me? Oh yes. A very long time.' He busied himself with plates, replacing cling film over sandwiches that, perhaps, would have to last for days. It was hard to tell just how broke they really were. I wanted to ask him a thousand questions, but he said, 'I've called a cab for you. It'll be here any minute. I do hope you'll come again, maybe stay over.'

'I'd like to bring the children.'

'I don't know ...'

'They're well behaved.'

'Perhaps. We'll see.' We stood in silence, looking at sun dipping behind the trees. 'You must take him with a pinch of salt, you know.'

'Ah.' My dreams of being a literary executor seemed to shiver out of focus. 'I see.'

'He gets these sudden enthusiasms.'

I'm his granddaughter, I wanted to say, not some stranger who's trying to diddle him out of his fortune. 'I understand. Don't worry.'

'He asked me to give you this.' He picked a frame from a high bookshelf, dusted the glass with his sleeve. My mother and father on their wedding day, black and white, she in a full-skirted white dress, he in a dark grey suit. Edward himself stood on one side, a woman whom I took to be Geraldine, his wife, on the other. Everyone was smiling. There was confetti on the ground. My mother looked very happy.

'Thank you.' I hugged the photo to my chest. 'It's beautiful.' I had never seen it before.

A distant beep of a horn, the crunch of tyres on gravel.

'Your car's here.'

Samuel helped me into the back of the cab, carrying bags, holding doors. I thanked him, he nodded and smiled. And, just before the driver pulled away, I looked up and saw, framed by the drapes of a first-floor room, the shock of white hair and the pale, half-smiling face of my grandfather Edward Barton. He raised a hand, gave a small, regal wave, and we drove away.

II
During

Chapter Five: Helen

THE WORST THING about adultery is the scheduling. With two men in my life the housework and childcare have to be squeezed into fewer hours, each minute of the day accounted for. And I have to take extra care over my personal comings and goings: I can't afford to run into certain people when I'm with Harry, and I don't want him to have anything to do with the children. It's a logistical nightmare which, frankly, is taking the fun out of things. It was all too easy when Richard was working away from home three weeks a month – but now, as contracts dry up, he spends more time at the main office in Acton, all too commutable from Balham. He's out of the house from 7.45 a.m. till 8.30 p.m. – I've encouraged him to go to the gym after work, which gives me a bit more time to sort myself out before he gets home. The benefits of this are clear to see: he's fitter, happier, more fun to be around. The downside is that his libido is supercharged, and he wants sex three or four times a week. This is wearing me out.

If I'm tired and distant it's explained by 'the course' – which, in a roundabout way, is true, although it's the tutor, rather than the workload, that's to blame. What started as a heat-of-the-moment fling has developed into an affair, and while it's usually me who suggests a date, and always me who pays for things, Harry remains keen both in and out of bed. We meet at his flat in Dalston, which is a pain in the arse to get to, but the parking isn't bad and I can usually manage an unhurried couple of hours, including a cup of tea and, obviously, a shower. Sometimes we even talk about my writing – after all, that's the point of the exercise, isn't it? In what little spare time I have, I've been writing a novel – well, more of a novella, it's only about 15,000 words long and I seem to be running out of steam. Harry is encouraging, and says that my exploration of the interior life of a modern mother shows great artistry, but I can't help thinking that if I spent less time driving to and from Dalston, sleeping with Harry and lying to Richard, I could write something much better.

I seem to be splitting into different people. Until now, I've never had to watch what I say to anyone, except possibly my parents, and nobody tells their parents everything. But these days I'm one person with Richard, another with the children, another with Annette, and quite another with Harry. Take yesterday. The morning started, as usual, with Radio 2 at 6.45 a.m. Richard went to the bathroom, I prepared breakfast, and we had our habitual, sacred cup of coffee together – black and strong – before we roused the children. We didn't say much to each other, just trivial words and long-standing jokes – but, in a way, this is the most intimate part of our day. We leaned against the counter top, looking out of the kitchen window at the signs of spring in the garden, we sipped our coffee and felt close and safe. Richard was warm and wet from his shower, the smell of soap on his skin. He patted me on the bum and went upstairs to begin the lengthy process of waking Ben and Lucy. I went to the bathroom, cleaned my teeth, heard the kids' voices raised in complaint as usual, then their footsteps thundering over my head, but all the soap in the world won't wash away the smell of betrayal.

The next couple of hours were fine. We ate breakfast, I washed up, discussed practical things, wrangled the children, saw Richard off to work with a kiss, got the children washed and dressed, an operation that I can carry off with military precision, then into the car and round the corner to pick up

Holly and Poppy. There was Annette fussing like a mother hen, we barely waved to each other, just a quick exchange – 'All right?' 'Fine, you all right?' 'Fine, see you later' – and off to school. Dropped the kids off, hurried over to Sainsbury's to load up on food, all of it stuff that could be prepared in the least possible time. Has Richard noticed that our dinners are somewhat rudimentary of late? If so, I suppose he puts it down to my writing.

Then home to attack the housework: washing machine loaded and on, hoover out, toys picked up and put away, ironing done, quick cup of coffee, a model of time-efficiency. And then it was time to change out of my workaday clothes and into my adultery outfit: a change of clothes for a change of personality. The traffic was bad between Balham and Dalston, but there is no practical alternative to driving: if I took a succession of buses, there would be no time left for sex. So I took the car paid for by Richard, the insurance, the road tax, the petrol, paid for by the sweat of Richard's data-analysing brow.

Harry lives in the upper half of a Victorian house in a quiet street near London Fields, satellite dishes sprouting from what were once elegant facades. It's a two-bedroom flat with a tiny box room that allows estate agents to call it a three-bedroom maisonette; I'm not sure how Harry affords it on a tutor's wages.

'Hey,' he said, opening the door in a V-neck T-shirt and a pair of grey sweatpants. On anyone else these would look shabby; when Harry's wearing them, all I could think of was what's inside, stretching the fabric. He was unshaven, his hair tousled – 'tousled'! But for the setting he was straight from the pages of Jackie Collins or Jilly Cooper. But this was a flat in Dalston, not a Hollywood bungalow or a Cotswold stud farm, and I was no fictional heroine. I was a married mother of two sneaking off for a bit of afternoon delight with a man all too aware of the effect that his hair, his stubble and the deep V of his T would have on me.

He kissed me on the lips as he closed the door, and my brain went blank, wiped by the power surge from his sharp bristles and soft mouth. I suppose we said something as we climbed the stairs to his bedroom, my hand in his, being led. There were endearments, expressions of desire, possibly even some conventional 'How are you?' and 'Very well thanks'. But then sex happened, and words were only there for their most basic functions. Very few were more than one syllable. 'Harder'. That's about it.

As soon as it was over, we tidied ourselves up. It didn't take Harry long; he simply pulled on the clothes I'd pulled off him earlier. His hair still stood up, but then he always looked freshly shagged, even at college. While I was brushing my hair in the bathroom, Harry was in the kitchen fixing coffee; he has one of those outsize espresso machines that have no place in a domestic setting, but which he adores, and tends with the same care other men give to cars and motorcycles. Coffee is important to Harry, part of his personal mythology as A Writer.

We sat at the pine kitchen table.

'So,' he said, 'how's it going?'

I knew what he meant. Not 'life in general' or 'this awkward but rather exciting situation we're in'. Not even my writing. 'It' is my attempt to secure the screen rights to *The Interlude*.

'Nothing to report, I'm afraid.'

He betrayed his irritation with the slightest wince, but converted it into blowing on his coffee, pushing the *crema* across the black surface in swirls. 'You did get in touch, though.'

'Yes.' I've written to Edward Barton's agent twice now, without getting a reply. He's represented by a very old-fashioned firm with offices in Bloomsbury – where else? – and I suspect they regard such issues as TV adaptations with a lofty distaste. Sooner or later I'm going to have to ring them and find out if the agent in question is still alive and working; I suspect neither.

'God!' said Harry. 'Agents! They're bloody useless at the best of times. They're preventing your grandfather from making a lot of money. He said I could do it. Most writers would kill to be on television.' Harry takes it for granted that his screenplay of *The Interlude* will be snapped up as soon as it's written. He hasn't yet decided whether it's a one-off or a six-parter.

'I'm sorry,' I said, as if this was my fault. 'I've been too busy to chase it up.'

'Just keep trying,' he said, squeezing my hand. 'I read your latest chapter, by the way. It's very good.'

'Thank you.' I knew this was flattery. My latest 'chapter', if you can call it that, was 2,000 words of notes.

'I think, with a little polishing, you'll have a very solid piece of work.' He looked into my eyes. 'Something worth sending out.'

'Well, that's wonderful.'

He heard the doubt in my voice. 'I mean it. You've got talent.' When Harry says things like 'talent', it's with a sense of ownership. He recognises it because he has it. Takes one to know one. The carrot was dangled, and I bit.

By two o'clock I was back in the car headed south. All might have been well were it not for a security alert that closed off London Bridge and snarled up everything between the river and Elephant and Castle; by the time I got to Kennington I was half an hour behind schedule. This presented me with a stark choice: go home and change, but risk being late to pick up the children, or go straight to the school, then face a barrage of questions from Annette about why I was all dressed up on a weekday afternoon.

On the whole, I preferred to be late.

The children were engrossed in a complicated game involving some sticks and a puddle, which meant they were muddy to the knees.

I drove to Annette's. 'I was getting worried,' she said as the children piled out of the car and spread the rest of the mud over her living room carpet. 'I was about to call you.'

I looked at my watch. 'Oh come on, Annette. Twenty minutes.'

She narrowed her eyes. 'You look flushed,' she said, accusingly. 'What have you been up to?'

'Nothing.'

'Have you been to college today?'

'No.'

'You only look like that when you've seen him. That tutor of yours.'

Okay, I wanted to say, I spent much of the afternoon straddling him, happy now? 'Don't be silly, Annette. Anyway, how are you? How's Glyn?'

'Fine.' She was not to be put off so easily. 'And how's Richard?'

Damn: I walked straight into that one. 'He's lovely,' I said, trying to sound cute.

'Yes, he is. And don't you forget it.' Annette looked stern, as if she were reprimanding one of her own children.

'What are you talking about?'

'I think you know.'

She'd guessed. How? What was the telltale sign? 'Don't be ridiculous.' I should have left it there and joined the kids in front of the TV, but I couldn't resist adding, 'And besides, I'll thank you to mind your own business.'

'Ah!' Her eyes lit up. 'I see. Okay.'

I shifted my feet and picked my cuticles.

'Helen, you must be careful.'

'I don't know what you mean.' I'm fourteen again, and my mum's accusing me of smoking in my bedroom.

'I think you do.' She laid a hand gently on my upper arm, and lowered her voice to a confiding contralto. 'Please just think about what you're doing.'

'I'm not doing anything.'

She ignored this. 'I've got no right to interfere.'

'Right.'

'But I'm your oldest friend, and I don't want to see you throw your life away.'

My life? What does she know about my life? My real life? My inner life? The bullshit I've been typing ... 'Thanks for the advice, darling,' I said. 'And now I'd better get those two home, as apparently I'm already running late.'

'Helen ...'

'Ben! Lucy! In the car.'

'Helen, don't be like this.'

I kissed her on one cheek. 'It's okay, Annette.' I kissed her on the other. 'I just have to start dinner. I'm cooking something rather special tonight' – actually it was baked potatoes and sausages – 'and I really ought to get on with it. Sorry about the mess.'

'Oh, don't worry,' said Annette, caressing Ben's shiny brown hair as he dashed past. 'I'll clean it all up.'

I got the children home and gave what was left of myself to them. And then Richard came in, and the kids went to bed, we ate dinner, washed up, wiped up, put away, poured a glass of wine and sat in front of a DVD, both of us too tired for conversation. We went to bed early, and when Richard put his arms around me and started to kiss the back of my neck I lay inert, hating myself until he gave up, sighed and rolled over. We lay back to back, neither of us sleeping.

And so my life continued, another day another lie, each night a little colder towards Richard until his advances stopped completely and we simply grunted 'G'night'. I lost a lot of sleep, and too much weight. I was looking haggard, but Richard never noticed, or if he did, he never asked me why. Annette's manner concealed a growing fury of disapproval. A crisis was coming – I could feel it, almost hear it, like a train speeding down the track towards me, whistle blowing, lights blazing, and I was powerless to get out of the way.

In the end, the crisis came from the most unexpected quarter.

I got home from Harry's one afternoon, and was tidying up the house when I noticed there was a message on my landline. This could only be from my parents; everyone else uses the mobile. I picked it up.

'It's your father here, leaving you a message.' He sounded tense; he doesn't like answering machines, and only uses them as a last resort. This had to be something important. 'I thought you might want to know that your grandfather died. Call me if you need to know more.'

No details, no expression of sorrow or concern. Just the bare fact, reluctantly given.

Edward Barton was dead. My first reaction was excitement.

Would you like to be my literary executor?

Oh my God, I thought, I can't wait to tell Harry! Now I control the estate!

And then I felt bad, and then sad – the old man I had last seen standing at that forlorn window, the distant figure from my childhood, the last of the great post-war authors, was dead. Dead. Not just in the sense of headlines and obituaries and estates, but dead in the sense of loss, bereavement, grief.

I rang my parents. My mother answered.

'I got Dad's message,' I said. 'I'm so sorry.'

'Yes,' she said, and 'Well.'

'Is he there? I'd like to speak to him.'

'He's just taking the recycling out at the moment.'

'Could you get him?'

'He's rather busy, darling.'

'Mum. This is important.'

She sighed, and I heard her distant voice shouting 'David!', and then, more impatiently, 'David! Telephone.' Silence – she didn't fill in the time by chatting – until a door closed and the receiver rattled.

'Yes?'

'It's me, Dad.'

'Ah. Hello.' He might have been talking to his bank manager.

'I'm so sorry about your father.'

'Right.' He cleared his throat.

'What happened?'

'Nothing.'

'I mean, how did you hear?'

'His secretary called on Monday.' It was now Wednesday. 'Apparently it was quite peaceful. He's not been very well for the last few months.'

'What was wrong with him?'

'He was very old, Helen.'

'But I mean what ... took him?'

'Pneumonia is what will be on the death certificate. They might as well put "shortness of breath". He was 94 years old.'

'Are you okay?'

'Me?' He sounded astonished by the question. 'I'm fine.'

'I don't mean your health, Dad. I mean, are you ... upset?' This was dangerous territory, but if a man doesn't grieve when his own father dies then something is seriously wrong.

'I've been expecting it for a long time.'

'But still ...'

'The funeral is the week after next.' He named the date. 'Although why it has to be such a long way off I do not know. I'm with the Jews on this one – get them planted within 24 hours, and be done with it. All this waiting around is ridiculous.'

Why, I felt like saying, does it disrupt your schedule? Was that your supermarket day?

'Will you let me know the details?'

'Oh, you don't need to come.'

'Dad, of course I'm coming.'

'You needn't put yourself out on my account, you know.'

I took a deep breath to calm my voice. 'I'd like to come for Grandad's sake.'

'I really can't see why.' He sighed. 'But I suppose if you want to come, you must. Please, Helen, don't bring the children. I don't want it to be a big thing.'

'Daddy, he's your father.'

There seemed to be no answer to that. 'Well, if you don't mind, I must get on.'

Of course: urgent recycling to do. 'Okay, Dad.' Let him grieve in his own way. Perhaps he needs to be busy, to pretend nothing's happened. Whatever problems he had with Edward aren't just going to evaporate. 'I'll call you at the weekend, shall I?'

'If you like.'

'And don't forget to let me know ...'

'I won't. Goodbye.'

A notification arrived from Stonefield, complete with black border, announcing the time and place of the service. No nonsense about 'no flowers by request'. A proper funeral, with a vicar and hymns and prayers over the coffin. Ashes to ashes, dust to dust, clods of earth, lilies and veils. Appropriately theatrical. No doubt Edward gave very precise instructions.

Richard insisted on accompanying me and the children. We have always agreed that we would not shield our children from death; when goldfish and hamsters have died, we've been quite upfront about it, no soppy nonsense about falling asleep. This, however, was their first encounter with human mortality, and although they'd never met their great-grandfather, Ben, at least, understood who he was and where he fitted in to the family line.

And so, on an overcast Wednesday morning in June, we drove up the M40, all dressed smartly, Richard and I in black. It was one of the last things we would do together as a family for a very long time. The children chattered away in the back, occasionally touching on the subject of death and burial and coming up with the usual howlers ('How will he go to the toilet?' asked Lucy). Richard and I didn't say much, and most of it was to the kids. He drove, and I looked out of the window. That train was getting closer, I could feel the ground trembling under my feet, and I knew, somehow, that Edward Barton's death would change things. Something had been decided. My life was no longer in my control.

The funeral was in the nearest village to Stonefield, a pretty little place with broad curving lanes, a proper green complete with duck pond, a war memorial, a couple of nice-looking pubs and even some thatched cottages. The children had never seen anything like it; for them, it was a trip into a bygone age. Ben hoped to see a horse and cart.

The church was a handsome sandstone building with a square tower topped off with four fancy finials, a St George's Cross flying from the flagpole, and a beautifully-tended churchyard. We took a pew near the back. The coffin stood on trestles near the altar, flanked by two enormous bouquets of white lilies that mixed with the scent of beeswax and candles. There were, perhaps, thirty people in the church when the service began. My parents sat halfway up, near the transept, although there was masses of space in front of them. My aunt Valerie sat alone across the nave. Samuel, Edward's secretary and factotum, was at the front. The rest of the mourners were very old. A good hard winter would see most of them off.

The service was short, the homily to the point, and the children were well behaved. Richard took good care of them, allowing me to concentrate on grieving. At one point, when the vicar said something about Edward's close and loving family, Richard squeezed my hand, and I realised that I had been daydreaming about Harry, noticing each detail of the scene, converting it into an anecdote to take back to him, dropping it at his feet like the faithful dog I had become. I turned to Richard, my heart beating as if I'd been caught out. Tears pricked my eyes, and Richard smiled in sympathy, a sad, loving smile. It was not for Edward I was crying, but for us.

We filed out to the waiting grave, and it was only then that my parents acknowledged us with tense smiles and nods. The children hung back, hiding behind Richard. If my parents could have hidden too, they would.

The coffin was lowered into the ground, Samuel threw some earth into the hole, and it was over. Richard took the children for a walk around the village while I faced the family.

My parents had little to say for themselves. Their faces were pale and immobile, their eyes dry. They thanked the vicar, they thanked Samuel, and they made small talk with me while glancing at their watches. When Aunt Valerie came to join us, their desire to get away became frantic. There was some mumbled nonsense about the traffic and the roadworks and they scuttled off to their car.

I waved them off, but they didn't wave back.

Valerie took my arm, and we took the well-kept gravel path around the church. The sun was breaking through a tear in the clouds, a few rooks were flapping around the trees, cawing from time to time, the perfect sound effect for the scene.

'Off they go,' she said, a grim humour in her voice. 'Running away as usual.'

Valerie is seven years older than my father, a stern, schoolmistressy woman with a strong jawline and a big nose – 'mannish', you would have called her once, and the fact that she remains unmarried makes me assume that she's lesbian. Not that there's any sign of a partner; discreetly tucked away at home, perhaps, another Barton family secret.

'How are you, Auntie Valerie?'

'I think we can drop the "auntie" now, can't we? You're not a child any more.'

'Valerie, then.'

'Or Val, even.'

'Okay.'

'And to answer your question, I'm fine. He had a good long innings and I wouldn't have wanted him to suffer any more.'

'Did he suffer?' My father hadn't mentioned this.

'You know what it's like these days. They keep you alive for as long as they can. Too long, in this case. All those antibiotics on drips, stuck into his poor old arms. Pneumonia used to be called the old people's friend, you know.' She snapped her fingers. 'A quick death when the time came. Oh well. He's at rest now.'

'Were you very close to him?'

'As close as anyone, with the possible exception of Samuel.' She nodded towards the gate, where Samuel was talking to a small group of elderly mourners. 'He was the one who did all the hard work. I hope he's going to inherit the lot. God knows he's earned it.'

I didn't mention my conversation with Edward about the literary estate, and for all I knew it had been forgotten. 'Did he leave much?'

'I should think that the estate's worth a couple of million, even after tax. Someone clever could make a lot more of it than that.'

'Edward said there was very little.'

'Oh, he said that, did he?'

'I saw him a few months ago.'

'Yes. He told me.'

'The old place seemed to be rather dilapidated.'

'That's because my father was a tight-fisted old sod who hated spending money on repairs. When my mother died, the

108

place started falling to pieces because he wouldn't cough up. It'll cost a good deal to get it to a sellable standard.'

'Do you think Samuel will sell it?'

'If he's got any sense he will. Samuel would be better off in a nice little flat somewhere, and none of us wants it.'

I wouldn't mind it, I thought, imagining the children running around the gardens, up and down the stairs, in and out of the French doors. I didn't picture Richard there.

'Time will tell, I suppose. When's the will to be read?'

'Ah, the reading of the will. It's so deliciously Agatha Christie, isn't it? The shocked faces around the table as the old white-haired solicitor drops the bombshell. I don't think it happens like that any more, sadly. It would be so perfect, like a scene from an Edward Barton novel. He always wanted life to be more like fiction. Like this.' She waved a gloved hand around the churchyard – the perfect golden tower, bathed in afternoon sunlight, the clipped yews, the cawing rooks. 'Like something from a movie, isn't it? Oh, he'll have thought it all through. When your whole life has been a fiction, you can't help it.'

'What do you mean?'

'You know,' said Valerie, quickening her step, 'once a novelist, always a novelist.' She coughed. 'Is that your husband?'

Richard was coming across the greensward, a child in each hand. With the sun behind him, he looked somehow two-dimensional. Lucy had picked up a large fallen branch, and was brandishing it like a weapon.

'We've been looking for ghosts,' she said, 'and this is how I kill them.' She thrust with the branch.

Valerie looked amused. 'That's a good girl,' she said. 'That's exactly how you should deal with ghosts.'

'I've been killing them too,' said Ben, 'but I've got a spell.'

'Clever boy,' said Valerie. 'I wish you'd tell me what it is.'

Ben jabbered some nonsense words, which Lucy picked up, and they ran across the graves, chanting.

'Well, Helen, Richard, it's been lovely to see you.' There was no wake, no 'after-party', and so we said our farewells at car doors. 'Do keep in touch.'

'Perhaps I'll see you when the old white-haired solicitor drops the bombshell,' I said, kissing her lightly on both cheeks.

She drove away, and I expected never to see her again.

Three weeks later we were invited to Stonefield when, said Samuel's letter, 'the testamentary dispositions of Edward Barton will be announced at 4 p.m. Dinner follows.'

I thought about what Valerie had said: every effect planned. Every scene imagined and staged. *When your whole life has been a fiction, you can't help it.* Was this to be the twist in the tale?

The solicitor was a disappointment: too young by half, he was barely my age, dressed in a nondescript grey suit, no gold-rimmed pince-nez, no air of mystery whatsoever. That aside, everything was perfect. We gathered, my parents, my aunt and I, in the living room sipping sherry and tea, which Samuel served from crystal decanters and silver pots. The room was cleaner than before; now that Edward was dead, Samuel had time for housework. The windows sparkled, and beyond them the garden was lovely in its spring splendour. Furniture had been dusted, frames polished. The glasses and cups from which we drank were spotless.

My parents sat side by side on a sofa, knees together, backs upright, saying very little. Valerie made conversation with the solicitor about the drive over from Banbury, local market days, traffic on the bypass, that sort of thing. Samuel was ill at ease, a servant suddenly thrust among his masters.

The solicitor looked at his watch and picked up his case. 'Well then,' he said, 'we'd better get down to business. I have other appointments.'

'Of course,' said Valerie. 'The dining room, I think you said, Samuel?'

Samuel stood at the connecting door, taking cups and glasses as they were handed to him. In just a very few minutes, the tables might be turned. He could order us about, and we would dance attendance, hoping for a few crumbs from the master's table. And there was the master's table, old oak, deeply polished, three chairs down either side and one at each end, a bowl of roses in the centre – pink and yellow, old fashioned, deeply fragranced.

'Oh, Samuel,' said Valerie, 'it looks lovely.' Samuel beamed, and clasped his hands in pleasure.

We sat, the solicitor at the head, Samuel at the foot, my parents on one side, Valerie and I facing them. I had a terrible desire to place my hands on the table and say, 'Do you have a message for anyone here?'

The solicitor clicked open his attaché case and withdrew a plastic file containing several sheets of white paper. Five pairs of eyes followed it to the tabletop.

'Right,' he said. 'I'll keep this short and sweet. The terms of Mr Barton's will are very straightforward, so there's nothing much to explain.'

Four of us stared at Samuel; Samuel stared at the roses.

'This will was made on the 12th of December of last year, whereby Mr Barton revoked all former wills and testamentary dispositions, et cetera et cetera.'

Samuel's eyebrows flickered in puzzlement.

'Shall I read the whole thing, with all the jargon, or just give you the main points?' He looked to Valerie, as the older child, for an answer.

'By all means dispense with the formalities,' she said. 'Let's have the headlines.'

'Okay.' The solicitor tapped the bottom edge of the document on the table, and proceeded. 'He appoints you, Valerie and you, David, as his executors and trustees.'

'Fair enough,' said Valerie. My father frowned, thinking of his recycling schedule.

'Right ... now then.' He scanned down, and read aloud. 'My trustees shall hold my residuary estate for the following persons ... Okay. Here we go. One per centum for the Royal Society for the Protection of Birds.'

My mother tutted audibly.

'One per centum to Age UK.'

The temperature in the room seemed to be rising.

'The sum of 500,000 pounds to my secretary and companion Samuel in recognition of many years of loyal friendship.'

That was it then. Half a million. Not quite the two million that Valerie had predicted, but not bad. Enough to buy a nice flat somewhere. Samuel wiped the corner of his eye, and nodded.

We all thought that was the end of it, but the solicitor held up his hand.

'The remainder of my estate I give and bequeath for her own use and benefit absolutely to my granddaughter, Ms Helen Barton.' He looked up at me, and added, rather redundantly, 'That's you.'

'Yes,' I said, and that was all I could say. The connection between brain and mouth was down. *The remainder of my estate*. What did that mean? The books and diaries that he'd promised me? Was there cash attached? What about the photos, even the paintings?

'The house?' said my father, in a strangled voice.

'Everything,' said the solicitor. 'Probate, obviously, will establish the value of the estate ... '

His voice whited out. The house? The *house*? And the rest of the estate – the money that Valerie had hinted at? The Barton Millions? Mine? My eyes were momentarily blind. When I refocused, everyone was looking at me.

'Well,' said my mother. 'I hope you're pleased.'

There was no mistaking the accusation in her voice.

'It can't be,' I said. 'He can't possibly have ... I mean, I only saw him that time. Samuel. My God, Samuel, did you know about this?'

'No, I didn't,' he said, and smiled. 'But I'm sure that's what he wanted. I'm very happy with what I've got.' A tiny wobble in the voice. 'More than happy.'

My parents got up. 'And now,' said my father, 'I think we'd better get going.'

'But dinner ...'

'The traffic was terrible on the way up, and I don't want to get stuck in the rush hour around Oxford. Come along, Rosemary.'

'Dad, please. You can't just walk out.'

'Thank you, Samuel. Good to see you, Val.' They didn't even look at me. A pall of shame and confusion hung over the room. The solicitor couldn't get out quickly enough.

'And I've got all this food ready,' said Samuel, the tears spilling down his cheeks.

I wanted to comfort him but how could I? He must hate me, I thought. The interloper, the inheritance thief. The scheming young woman who inveigled her way into Edward Barton's affections and somehow persuaded him to change his will. He would contest it, no doubt, claiming undue influence, or that Edward was not of sound mind. I felt like a dowdy English Anna Nicole Smith.

Valerie took charge of the situation. 'Well, this is a pickle,' she said, handing Samuel a wad of tissues and guiding him gently to the living room, where he sat down and cried quietly. 'Helen and I will make some tea. You take it easy for a minute.'

'It's all ready,' said Samuel, his voice muffled. 'All you have to do is boil the kettle.'

'Come on, Helen.' Valerie half pushed me out of the room. 'Did you know about this?'

'I swear to you, I had no idea.'

'He didn't say anything?'

'He mentioned something about being his literary executor, but that's all.'

'Right.' She folded her arms across her bosom, and nodded. 'Well, then, I believe you. I suppose he had his reasons.'

'He wanted to drive the final nail into this family.'

'What do you mean?'

'Not leaving anything to you or Dad. He wanted to make sure that none of us ever speak to each other again.'

'I don't think that's very likely.' She poured two large gins, added a splash of tonic to each and passed me one. 'Anyway, I never expected a penny from him.'

'But you're his daughter. Dad is his son. It's not right.'

'Did David tell you he expected to inherit?'

'No. But surely ...'

'Your father and I had no expectations. Whatever was due to us, we had a long time ago.'

Damn her, speaking in riddles again. 'What do you mean, Val? I wish you'd spell it out.'

'My father gave us a considerable amount of money when your parents married. He always said he wanted us to have it when it was useful rather than when we were already set up in life.'

'I see.'

'And when my mother died, there was another legacy.'

'Dad never mentioned that.'

'You don't surprise me.'

'Then why is he so angry with me? Why did they just rush off like that?'

'Your father is a very angry man for all sorts of reasons. Cheers.' We clinked glasses, and had a good long drink. 'Now let's go and keep poor Samuel company. Although he's not really poor now, is he? Half a million nicker. That goes a fair way, even these days.'

'It does,' I said, helping myself to ham and thinking that the residue of the estate – if Valerie was right about its extent – would go a great deal further. Apart from anything else, I suddenly had a very big house in the country, all its contents, and the Edward Barton literary estate at my disposal.

'Excuse me just a minute, Val,' I said. 'I need to make a call.'

'I'm sure you do.' She closed the kitchen door as she left.

It was Harry I called, Harry with whom I shared the news, and it was through his mounting excitement that I began to realise the full extent of what had just happened.

Much later in the day, after lunch and a walk with Val around the village, a drink in the pub and dinner back at the house, I phoned home.

No one answered.

I was very drunk when I went to bed; we all were.

I lay in a bed in a room in a house that I now owned and tried to see the future. But it was indistinct, and at last I slept. I dreamed of waking up in that bed in that room in that house with Harry beside me.

My father summoned me to discuss 'the matter of the will'. 'Don't let him talk you into anything,' Richard said. 'And for God's sake don't sign anything.' Harry said much the same. Both of them expected to share in my newfound wealth.

There was no pretence at hospitality, no little glasses of dry sherry, just instant coffee and down to business.

'Of course we all realise that the old man was not in his right mind,' said my father. 'The question is, how are we going to sort this mess out without involving a lot of expensive lawyers?'

I felt my cheeks burning; if I asserted my rights, I would seem like a very undutiful daughter indeed. Valerie stepped in.

'Just a moment, David. There's no "of course" about it. Daddy was in perfectly good mental health.'

'Don't be ridiculous. He can't possibly have known what he was doing.'

'Pure speculation.'

'He was 94 years old, Valerie. He was confused.'

'Ha!' Valerie pushed her cup away, barely tasted. The coffee was, indeed, revolting. 'When did you last see him, David?'

'That's got nothing to do with it.'

'I saw him in March,' continued Valerie, 'and I would say he was more with it than any of us. His legs were a bit weak, and his breathing wasn't great, but he was in full possession of his marbles. I won't have you saying otherwise.'

'But this will,' said my father, in a pitying tone, 'you have to admit it's just silly.'

'In what way?'

'Leaving everything to someone he hardly knew ...'

'His own granddaughter.'

'But for heaven's sake, Val ...'

'And what were you expecting, David? Hmm?' My father said nothing. 'Rosemary? What did you think he was going to do?'

'This isn't about us, Val,' said my mother.

'Then why are we here, may I ask?'

'I just want everyone to do the right thing,' said my father.

'Meaning that you want Helen to hand over the money to you, is that it? Or would you prefer the house?'

'Stop it, Valerie.'

'You know perfectly well that we had what was coming to us a long time ago. I can't believe you're trying to get your hands on more.'

My father's face darkened; we were in for a nasty scene. 'That is a poisonous thing to say.'

'Oh, really?' Valerie assumed an expression of cloying sweetness. 'And why would that be, brother dear?'

'You're impossible.'

'I seem to recall that when you got married, the old man settled quite a large sum on you.'

'And on you.' My father's voice was spiteful.

'I don't deny it. When it became apparent to all and sundry that I would never marry, he coughed up. He was generous, and fair. And let's not forget Mum's portion. That wasn't exactly chicken feed, was it?'

'Most of it went on Helen's education.'

'Are you going to invoice her for that now, David? Rather late in the day.'

I sat in silence, watching and listening, wondering what had poisoned the well of our family life.

'He caused nothing but trouble when he was alive,' said my mother, her American accent coming through as it always did in times of stress. 'I can't believe he's still causing trouble now he's dead.'

'I don't see any trouble here,' said Valerie. 'The will is perfectly clear, properly witnessed, and the only ones complaining are you.'

'What about poor Samuel?'

'Poor Samuel? He's a bloody sight richer than I am.'

'Oh God, Valerie,' shouted my father, 'why do you have to bring it all down to money?'

Valerie gave another bark of laughter, and the colour flooded to her cheeks.

'Look,' I said, and suddenly all eyes were on me. 'I know this is awkward for all of us, but we're a family, aren't we? We can sort it out without fighting.'

My father was about to say something, but thought better of it.

'I'm sorry if you're upset by the will. I'm in shock myself. It's going to change my life in all sorts of ways.' *And how*, I thought, imagining Harry in Stonefield. 'But there's no point in arguing. This was Edward's will. This is what he wanted.'

'Yes,' said my mother. 'To set us at each other's throats again.'

Again? 'Mum, please, this is ridiculous.'

'Ridiculous?' Her voice shot up, and she fought to bring it down. 'Yes, he's made all of us ridiculous.'

'It would have been better,' muttered my father, 'if he had died intestate.'

Valerie pounced. 'Oh yes, that would have suited you very well, wouldn't it, David? And what would have happened then? Let me think. The estate would have gone to the next of kin. Even after inheritance tax, that would amount to a pretty penny. And who would the next of kin be? Let me think ...' She rubbed her chin. 'Oh yes. His children. You and me.'

'Valerie, for God's sake ...'

'All right,' said my mother. 'That's enough. We must accept what has happened, I suppose. There's no point in arguing.'

'Who's arguing? Helen and I are perfectly content.'

'Oh shut up, Valerie,' said my father, and they were back in the playroom, lower lips stuck out in a sulk. He folded his arms and turned in his seat, staring out of the window.

'Well,' said Valerie, when we were safely in a cab going back to the railway station, 'I think we emerged from that relatively unscathed. Nothing quite as bracing as a big family row, is there?'

'I hated it.'

'Poor girl.' She squeezed my hand. 'I don't suppose you've seen your parents like that before, have you? I grew up with it. David always had a nasty temper.'

'Why is everyone so angry?'

'That's the question, isn't it? And I'm afraid I really can't answer it. Something happened to your father to make him that way. You know what it's like with fathers and sons.' She sighed, and relinquished my hand. 'All madly Oedipal, I suppose.'

We arrived at the station and boarded the train, riding in silence.

'It's a shame you never knew Billy,' she said when were approaching High Wycombe, where she got off. 'He was the real character.'

'Mum's dad?'

'That's right, dear. Oh, what a man he was! We were all in love with Billy. Great handsome athletic fellow he was.' So much for my aunt being a crypto-lesbian. 'And such fun! It was always a party when Billy was around. It's a tragedy that he died so young. He was a wonderful father, you know, whatever Rosemary says now.'

'They never talk about him.'

'No,' said Valerie, putting on her coat. 'That doesn't surprise me. Not much love lost between your father and Billy. They never got on.' The train slowed.

'Why not?'

'Long story, my dear, for another day. I was very fond of Uncle Billy. That's what I called him, although of course he wasn't a real uncle. Happy memories.' We were at High Wycombe. 'Oh well. Such a long time ago.' She kissed me quickly, a peck on the cheek. 'Lovely to see you, dear. And well done for standing up to them. It's about time someone did.'

'I'm not sure,' I said, but she was away down the carriage. She waved from the platform as the train pulled away.

Samuel wasted no time in moving out of Stonefield. Within a month the house and its contents were mine. Harry was eager to get started on the papers, and I took him down on a visit, eager to show off my new property.

We arrived at Stonefield at about eleven, and by quarter to twelve we were tidying ourselves up after a quickie on the living room sofa. Harry walked around the room picking things up, commenting on their quality. He weighed the silver frames like a pawnbroker, caring more for the value of the metal than the photograph it surrounded. It was a beautiful day, and he wanted to open the French doors on to the terrace. They were locked, of course, and I had the key.

'Come on, come on,' he said, impatient as I fiddled with the bolts, and then, when the door finally opened, he strode out to the lichen-covered terrace with the confidence of a new owner. 'Very nice. Some of these trees need to come down. Open up the view a bit, let some light in.' He turned to face me, the sun behind him, illuminating his curls. 'It's the beginning of a new chapter, babe.'

His shirt was still undone. 'Yes,' I said weakly. 'Something like that.'

I gave him the guided tour – he ran up stairs and down, bursting through doors. In Edward's room – the room where he died – he sat on the edge of the bed and bounced.

'Please, Harry,' I said, 'not there.'

'What's the matter?'

'This was his bed.'

'Hey.' He patted the space beside him, but I did not sit. 'I understand. You're upset. Grief is like …' He nodded a couple of times, to show deep understanding. 'A process. You have to go through it in your own time.'

'Thanks.' I remained standing.

'Where's the stuff?'

'Sorry?'

'The archive. The papers.'

'I'm not quite ready for that yet.'

'Come on, Helen. That's what we're here for, isn't it?'

'I don't know what you're here for.' I held the door open; he took the hint, and went on to the landing. 'I'm here to get my head round the fact that all this belongs to me.' I put a little emphasis on that last word.

'Yeah.' He hugged me – Harry, the great comfort-giver. I suddenly wanted, very badly, to see my children here. To hear the clunk of the car door, and Richard's voice shouting up the stairs.

'I understand,' said Harry. 'You're doing brilliantly.'

I wished he'd leave. I went down to the garden. He followed me and, sensing my mood, changed the subject.

'Hey, I forgot to tell you.'

'What?'

'I was talking to an agent friend of mine.'

'Oh, really?' I'd never heard of any 'agent friend' before.

'She was really interested in your stuff.'

'Seriously?'

'Yeah. She likes to keep an eye on the emergent talent that comes through my course. I don't bother showing her much, obviously.'

'Okay.'

'But I'm sending her yours.'

'Right.' I turned to face him, framed in the French doors. 'Well, thank you.'

'I think she's going to like it a lot. She says she's looking for new voices.'

'That's great.'

'Yeah.' He kissed me on the forehead. 'I'm pleased for you.'

We walked round the garden hand in hand, chatting about trivial things, the plants, the view, nothing about money or relationships or books. Perhaps Harry realised that he'd almost overstepped the mark.

'Now,' he said, 'how about doing what we came here for? Come on. Let me put these muscles to good use.'

The attic was reached by a set of pull-down metal steps that creaked and groaned as Harry sprang up and down, hefting dusty cardboard cartons as if they were empty. From the landing, I shifted them into a spare room; they weighed a ton.

'That's enough for today.' Thirty boxes stood in a broad-based pyramid. 'It'll take me weeks to work through all that.'

'There's more upstairs. He must have kept everything.'

'Doesn't surprise me.'

Harry put his arms around my waist, rocking his pelvis against mine in a slow waltz. He was sweating, and smelled of old paper and warm flesh. 'How about a sneak preview?'

'Not now.' I broke away. 'I'd better drive you to the station. I'm going to stay here tonight.'

'Alone?' He sounded hurt, and furrowed his brow.

'Yes, alone. I'm sorry, Harry.'

We parted in the station car park with a kiss. 'I'll let you know about that agent,' he said, waving as he jogged towards the platform.

Thirty boxes. Thirty-two, to be precise. I sat on a hardwood chair and stared at them, baffled by the task ahead of me. So much to do, and to what end? To research the life of a recently deceased, no-longer-fashionable author – and then what? Write a book that would sell five copies? Screw up my relationship with my parents so badly that it could never be unscrewed? Why not just put the boxes back in the attic, or sell them on eBay? There must be someone out there who would take them off my hands.

Why had he done this to me?

I heard Valerie's voice: *I suppose he had his reasons.*

And I remembered Edward's twinkling eyes as he sat in that old chair, rubbing his hands, so pleased that I'd agreed to take him on.

That's just wonderful. Thank you so much.

I knelt down and opened the first box. Papers. Covered in ink, covered in pencil. White paper, blue paper, pink paper, lined paper, plain paper. Paper torn from ring bindings, paper carefully folded or carelessly creased. Words, numbers, letter and lines, arrows and spirals, doodles and sums. Cashflow, phone numbers, names and addresses. My God, he'd thrown nothing away. Thirty-two boxes of waste paper. A hell of a lot of recycling.

That would please my father, wouldn't it? Week after week, sack after sack going to the dump for shredding and pulping.

The second box was the same, and the third, and the fourth. I rubbed a tear away; my hands were filthy by now, and the dust hurt my eyes. Was this all that was left of Edward Barton? Was this my great inheritance? A crumbling house that would cost more money to fix up than I could ever hope to sell it for, an unknown sum of money to be revealed by probate – probably little more than loose change, after Samuel had taken his cut – and a mountain of scrap paper? I had bitten into the apple, and tasted dust.

And then I opened the fifth box, sturdier and heavier than the others.

And that's when I found the diaries.

Chapter Six: Edward Barton's Diaries

March 1940

SINCE I AM TO BE a writer I had better start keeping some kind of diary not least because things happen so fast, people come and go so quickly to quote Dorothy, that I will forget it all unless I write it down. And if I survive the war, it would be nice to have something to look back on in my dotage.

Life goes on much the same as before and still no knock at the door in the middle of the night, so I suppose that Dr Rhys was as good as his word and wrote to the relevant people at the War Office, just as Eleanora said he would. In any case I have the important bit of paper in my wallet, and if anyone challenges me I am a polio victim. William says that acting and writing should be on the schedule of reserved occupations because we bring 'truth, beauty, light' to fighting men and 'remind them what they're fighting for'. If any of them saw the kind of rubbish that we put on, me twizzling around in a loincloth and William's hands all over me behind the curtain, they would throw down their weapons and join Hitler.

Now however things are very different and we have to give the boys what they want – songs and jokes and the obligatory bit of leg courtesy of Miss Lily Field, which is really all they've come to see. William still moans about Lily's 'lack of artistry' but I don't think she would claim to be anything other than what she is, a pretty little blonde with a sexy figure. She can dance, not the kind of expressive dance that Eleanora favours, but when it comes to tap she runs rings round the rest of us, quite literally. She knows thousands of popular songs by heart and can put them across with a saucy wink or a sentimental sigh as required. She learns lines like a machine and knows exactly how to get a laugh. She's been 'hoofing' since she was 12 and has played every theatre and music hall up and down the country so what she doesn't know about entertaining the boys ain't worth knowing.

When Lily joined our happy band, I tried my hand at what I thought was sophisticated comedy, which fell flat as a pancake and only worked because she sent the whole thing up and got big laughs where none was intended. Eleanora and William were furious, but Lily shrugged it all off. Since then, I'm writing only for her. The laughs get bigger with every new sketch, and now they're intentional. I am learning more about writing than I learned in three years of an English degree or blundering about in the symbolist mists favoured by the Moodys.

Eleanora is jealous. With Lily as the ingénue, Eleanora is obliged to be the mother, the duenna, the nurse, what she calls 'the crone parts'. I tried her out in a romantic scene and she was laughed off stage, she had the grace to take it with a smile but I could see that it hurt. William bolsters her up by saying she is still a great artiste, but art is not what Eleanora wants, she wants love, and it's a long time since William gave her any of that. If indeed he ever did. Of course there is the famous son about whom we hear so much, so they must have done it at least once.

Starved of drama on stage, Eleanora and William make up for it behind the scenes. They turn up at railway stations screaming at each other, which is bad, or not speaking at all, which is worse, because they then communicate through me. 'Tell my *wife* that she will never get that suitcase on to the rack.' 'Tell my so-called *husband* to give me my ticket.' And so on. Lily doesn't notice; she's buried in a movie magazine, or snuggled into her fur collar. Like a cat, she can sleep whenever she wants to. I am on eggshells not least because, when there's nothing else to argue about, they argue about me. William can always throw Eleanora's infidelity in her face, with some justification. She retaliates by saying, 'You're just jealous because you can't have him'. The more people listen, the louder the Moodys' voices get, playing to the gallery. Most of the dialogue would never make it past the Lord Chamberlain. Last week we were on a busy train to Aldershot when he denounced her as a 'whore!' complete with pointing finger, blazing eye and quivering beard, to which Eleanora stood up in her Lady Macbeth pose and replied, 'A whore I may be, but you, my dear, are a sodomite!' The other passengers clapped and laughed as she swept off towards the guard's van.

It's when we're in the theatres that things really get bad. William and Eleanora call them theatres; the rest of us call them mess halls, lecture halls etc., where they have set up a stage and some chairs. Our dressing rooms are rudimentary but we of the Art Theatre are used to that, having changed in toilets up and down the land; at least when we play military bases we have doors that close, running water and mirrors. I share with William, Eleanora shares with Lily, which leads to a great deal of storming in and out, slamming of doors and general fun and games. It's like living in a Strindberg play. The only respite is on stage, where we are witty and decorous. As soon as we're off, the claws are out again. Intervals are particularly bad. I wish I could share a dressing room with Lily. We get on perfectly well and there's none of that awful sex tension between us.

Sometimes I peep through the curtain at the boys in the audience and envy their easygoing camaraderie. Anything would be better than the hothouse atmosphere chez Moody. Perhaps I should report to the recruiting office and put an end to all this polio nonsense. It was a cowardly lie that has become a millstone round my neck. I should be doing my bit like the rest of the lads, squarebashing and learning the parts of the rifle and so on. At least in the army I might learn a trade, and be able to hold my head high in Civvy Street. As things are, I foresee a future of a) poverty and b) answering awkward questions about what I did in the war. Lily, at least, can marry well. I don't think that's an option for me.

September 1940

Humiliating experience at the recruitment office. After the storms and dramas of recent weeks beside which the bombing seems insignificant I finally mustered the courage to turn myself in – and despite my best efforts I could not convince them that I was fit for service. I must be the only man in London who's disappointed to be let off. I've met hundreds who are green with envy and some of them have offered me good money for my papers, or for the name of the doctor who signed them. Eleanora begged me not to go, she got quite hysterical which seemed daft but to her it would be like losing another son, she's already got one fighting somewhere, she knows not where, facing daily danger, and to lose me as well would be the final straw. It's somewhat chilling to realise that I've been little more than a surrogate son for all these years but when you get down to it Doctor Freud is usually right. Even William, who has spent so much time cursing me as a vile fornicator, begged me to stay – 'for the sake of the Company, dear boy'. Only Lily encouraged me to go, and has been looking at me more kindly since I announced my intention to sign up. She is going to be one disappointed blonde when I tell her I've been turned down.

The bombs are raining down on London every night and fortunately we've been on tour in Wiltshire, Gloucestershire and Somerset for most of that time. What will be left when we get home I shudder to think; William and Eleanora scan the newspapers for any mention of Kentish Town. We had a day off in Swindon and so I toddled off to the local army base where I demanded to see the officer in charge. This got me a brief interview with an incredulous sergeant who told me to bugger off, but I insisted and so after waiting in a corridor for nearly an hour I was taken to see a harassed little doctor who reminded me very much of my father, preoccupied, unfriendly and with an apparent inability to look one in the eye.

He looked over my exemption papers, asked me about polio, hummed and hawed, listened to my chest, got me to drop my trousers and had a look at my legs, and then said that he couldn't argue with his colleague's diagnosis, I had obvious signs of infantile paralysis and that I should look for a desk job. 'I'm sorry, Mr Barton, but there is nothing more I can do for you.'

Then I resorted to pleading, and he brought in a very nice Captain who was about 50 years old with grey sideburns and a grey moustache and looked a bit like Ronald Colman. He was sympathetic to my plight and explained that there was all sorts of useful war work I could do but if the doc said I was not fit for service, I was not fit for service. We had quite a heart to heart, I suspect he's the one they send all the nutcases to because he had a very sympathetic manner and he asked about my relationship with my mother and so on. I could see what he was driving at, he thought I was queer. Finally he got me to tell him all about Eleanora and he seemed very interested and mentioned that he too had been in 'theatricals' before the war, and he said he would be sure to catch our show, and then he shook my hand and said exactly what William has been saying for months – that we are doing valuable work keeping up the morale of the troops, reminding them of what they're fighting for and so on. Cheap innuendo and tap routines – our last great bastion against fascism.

So this is God's way of telling me that I am not meant to go to war, that they also serve who only ponce around in make-up.

And lo and behold who was at the show tonight looking very distinguished but 'my' Captain, laughing in all the appropriate places. Afterwards he came backstage and asked me if I would care to join him for supper, and I can't say I wasn't tempted but at that point Eleanora 'happened' to find us and assumed that the Captain must have been looking for her. She swamped him with her attentions and I had little choice but to slip away. When we were leaving the Captain was nowhere to be seen, Eleanora had frightened him off good and proper. We had an unpleasant scene overheard by our landlady in which she accused me of deserting the company etc., which I did not dignify with a reply. To be honest a night of being chased around a bedroom by an amorous army captain would be vastly preferable to Eleanora's worn-out routines. I tire of Strindberg. I'd rather be in a Noël Coward comedy.

May 1941

Great excitement in the Moody camp this morning as William received an official letter from the War Office. Eleanora screamed when she saw it and instantly assumed that her son was dead, and for once her hysterics weren't feigned. Even William was pale. I know very little about said son except that he hasn't been 'part of the family' for some years, but underneath all the petty dramas of their daily lives there runs a deep current of fear and sorrow for their lost boy, wherever he is. The arguments and scenes are a distraction just as I am. Something to occupy their minds while their son is away, and in danger.

Well, he is not dead but injured. Beyond that, there is little detail. Second Lieutenant William Moody (he has his father's name) has been 'wounded in action', it does not say where, and will be returning home, it does not say when. It could be anything from a scratch to an amputation. He could be a complete cabbage. For the rest of the day, William and

Eleanora were silent and preoccupied and couldn't even raise a decent argument between them. Eleanora disappeared and I found her in the yard smoking a cigarette, it was freezing cold but she didn't seem to notice. She was crying, her nose was running, and I would have comforted her but I heard her sob the name 'Billy!' as if her heart was breaking.

Christmas Eve 1941

Last night's show was the last one for a while as Lily is off to stay with her folks in Bristol. Eleanora and William are spending a quiet Christmas at home to which I am not bloody well invited. In the months of waiting for news of Billy they have become so quiet and introspective that I barely recognise them. This time last year as the bombs rained down they were busy planning new shows, sewing costumes, scrounging sheet music from here and there as if war was the most exciting game in the world. Now they're reluctant to go on, subdued on stage, the first to leave when the curtain goes down, and even on tour they shut themselves away in whatever miserable digs we have while Lily and I make what we can of local hospitality.

This leaves me with a rather painful dilemma. I can go home for Christmas and spend two or three days of silent recrimination with my parents, or I can stay in the flat and risk being alone. On the whole the latter is preferable even though I have very little money with which to eat. Still the flat is warm and I can catch up on sleep and writing, so I've made the decision and told my parents that I'm working. The relief in my mother's voice was quite clear even over the phone. I'm sure they will have the neighbours in as usual and they must be sick of trying to explain what I'm doing with my life. God knows what lies they've made up because I'm quite sure they haven't told anyone I'm an actor. Perhaps they're saying I'm dead. Direct hit in the Blitz? Heroic death as Spitfire pilot? Who knows. Anything is preferable to the shame of the theatre. And they don't know the half of it.

I might as well be hanged for sheep as for lamb. I don't have money but I do have youth, tolerable looks and thanks to wardrobe a decent suit of clothes, and if with all those advantages I can't rustle up a bit of seasonal cheer then the Luftwaffe has my full permission to drop a bomb on my head.

Boxing Day 1941

Feel like my life is splitting in two and I'm not sure this is a good thing or a bad thing and if we weren't in the middle of a war I might worry about it, but as things are I'll just take it as it comes. Everyone else seems to be with families or fighting overseas or stuck in one of the hundreds of military establishments we've played at, which means that the West End at Christmas is left to the outcasts and misfits. And so for a young man with the full complement of arms and legs and a reasonable measure of charm it is not difficult to find company even if it is queer. I spent Christmas Day in a very nice house in Richmond, where the bombs hardly seem to have left a scratch, with a very nice man called Alec whom I met in a pub in Leicester Square. He is the same age as my father and 'terribly interested' in my acting and writing and so on. He had fires burning in every grate and a larder absolutely crammed with black market goodies and some of the best wine I've ever tasted, and so all in all I had a very nice time and I shan't go on about the fact that 'it' happened but suffice to say that 'it' wasn't nearly as bad as I feared.

I spent a good deal of time in his bathroom staring at my face in the mirror looking for signs, but I look the same as I ever did, I have not developed a weak chin or fluttery eyelashes and I shall take jolly good care not to. Apart from the obvious attractions of the larder and the cellar, Alec was pleasant company, which I have missed in the last few years. We listened to Sibelius and Richard Strauss on his gramophone and we talked about books, and I was ashamed to admit that I have hardly read anything except Agatha Christie since leaving university. He said there was nothing wrong with Agatha Christie, he has a shelf full of her (many of them signed, I noticed), he applauded my taste and very tactfully suggested that as 'a young writer of such promise' I might like to try such and such. When I left this morning after my second 'peculiar' night he gave me a little packet of books. I opened them when I got home. *Brighton Rock* by Graham Greene, *Goodbye to Berlin* by Christopher Isherwood, *Hangover Square* by Patrick Hamilton. And tucked inside an envelope containing a letter on headed paper with his address and phone number wishing me a happy new year, and a five-pound note.

11 March 1942

Phone call this morning from William Moody no less, the first time I have heard from him in weeks, announcing that 'my son' is coming home at the weekend and there is to be a big party on Sunday to which 'absolutely everyone' is invited, oh and by the way would I be interested in a spot of work. ENSA has booked another tour of the camps; my heart sinks but I need the dough, I have been out of work since January. I am curious to meet the famous son, God only knows what William and Eleanora produced between them, I can only assume the worst.

12 March 1942

Up to Kentish Town for rehearsals. It's the same old baloney but I'm not the only one who's glad of the work. Lily Field is back and it looks like she's been having a lean time of it as well, she's not as plump and peachy as she was this time last year.

We've got a nice little three-week tour up in Cambs, Norfolk, Suffolk and we don't need much practice because we're still word perfect. After rehearsal Eleanora takes me aside for a 'quiet word'. She's looking old, and not just because she's stopped dyeing her hair (I suspect she can't get the henna), her face has started to sag and the lines round her mouth and eyes are suddenly deeper, I suppose it's the worry. 'You know, of course, that my Billy is coming back to us tomorrow,' she says. 'He's a very sensitive boy, and after what he's been through he's going to need complete rest.' Of course. I can just imagine the kind of neurasthenic wreck that she and William have raised. 'And so I hope you will be considerate and kind and not cause any trouble.' I don't know what you mean, I say, 'I've never caused you any trouble, Eleanora,' and put a hand on hers. She pulls away as if she's been burnt. Ah! The sting of guilt! 'Dear Edward,' she says, 'I know I can rely on you,' although she knows nothing of the sort.

'Oh Eleanora,' I sigh, and look at her with the big wet puppy dog eyes, as if I'm desperately in love but willing to sacrifice my happiness for hers, the noble renunciation scene, always goes over well in the movies. I wish I could think of some memorable line and doubtless I will later. Then she says, 'I hope I am not asking too much of you, dear Edward, but life is going to be very difficult for poor Billy when he comes home and I do so much hope that you and he will be friends. He needs friends of his own age.' I nod sagely and do the eyes again and say 'of course' but God only knows what he will be like. I imagine him as one of the creatures I've seen screeching around the Criterion Brasserie, all hair and scarves, but I suppose the army knocked that out of him. Then I say, 'If you need me just call, I'll be waiting,' sigh, gaze. Eleanora kisses me on the forehead and it's all very beautiful and spiritual which is quite a contrast to the old days.

13 March 1942

Dinner *chez* Moody. The famous son is not the least like I imagined him. He looks like a football player or a road mender – exactly the sort of person who would go to war and come back with an impressive injury (smashed leg at Tobruk) and a commendation for bravery. He is a little shorter than me, he has blond hair which he wears in a regulation short back and sides, and he's sturdy and strong looking, in other words not the faintest resemblance to William Moody Senior which makes me doubt that he had any role in the conception.

One thing they share is a taste for unpleasant scenes and you would be hard pressed to believe that this was the longed-for homecoming, hail the conquering hero and so on, because when I arrived there was an atmosphere that you could cut with a knife. William was upstairs in the attic, Eleanora was crying in the kitchen, this left Billy in the front room where I found him sitting in William's favourite easy chair, his foot up on a stool, smoking a cigarette and staring gloomily into the fire. He paid not the blindest bit of attention and so I was obliged to cough.

'And who the fuck are you?' were his first words of greeting, and had I not been the suave creature that recent years have made me I might have been quite discountenanced, but instead I strode forward extending a manly hand and said, 'Edward Barton, how do you do?' to which he was obliged to respond in kind. He did not get up, and for good reason: his left leg is encased in plaster and there was a pair of crutches leaning against the fireplace. He threw his cigarette into the fire and looked up at me, his eyes are very blue and very direct, and he said, 'I don't suppose you could pour me another drink, could you?' His empty glass was on the floor beside him and I sniffed it and knew that he wanted whisky.

'You seem to know your way around pretty well,' he said as I was pouring at the sideboard. I could see what he was driving at, he obviously thinks I am his mother's plaything, or possibly his father's, God knows what he put up with during his childhood. I said nothing but handed him a very large glass of Scotch.

'Water?'

'No.' He didn't thank me but he seemed to relax a little.

I moved to the other end of the fireplace, facing him. 'What happened to your leg?'

'Well fuck me,' he said, 'at last someone's asked. Those two have been pretending there's nothing at all the matter with me. I took a couple of bullets at Tobruk.'

'Ouch.'

'You can say that again.'

'And where have you been all these months?'

'What did you say your name was?'

'Edward Barton.'

'Do they call you Ted or anything? Teddy?'

'No,' I said.

'Mind if I do?'

'Call me what you like.'

'Right. Ted it is. Well, Ted, where have I been all these months? I've been in a shitty fly-infested army hospital in Cairo where I got so many infections that they were ready to chop my leg off, so they shipped me back to England with a bunch of other cripples and they've been patching me up in Queen Alexandra ever since.'

'Can you walk?'

'Not without crutches.'

'Will you be able to walk when the plaster comes off?'

'You're not scared of asking questions, are you, Ted?'

'No.'

'Not quite sure what's under here.' He rapped on the plaster with his knuckles. 'Might be a load of spam for all the doctors can tell me.'

'Does it hurt?'

'It itches like fuck.'

'Isn't that supposed to be a good sign?'

'Are you trying to cheer me up?'

'Not particularly.'

'Did *she* ask you to be nice to me?'

I thought of lying, but said, 'Yes.'

'Well thanks,' he said, and drained his whisky. 'I don't know if I'll be able to walk again. Fifty fifty. At best I'll have a limp. But hey ho, I'm lucky to be alive.' He looked round the room. 'Alive and back home. Whoop-de-fucking-do.'

'Another drink?'

'You bet.' He gave me his glass. 'And you're having one this time. You're not another one of their bread-and-milk brigade, are you?'

'Certainly not.' I poured, and we clinked glasses. 'Down the hatch, Billy.'

'Up yours, Ted.'

We drank. He wiped his lips on the back of his hand. On his wrists, protruding from worn cuffs, thick blond hairs caught the firelight. He was in civvies. Demobbed, then.

'And where do you fit in round here, if it's not a rude question?'

'I'm an actor.'

'Oh Christ.'

'And a writer.'

'Oh double Christ.'

'Don't hold it against me.'

'With them?' He jerked his thumb towards the back of the house.

'Yes.'

'Bad luck.'

'It's all right.' I was pretty certain that one or both of his parents were now listening at the door. 'They've been very good to me.'

'And why aren't you in the army?'

The direct question in return.

'Because I had polio.'

'Right.' He mulled this over. 'You look all right to me.'

'That's what I told the doctor.'

'Right.' Drink, wipe, cigarette, matches. 'A pair of cripples, then, aren't we?'

'I suppose we are.'

'Here's to it.' We drank again, and I refilled. The decanter, in which William pretentiously kept his whisky, was nearly empty and I, at least, was nearly drunk. Billy seemed untouched.

The door opened and Eleanora burst in, her eyes red but apart from that pretty well patched up, cigarette in one hand, scarf in the other. A very theatrical entrance. Billy rolled his eyes.

'Darlings,' she said, 'I'm so glad to see that you've introduced yourselves, dinner is coming along quite nicely, I think it's going to be a sort of stew, at least let's call it that, shall we?'

'Such a shame,' drawled Billy in a voice quite unlike his own, 'that you had to let Cook go, Mama.'

'Well, one makes these sacrifices,' said Eleanora, floating around the room like a heavy butterfly, 'in times of national crisis.'

'Ted here was just asking me about my leg.' His accent was back to normal – a far cry from his parents' outdated Mayfair lilt.

'Oh!' Her eyes darted to the door. 'Ted, indeed. We never call him that. Nobody calls you Ted, do they darling?'

'Are you at all interested in what happened, Mum?'

She put her hands over her hears. 'Mum! Ugh! Please don't call me that.'

'Very well.' The drawl was back. 'Mama.'

'That's better.' The crisis had passed, and she had avoided the gory details. 'I don't know where you pick this sort of thing up from.'

'The army, I suppose.'

'I suppose so, darling.' She fussed around, straightening antimacassars and tray cloths. 'Now, are we all right for drinks?'

'As long as the old man's got some more whisky stashed away, then yes.'

'Good heavens.' Eleanora looked at the decanter.

'Evaporation,' said Billy, and winked.

Dinner was entertaining. William sat at the head of the table, Eleanora at the foot, like a scene from a play, the paterfamilias and his dutiful wife. Billy was the prodigal son and I had obviously passed my audition as best friend and confidant. We managed rather well, although once or twice we forgot our lines. William talked about matters theatrical, puffing our little shows up to such an extent that you'd think we'd been headlining at the Palladium. Eleanora added little homely touches, gossiped about friends and relations of whom I had never heard. They avoided any mention of the war, or Billy's injury. I gather that he has in the past trod the boards, and might do so again if other work is not forthcoming.

'Edward can write something for you, darling, I'm sure,' said Eleanora. 'He's terribly clever.'

'I'll just make sure you don't have to do any tap dancing,' I said, and there was a clunking silence during which Eleanora and William stared at me as if I was Banquo's ghost. Then Billy laughed, throwing back his head, exposing his Adam's apple, and said, 'Tap dancing, that'll be the fucking day,' and his parents were so relieved they did not even comment on the profanity.

Eleanora cleared the plates – I have never seen her so domestic, I suppose she learned it in the theatre – and William passed round a packet of Players as if they were the finest Cuban cigars. We smoked and chatted and I was half expecting William to say, 'Shall we join the ladies?' but instead he did something even more amazing, he dug into his pocket and pulled out a couple of quid which he pressed into Billy's hand and said, 'Why don't you two toddle off to the pub?' I've never seen William give money away before, but Billy was all for it.

So off we toddled, rather slowly given Billy's crutches, to the Trafalgar on Kentish Town Road, which was smoky and rowdy and suited Billy just fine. I would normally have gone straight to the lounge bar but he dragged me into the public bar without discussion, there was no carpet on the floor and the smoke stung my eyes but the barmaid gave us a warm welcome and certainly had a twinkle in her eye for Billy, crutches and all. He ordered pints and even though we had been drinking heavily all evening he downed his in two gulps and ordered another.

'A good old London pub,' he said, when we sat down near the fire. 'I haven't been in one for years. I suppose there are some good things about coming home.' He drank. 'The beer, for instance. Better than the piss they drink in Spain.'

This was my cue to ask the questions that needed asking, i.e. where have you been for the last several years, why did you leave home, and so on. In a nutshell, William Moody Jr had an itinerant childhood tagging around provincial theatres with his parents, occasionally being shunted on stage when needed, and when the authorities insisted that he went to school at the age of twelve he was billeted with Eleanora's mother, Nanna Hamilton, in Essex. Life with Nanna was a bit rough and tumble – Eleanora isn't by any means as posh as she makes out, and it seems that her mother drank, so by the age of fifteen Billy knew a thing or two about life and could use his fists when one of Nanna's pals got 'a bit handy' as he puts it. He rejoined the family firm for a couple of years and was making a good impression as a juvenile lead, being blond and exceedingly handsome (he didn't say this but he didn't need to, all eyes in the pub were on him) but couldn't stand his parents' fighting. When he was eighteen he joined the International Brigades and went to fight in Spain, which gives you some idea of how bad his home life was.

Having survived that, it was only natural for him to join the regular army and as luck would have it he was posted to the Western Desert 'because I couldn't stand coming back to the cold and rain'. He worked on his suntan and saw action at Tobruk and here he is, lame in one leg, no educational qualifications and no idea what to do with the rest of his life. By pint number four he was getting a bit maudlin, wishing that Hitler would recommence aerial bombardment because he would rather have a 'quick clean death' than a slow lingering decay etc., but he perked up by pint number five and decided that what he really needed was a woman. This led to some inconclusive chat with the barmaid and a couple of girls who were sitting in the corner drinking gin and orange but eventually the liquor caught up with the heroic 2nd Lt Moody and I was obliged to escort him home before he fell over. This was not easy, even for the few hundred yards along Kentish Town Road, because he is a heavy bastard and there were the crutches to be managed, but I got him back to the house and on to the couch. There was no point in attempting to negotiate the stairs so I put rugs and coats over him and left him to snore. His head was turned to one side, resting on his crooked arm, the tendons and muscles of his throat standing out like sculpture in the museum. Although statues don't drool.

17 May 1942

Well now the inevitable has happened which makes things very awkward for all concerned but it's not as if I didn't see it coming, besides which it's none of my business what they get up to in their spare time, I just don't particularly like having my nose rubbed in it while I am at work. Still I am an actor and the very least I can do is keep my feelings to myself and behave like a gentleman even if this is beyond certain other people.

Lily is going around like the cat that got the cream while Billy has a look of stunned complacency on his face, like an idiot child. I suppose that is what 'love' does to you, or what people call love, which in this case is simple physical infatuation. The minute they met it was obvious where this was headed and I'm sure they would have done it right then and there were it not for the fact that Billy was still finding it difficult to walk let alone anything more strenuous. Their 'courtship' of the last few weeks has been odious in the extreme as they only seem to be satisfied when they are flirting in front of an audience – I suppose Lily Field is used to doing everything in public. Eleanora and William turn a blind eye, they're just glad that Billy's getting better, that the plaster's off and he can walk with a cane, and best of all from their point of view he's working for them again, taking up the romantic leads that he dropped when he rushed off to be heroic in Spain. I spend so much time writing material that I barely appear on stage, which suits me fine, I have no desire to make love to Lily on stage or off, I leave that kind of thing to them as likes it. So I churn out sketches by the yard in which Billy and Lily are given licence to parade their carnal appetites, much to the relish of our audiences, who like it coarse and strong.

The consummation came last night, and boy, didn't we all know about it. After two weeks in which Lily has been appearing a very long way down the bill at Collins, she deigned to come back to us for shows in Croydon and Brighton, and Billy was absolutely convinced that it was in Brighton that he was going to 'get lucky'. I'm not a gambling man but I would say luck had very little to do with this, Lily is what you might call a 'dead cert'. They spent the whole performance practically undressing each other on stage and then as soon as their make up was off (and in her case heavily reapplied) they went for supper somewhere, and I can just imagine what was on the menu.

I went back to the boarding house with William and Eleanora feeling very much the old maid. I am saying nothing to anyone apart from you, dear diary, although I am going to find it very hard to act the confidant when Billy dishes up the details as he doubtless will. I do think it's inconsiderate of him when there are so many other girls in the world, he has to pick one that we all have to work with. I can just imagine the ructions it would cause if I started sleeping with Eleanora again, although I have a perfect right to do whatever I choose, just as Billy has done. But when I think about my past intimacy with Eleanora I shudder; it's like a dream to me now, and a bad one at that.

23 May 1942

Back in London thank God and no need to see any of them for a week, which leaves me short of pocket money but fortunately I have friends who will see me right in that department, and after the stresses and strains of Brighton I think I've earned a bit of pampering. So I'm in Richmond for the weekend and I will let Alec take care of me, I'll be well fed and will have soft beds and hot baths and some intelligent company, which makes the other thing worth while, in fact I'm quite used to it now. Funny what you can get used to when there's a war on. Alec is generous and considerate and takes me seriously which is balm to the soul after a week of the Billy and Lily Show. I told him a bit about the situation and he quoted Shakespeare, 'lilies that fester smell far worse than weeds', Sonnet 94 apparently, I should remember this from university but I don't and shall have to look it up.

17 June 1942

Big smash-up after the show tonight with Billy storming off when the curtain came down and Lily bursting into tears,

God knows what it's all about, I'm immune to their dramas just as I'm immune to William and Eleanora's. Bloody theatricals, they're all as bad as each other and Billy for all that he pretends to be the great man of the people, war hero etc., etc. is no exception. Presumably they've had a row, it's usually one of three things a) Billy's drinking b) Lily's 'popularity' with the armed forces or c) what Billy calls 'playing for cheap laughs' on stage, though God knows they're the only laughs we get. He's terribly high and mighty about it all, he says the sketches I write are 'trivial' and even 'bourgeois' and we should be presenting material which reflects the world we are living in, the class struggle and so on. I can just imagine how well that would go down, I'm almost tempted to try it just so to see Billy and Lily running off under a hail of eggs.

25 June 1942

Billy down in the dumps today, says his leg 'hurts like fuck' and that he's going to have to go back to hospital to have it broken and re-set again, he's smoking and drinking too much and not sleeping, he's lost weight since he came home, he must be the only soldier in the land who thrived on army food. Of course it's all because of Lily who is not speaking to him except on stage and even then she manages to barb every line, much to the amusement of the audience. Billy sleepwalks through each performance, poor sod, I think I almost preferred it when they were all over each other because when Billy is in a blue mood, EVERYONE is in a blue mood, myself included.

So tomorrow we have a day off, thank God, but somehow I've allowed him to talk me into going out on the town. I would much prefer to spend the evening at home with the latest books and records that Alec has given me including a recording of Sibelius which I am very pleased with. But hey ho I suppose I should be flattered that Billy has chosen me as his drinking companion. I know exactly what will happen, we'll do the West

End pub crawl and I'll end up carrying him home drunk as a lord and bedding him down on the sofa again silly bastard.

27 June 1942

Last night did not go as expected, in fact it turned out to be surprisingly enjoyable and for the first time since the Prodigal Son returned I feel that he might be a friend worth cultivating rather than just part of the job. He insisted on coming to pick me up at the flat at 6 p.m. and arrived on the dot looking flushed and very pleased with himself because he walked all the way down from Kentish Town with only his cane for support, perhaps he won't have to go back to hospital after all. I thought that having a rest from Lily might have done the trick but I said nothing.

He was dressed smarter than I've ever seen him, in a jacket and tie even though it was a warm evening, this is what he calls his 'pulling clobber'. He's had his hair cut and the exercise brought colour to his cheeks, which have been looking sallow of late. And wonders will never cease, he brought a bottle of wine. Wine! Actual wine! Red, in one of those wicker basket affairs, it must have cost him a bob or two (if he didn't nick it from William's cellar that is). 'Hope you like it,' he said, and I half expected him to whip a bunch of flowers out from behind his back. I found a couple of wine glasses and didn't mention that they were a present from his mother because she couldn't stand drinking liquor from a teacup.

I poured the wine and Billy made himself comfortable, lounging around on the sofa and looking through my books and records as if he owns the place. 'Blimey,' he said, 'you read a lot, don't you?' which I couldn't deny. Then he said, 'What's this then?' and showed me the Sibelius LP which Alec gave me, so I said it was classical music, and he whistled. 'Didn't know you were so cultured, Ted, you'd better show me what I'm missing.' So I put it on and the first track is 'The Swan of Tuonela' which starts very very quietly. I was about to say something but he put his finger to his lips and sat up paying attention like a dog scenting a rabbit. When the cor anglais came in with that long ribbon of melody he gasped and then said 'Fuck' and then 'sorry'. For the next few minutes he was absolutely rapt and I had time to smoke a cigarette while the band played on. At the end when the strings were shimmering into silence he had tears in his eyes.

'Jesus Christ,' he said, 'what was that?' so I told him it's about a mythical swan who swims around the isle of the dead. He rubbed his eyes with the heel of his palm and said, 'Well I've been there and there weren't any fucking swans', but I could see he was upset about something and not, for a change, about Lily. I forget sometimes that he's seen things that I can not even imagine and this isn't the time to start asking him about it. 'I wish I had your education,' he said. 'The most I can manage is the three Rs.'

'That's all you need. You can teach yourself the rest.'

'Or you can teach me.'

'Depends what you want to learn.'

'Everything,' he said, and turned over a few books on the table. 'How about this for starters?' Shakespeare's *Sonnets* of course, which I borrowed from Alec (and like most things I 'borrow' from him like the gramophone I don't think he expects to get it back). 'William Shakespeare. Well we've got one thing in common at least, we have the same name.'

I took the book from him and opened it at the marker, Sonnet 94 of course. 'Try that,' I said. 'It's one of the really famous ones.'

He stumbled over the first couple of lines and handed it back. 'You read it.' So I did.

They that have power to hurt and will do none,
That do not do the thing they most do show,
Who, moving others, are themselves as stone,

Unmoved, cold, and to temptation slow,
They rightly do inherit heaven's graces
And husband nature's riches from expense;
They are the lords and owners of their faces,
Others but stewards of their excellence.

The summer's flower is to the summer sweet,
Though to itself it only live and die,
But if that flower with base infection meet,
The basest weed outbraves his dignity:
For sweetest things turn sourest by their deeds;
Lilies that fester smell far worse than weeds.

I don't think I put undue emphasis on the final line, but
Billy picked up on it. 'What's that? Lilies that what?'

'Lilies that fester smell far worse than weeds.'

'Fucking hell, you can say that again.'

'What do you mean?' – ha ha, as if I didn't know.

'Lilies that fester. Yeah. That's good, that is, Mr Shakespeare.
You hit the nail on the head there, Billy-boy.'

'Oh! I see what you mean.' Butter wouldn't have melted in
my mouth. 'Well, I suppose he had something of that sort in
mind. "Moving others are themselves as stone".'

This led to a line-by-line examination of Sonnet 94,
which I did my best to relate to the Lily Situation and by the
time we'd finished Billy was bursting with excitement. 'My
God,' he said, 'where do you get all this stuff from?'

'There are these secret places called universities.'

'Oh, right.' He looked glum. 'Fat lot of good they are to
me.'

'You should enrol.'

'Me? I don't think so. I'm thick. Teachers told me.'

'Of course you're not thick. Anyway, they're very keen on
getting ex-servicemen into higher education.'

'Well they don't know what else to do with us.'

He sounded bitter, and understandably so: he's been turned down for a handful of jobs because they don't want an injured man. 'I might as well spend the rest of my life reading poetry.'

'I'm serious. You could do a part-time degree.'

'What's the point?'

'You don't want to spend the rest of your life in crappy plays.'

'That's true.'

'So learn something useful!'

'Like this?' He tossed the Shakespeare aside. I can imagine that Billy was a very sulky little boy and I quite understand why his Nanna turned to drink.

'Not necessarily,' I said. 'You're always going on about politics. You could study that.'

'Huh. I can just imagine the sort of politics they teach in those places.'

'And what would that be?'

'How to keep the poor in their place. Why the British Empire is a wonderful thing and Trade Unions are the work of Satan.'

'I think you might be surprised,' I said, thinking of some of the comfortably off socialist firebrands I'd met in my college days. 'Why not go along to a couple of lectures? See how you like it.'

'They'd throw me out.'

'Were you like this at Tobruk?'

'Fuck off. Like what?'

'Easily defeated.'

'No.' He stuck his lower lip out, then picked up the *Sonnets* and threw them at me. The book landed face down, dog-earing the pages and no doubt cracking the spine. 'All right. You tell me where to go, I'll go. Bastard.' But he was smiling again.

We finished the wine and by now it was half past seven. 'I can't be bothered to go up West tonight,' he said. 'Let's go to the pictures.' So we went down to the Gaumont and saw *Casablanca* and at the end I was sniffling a bit and he put his arm round my shoulder and called me a 'soft cunt'. Then we had two swift pints at the Mother Red Cap and called it a night. He was wavering a bit as he limped up the hill but his last words to me were 'that's the best night I've had for fucking years' and that, I flatter myself, includes his nights with Festering Lily.

14 August 1942

On again, off again, on again, off again. The Billy and Lily Show has become the longest-running farce on the British stage. Even Eleanora is beginning to fret under the constant tension, while William absents himself and pretends nothing is happening. If they're 'on' they're inseparable, stuck to each other by the glue of sex. If they're off, anything goes – tantrums, physical violence, obscene tirades from both parties (my vocab expanding rapidly). She's quite capable of deliberately muffing a line, or dropping something, just to spoil things for him. Last week when we were playing in Aldershot yet again the audience stayed in their seats during the interval, which I couldn't understand (especially as there was a bar) until I realised that they were listening quite rapt to the dialogue from behind the curtain: 'Who are you calling a bitch?' 'You, you fucking bitch' and so on. The lines I write have a little more polish but when it comes to holding the attention of the basic soldier you really can't go wrong with a bit of the old Anglo Saxon.

Tonight is an 'off' night which means that I am Billy's best mate in the whole world, like a brother to me blah blah blah, and I get to hear all about what a ball-breaker Lily is, how she's only using him as a way of furthering her 'career' ha ha, how he wishes his fucking leg wasn't smashed up so he could go back to the war and the 'clean honest life of combat' as he puts it. Strikes me that Billy is inordinately fond of military life and his first instinct when faced with the complexities of family, sex, love etc. is to flee to the nearest combat zone.

Tomorrow or the day after I have no doubt all will be 'on' again and I will just be the funny university-educated bloke who knocks out stale jokes nineteen to the dozen and who might be good to sub him a few bob so he can take La Field out on the town. How many times I've paid for that young lady's dinner/drinks/dance/pictures I do not care to think but there's no point in bearing a grudge, I shall rise above it and one day I will get it all down on paper and make a fortune and that will be more than adequate recompense.

Anyway I have stopped asking about what the latest tiff is about, it always boils down to the same thing, it's like a seesaw, the only way it'll stop is when one of them gets off or the whole contraption breaks. I wonder if all people in love are like this? I don't know, having never suffered from the tender passion myself, certainly not with Eleanora. The nearest I've come is the pleasant friendship with Alec which continues calm and untroubled. I sometimes guess from looks that he gives me that he would like it to be something more than an occasional commercial transaction, and after a bad day with the Moodys I can't say I'm not tempted.

Just before we went on tonight Billy announced that 'we are going out dancing at the weekend', I thought he meant him and Lily but then he said, 'You have got some dancing shoes haven't you, Teddy?' He means to take me to the Hammersmith Palais 'to see how the other half lives'. He's been doing his best listening to my records Sibelius, Strauss, Verdi, etc. and now it's his turn to educate me. Obviously she has stood him up and he's taking me in her place, and I would be offended but for the fact that I have not been to a proper ballroom for years and I am curious to see Billy in his natural habitat. I suppose my black brogues will do as dancing shoes and I've got a couple of new shirts, thanks to Alec, so it's a date.

15 August 1942

Drunk and very tired, thanks to William Moody Junior not to mention the Billy Cotton Band and half bottle of whisky smuggled in WMJr's jacket pocket. Hammersmith Palais is huge and brightly lit and it was like walking into fairyland after making our way through the blackout, full of noise and smoke and faces, the sort of thing I'd usually run a mile from but Billy grabbed me by the arm, right to the middle of the dance floor and said, 'Right let's find us some partners and you can show me what you're made of.' Before you know it he had introduced himself to a couple of girls who were dancing together and said, 'Excuse me ladies but my friend and I were wondering if you might do us the honour', and suddenly I was gliding around the floor with a very pretty blonde as if we had known each other all our lives. Billy picked the short saucy-looking brunette, she only came up to his shoulder but she was certainly not lacking in other departments and in order to hold her close for the slower numbers he was obliged to press her against him. My blonde was more streamlined so we went round and round to one song after another, 'Don't Sit Under the Apple Tree', 'I Don't Want to Walk Without You', 'He's My Guy' and so on and so forth. Time slipped by. No conversation. Joy. Spontaneity. Movement and colour and laughter, Billy's eye catching mine as he whisked by with his girl in his arms, his bad leg trailing and halting as they turned but you'd never know from the smile on his face. Her eyes were closed, her lips parted, and when I looked back at my partner I found her scrutinising me with a very quizzical expression on her face. 'Your pal and my girlfriend seem to be getting on well,' she said. 'Do you want to sit this next one out?'

I said 'not really' because I wanted to keep on dancing, I wanted the merry-go-round to spin faster and faster, but she said she had to powder her nose and when I saw her half an hour later she was with another chap, this time her eyes were closed, her lips parted as they staggered from foot to foot, you couldn't call it dancing, to a sad smoochy number, something about 'somebody else is taking my place'. How very apt. Billy was nowhere to be seen and so I thought hey ho, time for Teddy to make his lonely way home, but suddenly there he was in the lobby, pissed as a newt, his hair falling over his face. 'Fucking hell I thought you'd pulled,' he said and suddenly we were out in the street and the fresh air hit me like a punch to the stomach. Billy was swaying around trying to get a lighted match to the tip of his cigarette without much success but between us we managed it, me holding his hand in place, and after he'd taken a big drag on it he stuck it between my lips, wet end and all. And so we marched in step, arms round shoulders, passing the fag back and forth, singing 'Don't Sit Under the Apple Tree with Anyone Else But Me' all the way to the underground.

28 August 1942

Show cancelled tonight because half an hour before curtain up to a full house in drill hall up in town there is still no leading lady. Too late says William to change things around and besides he is worried, he says Lily has been 'quiet and strange' the last couple of weeks and when he spoke to her last night she said something about 'family trouble'. Billy says he knows nothing, they haven't been on speaking terms for the last couple of weeks, it seems to be all over between them. I don't know what happened, I haven't asked and Billy hasn't volunteered the details, and since that night at the Hammy Pally there have been no more drinks or anything, he's unusually quiet as well. No backstage dramas, nothing.

And now she's disappeared and left us in the lurch. William had a word with the CO and the troops filed out very fed up. ENSA will not be pleased when word gets back to them and there's no earthly reason why we couldn't have cobbled something together between us, even if it was a revival of *Songs of Experience* with me prancing around in a nappy, at least that would have given them a laugh. But no, we may put up our pipes and be gone. William is grim-faced, Eleanora won't look me in the eye and as for Billy, he's disappeared before I can even ask him what's going on. So that leaves me with a free evening and no money in my pocket and so not being in the mood to kick my heels round the West End I call Alec and get the train down to Richmond.

29 August 1942

I wish I hadn't gone down to Richmond now because talking things over with Alec just made it worse. He said there is only one possible reason why things suddenly broke off like that: Lily is or was expecting a baby. Either she wanted it and Billy didn't, or Billy wanted it and she didn't, and she's kept it or got rid of it. Thinking about it I'm sure that Alec is right because it would have to be something really serious to make William cancel a show and nothing else fits. I can't decide which is worse: whether she's decided to have the baby and therefore force Billy to marry her, or whether she's got rid of the baby thus depriving Billy of a child and William and Eleanora of a grandchild. Alec said that 'she sounds like the manipulative type' and he was almost certain that Lily is trying to 'ensnare' Billy into marriage. Sounds plausible.

Mentioned that I'd gone out dancing and was surprised to discover that Alec is up to date with all latest songs and even has a collection of records by Andrews Sisters et al, 'my guilty pleasures' he called them, and he played me the latest Strip Polka which was very funny with lyrics about a stripper called Queenie and the chorus 'Take it off take it off cry the boys from the rear'. After a few drinks I was dancing around Alec's living room to Strip Polka and gave one of my best performances to an audience of one. This took my mind off things for the rest of the night and we had a gay old time but this morning I can't stop thinking about Lily and what may or may not have happened to her. Daren't ask Billy who is like a bull with a sore head.

Show back on tonight with Eleanora taking over Lily's parts until we can find a replacement, I can't bear to watch. It's too much like the Ibsen plays of yesteryear.

8 September 1942

New girl went on for first time tonight and is not half bad, anything is better than watching Eleanora in a Shirley Temple wig making love to her own son. Patricia doesn't have half the sex appeal of her predecessor but she's a quick study and more to the point she seems completely indifferent to her co-star. She is married and her husband is serving overseas so there's a big invisible KEEP OUT sign between her legs.

I will have to write some new material for her.

Also new boy started tonight, assistant stage manager who gets to come on for a few moments in a couple of sketches and seems absolutely thrilled at the prospect. He can't be more than 18 years old and he's as blind as a bat without his glasses, when he takes them off there are deep red marks on either side of his nose, but he's tolerably good looking and will do for kid parts. His name is Thomas and he's an eager beaver, wants to know everything about writing and acting and producing, smart boy, he'll go far. William told me to 'show him the ropes' and he now follows me around like a puppy, not sure if he's star struck because I am The Great Writer or whether his interests are more queer in origin but he certainly makes a welcome change from moody Billy Moody.

I tried to ask Billy for some details about Lily's departure and he bit my head off so I can only suspect the worst. She has left her lodgings in Bayswater and nobody has her family's address, she's just disappeared like a girl in a magic trick, in a puff of smoke. I found myself scrutinising the faces of the tarts on Shaftesbury Avenue the other night and thinking of an old James Elroy Flecker poem that was popular when I was an undergrad. Looked it up and was struck by these verses.

> Perhaps she cast herself away
>   Lest both of us should drown:
> Perhaps she feared to die, as they
>   Who die in Camden Town.
>
> What came of her? The bitter nights
>   Destroy the rose and lily,
> And souls are lost among the lights
>   Of painted Piccadilly.
>
> What came of her? The river flows
>   So deep and wide and stilly,
> And waits to catch the fallen rose
>   And clasp the broken lily.

18 September 1942

As we have the weekend off I suggested to Billy today that we might go out dancing again as I enjoyed it so much last time. My treat etc. He barely managed a civil response and walked off with a muttered curse as if I had made some kind of indecent proposal. Don't know what I'm supposed to have done. Felt very upset as had been looking forward to dancing again. Has he got a new woman? Is he still seeing Lily on the QT? Nothing would surprise me from that quarter and to be honest it would be best for all concerned if the river that flows so deep and wide and stilly would clasp the broken lily and do us all a favour.

Chapter Seven: Edward Barton's Diaries

6 October 1942

BILLY CAME ROUND after college absolutely boiling over with excitement, chasing me around the room wanting to talk about everything, how he was 'thinking again' and how his tutor is 'brilliant' and 'a socialist' who thinks that we will have some kind of English Revolution when the war is over, that 'the balance of power is held by the working classes' and so on. Seeing as this was the first time I've seen him smile for months I was pleased, and let him rave on until it was time for me to go to work. Billy was going to a meeting somewhere in town, doubtless to listen to some bearded vegetarian spouting lefty nonsense while the rest of the world goes up in smoke.

The show tonight was even more pitiful than usual. William has given up on everything, he seems tired and forgetful and has aged ten years since Billy got home. Eleanora is worried sick but puts on a brave face. Now that Billy has signed up at college we are down to a company of four, viz Patricia, Eleanora, Thomas and I, which is hardly what ENSA had in mind when they sent us out to boost morale but we do our best. Patricia is a sweet sensible girl and I keep telling myself I could do a lot worse, while Thomas is proving to be an adept actor with a decent tenor voice, he can carry a sentimental tune better than I can. Tonight we gave them half a dozen weak sketches about rationing, the blackout and so on, which they yawned and talked through, and they only really came to life for the Andrews Sisters number with Eleanora, Patricia and Thomas in matching wigs miming to Strip Polka while I operated the gramophone. Thomas threw himself into this piece of burlesque with considerable gusto and was rewarded with wolf whistles from the audience. He's learned amazingly quickly and is already asking me if he can write some new material. Well, why not? I'm fed up of churning out this kind of rubbish so good luck to him. Alec says I need to stop wasting my time on trash and concentrate on something more 'sustained and serious' and he's quite willing to make up the shortfall in my wages if I quit the company. He has also offered me a permanent berth in Richmond, which of course would save on rent.

24 October 1942

Billy came to the show tonight as we are still down in Wimbledon and he brought with him 'a friend from college', a serious girl called Geraldine, brown hair, good-looking rather than pretty, certainly not the sex-bomb type that Billy usually goes for. They sat in the front row and seemed to enjoy themselves, she laughed in all the right places and they both roared at the Andrews Sisters skit which is fast becoming the hit of the show.

Afterwards we went for a drink. Billy was on best behaviour, he took Geraldine's coat, found her a seat, went to the bar and then of course had to borrow five bob to pay for the drinks. She was very interested in everything to do with our work, asked all about how we organise the shows, who writes the 'wonderful' material, what the deal is with ENSA and so on, stuff that never occurred to Billy before and he sat there taking it all in as if it was the subject dearest to his heart. So although there was none of the smoochy stuff it was perfectly clear that Billy has designs on Geraldine. 'What do you think?' he said when the girls went to powder their noses.

'She seems very nice,' was all I could say, and she does seem exactly that. Nice, sensible and intelligent, just like Patricia. The sort of girl my parents would love me to bring home. Billy looked at me rather curiously, and I thought he was about to say something, but the girls came back and it was time to start putting on coats. Tommy lingered and kept asking me what I was doing, where I was going, and in the end I had to shoo him off to the station otherwise he'd miss the last train and the last thing I need is a lovestruck teenager on my hands.

Staying over in Richmond saves a lot of travelling. Tried to discuss the Billy/Geraldine situation with Alec but he got quite cross and said, 'Just for once can we talk about something other than your precious Billy?'

18 November 1942

Hammersmith Palais with Billy, Patricia and Geraldine, 'double dating'. Not much fun this time. Band no good compared to Billy Cotton, didn't play anything I could dance to. New shoes pinched like hell. B & G disappeared leaving me stranded with Patricia, who thank God knows how to behave herself in public and we kept up a very convincing performance of two young people having a lovely time. I was looking over her shoulder trying to see Billy in the crowd and I imagine she was going over her lines or composing shopping lists or something. In any case we stuck it out till half past ten by which time we both agreed that it would be sensible to beat the rush to the underground and off we went. On the way out of course there were Billy and Geraldine looking very pleased with themselves and in her case rather rumpled, doubtless I shall hear all about it in due course, whether I want to or not.

We sat together on the train, quite a jolly little quartet chatting all the way to King's Cross, anyone listening would think we were the best of pals. Billy kept going on about Geraldine's 'war work', she's got a job in a munitions factory even though she is training to be a teacher, he seems to think that this is much more noble than what I'm doing and kept saying how hard she works, what long hours she puts in, the deprivations of cold hunger lack of sleep etc. Well, good for you, darling, I wanted to say, try facing 200 randy squaddies on a Saturday night in Aldershot and then you'll know the meaning of hard work. But I just smiled and agreed with everything until my face ached and I wanted to punch myself in the teeth.

Got home and spent an hour furiously scribbling in notebook, ideas for a play rather like Coward's *Private Lives* but in a contemporary setting – war, blackouts, rationing and so on, where Coward is all silk pyjamas and champagne this would be make-do-and-mend and a pint of bitter, nobody knowing what the future holds, uncertainty, confusion, etc. Two young men both invalided out of the army, start off as best of friends but then make different choices embodied by the women in their lives. One goes for pleasure, a cheap sexy actress of the Lily Field type – the other goes for wealth and status, an older woman with a nice house, cultured, well-connected, a sort of mix between Eleanora and Alec.

It has potential. I even have a title. *Hors de Combat*. Will start writing tomorrow. What a hoot if it got put on with Billy and me in the leads.

25 November 1942

Work going well on *Hors de Combat*, I have a basic three act structure and some nice bits of dialogue. Tommy very interested in it, as in everything I do, and has helped by reading out scenes, always taking the girls' parts. Alec is full of encouragement and says that when I've got something ready he'll show it to a producer friend of his who is looking for just this sort of thing. So who knows if I work hard and avoid distractions I might make something of myself in 1943 if the whole world doesn't blow up in our faces first, tra la.

13 December 1942

William very ill. Show cancelled. Eleanora found him this morning in his usual chair yellow in the face and his mouth 'all crooked' and he is now in the Royal Free. Billy says it's nothing to worry about and that the 'old man' will be right as rain tomorrow and takes Geraldine out on date.

14 December 1942

Eleanora phoned in the middle of the night to say that William had died. She was very distressed and could not get hold of Billy, kept asking me where he was, why wasn't he there with her, and I couldn't very well say that I knew exactly where he was, he was screwing his precious Geraldine, so I kept my mouth shut. I made my way up to the hospital and there was poor old William under a sheet on the bed where he died, and Eleanora absolutely in bits. She cried like her heart was breaking. Who would have thought she loved William that much? And yet she grieved for him as if her world had ended. I wonder if anyone will ever grieve like that for me.

18 December 1942

Does not look like it's going to be the happiest of Christmases. Billy and Eleanora holed up in Kentish Town waiting for funeral, I have no wish to intrude. Needless to say all shows have been cancelled which leaves me broke but by no means idle, I'm working hard on *Hors de Combat* and occasionally trying out scenes with Tommy who has made some good suggestions. Spoke to Mother today, she sounded absolutely terrified that I was coming home for Christmas but no fear, I will put in an appearance on Christmas Eve and then go straight to Richmond.

22 December 1942

Frantic phone call this morning from Alec asking me if I had kept any letters he wrote to me and if so would I please destroy them right now. He sounded absolutely hysterical and when I finally calmed him down a bit he told me in a very shaky voice that the police had been round with a 'complaint' of unspecified origin and were asking all sorts of awkward questions about his friends and private life. Asked to see his address book, correspondence etc. but in absence of warrant were unable to force the issue. He suspects one of his friends has been blackmailed or arrested and the police are following up 'leads'. He is clearing out everything and 'throwing it on the fire' and urged me to do likewise. Said that Christmas is off, he's getting out of town and will be in touch when things calm down.

Felt quite sick when I put the phone down.

25 December 1942

Tommy came round at eleven o'clock this morning, standing on the doorstep in his big black overcoat and red wool scarf, his nose running because it was bloody freezing out. He said 'Happy Christmas, Edward' and presented me with a big cardboard box with a crepe paper bow on top. Inside there were six bottles of beer, a plate of chicken sandwiches, a dozen mince pies and even a couple of Christmas crackers, he said he'd 'borrowed' it all from his mum and dad and cycled all the way from Clapham to wish me Happy Christmas. Under the circumstances I could hardly turn him away, and he looked delighted when I invited him in. He chattered away and made coffee while I washed and shaved and dressed, and then we opened the beer and made a start on the mince pies. By two o'clock in the afternoon we were both a bit merry and very full of food and one thing led to another and now poor Tommy is even more devoted to me than before. I suppose I should feel remorse, but it was a more pleasant way of spending the day than sitting alone and so I felt nothing but gratitude. We got up at six o'clock and went for a walk around Regent's Park, which was pitch-dark and absolutely empty apart from a few geese and the occasional copper. Tommy was excited and kept pulling me behind trees bushes etc. for kisses as if it was all the biggest lark in the world, and what a lark it would have been if one of the coppers had caught us, but instead they tipped their helmets and wished us Happy Christmas. And then we went back to the flat.

14 February 1943

MOVING DAY. I'll miss the flat, but with no prospect of a job how can I possibly afford the rent? No alternative but to move back to parents which suits none of us. Packed up trunk and suitcases and struggled downstairs to find a cab, just as the postman was coming in with the very last delivery that I shall take at this address. A Valentine, thick white card with a bunch of dried violets stuck in the middle of a heart cut out of a gold paper doily, and a little verse inside about true friendship and the soul's companion and so on, no name but I didn't need one to know who it was from. Tommy. I left it in a bin on the street and got a cab up to Marylebone. Have not given Tommy my parents' address and see no reason why I should run into him in foreseeable future.

Lugged cases through station and got 10.45 train. Dad picked me up, hardly spoke a word on the drive home. Had lunch and went upstairs to start unpacking.

Tried to call Billy but no luck. Eleanora says he is more or less 'living with Geraldine', which strikes me as very selfish but Eleanora does not complain, he is still her blue-eyed boy and can do no wrong.

22 February 1943

Long semi-hysterical letter this morning from Tommy. I suppose Eleanora gave him my address, it was only to be expected. He accuses me of everything under the sun, seduction, corruption of a minor, breaking his tender little heart and so on, page after page of recriminations at the end of which he declares undying love, offers himself to me 'on any terms' and begs me to send him word.

Burned letter at bottom of garden.

Still no word from Billy.

16 March 1943

Sick as a dog when I got up this morning but fortunately have the house to myself so there is nobody to tut-tut when I get up at ten o'clock and eat breakfast in my dressing gown, and certainly nobody to count the bottles. Father at work, Mother spending a week with her sister, everyone seems to be getting very jittery about another Blitz but I'm as safe here as anywhere and I see no point in running. If it comes, it comes. And the way I felt this morning it's welcome, it wouldn't be any worse than the pain I was already suffering.

Spent last night in my room listening to records over and over again, the bloody 'Swan of Tuonela' and 'He's My Guy' by Harry James and his Orchestra until I was so pissed on Scotch that I managed to put a fucking great scratch across the latter. Now it sticks and jumps and I woke up after God knows how long of it just going 'he's careless about me – he's careless about me – he's careless about me' over and over again. Discovered that I had scrawled all over manuscript of play and pretty much ruined it so that'll be consigned to the flames as well. I seem to spend my whole time drinking or burning things these days.

6 April 1943

Letter from Eleanora this morning in which she relates news that Lily Field is dead. Killed by direct hit on a house in Bath where she was living with two other girls. Her parents have been writing to everyone in her address book and I suppose it makes sense that they would get around to M for Moody sooner or later. Don't know how the news was received in Kentish Town. Eleanora expressed usual amount of grief but the death does not touch her deeply, nor, I suspect, her son.

8 April 1943

Can not stop thinking about Lily Field. Last time I saw her she was so full of life, flirting with everyone, fighting with Billy, sulking, singing, dancing, and to end like that – a direct hit – there wouldn't have been much left of her or whatever was growing inside her.

10 April 1943

Phoned Eleanora and guess who picked up the phone? Billy. 'Hello Ted, how are you?' As if we'd seen each other yesterday. Sounded very chirpy. Still going to college, finding it hard, has to work in order to bring some money into the house, etc., but altogether 'not bad'. Then he said, 'Where are you hiding yourself, stranger, I haven't seen you for ages?' and I told him that I'd been living with my parents since February. He laughed and said we are 'a couple of Mummy's boys' and that we should 'paint the town red like we used to'. So we have a date for next week.

So good talking to him again that I quite forgot to ask about Lily.

14 April 1943

Got 5.20 train up to town and had time to kill so walked through Regent's Park remembering happy carefree student days, nearly eight years ago. I felt old and shabby and jaded compared to the young man who bounced through the park in 1935, intoxicated with freedom and discovery. The world, and I, have changed since then. There were hardly any flowers in the park, and everywhere you looked there were signs of a city exhausted by war – dirt, litter, fallen trees, the water in the lake was filthy. But the ducklings paddled around as usual, and even Hitler can't stop the daffodils, and by the time the sky had gone pink and the starlings were flocking I had a spring in my step and a song in my heart.

Met Billy in a pub off Tottenham Court Road, within spitting distance of my old college digs, at seven o'clock. He looked well, and was walking normally, the only sign of his old injury an occasional fretful rubbing of the knee. His hair was neatly cut and combed, the parting as sharp as a knife, glistening with Brylcreem, and he was wearing an old patched tweed jacket that once belonged to his father. It smelled of mothballs. When I walked into the pub he jumped out of his chair. Where had I been, what was I doing, what did I think about Italy and Hamburg and so on, had I read TS Eliot? He bought the drinks and seemed to have a very fat wallet, and it turns out that he's been mending roads for a living, the money is good and tonight would be 'my treat'. So after a couple of pints, which he sank rapidly despite talking almost non-stop, we wandered down into Soho. It was a pleasant evening and he carried the tweed jacket slung over his shoulder, suspended from one finger. Two fingers up he wore his father's old gold ring; I was surprised that he wanted any such memento.

I remembered another night, another year, walking through the London streets with his mother, *entrecôte* steaks and dry martinis at Le Relais, the building long gone now, smashed to rubble. Tonight it was liver and bacon and mashed potato and cups of strong tea at a cafe on Old Compton Street. Billy shovelled the food into his mouth, talking while he chewed, wiping his lips with the back of his hand. He finished before I was halfway through.

'Yeah, but you can't just be sitting there day after day doing nothing.' He seemed perplexed by the fact that I'm not working.

'Well, I'm writing,' I said, although the only 'writing' I've done recently has been insane drunken scribbling which ends up in ashes.

'Good man.' He rolled a cigarette, and picked bits of tobacco off his tongue. 'That's exactly what you should be doing. What is it?'

I almost said 'a play', but that dream had vanished along with Alec, so I said 'a novel', as I have vaguely thought about using some of the *Hors de Combat* material in that way.

'Fantastic! Is it about me?' Billy's teeth, when he smiles, are very large, very white.

'Actually, it's sort of about Lily.'

'Oh.' His face fell. 'Her.'

'I suppose you know.'

'Yeah. Poor kid.' He rolled the tip of his cigarette on the edge of the ashtray, carefully rubbing off the ash. 'So you're writing about her?'

'In a way.'

'Right.' He looked up at me. 'How?'

'What do you mean?'

'You didn't really know her, did you? And you certainly didn't like her much.'

'I liked her well enough.'

'Could have fooled me.' He was scowling now.

'How's Geraldine?' I asked when the silence had lasted too long.

Billy shrugged. 'She's fine.'

'You're still seeing her, then?'

'Yeah.'

'You don't sound very enthusiastic.'

'No, no, she's great. She's just ... you know. Women.'

I nodded, although my experience of the fairer sex is largely limited to Billy's mother. He seemed keen to drop the subject, but I wanted details. 'What's the matter?'

'Usual stuff, Ted. Wants a ring on her finger and a bun in the oven.'

'And you don't?'

'Not while there's a war on, no. What's the point?'

'Quite.'

'Anyway, I'm not ready for the old ball and chain. I'm only 24. I haven't done anything with my life.'

'What were you thinking of doing?'

'Dunno. Getting into politics, maybe.'

'Doesn't sound like much of a career.'

'That's rich coming from you.'

'Point taken.'

'Anyway, I can't afford a family.'

'But you're still seeing her?'

'Yes. If it's any of your business.' He sounded glum.

'And where is she tonight?'

'If you must know we had a bit of a row, okay?'

'What about?' My heart was beating fast.

'We were supposed to be going up to her mum and dad's tonight.'

'And you forgot?'

'No. Fuck that. I wanted to see you.'

I forced myself not to smile. 'Fair's fair. She has you every other night of the week.'

'Yeah.' He rubbed his knee and winced. 'She'd like to.'

I finished my food. 'Right,' I said. 'It's been good to see you, Billy.' It was nine o'clock; if I was going home, I'd need to get moving.

'What? The night is young.'

'But you have to work ...'

'Not tomorrow.' He smiled. 'Day off. Come on, let's go on the piss. I've got money.'

'But my last train ...'

'Oh come on, Teddy, you can stay at the house. Mum won't mind. She's always going on about how she wants to see you.'

'I don't know.'

'Please?'

That was what I wanted to hear. 'All right, then. But you'll have to let me pay you back when I have the ...'

'Oh fuck off, Ted,' he said, and ruffled my hair.

18 April 1943

Another full day writing. Everything seems to fall into place. A story that seemed banal as a play makes sense as a novel. Four characters and their mixed-up lives in wartime. I suppose there will be a thousand such books over the next couple of years but I can't stop writing it. Billy appears pretty much as he is – a wounded soldier. I'm a polio cripple, teaching at the university. Lily has become a singer with a big band, and the Eleanora/Alec character is a wealthy heiress with houses in Mayfair and Buckinghamshire. Stories and dialogue come as fast as I can scribble them down. Wish I'd learned to type.

11 May 1943

Billy rang from a phone box during his break, he's filling in a 'fucking great big hole' on Marylebone Road but has free evening tomorrow and wants to go out on the piss again. Another row with Geraldine? Told Mother and Father that I will be back tomorrow and this time I'm taking my toothbrush. Father muttered something about 'you should be out looking for work' and I told him that I am working, I'm writing, and he gave me a withering glare and said that he could speak to his manager about a position at the bank. I must earn some money but God only knows how.

13 May 1943

As I suspected Billy's sudden availability last night was due to the fact that he and Geraldine had argued again. She wanted him to go shopping for clothes – they've been invited to her sister's wedding, and Billy doesn't have a suitable suit – and he refused. This led to recriminations on both sides: she's trying to force him up the aisle, he's irresponsible and selfish, so Billy was in a pugnacious mood when I met him and seemed hell bent on proving something, to himself if no one else.

'How can I think about the future when we could all be dead tomorrow?' he said over the first of many pints in a pub off Baker Street. He had the *Evening News* in his hand, and the front page was all about 'new London Blitz threat'. It looks as if we may be in for it again. 'If I've only got one day left I don't want to spend it traipsing around Swan and bloody Edgar.' I said 'Quite right too! Live for the moment!', which was what he wanted to hear. He drained his pint – obviously road-mending gives him a thirst – and set up another. His hands, I noticed, were calloused, the nails grimy and bitten short. Mine, in comparison, are shamefully *soignées* – the only tool they've held recently is a pen.

He carried on in this vein for half an hour – gather ye rosebuds while ye may, the bombs may fall tomorrow – until I wondered what it was all leading up to. Then he made his big announcement: he's dropping out of college, not going back for his second year. 'What's the bloody point of it all?' he kept saying, and I had no ready answer. 'All they do it talk, talk, talk, but they haven't got a clue about what it's really like. The "working classes". The "urban proletariat". Try digging a fucking ditch at six o'clock in the morning and tell me about the urban proletariat! Fucking wankers.' He rolled a cigarette, and moistened the paper with his tongue.

'I thought you were all for it,' I said. 'Socialism, and so on.'

'Socialism!' He spat out a shred of tobacco. 'You talk to the blokes who are working on the roads, they don't want socialism. They want what the rich have got. They want to live in nice houses and they don't want to work for a living. They'll climb over your back if they think there's money in it.'

'But surely,' I said, 'people like you can make a difference. That's why education is so important.' I knew what I was doing, and it wasn't kind, but I didn't stop.

'I can't make a fucking difference,' he said. 'What am I? Some cunt who doesn't know whether he's a navvy or a fucking actor. I don't belong in the university, and I don't belong on the roads.' He looked up at me. 'I'm lost, Ted.'

'Course you're not. But if you don't like university, there's no point in sticking with it just for the sake of it.' And, I thought, if he drops out of college then he'll see less of Geraldine...

'Exactly,' he said. 'I knew *you'd* understand.' From this I gather that *she* doesn't. 'I'm sick of reading about life. I want to live life. Christ, if a bomb fell on us right now, right this moment, there would be so much that I haven't done.'

'Well let's hope it doesn't, then. Are you hungry?'

'I'm starving.'

We walked to Oxford Street and ate spaghetti in the Italian cafe opposite Selfridges. Billy calmed down with food in his belly. He even asked me what I'd been doing. 'Oh you know, writing,' I said, and he was so keen on the idea of 'my mate Ted' being a 'famous writer' that I rather exaggerated things, and let him think that the novel is as good as published. In fact I haven't shown it to a soul but I suppose now I will have to find an agent or something. 'It'll be great, Ted, you'll be rich and famous and we'll go swanning around the Mediterranean on a yacht,' he said, suddenly interested in the future now that it involved sunshine and luxury.

'And you?' I said. 'What will you be doing?'

'Oh, I'll be a movie star,' he said. 'Might as well.'

From this I gather that he is thinking of returning to the stage. So much for seize the day: Billy's just as worried about the future as I am, and the old man's meagre legacy can't last forever.

From the Italian we walked into Soho, drawn back like moths to a flame. The tarts were out on the streets, giving Billy the come-on (they don't bother with me), and he flirted back. Billy likes to be desired, even by professionals.

We did the rounds of the pubs from Berwick Street to Wardour Street to Dean Street to Frith Street to Greek Street, Billy downing a pint in each. I stuck to halves, and still felt pissed. He became maudlin, then excited, then sentimental.

'What the fuck are you doing,' he said, 'hiding away in your parents' house? You should be back here, where it's all happening! Life!' He gestured around the pub, a forlorn place with bare floorboards covered in fag ends; who knows what visions he saw in his mind. 'Come and stay with us.'

'I can't.' The idea of living between Eleanora and Billy and the ghost of William is too horrific to contemplate. 'Besides, according to you the bombs are going to start falling any minute. I'm safer in the suburbs.'

'No, Ted, I'm serious. You're dying out there.'

This was the first I'd heard of it. 'I'm all right.'

'But mate ... ' He put a hand on my shoulder. 'You and me. Eh?'

His eyes weren't quite focusing on mine. 'What's your point, Billy?'

'You're my pal, aren't you? I don't like you being out there.'

'I don't have much choice. I'm broke, remember?' I turned out my trouser pockets; a bus ticket and a bit of lint fell on the floor. 'No rent.'

'That's the point. You stay with us, you don't have to pay.'

'I couldn't do that.'

'Fuck off. You're going to be rich, right? You can pay us back when you're loaded.'

'By taking you on a yacht round the Mediterranean?'

'That'll do for starters. Come on, Ted, how about it?'

What did he want? A buffer between him and his mother? A shoulder to cry on, a refuge from the demands of Geraldine? 'I'll think about it.' The idea was not without its attractions; life with my parents is a protracted silence, punctuated by tuts and sighs.

'You'll do as you're fucking well told,' he said, pulling me to my feet as I struggled to finish my half. 'Starting tonight.'

We ended up in a tiny shoebox of a place on Shaftesbury Avenue, drinking Pale Ale out of bottles that the barman, a wispy little creature with acne and a lisp, served from a wooden crate behind a trestle table bar. How Billy knows of such places defeats me: the rest of the clientele appeared to be off-duty tarts and weary chorus boys from the nearby theatres.

We talked and talked about everything and nothing, the war news, the latest films, the 'crap' he'd been reading at college, until we were the only ones left and the barman was standing over us with a filthy rag in his hand waiting to close.

'Thanks sweetheart,' said Billy, getting unsteadily to his feet; either his wound was playing up, or the liquor had finally got to him. 'You're a little darling.' He pinched the barman's cheek, which brought colour to that sallow complexion, and we climbed the stairs to the dark street. It was past midnight, tubes had stopped running, and we had little option but to walk. This suited me, as I badly needed to sober up. Billy grumbled all the way up Tottenham Court Road, and when his leg hurt too much he put an arm round my shoulders and used me as a crutch.

In this manner we made our way to Kentish Town. It took well over an hour, what with stops for pissing in alleys.

'Don't worry about Ma,' said Billy when we were finally taking our coats off in the hallway, 'she'll be dead to the world. Come on. Let's have a nightcap.' The old decanter and glasses were in their accustomed place on the tray in the living room – a little dustier than before, but somehow there was enough whisky to cover the bottom of a couple of tumblers.

'Welcome home, Ted,' said Billy, throwing himself down on the sofa next to me. We clinked glasses, took a sip – and then, without warning, he leaned over and kissed me on the lips. My first thought was 'he hasn't shaved' and then 'he tastes of whisky' and then the enormity of what was happening dropped on me like a bomb. This was not the formal kiss of greeting or parting, or the stylised kiss of the theatre foyer – Billy was kissing me like he meant it, his lips parted, the weight of his body pushing me down. I did nothing at first – the alcohol made me numb, and fear paralysed me. But then, as he did not stop, I responded. I did what I had been longing to do since the moment I first laid eyes on him, in this room, all those months ago – I dug my fingers into his blond Brylcreemed hair, pushing around the sides of his head and then drawing him into me. I let go of my glass; it fell to the cushion, then rolled to the floor and broke with a dull crash.

Billy's mouth left mine. 'Fucking waste of good liquor, Teddy,' he said, then came back for more. His leg went over mine, and I could feel him pressing into me.

'Billy ...' I mumbled.

He broke the kiss. His hair hung down over his forehead as he looked into my eyes. 'What?'

'Is this ... what you want?'

He frowned for a second, perhaps unsure of the answer. And then he kissed me again. With one hand he was furiously unbuttoning his shirt, with the other he was grabbing my thigh. 'Fuck,' he said, rising to a vertical position and pulling the shirt over his head. A button flew off and landed with a rattle in the fireplace.

I've seen Billy's body a hundred times in dressing rooms and hotel corridors. We've shared rooms in digs. And I've always been aware, in a general sort of way, that he is well built, 'nicely put together'. But last night, in the dim light of that shabby living room, as he pulled his shirt over his head, his arms raised, his face obscured, I saw him for the first time as a thing of beauty.

I put my hand on his stomach, just below the navel, where there is a patch of hair. He grabbed it, and steered it down to the front of his trousers.

Somehow we made it up the stairs to his room, our clothes under our arms or, in my case, round my ankles, dropping things as we went, in too much of a hurry to care. Once the door was closed behind us, we gave ourselves to each other completely. It was like nothing I have experienced before. With Eleanora, I was an ardent if dutiful lover, doing what I believed was expected of me. With Alec and Tommy, I lay back and let them take what they wanted. But with Billy, heart guided hand and mouth, something between a dance and a fight. We lay naked on the bed, limbs intertwined, kissing and grasping and thrusting, unable to think beyond the moment, riding the waves of a gathering storm that, finally, released itself in a fury of passion.

Afterwards, we lay side by side, our hearts slowing, the sweat cooling. I held him in my hand and said, 'It looks like a rose,' prompted by God knows what poetic impulse. 'A rosebud on a long stem.'

He stroked my hair, said, 'Wanker' and pulled the covers over us.

We slept for a while, and woke before dawn, our mouths dry and heads pounding from drink, and sought respite from pain and uncertainty in another struggle towards oblivion.

When it was over I slept soundly, and when I woke Billy had gone.

14 May 1943

Eleanora put her head round the door; her hair was loose around her shoulders, and she wore an old kimono that might have been new in the twenties. She carried a cup of tea, which she put down beside the bed. 'There you are, dear,' she said in the kind of voice you'd use to an invalid, 'this'll make you feel better.' I propped myself up on one elbow and rubbed my eyes.

'What time is it?'

'Just gone eight o'clock.'

'Where's Billy?'

'He went out ages ago.' She perched on the end of the bed, and I was suddenly catapulted back into the years of our intimacy. How many times she had brought me tea in bed then. And now, like then, I was naked beneath crumpled sheets. I pulled them over my chest, and looked around for my clothes. They were hung over the back of a chair – not how they'd come off, of that I was quite sure. Billy had tidied up.

'Thanks,' I said, wishing she would go so that I could dress and leave and think about what had happened. My head hurt; Billy's must have been bursting. He drank twice as much as I did, and had more to regret.

'Take your time, dear.' Eleanora got up. 'Sounds like you boys made a night of it.'

'Yes.' What had she heard? 'Did Billy say anything?'

She stopped in the doorway, folding her arms. 'About what?'

'About me coming to stay.'

'No. Although of course it's always a pleasure to see you.'

'Right.' It was beer talk, nothing else. 'I'd better get up, Eleanora.' I needed to pee, and did not want her to see the state I was in, although she'd seen it often enough.

She closed the door softly behind her, and I closed my eyes, lying back on the pillow. The pillow where, last night, Billy's head lay beside mine. Had it really? Was it all a dream – a ridiculous fantasy brought on by boredom and frustration and too much liquor? I pulled the sheets back and there, written across the creased white fabric, was our testament. Yes, it was real – undeniably, physically real, done, a fact that could not be taken back. I smoothed the sheet, feeling the warmth of my own body, and made the bed. Let him remember when he returns.

'Must you go so soon?' asked Eleanora, when I appeared, dressed and at least partly washed, in the kitchen. She was polishing silver, a dirty apron over an old wool dress, her hair pinned up. 'I could make you some toast.'

'No thanks. I've got things to do.' This was not true; I would go home and wait – for what? For the war to end? For my life to begin? For Billy to call or write?

'A cup of coffee, then.'

'No, really.' The idea of chatting with his mother filled me with a strange dread. 'I'm late as it is. I slept much too long.'

Was that a smile on her face? A smirk? 'All right, then. Off you go.' She wiped her hands on her apron, and came to embrace me. 'So lovely to see you, dear Edward.' A light kiss on the cheek; surely she could tell. The truth must be there on my skin.

'Goodbye, Eleanora.'

I walked to Camden then through the park to Marylebone, watching the ducks with their little fluffy families, the blossoms hanging thick on the trees, the whole riotous spectacle of nature breeding and burgeoning and renewing itself, and I tried to think of what I had done – tried to frame my mind to the conventional remorse and despair, to feel myself exiled from the greater tides of nature and normality, but it would not come. Every regret was swept away by a surge of unbelieving joy. Billy loved me. Billy desired me. All the doubts and inconsistencies of our friendship, the long uncommunicative silences, the sudden bursts of boozy affection, were explained at last. This is what he had wanted, and feared. This was his true nature – and mine. Billy and Ted, Teddy and Bill, whose path to love and happiness had been as strange as any fairy tale, past monsters of doubt, the lurking threat of a jealous mother, an evil princess who tried to steal him away ... And now, like lovers should, we would be happy ever after. Yes, a wonderful fairy tale, and we were wonderful fairies, and I knew it at last and did not care. Nor did the ducks in the lake nor the petals falling like pink snow from the trees. All was love in the world, and I, at last, was part of it.

This feeling sustained me as far as Marylebone, where I smiled at ticket clerks and platform guards. I snoozed on the train home, and awoke with a shockingly clear image of Billy in my mind, that long-stemmed rose, and when I stood to get out at Chesham I took care to turn away from the elderly lady opposite me.

It lasted through the day, through the chilly lack of interest of my parents, and when I went to bed in clean sheets and clean pyjamas, bathed and shaved, my hair washed, I felt once again Billy's arms around me, the hard strength of his thighs between mine, the taste of whisky and the scratch of his whiskers, and so I fell asleep.

19 May 1943

Still no word from Billy. I spend the mornings calculating how long it could take a letter to get here from London. The possible delays and checks, the chances of Billy getting the address wrong, of an envelope falling out of the postman's sack. I test the telephone three or four times a day to make sure we have not been disconnected. But the postman comes as regularly as ever, and when the telephone rings, it is not for me.

20 May 1943

Called the house this evening, about nine, when Billy was most likely to be home unless seeing Geraldine. Eleanora answered of course. Said she would 'see if he's in', then there was the sound of muffled distant voices, hers raised, and finally the thump of approaching footsteps.

'Yes.'

'It's me. Ted.'

'All right.'

'How are you, Billy?'

'Fine.'

He didn't ask after me.

'Haven't seen you for a while, and ... '

He expelled air through his nose. A sound of contempt.

'I was just wondering if we might meet up for a drink or something.' *Something* ...

'I'm broke at the moment,' he said. And of course he knows that I can't pay. So that's that? The end of the story? No happy ever after?

'That doesn't matter,' I said, wondering how easy it would be to rob my father's desk for cash. 'My treat.'

He said nothing. Last week he loved me, he wanted me to live with him.

'How about tomorrow? Friday?'

'Can't. I'm busy.'

'Seeing Geraldine?' My voice went too high.

'Yeah.'

There was nothing more to say, but I couldn't bear to put the phone down, as if that fragile connection down a wire, through an exchange, from mouthpiece to earpiece, was all that held our friendship together. Once severed, severed for ever.

'Well, call me when you fancy going out. I'm not particularly busy. You know where to find me.' I was starting to gabble; he was silent. 'How's work going? Are you still managing to go to college?'

'It was a mistake, Ted.'

No; he can't mean that. He's talking about something else.

'Don't say that. I mean, getting an education is always a good thing ...'

'You and me. It was a mistake.'

I felt winded. 'Oh.'

Nothing back from him.

'Well, goodbye, then.' I wanted to be sick. 'Goodbye.'

He put the phone down – the last rattle and clank of the receiver shifting in his hands, touching the cradle, and then silence. Line dead. Severed.

I must have looked very green when I went back into the living room, where my father was reading the paper, my mother writing a letter.

'I'm going to bed,' I said.

They looked up, perhaps saw something, perhaps not. No comment was made. 'Goodnight then,' said my mother. My father grunted.

I lay in bed too tired for sleep, too numb for tears. It was a mistake. You and me. It was a mistake. Over and over again, no matter how much I tried to blot it out, no matter what hopeful explanations I invented. Of course he feels like that – it's a shock for him, just as it is for me, and we must both adjust. He's never done anything like that before – I, at least, had set foot on the primrose path, and although my friendships with Alec and Tommy caused me not a moment's remorse, Billy was not like me. He was – what? Normal. A soldier.

It was a mistake. You and me. A mistake.

My heart hammered in my chest, reaching up to squeeze my throat, and my bowels loosened until I thought they would empty.

Finally, long after my parents had gone to bed, when silence fell after the brushing of teeth and the flushing of toilets, I must have fallen asleep. I dreamed of Billy, and woke in tears to a grey light filtering through the curtains and the dead knowledge of a day, a life, alone.

18 June 1943

If I am queer – and I suppose I must be – then I can no longer live at home. I have found myself a job in a warehouse in Acton, and have taken a bedsit in Uxbridge Road, five minutes' walk from Shepherd's Bush. If I work long hours at the warehouse, lugging tinned goods and bottles, sacks of flour and sugar, I can pay my rent, feed myself and have enough at the end of the week for the pictures and a couple of pints. Or I save those few shillings by staying at home and writing. *Hors de Combat* is as good as it's ever going to be – it has an ending, at least, a fatuous happy ending that I wrote in a sort of anaesthetised daze – and I will get it typed up and sent out. Meanwhile, I shift crates. I am one of the few able-bodied men in the place, and the others look strangely at me, wondering why I can't die in battle like their brothers, husbands, sons and sweethearts. I wonder myself.

I have no one to talk to. Impossible to make friends at the warehouse. In the house where I live, doors stay closed. I see my neighbours like ghosts on the staircase, scuttling away at my approach. I am one of the loveless thousands that shuffle around London, exhausted, half-starved, minds dulled by the drudgery of war.

I don't know how long I can go on. Forever, I suppose. A lonely, loveless queer, limping towards an unmourned grave.

10 August 1943

Billy was sitting on my doorstep when I got home from work, smoking a cigarette, his back to me, shirtsleeves rolled up above the elbow. I fumbled in my pockets for my keys, pretended not to have seen him.

'Well you're a fucking slippery fish,' he said.

'Billy!' Surprise, a degree of pleasure, but on no account the ecstasy that I felt. 'What on earth brings you here?'

'I had to track you down like Sherlock bloody Holmes. Why the hell didn't you tell me you'd moved?'

'I didn't think you'd be interested.'

'Rang your house. Your mum, I suppose. Put on my best posh voice. "Hay say, is Master Hedward havailable to come to the telephone, my good lady?" She told me you weren't there. Gone away. Took no end of charm to get this address out of her.' He looked up at the front of the house, grimy paint peeling from decayed plaster, rotting windowsills, buddleia in the cracks. 'Not quite up to your usual standards, Teddy.'

'Beggars can't be choosers,' I said. The key was in the lock; he was obviously coming in. 'Anyway, it's a place to sleep.' What do you want, I wanted to ask. Have you got a bad conscience? Come to patch it up with a pint and a slap on the back, let bygones be bygones, then run back to Geraldine, your duty done, your conscience clear?

We got to my room, up three flights of stairs. Cracked brown linoleum covered the landing, and there was a smell of stale fags and sour linen that I had never noticed before.

The bed was unmade, and there were clothes hanging everywhere. Billy was my first visitor. He didn't seem to mind or notice. He went to the window, looked at the view up and down Uxbridge Road then drew the curtains. I busied myself with clearing a space to sit, kicking the worst of the dirty washing under the bed.

'You doing all right, Ted?' His voice trembled slightly, and when I looked up he was standing with his hands clasped in front of his stomach, his weight forward.

'I'm fine. Just a bit surprised to see you, that's all.'

He seemed to fall towards me, as if, had I not caught him, he would have hit the floor. 'Oh, Ted,' he said, his arms around me, his lips at my ear. 'God …' And then he kissed me. The bitterness of the last months melted away in the heat of that kiss.

We made love on the bed and on the floor, stopping only for cigarettes, unwilling to finish, prolonging the pleasure. Finally, when I lent him a toothbrush and he padded up the landing to the shared bathroom, it was nearly eleven o'clock.

He came back to the room bare chested, his trousers held up only by a button, hanging down over his hips. He was smiling. No anger this time. No hasty, silent departure. No regret.

'I thought you said it was a mistake,' I said, unable to hold my tongue.

He handed me the toothbrush, still wet. 'Yeah,' he said, 'it probably is. But some mistakes are worth making twice.'

4 November 1943

I am glad that the newspapers say we'll be bombed again by Christmas, because it stops me from looking forward. I live each day for what it's worth – and, on balance, each day ends on the credit side. Billy is staying with me in Uxbridge Road; every day brings some new proof. A toothbrush the first day, clean underwear, then shoes, suits, coats as the weather got colder, books, records that we can only play at very low volume. Each object a concrete piece of evidence, until the room is crowded with them. As crowded as the bed, a narrow single bed never intended for two grown men. I don't sleep too well, but I don't care. Billy sleeps like a child. We get up early, long before it's light, and have breakfast in a workers' cafe in Shepherd's Bush market, bright yellow light greeting us through steamed-up windows, bacon and eggs and thick white china mugs of tea. He goes to mend roads, I take the train to Acton and spend my days cheerfully whistling, talking, flirting with the girls in the stock clerk's office, making myself liked. In the evenings I buy a bit of fish or some eggs, some vegetables, whatever I can get, and try to rustle up something edible before Billy returns, dirty and starving, eating off chipped plates on a card table covered in newspaper. Once a week we go into town, blow our wages on beer and food, then come home. Home – one small room, 15 feet by 12, with a threadbare maroon carpet, cheap deal furniture, a dirty sink with a dripping tap and a mouldy old wooden plate rack, a cupboard in which to store food, a broken cane-backed chair and a narrow single bed.

A line of empty wine bottles filters the light from the dirty window through green glass, souvenirs of our nights listening to Sibelius, smoking cigarettes, reading aloud to each other, and making love.

In his more affectionate moods, Billy likes to hear poetry, and if it touches on love he can become quite demonstrative. 'Read that bit again!' he'll say, when I've given him something like 'Come live with me and be my love/And we will all the pleasures prove', and then, when he's repeated it to himself, considered it, parsed it, he'll jump on me, holding me in a headlock, rubbing the top of my head with his big lumpy knuckles.

In his bleaker moods – and they are frequent – Billy is silent and introspective, taking any remark of mine, even the offer of a cup of tea or a glass of wine, as a criticism. I know what these moods are about, and I wait for them to pass. Billy would love to live in a permanent present, in a shabby room with curtains drawn on an anonymous street, drinking and smoking and screwing, but even he can't keep the rest of the world out for ever. 'We can't go on like this,' he said one day, returning from work looking haggard and ill. 'It's fucking stupid.' What had happened? Had someone said something? Some joke about the queers, the nancies, that made him bunch his fists before he was forced to laugh along with the rest of them? I don't care about that sort of thing any more, but Billy minds terribly. 'I'm not like that,' he said.

'Like what?'

'One of those that has to hide.'

'I'm afraid it's necessary, Billy.'

'That's not going to be my life.'

'Then we must part.'

'Fuck off.' He scowled. 'You're being stupid.'

And so we go on and on until something distracts us or he takes his bad temper somewhere else. Back to Geraldine? I suppose so. I keep myself busy; I clean the room, wash shirts and socks and underwear, even visit my parents, anything to stop myself from thinking of what he might be doing. I cannot believe that he does with her what he does with me ... But I suppose he must. And I must tolerate it, as long as he comes home.

And then I feel again the fragility of this friendship, a thin, weak thread stretched to breaking point, and once it fails it can never be mended. I sit on the edge of the bed at eleven o'clock at night, midnight, one in the morning, waiting for his return, listening to every footstep in the street, every creak of the stairs, let it be him, let it be him ... And sometimes it is, and I'm too happy to ask for explanations. Sometimes he does not come back, and I wake to a dead, cold day as if it was all a tormenting dream.

So far, he has always come back. Sometimes after a day, sometimes two, but he always returns. I try to live without hope or fear but simply trusting the moment, weighing the happiness of my life with Billy against all the odds. And I know that I would take one night with him, one hour, against everything that the world, or Hitler, can throw at me.

Chapter Eight: Helen

So let me get this straight.

My grandfathers were lovers. And they shared my grandmother Geraldine – one as her boyfriend, the other, in time, as her husband. No wonder my parents are reticent.

I sat crosslegged on the top floor at Stonefield, surrounded by those 32 cardboard boxes, mounds of paper, teetering piles of diaries. My right leg had gone to sleep, and as I stretched it out it was assailed by pins and needles, but I didn't notice the pain.

My grandfathers – Edward Barton, whom I knew, and Billy Hamilton, alias Billy Moody, whom I did not – were lovers. For how long, or how seriously, I could not yet tell, but one thing was for sure, as I looked up from the yellowing pages of fading blue ink – Edward had been in love. Head over heels in love, sexually infatuated, transported by the rapture of first romance. And Billy? In love, or a drunken Narcissus, taking adoration where he found it? And what about Geraldine, the third point of the triangle? How much did she know? By what strange alchemy did Edward transform a necessarily clandestine affair with a man into a lasting marriage with his cast-off girlfriend?

Read on, said the diaries, and in the failing evening light, an ancient anglepoise perched above my shoulder, I did just that. The old, empty house creaked and ticked around me as evening progressed into night, and I read until my vision was blurred and my stomach rumbling. I went to bed and had fitful dreams of the dark streets of London in the blackout, of warm young bodies entwined in a narrow bed, and of danger on all sides.

'Good God,' said Harry, 'this is dynamite! I mean, this makes it a whole different story. The truth, Helen! The truth! He started with the mother, then he moved on to the son, and ended up marrying the son's girlfriend. It's ridiculous! It's fantastical!'

'It's also potentially very embarrassing.'

'What? You're not embarrassed by that sort of thing, are you? Sex? Come on.' Harry pulled the covers up to our chins; we were naked beneath them, and the worn satin felt slippery against my chest.

'I was thinking of my parents.'

'Oh, them,' said Harry. 'Well you won't amount to much as a writer if you worry about what your parents think.'

'But this isn't fiction, is it? This is reality. It's their fathers. How would you feel if you discovered that your dad was gay?'

'I'd be bloody astounded,' said Harry, 'seeing as my father is a lorry driver from Donegal.'

'And it's not just them. There's my grandmother too. Oh God, it's so complicated.'

'You owe it to Edward to tell the truth.'

'Why? He never did.'

'That's why he left it all to you. He wanted you to tell the truth that he couldn't.'

'But why should anyone know? It's so long ago, and so private and personal. And it's not as if Edward Barton is exactly a household name. It's not going to be on the front page of Heat magazine, is it? "Obscure English novelist's gay love romp with dead grandfather." Nobody's going to care.'

'But it adds so much to our understanding of his work.'

'Does it?'

'Of course it does!' Harry was playing with the hair above my right ear, which was starting to annoy me, and the more animated he became, the harder he pulled. 'Surely you can see that this is what *The Interlude* is all about! A married man with a secret lover. That's Edward.'

'Rubbish.'

'And if we tell the story correctly – if we can show the reality that informed the fiction – then we're on to a winner.'

'And how exactly do *we* intend to do that?'

'It makes for a much more interesting screenplay. I mean this is a six-part series, isn't it? Dipping in and out of the fictive realm. Shifting the iterative mode.'

'You really think you can do all that?'

'I'm sure of it.'

'And that anyone would be interested?'

'It's a completely new angle on period drama. And nobody else knows about it.'

'I assume my parents know.'

'They don't matter.'

I resented this; I can dismiss my parents, but I don't like anyone else doing it. 'I'll have to think about it, Harry. I'm not sure.'

'But I am.' He jumped out of bed, and I couldn't help noticing that he was excited, possibly at the thought of those shifting iterative modes. He paced around the bed, sometimes stopping at the window, leaning on the sill to present to my gaze his firm, furry backside. 'Think about it, Helen! Your grandfather, the conservative man of letters with his wife and children, friend of the stars, everything that the Angry Young Men of the 50s and 60s were rebelling against – and all the time he was having the most outrageous, scandalous sex life! You can't sit on this, Helen.' He was standing right next to me, his cock swinging between his legs. 'We have to share it.'

'They're my parents, Harry, not yours. It's my decision.'

'You have a duty here.'

'To whom?'

'To Edward Barton! To English literature! To the future!'

'To you too, perhaps.'

'What do you mean?'

'Well, you seem very keen on getting this project off the ground.'

'Of course I am, sweets.' He sat on the end of the bed and rubbed my feet through the covers. 'We're a team, aren't we? I want what's best for you.'

'Then you'll let me decide in my own way.'

He couldn't argue with that. 'Okay,' he sighed, and rejoined me in bed.

As I read further in the diaries, it was hard not to see things Harry's way. The story moved with a swift economy against the turbulent, dangerous last months of the war, as the bombing of London recommenced and the Allies made their victorious push into Europe. Edward and Billy's bedsit idyll continued into 1944, but Billy's absences grew longer and more frequent until even the lovestruck diarist couldn't ignore what was blatantly obvious to the rest of us – that Billy was still seeing Geraldine. In her sensible way she was a tenacious woman. Edward had to be hidden, disguised as a 'friend'; Geraldine stepped straight into the role of girlfriend and, at one point, fiancée. When Edward discovered this, the diary went into meltdown, page after page filled with incoherent grief and rage before a sudden silence.

Edward was at his most dangerous when he was silent.

Apparently conceding defeat, he took Billy on whatever terms he could get, putting up with his drunken, late-night appearances in Uxbridge Road, his erratic attitude to sex – one night more eager than ever, the next surly and rebuffing

– and never complained. He gave advice, lent Billy money which he knew he would spend on Geraldine. He put up with the indignity of playing gooseberry, accompanying Billy and Geraldine to the pictures or the pub and watching them 'pawing' each other, inwardly furious but, at the same time, delighted by his secret knowledge. Edward and Billy developed a private language, a code with which to arrange and describe their affair, which they would flaunt in front of Geraldine. The key word was 'rose' – a reference, of course, to the 'long-stemmed rose' that grew inside Billy's pants. 'When are you next seeing Rose?' Billy would ask as they took their leave of a suave, smiling Edward. 'Oh, I'm seeing her later tonight, I think,' Edward would reply, 'if she can get away.' 'I had a wonderful time with Rose last night,' he said to Billy just hours after they had been fucking in that narrow, creaking bed. Geraldine took it all at face value – or so Edward thought – and even asked after the mysterious 'Rose', hoping one day to meet her. 'Oh,' said Edward, 'it's a bit awkward really. She's engaged to someone else.'

Rose: the fatal heroine of *The Interlude*.

Perhaps, after all, Harry is right. This is the final piece of the jigsaw. Should I tell him?

Something holds me back. Respect for my parents, or a distrust of Harry's motives – I'm not sure.

Harry says that art does not think of consequences.

But unlike Harry, I do not consider myself as an artist. Among other things I am a wife, a mother and a daughter.

Since the bombshell of Edward's will things have fallen into place with disturbing ease. Everything conspires to push me in a certain direction – not altogether of my choosing. When the fact that we now owned a bloody great house in the country had sunk in, Richard and I spent a pleasant weekend going over the options. Move lock, stock and barrel to the country, selling up in London and using the money as capital for Richard to start up his own consultancy business? Keep both properties, dashing glamorously between the two, keeping the kids in London schools for now, but weekending at Stonefield with big, happy house parties? Or, most audaciously, sell the lot, pool the profits and start a brand new life in France/America/Italy/New Zealand? Places we've oohed and aahed over in films, or enjoyed on holidays. Money is no longer an object. Thanks to Edward Barton's bizarre bequest, the world is our oyster.

The interim arrangement is thus: I will spend the next few months gradually moving stuff down to Stonefield, making the place habitable and working my way through the papers. This will be my 'job'. Richard will be the primary parent (which he's perfectly happy with), and will stay in London, bringing the kids to join me at weekends. It's a serious curtailment of his working life, as he can only accept jobs within a reasonable distance from home, but we see it as an investment in our future as a family. Thankfully, we have Annette on tap for babysitting; Ben and Lucy feel almost as much at home with Annette as they do with us.

It's a wonderful chance for us. A great future for the family.

Then why am I still seeing Harry? His teaching commitments seem to be evaporating, and he prefers the comforts of Stonefield to the more urban charms of Dalston. Harry bathes in the golden glow of 'our' future success, unswervingly certain that *The Interlude*, adapted for television by him, will make his fortune.

So I am leading a double life, much like my illustrious forebear. But while Edward Barton's double life seems exciting and revealing and almost brave, mine seems mundane and cowardly and entirely unedifying. A married woman with a hardworking husband and two lovely children having an affair with a vain, needy man whose interest in her is financial:

it lacks poetry, doesn't it? Some people might even call it sordid. For all that Edward was manipulative and duplicitous, he was negotiating a world in which his affections were illegal and stigmatised. He could very well have gone to prison for seeing 'Rose'; he certainly would never have had a career as a writer if the truth had come out. I have no such excuse. My affair isn't illegal or dangerous, it's just selfish and immoral. Nothing ennobles it. I'm a married woman who wants to have her cake and eat it too, who's sacrificing her husband and children for the passing thrill of a new lover. Admittedly a very good lover, a mind-blowingly, gut-churningly skilled lover who makes me feel like running water, soaring music, swimming dolphins, but not somebody who's going to stick around once he's got what he wants.

I must talk to Annette. There is nobody else. My parents, Richard, Harry himself, are off limits. Annette will disapprove, she may even hate me. Perhaps that's what I need.

Rather surprisingly, Annette's take on the whole Harry situation was along 'cast the first stone' lines. 'I don't neces-sarily understand what you're doing,' she said after I'd given her a somewhat edited account, 'but I certainly don't judge.'

'The thing is,' I said, 'I feel so guilty.'

'Yes, that must be awful, but this is something you're going to have to work out for yourself.'

'Oh, but Annette ...'

'And I'm sure that you'll reach the decision that is right for you.'

'For me?' This wasn't going at all the way I'd expected. What books had Annette been reading? Had she joined a cult? 'What about Richard and the children?'

'I rather assumed that they would come into the equation.'

'Right.' It seemed as if the subject was closed. 'Well, thank you for listening.'

She looked at me over the top of her coffee mug, a level gaze that I knew very well.

'I know what you want, Helen. You want to pour your heart out, to share the ins and outs of this affair, then you want me to tell you what to do. You'll say how hard that will be for you, how much you've got to give up, and so on. We'll get through several cups of coffee and a whole packet of biscuits and you'll be no nearer a decision.'

'That's a bit harsh.' I felt close to tears.

'We know each other too well for this,' Annette said. 'You have to make a choice, one way or the other. I hope it's the right one for you. That's really all there is to say.'

'You disapprove of me.'

She sighed. 'I don't at all. Who am I to disapprove of anyone?'

'You're supposed to be my best friend.'

'And is that what best friends do, Helen? Disapprove of each other?'

'No. But they might sympathise a bit. Shoulder to cry on, and all that. I've done it for you often enough.'

'We were kids then. We're adults now.'

And that was the end of that.

My parents have announced that they want to visit Stonefield – the house, you'll note, not me. It's a beautiful house that seems to embrace you the moment you walk in the door. The view from every window is composed like a painting. My parents must have envisaged spending their retirement here. Perhaps they think that I will install them on an indefinite basis – after all, the place is far too large for me, and surely I don't want to uproot the children from schools and friends in London. They haven't come right out and said 'hand over the keys, bitch' but that's not their style. The indirect approach suits them better.

Harry has been making himself useful with roller and brush. In a world where creative writing courses did not exist, he could make a very good living as a painter and decorator, although I suppose it wouldn't sustain his image as an artist quite so effectively. I begin to wonder if he's not more skilled with the brush than the pen; I have yet to read any of his work. The novel for which he had such high hopes when first we met has been rejected so universally that Harry is exploring 'the very exciting potential of e-publishing'. He's shown me several treatments for 'our' adaptation of *The Interlude*, each more convoluted than the last, mixing fiction with Harry's reading of reality. I always think that if you've got a story the best way to tell it is from beginning to end, but this does not satisfy Mr Harry Ross. He's all about flashbacks and framing devices. He pesters me for more material, and sometimes gazes wistfully at the boxes of diaries and letters, but I have told him in no uncertain terms to keep his hands off. Perhaps, like Bluebeard's wife, he won't be able to resist, and will sneak in while I'm not looking. I hope not. For reasons that are not yet clear to me, I'm unwilling to give him the rest of Edward's story. I know that Edward marries Geraldine, and that their son marries Billy's daughter and then I come along. Harry could probably piece this together for himself if he thought less of narrative structure and schmoozing 'the independent sector'. He can keep up a sustained monologue on the subject while emulsioning a wall.

I am paying him for the work he's doing here. It's a good way of clarifying certain boundaries, at least until I make my mind up about the Big Question. Harry's in no position to refuse the money, although he gives me a sexy hangdog look every time I thrust the cash into his hand – a look that says 'Wouldn't it just be easier if we had a joint account?' Of course he believes that in the not-too-distant future the goose, in the shape of the Barton estate, will lay the golden egg, i.e. his TV version of *The Interlude*. Maybe he's right. I'd be mad not to

'Well,' said Harry, 'I can see you've got lots to discuss. I'll call you later, sweets.' He kissed me on the cheek, and bounced out, slamming the front door behind him. The subsequent silence was thick with surmise.

I was expecting Richard and the children to join me for the weekend. We're trying to get Ben and Lucy used to the idea of Stonefield as a potential future home, our current thinking being that we'll let Ben, at least, finish junior school before putting him into one of the excellent secondary schools round here, possibly the prestigious Stratford Grammar. Lucy, younger and more adaptable, could settle in any time, within a week she'd have half a dozen New Best Friends. During previous visits, they've explored the house and garden rather as they would a holiday rental, entranced and curious but always ready to go home. I'm waiting for one of them to say 'But Mummy, can't we stay here for ever and ever?'

I told Harry that I can't see him for a week or so, and that he's to put his TV plans on ice until I, as Edward Barton's executor, give him the green light. I'd more or less decided to put this nonsense behind me and commit myself to my husband and family. Harry was a moment of madness, a hot-lovin', brush-wieldin', creative-writin'-teachin' whirlwind who had blown through my life, dislodged a few cobwebs and could now blow off. Whatever we had was over. Like a good story, it had a beginning, a middle and an end. An interlude, if you like.

But then Richard rang to inform me that he and the children were joining Annette, Glyn, Holly and Poppy for a long weekend in Devon, it would be a fantastic opportunity for the kids to muck about together and it would give me more time to work on the Barton papers. He and Glyn would get some sailing in while Annette played mother hen. He made it sound like a bit of a penance, something he was prepared to endure for the sake of the children, and my work.

So that leaves me alone in Stonefield with only my grandfather's diaries for company. And when one is alone in Stonefield, one is utterly alone. There are rooks. There are squirrels. I think we may have a fox or a hedgehog; something is pooing in the flower beds. And that's about it.

I feel like a gambler who has held a winning hand too long. The game, it appears, has been played and won elsewhere.

I have a strange feeling of desolation as I return to the spare room, and the diaries.

Chapter Nine: Edward Barton's Diaries

13 April 1945

MET THIS MORNING with Leonard Leigh, the agent who is interested in representing me. His office is in Holborn, just behind the station, a poky little place that looks unchanged since King Edward was on the throne, but he seems to be the right man for the job. He counts several of 'the coming men' among his clients and since he's the only agent who's shown any interest I'm predisposed to like him. Leigh is a short, solid, dark-haired Jew, about 40 years old, handsome in a heavy-featured way, with a smooth face that must need at least two daily shaves. Expensively and conservatively dressed in a three-piece suit, the only artistic flourish a carnation in his buttonhole, as if he was going to a wedding.

He took me to a café on Kingsway, overlooking the trams trundling between Euston and Waterloo, and ordered coffee and cakes. He had read *Hors de Combat* and thought it showed 'great promise' – and then proceeded to tell me that the story was wrong, the title was wrong and even the name of the central character could be improved.

'You have to be aware of fashions, Mr Barton,' he said, as the waiter laid the spread before us. 'You write, at present, like Mr Maugham or Mr Waugh.' Apparently this won't do. 'When I show your work to editors, I must tell them that you are something quite new. The voice of the younger generation.'

He sipped his coffee, and dabbed cream from his lips with a linen napkin. 'The post-war generation.'

This seemed a little previous, as we are not out of the woods just yet. 'Oh, the war is a foregone conclusion,' he said. 'Publishers are looking for things that will do well in peacetime. Trust me, Mr Barton. The newspapers may tell us the war is not over. Mr Churchill may tell us that the war is not over. But I'm looking at what editors are buying, and it's all about newness, freshness, the future. The post-war generation,' he said again, obviously liking the phrase. 'And that is where you fit in.'

I took a mouthful of cake, but had no appetite. To be post-war, I will have to rewrite the whole book. I must have looked terribly crestfallen. I'd built my hopes up so much, certain that I'd found the man who would turn my stale dreams into the reality of ink on bound paper, and now he was fobbing me off with cakes and advice.

'Now now, Mr Barton. Don't frown like that. The most promising novelist of the post-war generation does not frown. He meets trouble head-on, with a cheery smile.'

'Does he?'

'I think, with a little judicious editing, that your novel could be ...' He linked his fingers over his bulging waistcoat, and scanned the ceiling, as if the *mot juste* were floating around up there. 'A startling critique of British manners and morals.'

'It could?'

'Your characters are brittle and hollow.'

'Right.'

'You guide us through the moral wilderness.' He looked at me. 'Don't you?'

'Yes, I suppose I do.'

'With the right title, we could make a very respectable sale.'

'Ah.'

I sipped my coffee. It tasted strong and very real; Leigh obviously knows where to get the good stuff. 'What sort of sum would you envisage?'

'Good question, Mr Barton. I should be very surprised if we did not bag a thousand.'

I whistled. 'Seriously?'

'More, if the title is right.'

'Does it matter that much?'

'It is paramount. And a really good illustration for the cover. One of the artists coming out of the War Office. Bawden, Ardizzone. Expensive, of course, and we may have to defray the costs, but worth every penny. And then there's your name.'

'Edward Barton.'

'Edward Barton.' He scanned again, apparently type-setting my name in his mind's eye. 'It will do, I suppose.'

'I could be Ted. Or Teddy.'

He shook his head. 'Oh no no no. Ted is redolent of the public bar, Teddy of the Mayfair club. Edward will do. A name that will serve you well for several decades to come.' He looked at me coyly. 'I think you have longevity, Mr Barton.'

'Really?'

'Why not? You have the sense to give the public what it wants, not what you want. You do not force feed it with things for which it does not yet have a taste.'

'I suppose so.'

'You deal with the sex side of things well, and without squeamishness, but within the limits of ... decency, shall we say.' By which I took him to mean that my couplings are explicit but conventional. I wonder if Leigh is queer? I hope not.

'I would like to send the manuscript out next week.'

'Good God,' I said, 'it won't be ready by then.'

'Of course it will. Work hard, work fast. We shall have a deal before the summer.'

'Really?'

'And a title, Edward. A title fit for an important post-war debut. Nothing fancy, and definitely nothing French. *Hors de Combat* sounds too much like *hors d'oeuvres*. Genteel, mincing. You need something hard and ... thrusting.' He drained his coffee cup. 'I leave it with you.'

He paid the bill, tipped generously and shook my hand at the corner of the street. And so, it seems, I have an agent.

14 April 1935

'Hard and thrusting' amused Billy greatly, and he had a few suggestions that would certainly not make it on to the shelves of WH Smith. He seems to regard my literary career as a bit of a lark, and while he's never lost his focus on the material benefits, neither has he shown any interest in reading the novel, whatever it's called.

He was drunk when he turned up last night. He seems more reluctant every time. I'm not blind: I'm losing him. The war is coming to an end, and he's thinking about the future. He doesn't want to be a road-mender for the rest of his life. He wants money and 'self-respect', which obviously he won't have if he's queer.

We talked and drank and finally went to bed. Billy slept, his head resting on my chest, my arm around his shoulders, soon dead from the weight of him. I gazed up into the darkness and thought about titles. *The Love Market. Love for Sale* – no, Cole Porter got there first, damn him. *Soul for Sale?* No: souls aren't hard and thrusting. If Leonard Leigh wants me to be part of the tough rackety post-war world then I must come up with something less aesthetic. *The Black Market? Black Market Love?* Sounds like a pornographic novel. *The Love Racket.* Yes, has potential.

Sleep on it, and talk to Leigh tomorrow.

16 April 1945

The Love Racket it is. 'You have understood me perfectly, Mr Barton,' said Leigh. 'I will send you a contract outlining our agreement. Welcome to the firm.' I wanted Billy to be the first to know but couldn't reach him. No one else to tell.

24 April 1945

Leonard has an 'expression of interest' for the novel, sight unseen, from a very prestigious publisher with whom he had lunch. 'I told him that you were hard, cynical and unromantic,' he said. 'They're looking for something fresh, something realistic – not dirty, exactly, but perhaps a little soiled. I told him you are the very man for the job and that *The Love Racket* is positively grimy.'

And so I set about begriming the manuscript, slipping in some unkind descriptions and reinstating a few passages that I'd previously cut. Well, I haven't seen Billy for over a week now, and I'm in no mood for kindness. Let 'em have it hot and strong, and if anyone complains I shall simply flaunt the size of my advance.

2 June 1945

I had a most unexpected letter this morning from Geraldine Shaw, Billy's mistress. Just one side of a piece of notepaper, perfectly bland until you read between the lines. She asks me to take tea with her on Sunday to discuss 'our mutual friend', and I don't think she means Dickens. I will go, if only out of curiosity.

9 June 1945

Geraldine is an extraordinarily nice girl now that I get to know her. And we have much in common: he's abandoned both of us. We met at Victoria Station and had tea in a chintzy little place off Eaton Square. Both of us were tired: I worked six days at the warehouse this week and most nights on the endless revisions that the publisher requires; Geraldine has moved from the munitions factory to teacher training college and is obliged to spend three mornings a week with unruly children in Battersea. We had both made an effort to spruce ourselves up, she in a fresh cotton dress and a little straw hat, me in a clean shirt and tie.

It felt like a date.

'Of course,' she said, after we'd worn out the excitements of classroom and warehouse, 'I never hear from Billy any more.'

'Oh no.' I shook my head and tried to put a laugh in my voice, as if we were discussing a wayward infant. 'Me neither.'

'He's out at the film studios every day now, apparently.'

'Really?'

'Met some director or producer chappie who thinks he could get into pictures.'

'Oh yes.' Queer, no doubt. 'Well, that's good. He always fancied himself as a movie star.'

'Yes.' She sighed, and pushed some crumbs around her plate. 'It's so hard to know what Billy wants.'

'Billy doesn't know that himself,' I said, thinking of the many nights when he's skipped from her arms to my bed. 'Apart from money, that is.'

'Oh, money.' She looked quite cross. 'Always on about money. If it's just a question of that, I can go to my father.'

'A substantial dowry?'

Geraldine frowned.

'If you want to call it that, yes. But he must do it all himself. Too proud to take a woman's money. Well, we'll see about that.'

'What do you mean?'

'He's got a new girlfriend.'

That took the wind out of my sails. 'Oh. Who?'

'Something to do with the studio. Someone's daughter.'

'I see. And I assume she comes with plenty of lolly?'

'Sacks of the stuff.' She poured more tea. 'Rather funny, considering he was such a red. Money is the root of all evil, property is theft and so on.'

'Billy's as acquisitive as the rest of us. More so, I suspect.'

'I can see him in ten years from now, a prosperous bourgeois with a plump wife, two children in prep school, and one of those horrid suburban houses with mock Tudor beams.'

Yes, I thought – and skipping off every couple of weeks for a bit of what he can't get at home. 'You never know,' I said, feeling bound to defend my friend, 'he might surprise us all and make a success of the movies. He's got the looks.'

'Oh yes.' Geraldine looked at me with her intelligent hazel eyes. I wonder what she saw?

'All he needs now is a bit of luck. They might go for him. Exemplary war record, smashed-up leg, rather romantic.'

'I suppose so. And then I shall be terribly proud to tell my children that I once knew the famous Billy Moody.'

'We'll be dining out on that for years to come.'

Geraldine laughed, and her tired, sad face lit up. 'Let's go for a walk,' she said, 'unless you're in a terrible hurry. It's such a lovely afternoon.' So we strolled up to the park and walked beside the Serpentine, arm in arm like any other young couple on a Sunday afternoon. Children were sailing toy boats, a band was playing, there were demobbed servicemen everywhere. Some of them gave Geraldine appreciative glances; she has fine legs and a slender waist. Others looked at me; I caught those glances and my cheeks burned. By the time we reached Bayswater Road we were laughing and chatting like old friends, even making jokes at Billy's expense. We parted at Marble Arch.

'I've had a lovely afternoon,' said Geraldine as we shook hands. She was wearing cream cotton gloves, slightly grubby at the fingertips; I suppose it's a long time since she had a new pair. 'Thank you so much. It does make a change to have someone actually listening to what I say.'

'I could listen to a great deal more,' I said, feeling suddenly gallant. 'May I take you out again?'

'Oh.' She blushed, and looked at her feet. 'If you'd like to.'

'I'd like to very much.' I knew exactly how to behave; haven't I played such scenes a thousand times in mess halls and freezing theatres up and down the country? I held on to her hand and said, 'Goodbye, Geraldine. You're a lovely girl. Billy's a fool.'

Her eyes were sparkling as she descended the steps into the underground.

Billy's girl. Billy's cast-off. How perfectly, neatly ironic. Well, Billy Moody is not the only one thinking of his future.

I felt restless, and the thought of gloomy Uxbridge Road was too much to bear, so I walked down to Leicester Square, knowing perfectly well where I was heading but pretending that my feet were simply wandering.

The Cross Keys at the bottom of Wardour Street is so notorious that even Billy knows about it. From the outside there's nothing at all unusual about it, but it would take a very thick skin to avoid the inevitable conclusion once you're inside. Even at opening time on a Sunday evening it was busy, and these were not your normal West End drinkers. Too well dressed, too busy with their eyes.

I took a seat at the bar and ordered a pint of bitter.

'Well well well,' said a voice at my right ear. 'If it's not the great Edward Barton.' I knew who it was before I turned round: Tommy, of course. I haven't seen him, and have barely thought about him, for two years.

'Good lord, Tommy,' I said, trying to sound hearty. 'How are you?'

'Bowled over,' he said. He looked thinner than before, as if he's not eating properly. 'Fancy seeing you in a place like this.'

I looked around the pub, feigning insouciance. 'Oh, it's not so bad.' I took a sip. 'And the beer's fine.'

'I see.' Tommy has taken to emphasising his sibilants. 'And of all the pubs in the world, you just happened to stumble into the Crossssssss Keysssssssss.'

'That's about it, yes.'

'Fancy.' He was deciding whether to let bygones be bygones, or to flounce out of the bar on a wave of self-righteousness. Curiosity got the better of him. 'So where have you been hiding since you broke my heart?'

'Shepherd's Bush.'

Tommy grimaced. 'I had no idea you'd sunk so low.' He eyed my glass. 'Aren't you going to offer me a drink?'

'Of course.' I still had money in my pocket; Geraldine had insisted on going Dutch. 'What will you have?'

'G and T, thanks.' The barman did the necessary. 'Make it a large one. He owes me.'

'Come on, Tommy. You're not angry with me.'

'Why shouldn't I be? You dropped me like a stone. And don't think I don't know why.'

'Please enlighten me.'

He looked arch, and rolled his eyes. 'Butter wouldn't melt, would it? Oh no. Not with Edward Barton.' He pronounced the name as if he had a plum in his mouth. 'I hear you're quite the author these days.'

'Who told you that?'

'Good news travels fast. Congratulations, I suppose.'

'Thank you.'

He took his drink, and appeared to be thirsty. It was not his first of the day; there was something unfocused about his eyes. 'And what about me, you're dying to ask?'

'Yes, Tommy. What about you?'

'Well the bombs missed their target, worse luck.' He grimaced at the taste of the gin; the skin round his mouth was papery. He was already looking old. 'So now I scratch a living in journalism.'

'Oh! A fellow writer!'

'Very funny. I do little squibs for the evening papers and the illustrated magazines. I could do something on you, if you like. When's your wonderful book coming out?'

'October.'

'Will there be parties?'

'I very much doubt it.'

'Shame. Better get yourself invited to some first nights, then. Get a pretty girl on your arm. Up-and-coming writer Edward Barton seen last night at the Duke of York's Theatre with the Honourable So-and-So. Or a rich American. They always go down well.'

'I suppose so.'

'Like your friend.'

'Who?' I knew, of course.

'Billy Moody. Or Billy Hamilton as we must learn to call him. Squiring that heiress around town. What a lovely couple they make.'

This was news to me. 'Billy Hamilton?'

'I take it that you and he are no longer as intimate as you once were.'

'I've quite lost touch with him,' I said, my heart beating like a tom-tom. 'Who's the heiress?'

'American girl. I forget the name. Her daddy is something big in pictures. Didn't you know?'

'I don't take much interest in all that.'

'But some of us have to take an interest. Some of us have to be grateful for what we can get.' He laid a hand on my arm. 'You weren't always so proud, Edward.'

'Proud?'

'There was a time when you were glad of my company.'

'Tommy, please ... ' The barman was eyeing us, and shaking his head.

'It's all right. I'm not going to cause a scene. Come on, Edward. Let's go for a walk.'

My second walk of the day. 'Where?'

'I don't know. Your place, my place, a bush in St James's Park, a room at the YMCA. What's the diff?'

'For God's sake, Tommy, don't talk like that.'

'If you don't want me, you have only to say. I can take it.' I felt, suddenly, the cumulative weight of loneliness, his and mine, threatening to crush me. I thought of Billy and his heiress, Geraldine and her grubby gloves and little straw hat, I thought of the pile of pages awaiting me at home, the prospect of another long night of cigarettes and headaches, and I said, 'Where do you live now, Tommy?'

'Bethnal Green. It's only a bus ride.'

I stayed the night, rose at half past five and made my way across town to the warehouse.

2 August 1945

A call from Leonard Leigh. 'Rejoice, dear boy!' A cheque has arrived for the first instalment of my advance, £600 – more money than I've ever had. Same again in October with publication. It doesn't seem real, as if the whole thing will evaporate like a mirage.

As soon as the money is in my account I will do three things.

I will hand in my notice at the warehouse.

I will buy Geraldine a new coat, as she was complaining just the other day that her winter coat has been repaired so often that it's 'more patch than coat'.

I will pay Tommy's rent so that he won't be thrown out on the streets.

That will leave enough to live on while I write another book, if I have another book in me. Leonard insists that I have. I am certainly not short of material – but it won't do, will it? Queer goings-on in bedsits in Uxbridge Road and Bethnal Green. No: I must change, I must disguise. Edward Barton writes about passionate men and beautiful women, and for the kind of money that Leonard is talking about I'm willing to alter the pronouns.

10 August 1945

Cheque has cleared. With uncanny timing, Billy paid a call for the first time in weeks, looking healthy and prosperous in a clean shirt and new trousers, his hair well cut, and a bit more meat on his bones. In fact, he looked exactly like a movie star.

'So,' he said, looking around my room as if he was the Queen visiting the slums, 'you're still here then.'

'You know me, Billy,' I said, in my light comedy voice. 'Steady Teddy. I don't just disappear.'

'Still working at the warehouse?'

'I gave notice today, as a matter of fact.'

'Good for you, mate.' He seemed distracted, and wouldn't sit. If the room had been big enough, he'd have paced up and down – but here you can manage step-step-turn, step-step-turn. 'Well. That's great.'

He wanted something, and knowing Billy it was one of two things. One was money. Well, if he wanted money – or the other thing – he'd have to ask for it. 'How's the movie world?'

'Oh yeah. Yeah. Fine. Really good, actually.'

'Well that's marvellous, Billy.'

He frowned; I was not playing my part. What did he expect? Did he think I'd been waiting in a state of suspended animation for him to turn up?

He lit a cigarette. His hands looked manicured, the nails clean and trimmed. No longer a labourer's hands. He shook the match out, and said, 'War's over, then.'

'It certainly looks that way.'

'Atomic bombs, eh?'

'Terrible.'

He grinned. 'Yeah. Terrible.' He puffed on his cigarette. 'Seems weird, doesn't it? Peace.'

'It's been a long time.'

'Six years.'

'Indeed.' Suddenly it was not the war we were talking about.

'The world's changed, Ted.'

'I suppose so.'

'We've all changed.' Puff, pace, turn, puff. 'I've changed.'

'Yes, you have.'

'The thing is, Teddy ...'

'Yes, Billy?'

'I mean, we've got to think about the future now, haven't we?'

'Absolutely.' I sat with my hands resting on my thighs.

'We can't live in the past.'

'No.' This was the brush-off, then. Thanks for everything, the nights spent in each other's arms listening to Sibelius, drinking cheap wine, smoking endless cigarettes. Thank you and goodbye.

'I've met this new bird.'

'Oh, really?'

'She's a Yank.'

'Wow.'

'Yeah.' He stood in front of me, close, looking down into my eyes. 'Her dad's a big producer.'

'Ah.' And he doesn't want a queer son-in-law. 'I see.'

'He's a great guy. Thinks I have a future in pictures.'

'Gee. Swell.'

'Fuck off, Teddy.' He reached down and rumpled my hair, then gingerly withdrew his hand.

'Have you come to say goodbye?'

'What?'

'That's what this is leading up to, isn't it? Let's bury the past, forget what happened, pretend that we're just good friends. Or not even that. Pretend we barely know each other.'

'No. I just ... You know.' He held his hands by his side, palms facing me. I wanted to stand, grab them, put his arms around me. I still loved him.

'I don't know, Billy,' I said. 'Unlike you, I can't turn it on and off like a light. It takes me a while to get used to things.'

'Right. Like seeing Geraldine, I suppose.'

'Geraldine and I are ...'

'Just good friends?'

'Don't sneer at me, Billy. I like Geraldine. She's a nice girl.'

'Yeah.' He laughed through his nose. 'And a good fuck.'

I didn't know whether to hit him or start crying. 'That's a rotten thing to say.'

'Is it? Don't see why.'

'And what about your new bird, then? Is she a good fuck?'

'None of your fucking business.'

'Or is that why you're here? She not putting out?'

'Bollocks, mate. I get plenty.'

'Good.' I swallowed a mouthful of saliva. 'And so do I.' No need to tell him from whom; let him jump to his own conclusions.

'Right.'

There seemed little else to say. 'So is this it, Billy? Our brave new world? Chucking old friendships out the window?'

'No.'

'That's what it looks like to me.'

'I didn't say that.'

'Then what? What do you want?'

'Don't know.' He put his hands in his pockets, and stared at his feet like a sulky child. 'You're still my best friend.'

'I'm glad to hear it.'

'But the other stuff ...'

'I've never told anyone, you know. I'm quite discreet.'

'Good.'

'And so are you, I expect.'

'Yeah. I'm not about to shout it from the rooftops, am I?'

'I shouldn't imagine so.'

He relaxed and shrugged, and suddenly the air in the room seemed thick with the promise of sex. 'Got a cigarette?' I asked him, but before I finished the request he grabbed my tie and pulled me into a kiss. The war may be over but some things, it seems, are not.

8 February 1947

Publication day. My photograph has appeared several times in the press – I look 'handsome and distinguished' (according to Geraldine), 'like a God' (Tommy) and 'poncey' (Billy). My parents have not commented.

Second instalment of money also comes today and just as well: I can't stand Uxbridge Road much longer. Four walls, a narrow bed, the smell of the toilet ... This is not how 'one of our most promising post-war novelists' (*Daily Mail*) is supposed to live, although Leonard says it has 'a bohemian quality' i.e. I'm not some posh twit with a silver spoon in his mouth. He's arranged for a photographer to take pictures of me heating up a tin of spaghetti and posing by the hot water geyser. Leonard is absolutely adamant that I am not identified with the Waugh-Maugham-Rattigan-Novello-Coward crowd, 'the dressing gown brigade' as he calls them. He is very keen on the idea of Geraldine, and encourages me to tell journalists that I am 'engaged' to a schoolteacher. When I point out that this is not true, he waves it aside. 'Fiction, Edward, fiction. That's the name of the game.'

And Geraldine is very agreeable company. We go to the cinema and have intelligent discussions about the films. Sometimes we go to the theatre. We read new books, we go for walks in the country and drink a lot of tea. She reminds me of the girls I knew at university – nice, sensible young women who don't go in for politics, don't turn up drunk at three o'clock in the morning and don't start screaming just because you haven't phoned them. Compared to Billy and Tommy, Geraldine is restful and refreshing. The sort of girl I should marry – would have married by now, if the war hadn't come along and thrown our lives into chaos.

We could have a very pleasant life: a proper home with a garden, meals on the table at the appropriate hour, a nice room in which to work, roses at the window, a cat sleeping on a chair. Children, even.

Can I change? I'm 30 this year. I should know what I am by now. Tommy says he knew when he was four.

Going for dinner tonight with Leonard and Mr Warren, my editor, at Le Caprice, which, Leonard assures me, is very much the place to be seen. I am taking Geraldine.

17 February 1947

Letter from Billy inviting me to the studios for an 'insider tour'. I am to escort Eleanora. This is one function to which I will not be taking Geraldine. Billy remains a sore point.

2 March 1947

Eleanora looks well considering that she must be – what? Fifty? More? She's settled into the dowager role, and even though it's many years since she stepped on to a stage she is just as theatrical as ever. The house in Kentish Town looks run-down, like it needs several hundred pounds spent on it, but who has that kind of money these days? The paint's peeling and the windows are filthy or, in some cases, boarded up. I shudder to think what it's like inside.

Eleanora's personal appearance was immaculate, if not quite suitable for daylight. The grey hair that appeared during wartime had returned to her signature red, no longer piled up on top of her head in the Edwardian manner but professionally cut and set. Is Billy paying her hairdresser's bills? She was wearing a beaded black dress, a long amber necklace, and a good black wool coat that I'm sure was made over from something she used to step out in before the war. If I looked closely I would see moth holes patched over with darning wool, cuffs and collars turned – but I'm too much of a gentleman to look closely. Her face was fully powdered and painted; a less forceful woman than Eleanora might have looked clownlike.

'Edward, my darling,' she said, locking the front door and pulling on black satin gloves. 'How well you look.' She took my hand and descended the steps – always making an entrance, even if only into Kentish Town Road. 'And may I say' – kiss, kiss, one on each cheek – 'how very proud I am of you.'

'Thank you, Eleanora.'

'I always you knew you had a wonderful talent.'

'Have you read the book?'

'Of course. It's marvellous.' She took my arm and we walked to the station. 'So clever.'

'I'm glad you like it.'

'And now we're going to see my son, the film star. Oh, my dear, I have become quite unbearable. None of my friends are speaking to me any more, I'm so swanky. My son the film star, my dear friend Edward Barton the novelist.' She giggled. 'And I let them think that once upon a time we were more than friends. Is that very awful of me?'

'Not at all.'

'Of course they don't believe me, and why should they? An old bag like I am now.'

I picked up the cue. 'But you look wonderful, Eleanora. Really.'

'Bless you, dear. I do my best. But I don't suppose I shall ever play Juliet again.' She sighed. 'I might do a rather nice line in mothers and duchesses and so on. Billy says the studios are crying out for properly trained actors. They're mad about the English in Hollywood, apparently. Wouldn't that be hysterical? At my age. They say the sun plays havoc with your complexion out there. I should have to acquire a range of very large hats.'

'I can just picture you, darling, sitting by the pool, surrounded by handsome young men.'

'Wouldn't that be lovely?' She looked up at me, a naughty glint in her eye. 'I'm sure they're ten a penny out there. And why not, indeed? I've been a lonely widow for far too long. I miss the company.'

She squeezed my arm. 'Don't worry, my sweet, the old bag isn't going to pounce.'

Failing to think of the right reply, I gave a light social laugh.

'Anyway, I'm sure you have absolute shoals of other fish to fry.'

'Well ...'

'A rich, handsome, talented boy like you. You can take your pick.'

'Eleanora, really.'

'And have you ... picked?'

We reached the station. 'Here we are,' I said, and busied myself with buying tickets. For the rest of the journey Eleanora restricted herself to commenting (loudly) on other people's personal appearances, referring to my 'recent novel' and her son's 'forthcoming picture' and when we got off the train one young woman asked us for our autographs. Eleanora signed the back of an envelope as if it were the most natural thing in the world. 'And my dear friend, the famous novelist Edward Barton, author of *The Love Racket*. Got that? *The Love Racket*.'

I handed her down from the carriage. 'You see, darling, you need someone like me,' she said. 'I'm not ashamed. My mother worked on a fruit stall.' She lapsed into stage cockney. 'Getcher lovely pippins!'

'You're a marvel, Eleanora,' I said, remembering stories Billy had told me of his grandmother, the man-mad drunk who looked after him when his parents were too busy to care.

A car was waiting outside the station, a uniformed driver holding up a card that read BARTON. Eleanora gave a squeal of delight as he opened the door for her.

'I expect you know my son,' she said, leaning forward in her seat. 'Billy Hamilton.'

'Yes, ma'am,' said the driver, never taking his eyes off the road.

'This is his third picture,' she said. 'He has lines in this one.'

'Yes, ma'am.'

'I suppose you know all the stars, don't you?'

'Yes, ma'am.'

'Dirk Bogarde and Laurence Olivier?'

'I have had the pleasure, ma'am.'

'Hear that, Edward? My good friend, the novelist Edward Barton.'

'Sir.'

The studio gates swung open and we were deposited outside what looked like a factory, an ugly, low, redbrick building with rows of curtainless windows and worn concrete steps. I'd played at military bases with more glamour than this. Eleanora behaved exactly as if it were His Majesty's Theatre, greeting everyone – harassed typists on their coffee break, electricians, portly men in three-piece suits – with the same jovial grandeur. Finally we were commandeered by a short fellow with a clipboard and a corduroy jacket who was, he said, our guide for the day. 'Our Virgil in the underworld,' said Eleanora, taking his arm. I trailed in her wake.

After the tour we were deposited outside one of the sound stages – an enormous hangar with sliding doors – and told that 'they will be breaking in about five minutes. Please keep quiet'. Eleanora conversed in her best stage whisper, rolling her eyes and gesturing like a silent movie queen. She was especially animated whenever a man in a suit was in sight. It occurred to me that, for Eleanora, this whole visit was an audition.

The red light went out, the doors trundled open, and we were stampeded by a dozen young women in bathing costumes running for the warmth of dressing rooms, their brown-painted skin covered in goosepimples. Bringing up the rear was Billy, pulling a towelling dressing gown over a pair of swimming trunks. His hair was slicked up, a pair of sunglasses perched on the crest. Make-up covered the scars on his leg. 'Welcome to the Riviera,' he said, tearing his eyes away from the bottoms jiggling across the tarmac. 'Feel that lovely Mediterranean sun!'

'Billy, darling.' Eleanora kissed the air on either side of his cheek. 'How thrilling this is.'

'Mum.'

'Ssssh! Don't call me that!' she shout-whispered. 'I want them to think I'm a star, incognito.'

'Teddy, mate.' He shook my hand. 'Great to see you.'

'And you. I hear you have lines.'

He struck an Olivier pose, held out a hand and declaimed, 'Hey, who's coming for a swim?' Eleanora applauded, tapping her gloved fingers together, as Billy bowed. 'Well,' he said, 'it's a start. Makes a change from standing around in a copper's uniform or falling off ladders. Anyway, give me two ticks to get dressed and we'll get some chow.' He jogged off to the dressing room, his gown flying behind him.

'He looks well, doesn't he?' said Eleanora.

'Indeed.'

'Such a handsome boy. I can't think where he gets it from.'

'Oh, his father, of course.'

Eleanora punched me lightly on the arm. 'Cheeky!' She looked around for an audience, but found none. 'I wonder if we'll meet the famous Laura.'

'Is that her name? Miss Moneybags?'

'Dear me, Edward, that won't do.' She straightened my tie. 'One never shows jealousy in front of a rival.' She brushed dust from my lapel. 'One is at all times charming. Remember that.'

A rival? What does she know? 'Thank you, Eleanora.' A long black car glided past us, and she was distracted by its contents. 'I'm sure that was Ronald Colman.' She took a couple of steps. 'I wonder if he remembers me.'

'You knew him?'

'Of course, darling!' She put a hand to her bosom. 'One knew everyone.'

Billy returned, dressed in a loud check jacket and an open-necked shirt. 'Come on. I'm starving.'

'Where are we going? The staff canteen?'

'Boss's office. He wants to meet you.'

'Me?' Eleanora was all gracious surprise. 'How sweet! Nice to know that one is not completely forgotten.' We set off at a smart pace towards the front offices. 'To feel, after all, that one's work was not entirely in vain.'

The boss's office was distinguished by a brass plaque on the door and dark blue fitted carpets that looked as if they might have come from a cinema. A long table was laid up with knives and forks, three large foil-covered plates along the centre.

'Welcome welcome welcome!' This was unmistakeably the boss – large of stomach, florid of complexion and broadly American. 'Henry Casselden at your service. Hey, Billy, thought you said you were bringing your mother, not your sister.' He took Eleanora's hand and raised it to his lips. 'Pleasure to meet you, ma'am.' Eleanora actually curtseyed. 'And you must be the writer fellow.' He slapped me on the back. 'Okay, okay. Great. Billy, pour drinks.'

'Sure, Mr Casselden.' Billy sounded American. 'Whisky and soda for you, sir?'

'You know how I like it.'

'Sherry, Mum?'

'Yes, dear, thank you.'

'Ted?'

'Scotch will do fine.' Billy drank only soda water.

'Please, have a seat. Take the covers off, Billy.' Casselden sat at the head of the table, a large floral arrangement blocking his view. 'And lose the salad.'

'Sure, Mr Casselden.' Billy bustled about like a waiter.

'Where's my daughter?'

'She said she'd be here, sir.'

'She'd better be. Okay, folks. Dig in. Nothing fancy.'

There were salmon sandwiches, ham sandwiches, slices of gala pie, halved tomatoes. I filled my plate; Eleanora nibbled daintily, although I'm sure she was ravenous.

'Well, well, this is fine,' said Casselden, glancing at his watch. I was not sure what was expected of us. Casselden looked like the kind of man who enjoyed talking about himself, so I started asking questions.

'I understand you are a producer, sir.'

'An executive producer, son. Top dog. The buck stops here.'

'I see. And how long have you been in England?'

'Just about a year now, is it, Billy?'

'About that, sir.'

'And do you see potential in the British studios?'

'Sure do.' Casselden pushed away a plate of untasted food and lit a cigar. 'Cheap labour over here. Cheap studios. In America, Jesus, pardon me, lady, but the unions are getting a stranglehold. Over here, you can get the job done.'

'And we have the great tradition of acting, of course,' said Eleanora, sounding regal.

'Sure, sure. Some of the Brit actors are okay.'

'Well, I rather think we are more than ...'

'Your boy here.' Casselden waved his cigar at Billy; ash dropped on to the table. 'He's got something.'

'Of course he trained with his father and I ...'

'The girls in the publicity office like him. That's my usual test.' He looked at his watch again, and frowned. 'Now where is that damn daughter of mine?'

'I'm sure she's on her way, sir.'

'She'll be late for her own funeral. Ah.' A bustle at the door, and a flurry of fabric, announced the arrival of the heiress. 'Hey honey. Thought you weren't coming.'

'Sorry, Daddy.' Her face was peaches and cream between a fur collar and a felt hat. The accent was softer than her father's. 'I swear that driver takes the longest possible route. How do you do. I'm Laura Casselden. You must be Mrs Moody.' She beamed at Eleanora, who beamed back. 'Delighted to meet you.'

'My dear.'

I was ignored. 'Oh, Daddy, what on earth are you doing, smoking at the table? Really!' She took the cigar from his fat fingers, and looked around for something to drop it into. Eventually she found the water jug.

'Christ, kid, that's Havana! That's ten bucks up in smoke.'

'Better for you.' She flapped her hand in front of her face. 'Disgusting smell, and you know what the doctors say. Billy, darling, how did it go today?'

'Fine, fine.' Billy fussed around her, taking her coat, pulling out a chair. 'Great to see you, baby.'

Casselden frowned again; I'm sure he has a strong aversion to gold-diggers. The fact that Billy's got this far means that someone takes him seriously as a suitor. It must be Laura; the old man surely wants her to marry money or a title. And Eleanora, for all her airs, does not have the whiff of aristocracy. Oh, how easily I could bring this house of cards crashing to the ground! Just a few words would do it. Three little syllables. 'I've fucked him.' Cue screams, tantrums, darkness at noon.

'What a beautiful dress, my dear,' said Eleanora, eager to appropriate her potential daughter-in-law. 'Don't tell me.' She pressed a finger to her temple and closed her eyes. 'Worth. Am I right?'

'Yes! How clever!'

'One develops an eye.'

'Oh, one does,' said Laura.

Her father looked a little less hostile. I heard the faint pre-echo of wedding bells. Now, Edward – lean back in your chair, put your hands behind your head and utter those three syllables before it's too late.

'Well, well,' said Casselden, getting to his feet. 'I must get back to work. Billy – don't let my little girl make you late on set.'

'No, sir.'

'And Laura – keep off the sauce, baby.'

'Oh, Daddy.'

'Pleasure to meet you, ma'am.'

He bowed towards Eleanora, ignored me, and left.

'Honey,' said Billy, 'this is Ted that I was telling you about.'

Laura tried to remember, and failed. 'Oh yes?' She never took her eyes off Billy.

'Ted's written a book.'

'Oh it's marvellous,' said Eleanora, leaning towards her new friend. 'You simply must read it.'

'Billy, sweetie, are we going to Murray's tonight?'

'Sure, baby, if you'd like to.'

A bell rang outside – the end of playtime. 'I'd better go,' said Billy. He'd barely eaten a thing. 'Mum, Teddy, thanks for coming. Sorry to dash off.'

We stood; Laura remained seated, angling her perfect face for Billy to kiss. 'Oooh! Baby, you smell of embrocation!' Billy shrugged, and left. Laura stretched out her legs and lit a cigarette.

Eleanora and I took our leave. I deposited a copy of *The Love Racket* with an uninterested girl in the front office; if it ever gets to Mr Casselden, he will never read it.

17 August 1947

Eleanora called this morning, very excited, to discuss 'the wedding', to which she had just received her invitation. It's in November, at a church in Marlow Bucks, with reception at Casselden's house on the river. Sounds like a very swanky do and we shall all have to be in best bib and tucker. There will be press no doubt.

Tommy thinks he will be coming with me, I don't know quite how to break it to him. He brought new curtains that he has made for the kitchen, cheerful gingham, which he put up. He's determined to make his mark on the new flat, to impress me as a nest-builder and homemaker. He uses the first person plural, future tense, a lot in conversation and I imagine he sees himself moving in at some point. While in the bath together we drank a toast to 'the happy couple', meaning Billy and Laura, but from the look on Tommy's face, his eyes sparkling beneath the strands of wet dark hair, he was also thinking about us.

22 August 1947

My invitation to Billy's wedding has still not arrived. Knowing him he's probably sent it to the old address in Uxbridge Road, although he knows perfectly well that I've moved. Not that he's visited me in Putney. I shall have to get Eleanora to do some discreet chasing, if she's capable of such a thing.

28 August 1947

At last, an envelope addressed in Billy's handwriting, too flimsy to contain a nice thick invitation. Instead there's a sheet of studio notepaper in which Billy informs me that he hopes I won't be too upset, circumstances beyond his control, there is a very limited number of guests he can invite to the wedding, immediate family only, there will be a big celebration 'at a later date' to which I can come with the rest of hoi polloi, and it's signed 'Billy Hamilton', the final insult. Does he fear those three little syllables that I could so easily utter? Or have I been struck off the list by Laura – or her father? Is there some whiff of scandal? Has Tommy been talking? I've asked him often enough not to betray my confidence but I might as well have told the whispering grass, 'cos it done told the trees and they done told the birds and bees and now everybody knows.

18 October 1947

Sent MS of new novel *Rations of the Heart* to Leonard today. Hope he likes it. It's better than *The Love Racket*, and it would make a wonderful movie: classic love triangle, this time about a woman whose missing-presumed-dead husband comes back from the war, only to find that she's started a dull new life with a dull new man. Of course I'm the heroine, Billy's the returning hero and Tommy is the little clerk who wants to make a home in the suburbs, but nobody needs to know that. And the twist in the tale is that the noble not-so-dead soldier is an idol with feet of clay that go right up to his armpits, a liar, a swindler who has profited from the war and is now attempting to blackmail his wife. Nasty, cynical but with a satisfyingly moral ending, so we can all feel good when it's over. Dreary little bank clerks and their humdrum wives will lap it up.

27 October 1947

Lunch with Leonard and Warren the editor. All delighted with *Rations of the Heart*. Leonard kept winking at me; he's waiting for Warren's official offer, and you could practically see the pound signs in his eyes.

15 November 1947

Billy got married today.

Interesting meeting with Leonard and a chap from Rank who is interested in the screen rights for *The Love Racket*, and possibly also for *Rations of the Heart*. Nice suave fast-talking character who peppered his speech with Americanisms. Kept saying 'You are the voice of the new generation' like a parrot. Geraldine most amused. When I take Geraldine to business meetings they treat me with a great deal more respect. I suppose she answers any questions they may have. She blows away the mists of ambiguity. She makes me look richer, more successful – more worth the money.

Leonard expects Rank to option the books, which means another cheque. Added to the advance for *Rations* this means I have earned more in 1947 than I did in the entire six years of the War.

18 November 1947

Tea *chez* Eleanora. The old place has had a much-needed lick of paint. I suspect that Eleanora is planning to sell it.

Of course she was bursting to tell me all about the wedding. I had already decided that I would be interested, amused, nothing more. I would refrain from asking too many questions and I'd be happy that it all went off so well (if it did), sorry if the whole thing was a debacle.

She held a sort of *levée* in her bedroom, lolling around with tea things spread out all over the place; the 'parlour' as she now calls it is being decorated. 'Well, my dear,' she said, making herself comfortable against a pile of pillows, 'it was absolutely outrageous. I mean, the flowers alone must have cost more than you and I see in a lifetime. Although perhaps not you. Not now.' She reached over and felt the lapel of my jacket. 'The prosperous, successful author.'

'Go on about the wedding,' I said, my resolutions to be aloof already crumbling.

'Oh, you should have seen her coming down the aisle! Decked out in enough old lace to cover a bus. She looked like a giant meringue.'

'Sounds lovely.'

'And you could barely see Old Mr Casselden for all the frills and flowers. But there he was, leading the heifer to the altar, looking as if he'd rather be anywhere else in the world. I don't think Billy is the son-in-law he'd have chosen, and even though I charmed the very birds out of the trees he seems to think that we are rather *infra dig*.'

'Americans don't understand breeding.'

'Anyway, the church was packed. I think they just rented a whole load of extras.'

'Pity they couldn't squeeze me in, then.'

'And apart from me there was no other family.'

'Billy's friends?'

'Billy doesn't have *friends*, darling. Apart from you.'

'And I was not invited.'

'Of course he had a best man and ushers and that sort of thing. They all looked exactly the same. Handsome young men with greasy hair and strong jawlines. Actors.'

'And the bridal party?'

'Quite a gaggle of them, all in the most disgusting candy pink dresses I've ever seen. I thought my teeth were going to rot just looking at them.'

'What about her mother?'

'Conspicuous by her absence.'

'Does she have one?'

'I imagine like most people she's had a mother at some point in her life, but you know what Americans are like, particularly in the entertainment business. They divorce on a whim. Not like us. I stuck it out with William through thick and thin. Of course, we had our little differences of opinion ...'

'Well, I wish them all the luck in the world,' I said, wishing that my cheeks did not betray my feelings so much. 'I'm sorry that he didn't want me there, but we can't have everything in this life, can we?'

'We certainly can't, darling. Life, I have discovered, is the art of the possible. We must settle for what we can get.'

28 November 1947

Tommy arrived at the flat looking like death, as white as a sheet with huge circles under his eyes, unshaven, his hair sticking up, his collar dirty. Not, in short, his usual smart self. Turns out he'd been in police custody for the last 36 hours following his arrest for 'importuning' in a public lavatory near Charing Cross Road. He swears blind that he didn't do a thing, merely glanced sideways at a gentleman who occupied the adjacent stall and then felt the long arm of the law. He was taken to the station, charged, appeared in the magistrate's court this morning, pleaded guilty and was fined. So he now has a criminal record.

'I'm so sorry, Tommy, it must have been awful,' I said, as if he'd just told me that he'd had a spot of bother with his income tax. 'But you'll know better in future.'

'What's that supposed to mean? I didn't do anything! They were waiting for us! I wasn't the only one, you know.'

'You were in the wrong place at the wrong time.'

'It's not fair.'

'You should be more careful.'

'I am careful!'

'I'm very glad to hear it.' And I am. 'I hope they didn't ... question you.'

'Of course they did. They wanted the name and address of every queer in London.'

'My God, Tommy ...'

'Don't worry. I didn't tell them anything. I played dumb. Bastards.' He almost spat. 'I'd like to kill every last one of them. Get a gun and start shooting.'

'Calm down. You've had a shock.'

'Oh Edward,' he said, coming too close and looking up into my eyes, 'I wish we could get away for a while. Go somewhere warm and sunny where we don't have to worry.'

'I've heard Bognor is lovely,' I said.

Tommy sighed.

'You don't take anything seriously.'

'On the contrary, I take things very seriously indeed. And I think we need to be very careful. Very ... discreet.'

'So what am I meant to do? Piss in my pants because I'm too discreet to use a public bog?'

'I'm sorry for what happened, but there's nothing I can do about it.'

'You could try comforting me.'

'There there,' I said, stroking his arm.

He stood very still, looking at me. 'You disgust me some-times.' He walked out of the flat, slamming the door behind him. I suppose it would be best if I do not see Tommy for a while.

10 December 1947

Sent out Christmas cards today. Do not have an address for Billy and don't expect to receive one from him. Asked Geraldine if she would like to come up to my parents' over Christmas some time, all very casual, she said she'd love to.

11 December 1947

Christmas shopping. Got the thing I want for Geraldine, which I will give her when she comes to visit. If you're going to do these things you might as well do them properly.

18 December 1947

Horrible letter from Tommy accusing me of abandoning him, hinting in the most roundabout way at blackmail, 'obviously you know that I would never do or say anything to hurt you' – just reminding me that he could do if he so chose. On and on page after page alternating between improper declarations and wild accusations. Typical queer hysterics. How glad I am to leave all this behind.

26 December 1947

Nice crisp bright day and for once parents were on best behaviour because they are meeting 'your lady friend'. Mother up at 6 a.m. cleaning the house even though it's already spotless. Her face was glowing. I suppose she thought this would never happen.

Geraldine looked very smart in her new coat and some gloves that I gave her last week. I was proud. She kissed my parents, and my father became quite talkative. We had a glass of sherry and there were shining eyes and rosy cheeks all round. We went for a walk around the village while mother prepared lunch, and Geraldine was charmed with everything, the church, the green, the houses, the Christmas decorations, and seeing it through her eyes I was charmed too. We stopped at the pub for a quick drink and it was here, as planned, that I popped the question.

I am pleased to report that Geraldine accepted. I gave her the ring, which looks well on her finger. I suggested that we might not have a very long engagement, that we should be married in the first half of next year, and she agreed. I felt as if we ought to shake hands to conclude the deal, but instead she offered her cheek and I kissed it. We finished our drinks and went home for lunch. I did not tell my parents.

All in good time.

A spring wedding, then, or early summer. Just immediate family and a few carefully chosen friends. And obviously that will not include Billy.

III
After

Chapter Ten: Helen

EDWARD BARTON'S DIARY, so full and detailed until now, clams up completely at the point of marriage. It becomes little more than a schedule of appointments, with occasional annotations, schedules of income and expenses and baffling little symbols that hint at a secret life. Edward must have feared that his wife would pry – and, if she did, the diaries were quite blameless. The wedding came off without incident, and judging by the lists of caterers, entertainers, waiters and guests it must have been a lavish affair, even with rationing. After a suitable interval, Geraldine was pregnant – Edward recorded the news dispassionately, and on 2 January 1950 he announced the birth of a daughter, Valerie, at 5 p.m. On the same day Edward had a meeting with his agent, Leonard Leigh, to sign contracts with a new publisher, Bond and Lock, for a third novel, *Leave Before Dawn*. The size of the advance is recorded; the weight of his newborn daughter is not.

Billy disappears, leaving barely a ripple. Edward maintained contact with Eleanora – there were lunches at the Criterion Brasserie, just the two of them, while Geraldine nursed the baby at home in Putney. Eleanora, observant old gossip that she was, must have kept Edward up to date with her son's doings, but these went unrecorded. I know that Billy became a father in 1951 when my mother was born in Los Angeles. How did Edward react when he learned that they'd called her Rosemary? Was it a coincidence that that fatal flower

You might think, from a resumé of Edward Barton's career, that he sailed through life from one success to the next, finally dropping anchor in the safe haven of Stonefield where he enjoyed a long and comfortable retirement. The diaries and scrapbooks bear witness to his continued fame: he was regularly interviewed, he appeared on chat shows and game shows, he provided opinion pieces for the newspapers, and as the decades slipped by his opinions, like his appearance, fossilised into a parody of the conservative English gent. He represented a disappearing world of steam trains, repressed emotions and wearing a hat in public. He never wrote another novel.

I'm left with scraps of paper cut from magazines and newspapers, diaries that are merely lists and indecipherable symbols, the trash left by a man too long in hiding. Births and marriages – including my own – are recorded with as little embellishment as deaths. The passing of Geraldine, of Eleanora, of his own parents, is simply stated. My visit to Stonefield last year is marked by my name and a time. An appointment with his solicitor a few weeks later shows when he changed his will. And that's it.

I feel like I've bitten into the apple of Sodom, and got a mouthful of ashes.

Time for a major trip to the recycling centre. I've consolidated all the worthwhile stuff – the diaries, the drafts, some of the more interesting correspondence – and I'm trashing the rest. In the old days I could have had a large and very satisfying bonfire. I'm rather surprised Edward didn't do so. Perhaps, after all, he wanted someone to know the truth.

I managed to clear the attic. It will make a nice bedroom one day, possibly with en-suite bathroom. The remaining boxes were full of uncorrected proofs, piles of old *Country Life* magazines which I can't be bothered to sell on eBay, utilities bills going back to the 70s. I emptied them into black plastic sacks and stacked them in the hall.

And then, weirdly, as I was upending the last dusty box into the last plastic sack, my eye alighted on a thick manila envelope, worn and torn at the edges, some very old stamps in the corner and Edward's address scored through. Written across the front in biro were the words THE HAPPY ENDING.

Strange, I thought; there's been nothing else like this. And it was at the bottom of the last box, stacked right in the corner of the attic, the least accessible place in the house. Almost as if it had been hidden.

I opened the envelope; the brown paper frayed into fibres against my damp fingertips.

Inside was a sheaf of A4 paper held together with a rusty bulldog clip. The pages were typed, with a few corrections in ink. The front page read 'THE HAPPY ENDING by Edward Barton'. Beside it, in Edward's beautiful handwriting, were these words.

'This is the last thing I wrote. It remains unpublished on the advice of my agent and my solicitor. Edward Barton, 1966.'

The lost work. The final testament, the Dead Sea Scrolls, the Rosetta Stone that would explain all. My hands tingled, my cheeks flushed. It was too ridiculous, too melodramatic. The last thing in the last box, salvaged by chance as the whole lot was headed for the dump. Dramatic music, cliffhanger. I remembered Auntie Val's words at the funeral. 'Like something from a movie, isn't it? Oh, he'll have thought it all through. When your whole life has been a fiction, you can't help it.'

Well that turned out to be truer than I expected. Edward's whole life was indeed a fiction, a lie – and Valerie must have known it. I shouldn't be surprised that he'd planned these final scenes. It was very convincing on the surface: the hidden manuscript, forgotten for over 40 years, coming to miraculous light. But Edward knew, well before his death, that I was to be his executor. He must have anticipated that I would go through every box, looking for something worthwhile. He counted on my greed and curiosity to get me all the way to the bottom of the pile. He chose me well. My parents would have chucked the lot, unopened.

So here it was, Edward Barton's last word, forty pages of rust-stained, unpublishable truth. His agent's worst nightmare. A legal hot potato. Scandalous, possibly libellous, and maybe – just maybe – honest.

Chapter Eleven: The Happy Ending

ONCE UPON A TIME there was a man called Edward, who lived in a big house in the country with his wife Geraldine and two children, Valerie and David. Geraldine and the children were very happy because they had a lovely house with a big garden, they had nice clothes to wear and delicious food to eat, and they never had to worry about anything because Edward was sitting on a big pile of gold.

Edward should have been happy too, but he wasn't, and although he had a lovely wife and children, a lovely house and garden, lovely clothes and lovely food and a lovely big pile of gold, he was lonely. Because once upon a time, a long, long time ago, Edward had a friend called Billy whom he loved very much indeed, and Billy loved him too, just as much.

But Billy was dead.

And now Edward's wife and children seemed like strangers. The house seemed like a tomb, the food had no taste, and the pile of gold was cold and comfortless. Edward was alone with his memories of Billy, and nothing he could do would bring him back. Sometimes he thought he'd found a new friend, but they were never the same as Billy. They ran away, or they robbed him or hurt him, and in the end Edward preferred to be on his own. At least that way he could live in the past, and count his gold.

He did this for many years, and everyone said how clever he was, how kind, and how rich. Edward smiled and said thank you, and he watched his children growing up and told himself that they were the ones that mattered now, not him. They would have happy comfortable lives, they would want for nothing and they would never know what it was like to be sad.

But one day, sitting on top of his pile of gold, Edward heard a voice. Not even a voice, but a whisper. It could have been the rustling of a leaf on a tree, or the wind sighing in the chimney. It could just have been the coins shifting in his pile of gold. But he knew it was none of these things, because he'd heard it quite plainly. It had said a name. His name.

Teddy.

That was a special name, a secret name that only one person ever called him. He listened for the longest time, and just when he thought he'd imagined it he heard the voice again, calling softly from a long way away: *Teddy*.

After that, for days and days, weeks and weeks, he heard Billy calling his name more often, until finally he heard it all the time. He started to listen to the voice, and he realised that it was telling him a story. It was a story that he'd always known, like a fairy tale, something long forgotten, locked away in his memory, waiting for someone to come along with the key.

And so Edward listened to the old forgotten story, and when he knew it by heart he decided to write it down so that he could never forget it.

And this is what he wrote.

Liverpool has always seemed to me a place of departures, a liminal place where people wait to get away. I came here often enough during the war, when we performed in army camps and community halls, and despite the blacked-out streets one was always conscious of the sea lapping at the harbour walls, the ships waiting to carry people off, to death in the Atlantic or a new life. The voices of seagulls carry through the damp, misty air, a hoarse song around this isle of the half-dead, their shapes sometimes visible in the sky, white wings spread against the gloom.

Now I was back, years after the war, and once again I was singing for my supper. Not as an actor this time, telling jokes and dancing and romancing the leading lady, but as an author promoting my new book. I was halfway through a tour that had taken me, for the first time, to Scotland, where I'd gone down very well with the genteel ladies of Edinburgh who told me my books were 'quayte entertaining', and on through the more prosperous cities of Yorkshire and the industrial north. My agent accompanied me, partly to smooth out any problems, partly to keep an eye on me, but despite his vigilance I slipped the leash in Glasgow and Leeds to find company of a less literary nature. Those young men – Colin in Glasgow, Keith in Leeds – spent a pleasant night in a good hotel and left in the morning a few pounds richer, a small price to pay for their discretion. My agent scrutinised my face at breakfast, looking for signs of debauchery, but found none.

We arrived at Lewis's department store in Liverpool to a packed room. I read well, they laughed in all the right places, gasped when they were meant to gasp, and when I'd finished they obediently bought books and queued up to get them signed.

I must have been thinking of the past, and of all the stories that had gone into the making of my fiction, because I shuddered as if someone had walked over my grave, and when I looked up there was a bulky figure looming over me.

Of course it was Billy.

'Hello, Mr Barton,' he said. 'Would you sign this for me?' He offered my own book, open at the title page. *Leave Before Dawn*, by Edward Barton.

'With pleasure,' I said, playing my part. 'Who shall I sign it to?'

'For Rosemary,' he said, looking down into my eyes. 'She's my daughter.'

I found it hard to focus on the page as I wrote 'For Rosemary, with best wishes from Edward Barton'. 'What a lovely name, Rosemary,' I said, stressing the first syllable with a feather's weight. I handed the book back. It was hard to see his face with the light behind him, but I recognised the hands, big, square hands, gold hairs shining on the wrist, the nails dirty and bitten. No watch. Cuffs not as clean as they could be, and frayed.

'Thank you.' He took the book and stepped aside. The next person took his place.

'No, Billy, wait. I must talk to you.'

But the queue was pressing forward, and Billy was pushed away. 'I'll see you, Ted,' he said, and was absorbed by the crowd. Someone in front of me coughed.

'Hello,' I said. 'Who shall I sign it to?'

I forget the names – Gladys and Catherine and Hilda and Joan, Nigel and Geoffrey and Mark – but I scribbled and smiled, smiled and scribbled, talked to the press, posed for photos, always someone wanting my attention, my agent watching me like a hawk.

The streets were quiet when we finally left, a fine drizzle blowing in from the sea, haloing the streetlamps. A ship's horn blew from the docks, a muffled note of grief. I could have bellowed along with it.

We were due at a reception where I would be introduced to some local worthies, photographed and made much of.

I made my excuses and left, walking towards the sound of the horn, and turned down a side street where I could no longer hear my agent's voice calling after me.

Footsteps followed me. I increased my pace; they increased with me. Of course! What a fool I'd been, a man in a suit, an obvious target, walking alone after dark in the back alleys of a notoriously dangerous city. I felt the hand on my shoulder, smelt the tobacco breath, and waited for the first blow, fear tightening my stomach and shooting pain down my legs.

'I thought you'd never fucking leave.'

I turned. 'Billy.'

'The bad penny. You must have known I'd turn up eventually.'

'I thought you'd gone to America.'

'No.' He waved a dismissive hand. 'Not for want of trying.'

'What's the matter?'

'They won't let me in. Member of banned organisations.'

'The Communist Party? That was a long time ago.'

'That's what I said.'

'But you've got a wife and child over there.'

'Yeah. Not that you'd know it.'

'Surely she can do something? Her father?'

'I'm sure he's doing everything he can to keep me away,' said Billy. He took my arm and steered me deeper into the labyrinth of streets around the docks. 'It's good to see you, Ted.'

'You too, Billy.' I had still not had a good look at him. In the light of occasional streetlamps he looked heavier than before, his features coarsened by age and alcohol. 'It's been four years.'

'You didn't invite me to your wedding.'

'You didn't invite me to yours.'

'You married my bird.'

'You'd finished with her, as I recall.' We walked on. 'And with me too.'

'Oh fuck off, Teddy.' We passed out of a pool of light, into the darkest part of the street, tall buildings sheltering us from the eye of the moon. He pushed me against the wall, damp bricks rubbing against the back of my coat. 'Enough words.' He kissed me, our teeth knocking together painfully. His breath was sour from too many cigarettes, cheap coffee and a bad diet, and as I held him to me I could feel that his body had softened. But for all that, for his brokenness, his failure, the wreck of his marriage and the strange, sad death of our friendship, I loved him more than ever. We kissed like drowning men sucking air from each other's lungs.

'Better,' he said, breaking at last and spitting on the ground. 'Where to now, Gunga Din?'

'Your place or mine, I suppose.'

'I live in a shithole in Bootle.'

'I've got a suite in the Adelphi Hotel.'

'Come on then.' He put an arm around my shoulder and led me out of the darkness.

Time had not been kind to Billy. The dashing young war hero with the romantically smashed-up leg was gone, the movie-star jawline blurred and indistinct, the slick gold hair now thinner and duller. Since his wife left him to give birth in her native land, he'd been stranded and out of work, and when the cheques stopped coming he went back to labouring, eating in cafes, living in rented rooms and drinking his wages. He'd got in with a good gang in Liverpool, he said, and had regular work while waiting for the call to come; as soon as Laura's lawyers cleared the paperwork and wired the money he'd be on the first boat out of there. It was, he said, just a matter of time and bureaucracy, but he was kidding himself. Pop Casselden, I'm sure, was doing his damnedest to make sure that his no-good son-in-law stayed on the other side of the world, and for Laura, out of sight was out of mind. No doubt the child Rosemary was raised by maids, while Laura broke her marriage vows with every ambitious actor that crossed her path.

Billy told me all this in bed that night, his head resting on my chest, rising and falling as he smoked cigarette after cigarette. I listened and stroked his hair and smoked one for every five of his. I told him little about my life; he was not curious. No need to tell him about the Colins and Keiths, those eager, quickly forgotten bodies who rushed in to fill the vacuum that he left. It was enough that we were together again. Perhaps I was a refuge from loneliness, a source of cash – but when we made love in the dim light of a Liverpool dawn it seemed as real and true as it had ever been; more so, now that he was so broken and low. To love Billy before was easy, and he accepted love as he accepted his reflection in a mirror. Now, with the bitter taste of his loneliness in my mouth, it felt as if I had passed a test, that my love for him had survived the refiner's fire.

At last we composed ourselves for sleep, his curved back pressed into my stomach, his legs drawn up. My hand rested on his knee, and my fingers traced the familar crooked shape of a long, blue-grey scar.

In the morning we went to Billy's digs in Bootle, I paid what was owing to his Irish landlady while Billy packed his few belongings into a cardboard suitcase. We left Liverpool by a lunchtime train, travelling south to Birmingham, the next day to Oxford, and then to Guildford, Southampton and Bristol. Billy shared my bed every night, accompanied me to readings and dinners, and when my agent asked the inevitable awkward question he was quick with an answer.

'He owes me one, mate,' said Billy, with a wink. 'He married my bird.'

Geraldine was amazed when I told her who I'd met in Liverpool, and baffled when I invited Billy to Valerie's christening. Of all the people in the world he was the one she least wanted to see – but I played on her heartstrings, said that he was down on his luck, missing his baby who was far away across the ocean, and by the time I'd finished she was as eager to invite him as I was.

And so Billy came, and after some initial awkwardness he and Geraldine were chatting like old friends. Valerie took to him immediately, and was happy to be held, looking up into his face, giggling, putting her finger in the cleft of his chin.

When everyone had gone, and my hand ached from handshakes, none firmer than Billy's, I washed up while Geraldine put the baby to bed. At last, as I sat in the living room drinking whisky and smoking a final cigarette, she came in to empty the ashtrays. I pulled her on to my knee and kissed her. She squirmed and wriggled, but when she returned my kiss she was as eager as I. We went upstairs, and she emerged from the bathroom wearing a nightgown I gave her for Christmas, her hair gleaming from the brush and something fragrant on her skin. It was the first time for many months that we were together as husband and wife.

Chapter Twelve: Helen

RICHARD WAS SITTING at the kitchen table when I arrived, summoned by text. 'Come home. Stuff we need to discuss.'

The house was surprisingly, I might even say suspiciously, clean, and there was no sign of the children. No unwashed plates of uneaten fish fingers and baked beans, no toys scattered about the place, no voices. Just Richard, in a white shirt and a loosened red tie, his arms resting on the tabletop, as if starting a business meeting.

It was so quiet that I could hear the buzzing of the fridge. I tried to make some noise by jangling my keys, rummaging in my handbag and so on, but Richard remained silent and seated.

'Is there an agenda?' I said.

'No.'

I looked around the kitchen, trying to find something to comment on, to distract him from what was coming. I already felt in my heart what it was, but if I could keep my brain busy I need not know it. And not knowing something means it's not happening. But there was nothing: everything was in its proper place, everything clean. No post to open. No new paintings on the fridge door. Nothing. As antiseptic as an operating theatre before the first incision.

'Helen, we need to talk.'

'I'm all ears.' I sounded stupidly jovial, but I couldn't help myself. Nothing bad could happen if I kept smiling.

'I'm having an affair with Annette.'

I kept smiling.

'Did you hear me? Annette and I ... we're having a relationship.'

The fridge buzzed, clicked, shuddered and was silent. Nothing left, not even a bird singing. Not even the blood flowing past my years. Perhaps it had stopped. Perhaps I was dead.

'I'm sorry, Helen. But you have to know.'

'How long has it been going on?' I needed to ask questions, to gather information, or I'd start screaming.

'About six months.'

I made rapid calculations. 'After my grandfather died.'

'Yes. After that.'

'I see. When I wasn't around you just started sleeping with my best friend.'

I expected an angry denial, but Richard said, 'Basically, yes. That's how it was.'

'Right.' It would have been easier if we could fight, but he was determined to be direct and honest. It was one of the things I loved about him. 'And how does Glyn feel about this, may I ask? Has he been informed?'

'Annette and Glyn have separated.'

'What? That's impossible. She'd have told me about it.'

'Nevertheless it's true.'

'So you and she are going to just ... What?'

'We don't know exactly, yet.'

We. That used to mean us – Richard and I. Now it was Richard and Annette. One little shift of such a small word, and my world was in ruins. 'Where are the children?'

'With Annette.'

'How dare you?'

'They've been practically living there since you left us, Helen. Hadn't you noticed?'

'Left you? What do you mean?'

A bloody stupid question, and he had every right to be sarcastic, but he just said, 'That's what pushed us together, really. Looking after the children.'

'You mean it's my fault? Because I've been taking care of my grandfather's estate and trying to establish a future for us there ... To make some money out of it ...'

'No, that's not what I mean at all. But you were never here, and someone had to look after the kids.'

'So Annette just stormed in and took over, did she? Oh yes, I can see her doing that. She couldn't wait to get her hands on them. Or on you. She's been waiting all this time until my back was turned, and then ...'

'Helen.' His voice was hard and stern.

'What?' I sounded hysterical.

'It's not like that.'

'Then would you kindly tell me how it is?' Tears were starting to flow, and snot was bubbling out of my nose. I was here – at home – in my own kitchen, where I made the children's dinner, where I cooked Sunday lunch, where Richard and I shared our sacred first-thing-in-the-morning cup of coffee – and I was about to lose it all. The picture was going out of focus, blurred by tears, dissolving.

'You left me, Helen.'

'I did not! I've been working.'

'Oh God.' He put his hands over his face, and for the first time didn't look like a data analyst. 'Do I have to spell it out?'

He knows. 'I think you'd better.'

'I know about you and ... that man. Your tutor.' He swallowed hard. 'Harry Ross.'

The name dropped into the room like a brick.

'I see.'

'It's true, then.'

'Did she tell you?'

'Annette confirmed my suspicions, yes.'

'"Confirmed my suspicions". Right. And you thought that gave you the right to start sleeping with her, did you? Just because of something Annette tells you that I discussed with her in confidence.'

'But it's true, isn't it, Helen? You and he have been – you know, together, for a long time.'

What was I going to say to that? A flat denial? 'Oh God, this is awful.'

'Yes. It's awful.'

'What are we going to do?' I reached out for his hand, but he moved it away.

'I think we're probably going to get a divorce.'

'But Richard ... the children ...'

'It's too late for that, Helen.'

I got up and scraped my chair over the floor tiles; it sounded like a scream. 'Too late?'

'Sit down. We have to talk.'

I blundered out of the kitchen, barely able to see, and ran from the house. Richard did not come after me.

Nothing stands between me and the pain but time, and time is the thing I cannot endure. So I sit here alone in Stonefield drinking gin; alcohol buffers pain and speeds the clock and somehow helps the day to end. It's not much fun in the morning, or when I wake with a bang in the middle of the night, panicking, my heart pounding, face-to-face with the realisation of what I've done. I've lost my husband and my children, I've thrown them away, and no matter how much I blame Annette or Richard or even Harry, I know it's nobody's fault but mine.

But that feeling doesn't last too long, and certainly can't survive a very strong gin and tonic. More gin than tonic.

Children forget quickly. By now Ben and Lucy think that they have always lived with Holly and Poppy – God what stupid fucking names – that Annette is their mummy and that I am ... what? A lady who used to pick them up from school sometimes? Annette's house is their home, now she's got Glyn out the way. They've all been on holiday together. What fun. And I'm alone in Stonefield with dead crumbling paper and the ghost of a man whose dishonesty has poisoned all our lives.

A letter arrived this morning, recorded delivery, which meant that I had to stagger downstairs in the clothes I fell asleep in, clutching my head, looking like death. The postman glanced up at me and quickly glanced down. I'm sure I stink of liquor. Rumours of the mad woman at Stonefield will be spreading round the village.

It was from a firm of solicitors.

Dear Helen Barton

I act on behalf of Mr and Mrs David Barton in the matter of your proposed biography of Edward Barton, deceased. I hereby request you to cease preparation of any such publication as it would constitute a breach of my clients' privacy and would also be considered defamatory. My clients absolutely and irrevocably decline permission to publish any of the materials contained in the estate of Edward Barton dec'd and any attempt to do so will be in breach of intellectual property laws.

Yours sincerely, etc.

I read it once, then again over a cup of coffee, then again while lying on the sofa wondering if it was too early for the first drink of the day. How very like my parents to communicate through the medium of solicitors. They could so easily have come to see me, put their case, told me the reasons why they were so upset, and we might have discussed it like reasonable human beings. Instead they went to law, preferring to pay a stranger to issue me with threats.

Big mistake. I've got enough bullshit in my life without this. If my parents are so uptight about the fact that their fathers were lovers, then tough. It's time they dragged their attitudes into the 21st century. It's time the doors were blown off this particular closet and the truth taken out and examined. Maybe then we can all move on. If I had any doubt about the necessity of writing something about Edward Barton, this changed my mind. I'll read the rest of *The Happy Ending*, and if it's any good I'll see about publishing it with a long biographical introduction and, perhaps, edited extracts from the diaries. You thought you knew all about crusty old Edward Barton with his tweed jackets and pipes and conservative attitudes, you laugh at the film and you ignore the books, but just wait till you hear the truth. Barton back on the agenda, the books back in the shops – and maybe Harry Ross will get to write that TV adaptation after all. Why not?

They can threaten injunctions till they're blue in the face, but there are no grounds. The intellectual property argument doesn't stand up, because Edward left everything to me – and I can do what I like with it. As for invasion of privacy: whose privacy? I'm hardly going to start revealing details of my father's recycling schedule or my mother's taste in fleece dressing gowns. And it's not defamatory if it's true, and I shall make damn sure than anything I say about the living is checked and checked again. I can say what I like about Edward, about Billy, about Geraldine – because you can't libel the dead.

No word from Richard for three days. I suppose that he, like my parents, will communicate through solicitors.

A big branch fell off a tree last night, right on to the roof, smashing a lot of tiles and breaking the attic skylight. I didn't even hear it, I was so drunk. I will have to get around to fixing it because rain is getting in.

For the time being I've placed buckets and bowls under the worst of the drips.

The house feels cold no matter how high I have the heating, the warmth just seems to fly through the windows and doors. I am never comfortable.

Harry has been calling but I don't answer. I can't tell him what happened. I suppose if he really wants to see me he'll come around. Perhaps he thinks I've gone back to my husband and am avoiding him.

That's a laugh.

Chapter Thirteen: The Happy Ending

(continued)

THE HEAT HIT US as soon as we stepped off the plane, slamming up from the tarmac, taking our breath away. Valerie squealed, Geraldine said 'oh my goodness' and started fanning herself with a magazine, while Billy ran ahead whooping and laughing. It was the first time he'd been out of England since he was shipped home from Cairo with a mangled leg and a fifty-fifty chance of walking again. You wouldn't have believed that, looking at him now, arms in the air, executing a jig of delight, grabbing Valerie's chubby little hands and swinging her around in a big circle, making aeroplane noises. You wouldn't have believed this was the same seedy individual I'd found haunting the wet streets of Liverpool; in recent months he'd been in the gym, lost weight and fixed his teeth. His eyes were sparkling again, and so they should. He was loved.

Billy spoke less now of going to America. He was reconciled to his life in England, with me footing the bills and paying the rent on a flat where we could be together. If he was missing his wife and child – a child he had never seen – well, he had mine as a substitute. Geraldine accepted him as a friend, Valerie loved him as an uncle, and nobody raised an eyebrow when it was proposed that he should join us on holiday. We flew first class to Nice. I reserved a family suite at the Negresco, and for Billy a small penthouse on the

Promenade des Anglais where it was understood he could entertain in private.

I left Geraldine to unpack, and escorted Billy to his quarters; his French barely extended beyond 'parlay voo'. We registered, and carried the cases up eight flights of stairs; the room had views up and down the bay from a tiny balcony with fancy blue wrought-iron railings and a faded red-and-white striped awning. Billy rushed around looking at everything – the brass bedstead, the floral wallpaper, the strange candelabra light fittings, the rickety wooden nightstand. He laughed at the toilet – one of those archaic affairs that's little more than a hole in the ground – and puzzled over the bidet. Finally he discovered the balcony.

'Jesus, Ted, feel that sun!' He stood on the worn tiles, white with salt, and stretched up his arms. 'It feels so good to be here!' He stripped off his shirt, rubbing the sunlight over his body as if he was washing in it. 'Oh, man alive.' He closed his eyes and leaned his elbows on the railings, sticking his backside into the room.

He said something, but I wasn't sure I heard it right, and so I moved closer to the window. 'What did you say?'

'I said fuck me.'

'Are you sure?' He wasn't usually keen, and had certainly never come right out and asked for it before. Perhaps this was a measure of how grateful he was for the holiday.

'Yeah.' He unfastened the top of his trousers and pushed them down to his knees. His bum glowed white in the gloom of the room. 'I want it.'

I stood behind him, gripping his hips, pressing myself against him, both of us looking out at the bay, the cloudless blue sky above it, the busy beaches and streets below.

'Come on, Ted. Do it.'

There was a bar of soap in the bathroom, and while I worked up enough lather for the job, Billy kicked off his shoes and pulled off his trousers, turning them inside out in his hurry. The soap was going to sting, but neither of us cared. He stood with his feet apart, strong legs braced, hands gripping the top of the iron railings, and I entered him without preliminaries. He bit his arm, and I heard him grunt, his slicked-back hair falling over his forehead. A gentle salty breeze blew around us, billowing the curtains into the room, and we moved on to the floor, the sun hitting my back as I screwed him to the carpet. He looked into my eyes as I did it, and I saw there no shadow of betrayal.

Billy made himself useful in all sorts of ways. As Valerie's favourite babysitter he gave Geraldine and me plenty of time to ourselves, and as this holiday was in part a delayed honeymoon we spent most of it in our Negresco bedroom, making up for lost time. Marital relations, never exactly passionate, had ceased altogether with her pregnancy – but now, I suspected, she was ready to conceive again. As we had not discussed a second child, I took good care to use protection, expecting on each occasion that she would stay my hand.

Billy also came in handy when I wanted to work; he would take Geraldine and Valerie to the beach, leaving me free to sit in my room, sketching out plots for future novels, all of them distinctly triangular in shape. I wanted more than anything to write down what was happening here and now, to tell the truth rather than dressing myself up as a frustrated housewife, or transforming Billy into a heartless *femme fatale*, but I could imagine all too well my agent's reaction to any such initiative. And so I would remain in lucrative disguise, until such time – if ever – that the world was ready for the truth.

More often than not I used my 'writing time' to sleep. Having two lovers on one holiday was taking its toll, and I was no longer 20 years old. I wondered if either Billy or Geraldine had noticed my appetite for oysters and rare steak.

One afternoon I joined the family on the beach. Geraldine was on a lounger underneath a parasol, her wet hair held up by an elastic band, her limbs shiny with oil. Billy and Valerie were playing by the water's edge.

I sat down on the sand. 'Have you been in?'

'Yes,' said Geraldine. 'It's lovely. How's the work?'

'Splendid.' I watched Billy lift my daughter as if she weighed no more than a feather, and place her on his shoulders. Thus burdened, he charged up and down the beach, kicking up great plumes of spray; Valerie screamed with joy. 'Look at them. He's as much of a kid as she is.'

'He's missing his little girl.'

'He's never even seen her.'

'Oh, Edward!' She sounded cross. 'How would you feel if you weren't allowed to see Valerie?'

'I can't imagine the situation will ever arise, will it?'

'Of course not.' She settled her sunglasses on her nose; they had slipped down, allowing me a glimpse of the pain in her eyes. 'That bloody wife of his. I could wring her neck.'

Billy jogged up the beach and delivered Valerie into her mother's arms. 'She needs the loo,' he said. 'That's where my duties end.'

Mother and daughter made their way to the *toilettes*. I noticed how attractive Geraldine looked in her turquoise swimsuit; it had not escaped Billy's notice either. He gave a long, low wolf-whistle. 'You're a lucky sod,' he said.

'I've got the best of both worlds, haven't I?' I said, staring none too subtly at the front of his minute black swimming trunks.

'You'd better watch out,' he said.

'Why?'

'See the way the French blokes look at her?' He nodded up the beach, where heads were turning in the direction of Geraldine's turquoise *derrière*. 'Always someone ready to take her off your hands.'

'Don't worry about me,' I said. 'I can take care of my wife.'

'I hope so,' said Billy, stretching himself out on the sand, in full sun. He put his hands above his head, extending his arms, bunching up the muscles in his thighs and stomach. A couple of young women in bikinis watched him as they passed, whispering behind their hands. Billy sat up and waved, and they walked away, giggling and looking back.

After two weeks of sun, sea and sex, we were all ready to go home. Valerie got a tummy bug, and was grumpy and hard to please. Billy was restless; it was too much to expect him to be faithful to me for so long, especially when surrounded by such temptation, and however passionate he was when we were together, I was not blind to the other side of his nature. He wanted 'the best of both worlds' too – more than me, in fact. I'd have been happy with Billy and only Billy for the rest of my life. But no two men are made the same, and it would have been suicidal folly to force him to make a choice.

Of all of us, Geraldine was the happiest. She floated around Nice with a smile on her face and a glow on her skin – a suntan, of course, but something more, the look of a woman well loved. Those naps and oysters had paid off. Finally even she succumbed to Valerie's tummy bug, and spent the last two days rushing off to the bathroom to be sick.

When we got home, after a long day's travel, and had unpacked and got Valerie settled, we sat in the living room and opened a bottle of duty free wine. Geraldine took only the smallest amount and when I asked her if she was feeling unwell, bit my head off. I put it down to fatigue and homecoming blues.

She was no better the following morning, the following week or month. Her mood deteriorated and she was often tearful, spending all her time looking after Valerie, none with me. Any physical overtures were curtly rebuffed. At last, over dinner six weeks after our return, she said she had something to tell me.

Of course, she was pregnant.

Nine months later, little had changed. Geraldine was bigger, Valerie was older, Billy still waited for the call that never came, and I was correcting the proofs for *The Interlude*, the book I started in France. It seemed stale and artificial compared to the reality of my life, but my agent and publisher were delighted, and advance sales suggested a success that would put my previous efforts in the shade. There was already talk of a movie deal, of a big name director and proper stars. This, said my agent, was the book that would set me up for life – and just as well, with the impending addition to the family. If he'd read the notes I'd been making recently, he'd have had a heart attack. But I was careful. Nothing was lying around. Things got burnt.

Geraldine went into labour, and I drove her to the hospital. She was happy to be left, and the nurses were eager to get rid of me; Sister said she'd telephone just as soon as there was any news. I called Billy, and arranged to meet him in town for a night of old-fashioned drinking, a pre-emptive wetting of the baby's head, the prelude to two or three bachelor nights.

I took him for dinner at an Italian restaurant on Frith Street, where he pitched straight into the aperitifs and guzzled half a bottle of wine before the starters arrived. He seemed glum and preoccupied, drinking to blot something out, just as he used to during the war, when his leg hurt and his sex life troubled him.

We finished eating, and I looked at my watch. 'Half past nine. Geraldine's been in labour for nearly twelve hours. It must be on its way by now.'

Billy struggled for words.

'Oh ... that's fantastic.' He took a large drink. 'Hope she's okay.'

'She's in very good hands.'

'Shouldn't you be there, or something?'

'I don't think I'd be very welcome.'

'But supposing ...'

I held up my hand.

'Billy, nothing will go wrong. They will call me as soon as there is any news.'

'Then you should be at home.'

I gestured to the waiter to bring the bill. 'Whenever you're ready.'

'You want me to come?'

'Of course.'

'To your place?'

'I need to be near the phone.'

Lust and propriety battled in his mind; I could practically hear the cogs turning. 'Come on then. I need a nightcap.'

We took the tube back to Putney, and I rang the hospital while Billy poured drinks.

'All quiet on the western front,' I said, and we clinked glasses.

At first, when we went to bed, he was distant and unresponsive, letting me do all the work. I stopped and looked up from between his legs. One arm was thrown across his eyes, his lips parted. He was drunk; I wondered if he was asleep.

'Penny for your thoughts,' I said, and felt the tension in his muscles as if he were about to bolt. And then he relaxed, opened his arms and took me in them.

The phone rang at seven o'clock. I was the proud father of a son, born at 4.30 in the morning. Mother and baby were doing well, and I could go and see them at lunchtime. I told Billy, who was lying in bed looking very green around the gills; we'd only had a couple of hours' sleep.

'Congratulations,' he said, 'that's wonderful news.' His eyes were bloodshot, his face haggard as he went to the bathroom. A few moments later, I heard him retching.

When finished copies of my new book arrived, I presented a signed copy to my wife, who was far too busy to read it, and had one couriered at great expense to Billy's address. I should have known from the silence which followed that he was displeased, but I was too busy being feted by publishers and interviewed by journalists in a specially hired suite at the Savoy to notice. At last he telephoned, and said only 'I need to see you'. We made a rendezvous at Euston Station.

He was standing under the clock as arranged, smoking and checking his watch. As soon as I arrived he grabbed my elbow and steered me out of the station. 'You're late,' was all he said.

We walked quickly into Regent's Park. It was a beautiful warm morning, and the flower beds were full of early daffodils, there was blossom on the trees, and the birds were singing. Just like the first time ...

'Lovely day,' I said. 'You can feel the sun.'

Billy didn't want to talk about the weather. 'How dare you?' he said, stopping dead in front of me and putting a hand on my chest, almost knocking me backwards.

'I beg your pardon?'

'You beg my pardon? You'd better fucking beg my pardon all right.'

I took refuge in good manners. 'What appears to be the problem?'

'Appears?' His face darkened, highlighting the network of broken veins that were appearing around his nose and cheeks. 'I'll tell you what appears to be the fucking problem, mate. Your fucking book, that's what.'

'You didn't like *The Interlude*, then.'

'You bastard.'

'Well I must say, I've had better reviews.'

'How dare you?' His jaw was jutting forward, thick veins standing out in his neck and forehead.

'I don't know what you're so upset about.'

'I'm not stupid, you know.'

'I never said you were.'

'Look ...' His fists were bunching, and I thought he was actually going to hit me. Instead he took two paces away, and breathed hard. 'How could you do it, Ted?' he said at last. His face was pale and clammy.

'Do what? Give me a clue.'

'Write this crap. About us.'

'About us?'

'Okay – about me, then. I don't give a toss what you say about yourself or even Geraldine, although God knows the poor girl doesn't deserve it. But leave me out of it.'

'You flatter yourself, Billy. Not everything I write is about you.'

'So I suppose it's a coincidence that the girl is called Rose, then?'

'Well, that ...'

'And that the hero drops out of university.'

'That's just a minor detail ...'

'And they carry on an affair right under his wife's nose. His wife and child. And all the while this "Rose" is waiting to go to America. Oh God, you are a bastard.'

'Please, Billy.' He was walking away from me up the path. 'It's not that simple.'

'Fuck off.'

'You must listen to me!'

He turned round, and now his face was red, spittle on his lips. 'I've listened to enough from you! Jesus Christ, what do you think I am? Some kind of whore?'

I wondered if he was drunk. 'Of course not.'

'You think you can treat people however you want just because you're the one with the money and the family and the big name. Well let me tell you, Edward Barton, you better start treating people right. Because otherwise ...'

'Yes? Go on.'

'You know.'

'Are you threatening me, Billy? Is this blackmail?'

'Oh what's the use?' His shoulders relaxed, and I thought – good. He's blown off his steam, now we can get back to normal. 'You can't help the way you are. You're like a vampire, Ted. You suck, suck, suck and when you've got what you want you spit it out.'

'I never heard you complain before.'

Bad timing. 'I'm warning you, Edward,' he said, in a cold, emotionless voice. 'Keep away from me in the future. From me and my family.'

'What are you talking about?'

'You're a cruel bastard. You don't care about anyone except yourself. You've played me like a fiddle for all these years, and now I've had enough.'

'Billy please. This is ridiculous. If I've upset you ...'

'Oh, forget it.' He walked away from me, back towards the busy Euston Road.

'Billy!' I shouted, but he did not stop or turn, and I did not see him again for seven years.

Chapter Fourteen: Helen

IT IS BEN'S NINTH birthday on Monday, and we are having a party today, Saturday. All his friends are coming, and it is only right that both parents should be there as well. And so I am standing in front of the bathroom mirror trying to make something presentable out of the pouchy, flushed face that I see before me. Too much booze and too much crying. A heavy-duty concealer helps, but no duty is heavy enough to erase me completely, and that's what I want. A clean page. A fresh start.

The party has been arranged by text – the best medium for conveying information with no shade of emotion. But even from these exchanges I gather that Annette will be present with Holly and Poppy, and that Richard has invited my parents without consulting me. So I will be walking into a room containing my husband and his mistress who is trying to steal my children, and two people who are threatening me with lawyer's letters. All that's needed is a surprise appearance by Harry Ross, demanding sex and/or the rights to the Barton estate, and the party will be complete. I wish I had some tranquilisers. I rummaged through the medication in the bathroom, but all I could find was laxatives, and they're the very last thing I need.

I'm taking the car, as I have a large and unwieldy present for Ben, which I don't fancy manhandling on public transport. I've become a typical divorced parent before I'm even divorced, trying to buy my child's affection with an outsize gift. It sits on the back seat of the car, alongside a briefcase containing Edward's unpublished manuscript and other papers.

'It remains unpublished on the advice of my agent and my solicitor.' Who was he trying to kid? An explicit account of a homosexual affair conducted under the wife's nose, with soapy fucks in rented rooms and drunken couplings in the marital bed at the very moment she's in hospital giving birth? In 1966? He used real names, for God's sake. There would have been a scandal and certainly a divorce. Is that what he wanted? Maybe, for one brief moment in the 60s, as he saw the world changing around him, Edward wanted to throw off the shackles and live openly. If so, it was a passing fancy. He remained married until Geraldine's death, and after that it was too late and nobody cared.

I see now why he never published again. Those last words from Billy – 'you're like a vampire ... you don't really care about anyone except yourself. You've played me like a fiddle ...' Oh, they must have cut deep. So deep, indeed, that part of that speech, the oft-quoted 'You've played me like a fiddle', found its way into the screenplay of *The Interlude*. It's not in the novel; I've checked. Even after all that happened, Edward couldn't resist stealing Billy's best lines just one more time, casting himself as the abused lover. But with Billy gone, there was nothing left to steal. I wonder if Geraldine ever found out. Is that what poisoned my parents' lives – the bitterness, passed on from their parents, of this endless betrayal?

That would make good party small talk. 'Hi Mum. Hi Dad. You know that injunction? Is it because Grandma found out that Grandad was fucking Grandad?'

I remember Edward in his room, the figure behind the curtain, hooking me and reeling me in, playing me like a fish, or like a fiddle, if you prefer. Even then, so close to death, his nerveless fingers were meddling with other people's lives. Did he realise that, by giving me the house and the literary estate and all that money, he was handing me just enough rope to hang myself? Because that's what it amounts to. Without my inheritance I'd have been of precious little interest to Harry, and we'd soon have tired of our frantic afternoons in Dalston. The whole bloody mess might have been forgotten, a hiccup in my marriage, nothing more. Instead I have an irritable lover and a pending divorce. So much for my literary aspirations. If that's what creative writing classes do for you, I wish I'd never enrolled. The novel I was working on has long since been shredded. One thing the world does not need right now is more fiction.

The party was in full swing when I arrived, children running everywhere, adults packed into the kitchen where sausage rolls were being taken out of the oven – my oven – by Annette. She was wearing my apron and using my oven gloves. She had the decency to blush when she saw me, although it could have been the heat from the oven acting on her naturally florid complexion.

I should have been here to help with the preparations. What do I mean, help? A party for my son, in my house? I should have been in charge. I should have sent out the fucking invitations. I should have been here ...

I stopped in the doorway, took a couple of deep breaths to quell the panic, and looked around for a drink. There was abundant squash.

'Hi, Helen,' said Richard, squeezing past me with a large pile of paper plates that he dumped into the bin. 'Want a cup of tea or something?'

'That would be lovely. It's okay, I can help myself. I think I know where everything is.'

He gave me a warning glance. *Not now*, it said.

Ben ran up and hugged me. Oh Christ, I needed a drink, I needed tranquilisers, I needed my children and my husband and my life back, not this distorted picture, this bad dream, another mother in my place.

'Hello darling.' I kissed the top of his head. 'Want to see what I've got for you?'

'Yeah!' He dragged me to the car, passing my parents in the hall. Even they had got here before me. Did Richard deliberately tell me to be late? Trying to make me look bad? Trying to minimise the amount of time we were under the same roof? My mother quickly looked away. My father ignored me completely.

'Here we are!' My voice was high and hysterical as I pulled the huge plastic bag from the back seat. 'Hope you like it!' Ben snatched it and tore the paper off, revealing the massive box of Lego.

'Got it already,' he said.

'Oh.'

He put it back in the car. 'Doesn't matter,' he said, and ran off to join his friends. I felt as if I had swallowed a fistful of laxatives after all, and had to run to the upstairs bathroom. Glyn was standing in the living room, drinking from a bottle of beer. He smiled and raised it to me as I hurried past.

Locked in the bathroom I could smell alcohol seeping out of my pores, the stench of desperation. There was cologne in the cupboard; at least she hadn't moved that. I doused myself and returned to the fray.

'Helen! How are you?' Glyn was his usual cheerful rotund self; he did not look like a man whose wife has walked out on him.

'I'm fine,' I lied. My guts, so suddenly emptied, hurt like hell, and I still felt panicky. I found my eyes straying to his bottle of beer, the condensation sparkling on the glass, so refreshing ... 'And you?'

'Never better.' He bent his knees, an annoying gesture of self-confidence like a comedy copper. 'Never better.' Did this mean that his life seemed fresh and new since he ditched his wife? Or ... could it mean ...

'Annette looks well,' I said. 'I just saw her in the kitchen cooking about a thousand sausage rolls.'

'You know Netty. Never happier than when she's feeding the five thousand.'

He doesn't know.

'How is her cooking these days?'

'Excellent.' He patted his large, solid stomach. 'Probably too good, in fact.'

She hasn't left him. It was a lie.

'Oh, that's nice,' I tried to think of the next question. 'Have you been on holiday?'

'This is like being at the barber's,' he said, and laughed at his own wit. 'Well, we all piled down to Devon, you know about that. Shame you couldn't join us.'

'Ah, yes.' *He was there.* 'I'm sorry about that, but you know ... Work.'

'You don't have to tell me.' Glyn likes us to believe that he's the hardest-working man in the land. 'How's it going, the great project?' He enclosed the last two words in finger quotes.

'Not too bad. I'll be glad when it's over though.' I looked round the room, wondering how many people knew what was going on. 'Get back to normal. Be a full-time mum again.'

'We don't mind having your two around. They're no trouble.' Either Glyn is the best actor in the world, or Richard had misrepresented the situation.

'Daddy! Daddy!' Poppy came storming into the room; like her parents, she's built along spherical lines. They bounced off each other and wrestled. This looked like happy families to me.

Richard was standing in the doorway. He could hardly run away, not in front of all these witnesses.

'So, Richard.'

'Helen.'

'This is nice.'

'Yes.'

'I know this isn't the time or the place,' I said, in a conversational party tone, 'but I think you should know something, in the interests of honesty and fair play. I am no longer seeing Harry Ross.' This wasn't strictly true, but it soon would be. 'What happened between us was a mistake.'

'I don't think we can ...'

'A big mistake, I grant you.'

Richard said nothing.

'I wonder if we can?' I said.

'What?'

'Start again.' He looked out of the window. 'Together,' I added, in case he thought I was offering him freedom.

'Look, Helen, you're right. This isn't the time or the place.'

'Can we schedule something?' I tried not to sound sarcastic, but it was hard.

'We'll talk,' he said, and went about his hostly duties. It felt like I'd caught him out. I experienced a flush of exultation, quickly doused when I ran into my parents. They were trying to leave.

'Oh, hi!' I said, casual, but delighted. 'How are you?'

'Your mother's got a headache. We're just off.'

'That's not actually true, is it?'

'I beg your pardon?'

'Look, it won't kill you to talk to me. Nobody's going to tell your solicitor.'

'That's not funny, Helen.'

'Sorry, no, it's not, is it. Unlike your lawyer's letter, which was an absolute hoot.'

'Come along, David.'

'Before you rush off,' I said, 'I think you should know that I've taken legal advice of my own.' Another lie, but what's the difference? 'And I'm afraid you don't have a leg to stand on. I can publish pretty much what I like.'

'No you can't.'

'But in the interests of family harmony, I'd be more than happy to discuss your concerns.'

'There's nothing to discuss,' said my father, his lips so pale they disappeared.

'As far as you're concerned, Dad, there never is. Easier to pay a lawyer to do it for you, right? But I think for once in our lives we need to sit down as a family and work things out.'

'Is that what you've done with Richard?' said my mother.

'That's a bit below the belt, Ma.'

'Well, I mean ...'

'Because as I'm sure you know, Richard and I are having a few problems at the moment, which we're trying to resolve. Don't look so crestfallen. I might begin to think that you want my marriage to break up.'

'Don't be silly.'

'I might even suspect that you'd been stirring the pot.' They tried to get past me, but could not do so without making an exhibition of themselves. 'What are you so frightened of?'

'We're not frightened,' said my white-faced father. Was he sweating? 'Don't be so stupid.'

'When did you find out?'

My mother's eyes flew wide, and she barked, 'What?'

'About Edward and Billy?'

They froze for a moment, then my mother said, 'Oh Helen, I wish you'd keep your nose out of other people's business. You always have to pry.'

'Thanks, Mum.'

'You think you know all about us, don't you? But you have no idea.' Her voice was getting louder, and people were glancing at us. She checked herself. 'Everything's very simple in your world – black and white, good and bad, right and wrong.'

Under the circumstances, I could hardly agree.

'But real life's not like that, Helen. Real life is ... ' She racked her brains for the right word. 'Real life is dirty.'

'Dirty? For God's sake, Mum, they were in love.'

'Oh Jesus Christ,' said my father, not caring how loud he spoke. 'You think that's what this is about? Love? You stupid, stupid girl.'

'David, no.' My mother was crying, and fumbled in her bag for a tissue.

'Look what you've done.' Dad's face was dark now; this was not good for him. 'Come on. We're leaving. And you, Helen ... You just keep away from us.'

They marched out of the house, leaving the front door open. In the living room, voices were raised in artificial jollity, masking the awful silence.

I waited until their car had pulled away, made small talk with a few friends, and then, when no one was looking, I slipped out without saying goodbye to my husband or children.

Back at Stonefield, I got pen and paper and sat at the dining room table with a large glass of white wine, the bottle recorked and back in the fridge so that I would have just the one. After what I'd been through, I needed it.

I drew two lines down the page, creating three columns. At the top of them I wrote *Richard – Mum and Dad – Harry*.

Under 'Richard' I wrote the following.

Is he telling me the truth about Annette?
Are they lovers? If so, how serious?
Have they told Glyn? I don't think so.
What do the children know?
Does Richard want a divorce, or is this just revenge?
Why did Annette tell him about Harry? To get him for herself?

Does Richard believe me when I say I've finished with Harry? (Have I? See col. 3)
Would he consider taking me back?
What can I do to influence his decision?

Under 'Mum and Dad' I wrote:

If it's not Edward and Billy's affair that upsets them then WHAT?
What happened after Geraldine died?
Why did Dad fall out with Edward?
Why does Mum never talk about her childhood?
What were the circumstances of their courtship?
Why are they so unpleasant to me and their own grand-children?
Are they upset about the will? If so, why?
What does Valerie know?
What does Samuel know?

Finally, under 'Harry' I wrote:

Have I really finished with him?
If so, has he got the message?
Was he ever interested in me, or just the Barton estate and the money?
If Richard refuses to take me back, do I have a future with Harry?
Should I tell him about *The Happy Ending* or should I withdraw all permissions?
If I chuck him how will he react? Is he a threat?

Lists always make me feel better. In that far-off time when I was a wife and mother, I always started the day with a list – school activities, shopping, engineers to call, stuff to take out of the freezer and so on. Ticking things off meant that my life was progressing with a purpose, and I was not above writing something down that I had already done, just for the pleasure of ticking it off.

Now, if I could just get a few ticks on this list, all would be well. I stared at the paper, fantasising little red check marks against each item, and when everything was done I would be safe. Back home with Richard and the children – because that, above all, is what I want now. I would give up anything – the house, the money, the poisoned chalice of Edward's legacy – to be plain Mrs Richard Coleman again.

I linked my fingers, stretched my arms and cracked my knuckles. Every journey starts with the first step, and so on. I would call Valerie, and write to Samuel.

And I must call Harry, of course. I have to answer those questions.

Chapter Fifteen: The Happy Ending

(conclusion)

SEVEN YEARS CHANGES so much. In seven years my children grew up, and my marriage fell apart. After the birth of my son, my wife had no interest in resuming the relations that had led to his birth. We weren't unhappy, unlike so many of our friends who had blazing rows at cocktail parties. We lived serenely under one roof, we ate meals together, even went on holiday. I think we were good parents. Valerie and David wanted for nothing, went to excellent schools and had a stable home environment. Money kept rolling in from books and movies and clever investments. I had no need to work. Every so often my agent would invite me for lunch and after the usual chit chat would ask when he might expect a new novel. My answers grew ever more evasive, and after a while the lunches stopped. We both knew why. I had nothing left to write about.

I was not idle. After *The Interlude* was published, I rode the crest of popular success for three solid years. When the film was made, I involved myself in every aspect of production: script, casting, locations, shooting, turning up at studios in an advisory capacity, earning my credit as 'associate producer', for which I fought long and hard. Along the way I made friends with Laurence Olivier and our director Anthony Asquith; they were among the first to dine with us at Stonefield, a lavish pile I bought for cash. I was even 'spotted' out on the town with Jayne Mansfield, which led to a couple of gossipy paragraphs in the papers. She played her part, and I played mine, and by the time the film opened we were supposed to have had a mad affair just like the one in the story. Clever, and effective. The grosses were huge.

The truth was rather different. Miss Mansfield was, in private life, Mrs Miklós Hargitay, and the only romance that I enjoyed was not with the blonde star but with a young actor who played a minor role on screen and was valued by Asquith and many others for his off-screen discretion. He was handsome and co-operative and not averse to gifts.

When the film opened in America, I was obliged to travel to Los Angeles, New York and Chicago to attend premieres, talk to the press and sign books. Jayne Mansfield was my entrée to the American market, and thanks to her I made a very great deal of money, for which I will always be grateful. It was not possible to fly my actor friend across the Atlantic, but his place was quickly taken by others. Nature abhors a vacuum.

I often wondered if Billy might be in the audience, if his silhouette might loom over me as it had done before, 'Good evening Mr Barton', the accent perhaps Americanised by now, and we would be friends again. It never happened. I might have passed him on the street and not known. He could be living on the next block. I didn't even know if he was in the country. I called information on both coasts, asking after a William Moody or a William Hamilton, but none of them was Billy.

And so, in time, I forgot him. Time and money and other bodies wore away the traces he had left, until there was nothing, just the vague sense of something missing, as elusive as a dream that dissolves on waking – and that was all, gone as soon as it had come.

In 1963 I was invited to New York for a sort of literary jamboree, paid for by my American publishers, a week of events during which I would get up on my hind legs at various dinners and talk about how wonderful it was to have one's books made into films. I extended my stay by a fortnight on the pretext of researching a new book. The publishers hoped for something like *Breakfast at Tiffany's*, and coughed up for the accommodation. I had no intention of writing any such thing; the most anyone would get out of the trip was a 2,000 word feature for one of the Sunday papers about why I found New York so vulgar. But I appreciated their faith in me.

I arrived in New York not as I would have chosen, by boat – there is something about the melancholy of sea travel that will always appeal to me, and it has served me well. Instead I flew to America in a great white bird, circling Manhattan before coming into land at Idlewild. I wondered who was waiting for me on that island of spikes and ravines, what faces, what bodies.

But of course it was Billy that was waiting for me at journey's end, Billy that I'd crossed the ocean to find.

He could hardly fail to notice that I was in town; I was famous enough by now to get my picture in the papers, and there was still some mileage in the Jayne Mansfield connection – she was back in the headlines for baring her breasts on screen in a desperate attempt to revive her flagging career. One was accustomed by now to being asked about her; people liked the idea of the egghead writer and the blonde bombshell, and I benefited from Arthur Miller's leavings. I was even on television – *The Tonight Show*, which secured my place on Olympus. I was not exactly mobbed in the street, but I was not short of company. I was careful, picking my playmates from within the entertainment industry, which assured a certain amount of discretion. There were restaurants and clubs in New York where one could dine *à deux* without raising eyebrows.

I was staying in an apartment on Fifth Avenue, one of those places with a liveried doorman and an extensive awning; it belonged to someone very important in the New York publishing world, I never found out who. It afforded me spectacular views and total privacy.

This time Billy didn't have to stand in line to meet me. I was coming out of a bookstore one evening, and had just shaken off the last of the fans before walking uptown to meet the companion *du jour* at a cocktail bar, when a long black limousine glided alongside me, coming to a halt a few yards ahead. The door opened. I wondered for a moment if I was being kidnapped; one heard of such things. 'Get in, Teddy.'

I stooped down and looked into the back of the car and there he was, Billy Hamilton himself, beautifully dressed in a dark blue suit, his black shoes as shiny as mirrors.

'Good God.'

'Not quite. Just me. Are you getting in or not?'

'I have a date.'

'Yeah. With me. Get in and shut the door.' I did as I was told. 'Fifth Avenue, isn't it?'

I answered like an automaton. 'Yes.' The car slid up the road, the chauffeur silent and uniformed.

There was enough room in the back for us to face each other without touching. The interior was lined with cream leather and polished walnut. There was an ashtray in the armrest. I'd lived in places smaller than this car – a bedsit in the Uxbridge Road, for instance, where two young men had drunk red wine and made love while Sibelius played on a borrowed gramophone.

'You look prosperous, Billy.'

He patted his gut, which was as flat as ever. 'You mean fat?'

'No.' I gestured around. 'All this. The limousine.'

'Can't complain.' He felt the material of his lapel with forefinger and thumb. 'All paid for too.'

'Good for you.'

'I saw you on the telly.'

'Indeed.'

'Big star now.'

'I suppose.'

'Easy to find.'

'Apparently.'

We turned into Fifth Avenue. Six blocks to go. Would he state his business? He kept looking at me, smiling an enigmatic smile. 'I suppose you live in New York now, Billy? Or are you just visiting?'

'We have a place here.'

'Do we indeed?'

Five blocks to go.

'Rosemary's in school here.'

'She must be quite grown up now.'

'Fifteen.'

'Good lord.'

Four blocks.

'I try to spend a good deal of time here too.'

'Right.'

'When I'm not in LA.'

'Of course.'

'She comes home for vacations.'

'How nice.'

'Yeah.'

Three blocks. What did he want?

'And your two, Ted. How are they?'

'Both well, thank you. Valerie's sixteen. Quite a young lady. David's ten.'

Billy whistled. 'Ten!' He scratched his chin. 'He's growing up fast. Bet he's a good-looking lad.'

'I suppose so.'

'Like his dad.'

Two blocks. He put his hand on the armrest.

'Ted.'

'Yes?'

'I'm sorry we lost touch.'

'Well ... You made yourself quite clear ...'

'Oh, that.' His hand crossed the divide, came towards me. 'I was angry. That was a bad time for me.'

'Yes.'

'I'm sorry.'

'That's quite all right.'

One block.

'All forgiven?'

'There's nothing to forgive, Billy. I never had anything but the fondest thoughts of you.'

'Really?'

'Of course. You know that.'

The limousine was slowing down, pulling in, the doorman stepping forward expectantly.

'Good.' Billy adjusted his tie in the dark glass of the partition, reached across and opened my door. 'Come on, then.'

'You're coming up?'

'You don't think I'm letting you go now that I've gone to all the trouble of finding you, do you? Of course I'm bloody coming up.'

'What about your wife?'

Billy stepped into the carpeted lobby, approving the potted palms, the gilt fittings. 'Laura's dead,' he said, in a light, conversational tone, as if he was saying 'Laura's fine'.

'What? Dead?'

'She died a long time ago, Ted. Cancer.'

'I'm sorry.'

'Don't be. I'm not.'

So that was where the money came from. Billy had inherited the lot – daughter and all.

We stepped into the elevator, and Billy shut the gates with a clang. 'What floor?'

'Top.'

'Good.'

We shot skywards, and long before we reached the first floor we were locked in a passionate embrace.

How can I describe my experience of Billy without descending into pornography or cliché? 'We were locked in a passionate embrace' is bad enough. I have no wish to describe the mechanics of who did what to whom; I am of the wrong generation, class and nationality for this. I can use four-letter words, have done in this very manuscript to describe our couplings – but not to describe the emotions that I felt in that apartment high above Fifth Avenue, reunited for the first time in seven years with the man whom I loved above all others. I felt lost, and I felt found. I wanted to live like this forever, and I wanted us both to die. I wanted to tear his throat out, to plunge my hand through his stomach and up to the heart, and yet I would have killed anyone who harmed a hair on his head. The little chip of ice that pierced my heart so long ago suddenly melted, and I was swept away, washed clean in a hot salty tide. It sounds so crass, so smutty when I try to write it down. But for those moments when I was with Billy, nothing else mattered. The world had constricted to one room, one bed, two bodies that had no limits of 'him' and 'me'. We knew each other so well, and neither had forgotten a thing – knew exactly how to please the other, and in doing so please ourselves. There was no giving and taking, just sharing, just being.

Enough. I verge on the Lawrentian, which will never do.

At the climax, I felt that I had achieved some kind of unbreakable psychic union with Billy, something far beyond the mere action of tissue upon tissue. We had reached Nirvana, and we would never leave it. We would be together forever.

I was so wrong, and so right.

Afterwards, we lay as we always had, smoking. The bed was big enough for four, and there was no need to entwine ourselves, but habits formed in a creaky single bed were hard to break. We were older now, both of us in our forties, and although Billy had lines on his face, less hair on his head and more on his chest, to me he was more beautiful than ever.

It was dark outside, but the light and noise from the street still found its way up.

'A lot to catch up on,' I said, stroking his hair.

'Yeah.' He blew smoke out through his nose. 'Suppose so.'

'What do you do for a living, for instance?'

Billy wriggled against me; even at our advanced age, we'd soon be ready for Round Two. 'This and that. Managing investments, playing the markets.'

'Acting?'

'Nah, fuck that for a game of soldiers.' His accent had not crossed the Atlantic. 'What's the point? I hate the movie business.'

'Right.'

'No offence.'

'None taken, I assure you.'

'Laura left me very well off.'

'So I see.'

'Me and Rosie.'

'Ah. Rosie.'

I remembered London, and the bitter things he said.

'I never forgot you, Ted,' he said. 'It was always you.'

'Ah.' I was crying, I wasn't quite sure why – I suppose because I'd waited to hear these words for so long.

'It wasn't easy for me.'

'I know.'

'I mean ... with a bloke. With you.'

'I understand.'

'Don't suppose it was easy for you either.'

'I never had a moment's doubt, Billy.'

'Right.' He turned over and kissed me on the lips. 'You're still married though.'

'Yes. I am.'

'Funny world, isn't it?' He kissed me again, harder this time, and his hand went down between my legs. 'Wow. Ever-Ready Teddy.' He grabbed my wrists, pinned them above my head in one huge hand and spun me over.

I am spinning still.

The days we spent together in New York City were very happy. Cloudless, I might say. We did all the things that lovers do – we walked in Central Park, we took the Staten Island Ferry, we had cocktails in the Rainbow Room and we saw the show at Radio City. We ate hot dogs from street vendors, and we ate steaks in the best restaurants. I took Billy to literary parties, and he behaved impeccably, charming the wives, telling tall tales about our shared *vie de bohème*, when we were actors in wartime, me with my polio, he with his smashed leg, always ending with the punchline 'and then the bastard stole the girl I was going to marry'. He loved the limelight, and I gave him every opportunity to shine.

We visited Rosemary – Rosie, as he called her – at her expensive private school in Connecticut; she was a quiet, thoughtful girl with little of her mother about her. Beautiful, in an unresolved way – she could be plain in later life, but for now she had the sheen of youth. She blossomed in her father's presence, took his arm and wouldn't let go, kissed him and fiddled with his hair, his tie. We went for lunch in a nice restaurant, and went sailing, and by the end of the weekend she was calling me Uncle Ted.

Sometimes we went to the theatre; most of the managements were happy to give me complimentary tickets. More often, we ate early, strolled through the twinkling Manhattan streets and then home, saying goodnight to the doorman before taking the elevator to our penthouse paradise. I paid for everything; it never occurred to me to do otherwise. Perhaps this should have made me suspicious, but I was in love. I could not spend enough on him. I would have given him the moon.

The days flew past. I could not envisage our parting. When I thought about the future, I saw only a grey haze, like an untuned television screen. Of the last seven years, I pieced together a narrative from hints and fragments. When we parted in London he'd given up all hope of coming to America to start a new life with his wife and daughter; Laura did not reply to his frantic letters, and eventually her father informed him that divorce proceedings would soon commence. Billy sank into depression, living with his mother, picking up what work he could, drinking too much and watching my star rise with a mixture of fury and pride. Nothing came from California: no divorce papers to sign. And then one day, quite out of the blue, a phone call from Laura herself, telling him that she had breast cancer and maybe a year to live. There was a ticket in his name at Thomas Cook.

When Billy arrived in Los Angeles his wife was a living skeleton attended by an army of nurses, unable to leave her bed. Lawyers hovered, imploring her to sign the papers that would effect her final separation from Billy, but it was never the right time; even at the end of her life, she defied her father. Marrying Billy was the one thing that she had done for herself, proof that Laura, the pampered daughter of the Hollywood millionaire, had made one little stab at independence. Divorcing Billy would have been a final defeat. 'She told me,' said Billy, 'that the only thing that made it worth staying alive was seeing how pissed off the old man was.'

'She must have loved you still,' I said, thinking it highly unlikely; from the little I knew of Laura, she was not the romantic type.

'I think she did,' said Billy, who was keen on adoration.

And so, with his wife safely under ground and her fortune in his name, Billy and his daughter relocated to the East Coast. His friends were hard drinkers with bachelor apartments and independent wealth; I don't think any of them had to get up for work in the morning. We met them in bars on the upper West Side, smart places where sharp-suited men and elegant women performed elaborate courtship rituals, and drank like fish. There was much back slapping and obscene banter, much competition to settle the bar tab at the end of the night. Billy filled me in on who'd fucked whom, who was broke, who was a drunk. It was an unpleasant world, superficial and bitchy, and when I said as much to Billy he merely laughed and said in that case he'd be careful not to take me to any of his downtown haunts.

We never went to his place, an apartment on 18th Street that he shared with 'a couple of other guys'; it was one thing to parade his famous English friend around the bars, but quite another to have him hanging around the apartment. Needless to say his roommates 'don't know about me' and he was in no hurry to enlighten them. If his in-laws found out about the other side of his nature, Rosie would be taken away from him. It seemed like a legitimate fear, and I didn't press matters. Anyway, who needed a bachelor pad on 18th Street when we had a Fifth Avenue penthouse? We had a huge bed, a ridiculously luxurious bathroom with a shower so hot and powerful it made me laugh every time I got in it, deep carpets on every floor. For two people trying to cram a lifetime's love into two short weeks, it was a very convenient accommodation.

Two days before I was due to fly home I had a meeting with an advertising agency that was offering me a very large amount of money to endorse a certain brand of whisky; all I would have to do is be photographed 'looking English' and provide a specimen of my signature which would be appended to a laudatory statement about this excellent distillation. The sum in question was more than even I could reasonably hope to be paid for a new novel. I left Billy to his own devices for the day, and reported to the offices, eager to sign my soul away. In my mind I had already spent the money. I would return to New York in a couple of months, take an apartment of my own and then, perhaps, we would travel to the coast, to Connecticut, Massachusetts, Maine. Perhaps I'd have to write a few more books to pay for it all. On the way home from the photo shoot, I was already sketching out plots in my mind.

A young black man accosted me outside the apartment block on Fifth Avenue. He was smartly dressed, his hair carefully brushed into a side parting; I recognised him as one of Billy's West Side drinking buddies.

'Mr Barton?' he said.

'Yes.' I tried to remember his name, and drew a blank.

'I'm sorry to pounce on you in the street like this, but, you know ...' He cocked his head towards the liveried doorman, who was frowning.

'Oh, good heavens. This gentleman is a friend of mine,' I said. We entered the lobby.

'It's Samuel,' he said, shaking my hand. His cuffs were dazzling white, fastened with gold cufflinks in a Japanese design. Expensive.

'Samuel, of course.' What did he want? A handout? A little light blackmail? The doorman was still watching us. I did not wish to compromise my generous, unknown host.

'I'm sorry,' said Samuel, looking down at his shiny black shoes.

'That's quite all right.'

When he looked up again, his eyes were full of tears. 'It's Billy,' he said. 'He's had an accident.'

'Oh.' The shock was inside me, but still small and cold. 'How bad? Tell me straight away if he's dead.'

'He's not dead.'

'Thank God.'

'But it's bad. Very bad.' He brushed a fat tear away with the back of his hand. 'They don't think he's going to make it.'

I sat down in one of the leather armchairs that dotted the lobby. Samuel stood over me, anxious, solicitous.

'What happened?'

'He was crossing over Broadway. He was hit by a bus.'

'A bus?' My first image was of a red London double decker; this could not be right.

'Yeah. Turning the corner from 23rd Street. Didn't see him, I guess. Going too fast. I told him to take more care. Always looking for traffic coming from the wrong direction.'

'What's broken?'

'His leg.'

'Oh, his poor leg.' But that's all right, I thought. People don't die from broken legs. He got through worse at Tobruk. He's not going to be defeated by a bus.

'But there are internal injuries, the doctors say.'

'Oh.' I felt sick. 'What?'

'His ... ' Samuel gulped and gasped, a wheezing treble note. He took a moment to right himself. 'His liver, I think. The bus ... went over him.'

'I see.'

'He wants to see you.'

'He's conscious?'

'Yes. He wants you.'

'He asked you to come and get me?'

'Yes.'

And why were you by his bedside? Who are you to him, Samuel? 'Then we must go.' I marshalled what was left of my sangfroid, and asked the doorman to find us a cab.

Curtains were drawn around the hospital bed, and when we arrived a pretty young nurse told us that the doctors were just examining Mr Hamilton now, and we would have to wait for a few minutes. She would not tell us how Billy was, other than to say that he was 'stable'.

'Stable is good, right?' said Samuel, his hands clasped in front of him.

'The doctors are seeing him now, sir.'

'But he's out of danger?'

'They'll be able to tell you much more in a few minutes.'

I knew then that Billy was going to die.

We waited in the corridor like two expectant fathers. I tried to make conversation; anything, even the most banal chit chat, was better than the screaming silence.

'What do you do, Samuel?'

'I'm an actor.' It did not surprise me; he too could play his part, keeping the dialogue going. 'At least, when I'm working I'm an actor. It's not easy out there.' He nodded in a direction that I supposed indicated Broadway. 'There just ain't enough Lorraine Hansberry plays to go round.'

'Have you worked in films?'

'Yes, some. That's how I met Billy, out in Hollywood.'

'I see.'

'We worked on a couple of pictures together, before he gave it all up. Shame, really. He was pretty good. Could have made a go of it.'

'And now you've relocated to New York? I suppose that's where the theatre work is.'

'Well, yeah ...' He sounded undecided, and glanced at my face, trying to read the signs. 'Of course, if you're serious about it, this is where you need to be. The Great White Way.' He grimaced. 'With the emphasis on the white.'

'And how long have you been here?'

'A few years.'

You moved here with Billy.

'Perhaps you're one of the famous roommates one hears so much about.'

'Er ...'

I'd wrongfooted him. This was unkind. The nurse trotted into the corridor.

'You can go in and see him now,' she said. 'But I must warn you, he's been given sedatives to help with the pain. He might not make a lot of sense.'

'That's quite all right.' We followed her on to the ward; Samuel held the door for me, and I preceded him. He was, I guessed, about half my age, early twenties, a very handsome, very presentable young man. Struggling to find work, but wearing smart clothes and some fancy gold cufflinks. Someone's picking up the tab.

'Mr Hamilton?' The nurse bent over the bed, speaking softly and smoothing the covers with cool hands. 'You've got some visitors.'

'Samuel?'

'Don't try to sit up. They're right here.' She indicated a couple of chairs, and we sat.

'I'm here, Billy,' said Samuel, his eyes full of tears. He sat with his hands clamped between his knees, as if to stop himself from touching the body in the bed.

Billy's face was unmarked, apart from an abrasion on the left-hand side of his forehead, a few grains of dark dried blood clinging to the roots of his hair. The bedclothes were pulled up to his chest, held away from his body by a frame. His left arm lay outside the covers, a drip plumbed in at his elbow.

'Did you find him?'

'I found him, Billy. He's right here.'

Billy struggled to bring his other hand out from under the sheets, but the effort was too great. He licked his lips and squinted, as if a bright light was shining in his face. 'Ted?'

'Hello, Billy. What on earth have you been up to?'

He laughed through his nose, and there was a thin trickle of pink fluid from one nostril. The nurse wiped it away.

'Wasn't looking where I was going. Bloody stupid.' He sighed deeply. 'Big bus.'

'So I gather. That wasn't very clever, old man.'

'Wasn't very clever ...' He winced, and closed his eyes for a while, but the breathing was regular. 'Samuel.'

'Yes?'

'C'mere.'

Samuel bent over the bed, listening to whispered instructions. 'He wants to talk to you alone, Mr Barton,' he said. 'Nurse? Is that okay?'

'I'll be just outside,' she said. 'If you need me.'

She and Samuel slipped away.

'Ted.'

I pulled my chair closer to the bed, and found the outline of his hand under the sheets. 'What is it, Billy?'

'I've got to tell you something.'

'Go on.'

'Whatever happens ... to me, and in the future, right ...' He licked his lips again, and seemed to be in pain. His face was horribly pale, the skin damp and clammy. 'I've always loved you, Ted.'

I could say nothing.

'I've done some fucking stupid things in my life, I know it. I was always a wanker.'

'No you weren't.' I was angry with him for speaking ill of the nearly dead.

'It's okay. I just want you to know that it was always you, Teddy. From the very beginning. You believe me?'

'I believe you.' My chest was heaving.

'Whatever happened after that ... I know it was all a fucking mess. But it was always you.'

I took a deep breath and tried to slow my pulse, just as I used to before going on to a hostile audience of squaddies. 'The last two weeks have been the happiest time of my life,' I said. 'I love you, Billy.' My voice broke.

'I love you too, Ted. Always did. Believe me, don't you?'

'Yes.'

'It's important.'

'I believe you.'

'Sure?'

'Yes!'

He frowned again and turned his face away. The tendons of his neck were just as sculptural as ever. But below the chest? Under the sheets, beneath the frame? What was left?

'Billy.' He did not respond. 'Billy? Are you all right?'

I wasn't sure if he was conscious, and called the nurse. She waited for me to leave.

Billy died without recovering consciousness. I left Samuel weeping in the hospital, and walked back to Fifth Avenue where I drank the best part of a bottle of the whisky that I was advertising.

When I regained consciousness my clothes were in tatters all over the apartment, there was broken glass on the floor and vomit splashed around the bathroom. I had cut my feet and bled on the sheets and carpet. I felt excessively ill. I checked my watch; my plane was due to leave in approximately four hours. I phoned the airline and cancelled my flight.

I cleaned up the apartment as best I could; any damage I would pay for through my publishers. I packed a bag, tipped the doorman and took a taxi to a hotel in Chelsea. I did not tell anyone where I was, and I did not leave the room for the best part of a week. I can not describe the pain that I experienced, not because my literary powers fail me, but because to do so would bring it back. Four years later, I can't think of Billy's death with anything approaching equanimity. Part of me died with him.

After what seemed like months of drinking myself into oblivion every day, living in one New York hotel after another, each one cheaper and dirtier than the last, I realised that I must resume what was left of my life in England. There was nothing for me in America, just cheerless rented rooms, loveless commercial transactions and the clawing pain of loss. Without Samuel, who tracked me to each new temporary address, kept me out of trouble and forced me to communicate with my wife, I might have ended up drinking Thunderbird out of a brown paper bag with the rest of the bums on the Bowery. But Samuel picked me out of the gutter, cleaned me up when I'd puked on my shoes or soiled my pants, even frogmarched me to the barber's for a haircut and shave. When the time came to return to London, I took him with me; the thought of making an Atlantic crossing on my own filled me with panic.

Rosemary stayed at her private school in Connecticut, and went west during the vacations to live with her mother's family. Samuel and I returned to England by boat. I needed time in which to prepare myself, and a sea crossing affords a very agreeable period of suspension. I sat on the deck when possible, or in my cabin if it was wet, and thought about Billy, repeating to myself the last words he said to me.

I've always loved you.

It was always you.

Over and over again I heard those words, saw his pale face, felt the urgency in his voice. *You believe me? Sure? It's important. I've always loved you. Whatever happened, it was always you.*

He came to me in my dreams, repeating those words. I recalled details of those final weeks – the passion of our reunion, the simple equation of our happiness together – and everything fell into place. It was always us. Despite the times we lived in, the people that we were and the wide cold distances that came between us, it was always us.

When I arrived in Southampton, with Samuel two paces behind me carrying the suitcases, I believed that I could go on. I had loved, and been loved. Geraldine was there to meet me with the children, waving and smiling, and I went to them with a kind of exhausted relief. To the thousands of people at the docks that day, it was just another happy reunion. But if they saw joy on my face, if they sensed the bliss that comes at journey's end, it was because I had found a home for Billy in my heart.

And he has never left it.

Chapter Sixteen: Helen

'AND YOU DON'T think he ever intended to publish it?'

'I'm quite sure he didn't. I think he just wanted to write it down, maybe to persuade himself that he'd told the truth on some level, even if nobody read it in his lifetime.'

'Right.' Valerie nodded, a short, businesslike nod, and lit a cigarette. 'I know I shouldn't, but just recently I've had the urge again.' She inhaled, exhaled. 'Makes one feel like a teenager sneaking fags up on the playing fields.' We were sitting on the terrace at Stonefield, drinking coffee in the sunshine. 'Well, you'd better give me the headlines. Get me up to speed, as they say.'

'You probably know it already.'

'I've no doubt I do.' Laugh lines appeared round Val's eyes. 'And more.'

So I told her about the reunion in Liverpool, the affair conducted behind Geraldine's back, the French farce of their holiday and the subsequent bitter separation in Regent's Park. I told her about New York, the fairy tale fortnight high above Fifth Avenue, Billy's death and Edward's bittersweet return to England, with Billy in his heart – the 'happy ending' that enabled him to carry on for so many more years.

Valerie listened attentively, and did not interrupt.

'And that's about it,' I said. 'It's quite moving in its way.'

'I'm sure it is. Poor old Dad.'

'You don't sound very surprised.'

'Surprised? Good Lord, why should I be? You don't have to be Miss Marple to work that one out.'

'You knew about him and Billy?'

'I guessed for a long time, and then it was confirmed.'

'He told you?'

'Mum told me.'

'She found out?'

Valerie laughed. 'I'm sorry, dear, I shouldn't laugh, but you look so solemn and surprised. She knew before she married him.'

'Then why marry?'

'She didn't get such a bad bargain. He was a good father, there was plenty of money, and he never disgraced himself.'

'It sounds so businesslike.'

'Isn't that what marriage is? Not that I'd know, old spinster that I am. But it worked for a long time. That's more than can be said for a lot of marriages.'

'Yes.'

'Sorry darling. Me and my big mouth.'

I swallowed and coughed and said, 'Do you think I could have one of those cigarettes?'

'When did you say that piece was written?' said Val, lighting me. '1966?'

'Yes.'

'Hmm.' She seemed to be calculating. 'And there's nothing later than that date?'

'Just the diaries, which reveal nothing.'

'Right.' We smoked for a while in silence, watching birds hopping from bush to bush, and then she said 'Helen' in a slow, uncertain voice.

'Yes?'

'How much do you really want to know about your family history?'

'Everything.'

Finches and tits came and went. She took a final drag on her cigarette, extinguished it carefully and flicked the butt into a flower bed.

'There's something that nobody's ever told you.' She wasn't smiling any more.

'Oh? Another skeleton in the closet?'

'I'm not sure it's my secret to tell ... But I think you ought to know.'

'I've coped with the fact that my grandfathers were lovers.'

Valerie looked closely at me. 'Given everything else that's happened. I don't want to ...'

'What?'

'The thing is, Helen, I don't like secrets. I grew up surrounded by them, and I've seen what they do to people. They're like cancer.'

'Yes.' I thought of the horrible mess of my home life, the lies and deceptions that seemed so harmless to start with.

'I've been struggling with this ever since Dad died. Every day I've expected the phone to ring.'

'What do you mean?'

'I thought you'd have ... found out.'

'Well, haven't I?'

'You've found what he wanted you to find. All stage-managed, like everything else in his life. Lift the curtain and there it is, beautifully arranged and lit.'

'When you said you've been struggling ...'

'I've been trying to decide whether to let sleeping dogs lie.'

'I'd prefer the truth.'

'Whatever it is?'

'Of course. What's so awful?'

'Helen, when you rang me up last week you said you needed to ask me something. What was it?'

'About Mum and Dad.'

'Go on.'

'Will you tell me the truth?'

'Do you want me to?'

This was exasperating, and I showed it. 'Yes! For God's sake, Val, we're going round and round in circles. Can we just cut the crap?'

She looked angry for a moment – I saw the resemblance to my father – but then her shoulders relaxed, and the grim line of her mouth softened. 'I think I need a drink, darling. Would that be awful? A large G&T? I feel as if I'm about to do something stupid.'

'I need one too.'

Minutes later, we were sipping our gins, for all the world like two provincial ladies discussing flower arrangements.

'Fire away then, before I lose my nerve.'

'All right.' I had my list of questions in my hand. 'Why does Mum never talk about her childhood?'

'Because she had a bloody miserable childhood. Her mother was a bitch – sorry. That's your grandmother I'm talking about.'

'It's okay. I never met her.'

'The only love that Rosemary ever got before was from Billy. She absolutely adored him. Well, we all did. He was just ... ' Val sighed. 'So alive. So much fun. Everyone else seemed as if they were half asleep. He was wide awake, in full colour. Oh yes. Billy.' She wiped her eye. 'You couldn't help loving him.'

'Edward certainly couldn't.'

Valerie opened her mouth to say something, but thought better of it. 'Next question.'

'Okay. How did my parents meet? Tell me about their courtship.'

'It was love at first sight, I can tell you that for sure because I was there. What the French call a *coup de foudre*. I've never seen it before or since.'

The gin was starting to affect me now, and I felt a great upsurge of affection for the young lovers my parents had once been.

'Rosemary came into her own money when she was 21, and the first thing she did was clear out of California, where she'd been living with some hideous aunts, and go to New York City. The place where she'd been happy, the place where she had friends. All those nice girls from nice families that she went to school with. So she got herself an apartment in Greenwich Village, which was quite daring of her, with another girl to share, and enrolled at Columbia to study ... Oh, what was it? Law? Something like that.'

'You're joking.'

'No, darling. She never finished it. Trouble is, she had all that money, she didn't need to work. And then, like many an American heiress before her, she wanted to see Europe.'

'Very Henry James.'

Valerie took a big gulp of gin. 'So she came to England, and the first person she looked up was Uncle Edward. Dad was absolutely delighted. He threw a big luncheon party to welcome her – tables out here on the terrace, it was a lovely day in May, all the best linen and silverware, flowers everywhere, Samuel worked his socks off for days as you can imagine.'

'Of course.'

'I'd long since left home by then, I was living in London and working in a rather dreary secretarial job with vague thoughts of marrying the boss.' She laughed through her nose, and poked a slice of lemon with her finger. 'Not that that came to much. Anyway I was always glad of an invitation, and I was quite intrigued to meet this American girl that I'd heard so much about. You see, Billy had acquired a sort of mythical status in our family; Dad was always reminiscing about him, their time in America and so on, and naturally I'd heard a good deal about Rosemary. She was such a young *lady*. So well educated, such lovely manners, so intelligent. I was half prepared to hate her, but you just couldn't. Oh, she was lovely, your mum. She walked through those doors, arm in arm with Dad, wearing a very simple cotton print dress, green with a little pattern of daisies on it, white shoes, everything clean and fresh. I felt like a terrible frump in my velvet trousers and one of those ghastly embroidered tops one used to wear. She just looked ... gorgeous.'

'Hard to believe.'

'She stood there taking it all in, the garden, the table laid for lunch, the flowers and all these people standing up to shake her hand, and then she saw David. He was sitting in a chair just staring at her, and I don't think he could actually get up, poor thing. Poleaxed. Mouth open. Love hearts in his eyes, bluebirds tweeting around his head. Dad said something like "where are your manners, David?", and I giggled, and I remember Mum giving me a very sharp look. I thought nothing of it at the time, but ...'

'What?'

Val collected her thoughts. 'From that moment on, there was nobody else in the picture, just Rosemary and David. They could not take their eyes off each other. Rosemary was very polite, and she tried to pay attention to what was being said, but she kept straying back to David. As for him – well, I'd never seen him like that before. He was my kid brother. I still thought of him as a bit of an oik. Suddenly he'd been transformed into Sir Lancelot. I must have said something to Mum when we were clearing away, like "I think David's rather smitten", and she absolutely bit my head off.'

'Weird.'

'I was used to that sort of thing, though. My mother never thought much of me. David was the apple of her eye. I thought, "Serves you right, another woman's come along and she's going to steal your darling boy away." Rotten, wasn't I?'

'I don't think so.'

'Anyway, that wasn't it.'

'Sorry?'

'You see ... ' Again, the arrested word. 'They became inseparable. I thought it was very sweet – they were like children who just delight in each other's company. They went everywhere together – David showed her around London, they had days out in the country in Dad's car, picnics, all that sort of thing. Terribly romantic.'

'They were in love.'

'And how! Dad was delighted. He thought it was a perfect match, uniting his son with Billy's daughter. I expect he had all sorts of wildly symbolic ideas about it. He did everything he could to encourage the match. My mother, on the other hand, was dead against it.'

'Why?'

'We couldn't understand it. David was terribly upset because she'd fly into rages with him for no apparent reason. I thought it was the menopause, she was the right age. But the more serious the affair became, the worse she got. I'd hardly ever seen my mother angry before – she was quite a placid woman by nature. Then suddenly she went off the rails. Poor Dad – he thought she'd gone quite mad.'

'Billy, I suppose.'

'Yes.'

'Because she knew about Edward and Billy?'

'You'd understand it, wouldn't you, if she never wanted to have anything to do with Billy or his family ever again?'

'Quite.'

'But there was rather more to it than that, as it turned out. And this is where my job gets so difficult.'

A brisk wind blew across the garden, sending the birds flying up from the branches. I shivered. 'Shall we go inside?'

'No. Don't stop me now, or I'll never tell you. Buggeration, I've finished my drink.'

'I'll get you a ...'

'Sit down!' She sounded at the end of her tether. 'I'll have a fag, that'll have to do. I've got to tell you this, Helen. It's not right that you don't know.'

The bushes were moving around in the wind as if a large, blundering animal was about to break into the garden.

'You're frightening me,' I said, trying to put a little laugh into my voice.

'Of course nothing my mother said could stop them. Nothing like a little parental opposition to drive young people together. I don't know quite what happened, whether my father confronted her or whether she just gave up trying, but the wedding went ahead, of course, and it was a lovely day. My mother played her part, there was no unpleasantness, and Dad was smiling like the Cheshire cat. A few months later, you came along, darling.'

'Ta-dah.' My voice sounded flat and dismal.

'My mother was never the same afterwards. She was often depressed. A lot of women get like that in middle age; I've had my moments, to be honest. But with her it was different. She was withdrawn and miserable. She lost weight. I don't suppose you'd remember ...'

'Not really. She was always just an old lady to me.'

'Nobody was surprised when she got cancer. She was, to coin a phrase, riddled with it.'

'I'm sorry.'

'The last couple of years of her life weren't much fun. We did what we could, but ... Well, that's an old story. She was only 64 when she died.'

Valerie smoked in silence. This could not be the end of the story. Where was the punchline? The key to the riddle?

'What's left on your little list, darling?'

'What happened after Geraldine died? Why did Dad fall out with Edward? Why are Mum and Dad so unpleasant to me?'

'You haven't guessed?'

'No.'

'Oh dear. Then I shall have to spit it out.'

I was going to say 'I wish you would,' but suddenly I wished she wouldn't. I was shivering, and it wasn't just the cool air; I was afraid. My shoulders shuddered as if someone had passed behind me; I looked round, expecting to see ... who? A ghost? Harry? Samuel?

'I told you I didn't always get on very well with my mother, but towards the end we were forced into a sort of understanding. I looked after her. Dad hated hospitals, and David and Rosemary were so busy with you – so of course it fell to the spinster daughter to pick up the pieces. I didn't mind. I have a very strong sense of duty, as you have probably guessed by now. As she became more and more helpless, she softened towards me. In the last months of her life, we had the best part of our relationship.'

'That must be some comfort.'

'Yes and no, darling. You see, she told me things.'

'Ah.'

'A lot about her childhood, her parents and so on. How she met my father, and why they married. She confirmed everything that I'd guessed about him, so it didn't come as too much of a surprise. She was quite relieved to tell someone at last. All those years she'd been married to a gay man, and I don't suppose she'd mentioned it to a soul, just kept up appearances as women did in those days. I took it rather well, even if I do say so myself, and she was pleased about that. So she must have decided that she could tell me anything. She wanted to unburden herself, that's what she said. She didn't feel she could go to the grave with this big secret.'

'Right.' I swallowed hard, and took another of Val's cigarettes.

'I wish to God she had. Why did she feel the need to let the cat out of the bag? Nobody would have been any the wiser. But no, she had to open Pandora's Box, didn't she? I'm getting muddled now, Dad would have said, "You're mixing your metaphors, Valerie".'

'And what was in there?'

'Sure you want to know?'

'I am going to scream in a minute.'

'She told me that David was Billy's child.'

'Oh, well that isn't such a ...' I was going to say 'surprise'. And of course it wasn't really a surprise; it was so obvious. What I hadn't anticipated, in my glib acceptance of adultery, were the implications of that simple fact.

'So, of course,' said Valerie, 'David and Rosemary ... your parents ...'

'Are brother and sister.'

'Half brother and sister, if that's any consolation. But yes. That's about the size of it.'

'And I ... I am the product of incest.'

'That sounds awfully melodramatic, darling.' She reached out to touch my arm, and that's when the scream finally came. 'Don't touch me!' I jumped to my feet, pushing the white metal chair over; it clanged and clattered on the flagstones. 'Don't ...'

I ran into the house, up to the very top, to the room where Edward Barton's hateful boxes were neatly piled, concealing within them the poisonous secret of my parentage. I stood in the doorway, my hands grasping the hair on either side of my head, and listened to myself screaming.

I spent an hour kicking the skirting board, saying 'shit' and then saying 'shit' even louder as some new refinement of horror occurred to my whirring mind. *My parents are siblings ... They found out after I was born ... That's why they stopped speaking to Edward ... That's why they're so weird to me and the children ... That's why they freaked out the moment I mentioned a book about Edward's life ... That's why they would do anything to stop me. They were trying to protect me from the truth.*

Eventually I calmed down enough to splash cold water on my face, blow my nose and descend on shaky legs to the living room, where Valerie was sitting in an armchair, her knees together, her hands folded in her lap. She started when she saw me, and looked guilty.

'I'm all right, Valerie. I'm sorry. I just ...' I waved my hand towards the upper floors.

'I shouldn't have told you.'

'I suppose it's certain, is it?'

'What, that Billy was David's father? I think so. There's never been a DNA test or anything like that.'

'Then he could be Edward's son. Geraldine might have been wrong.'

'Sit down, dear.' I sat. 'You never knew Billy. He was dead long before you were thought of. If you had, you'd see that it's true. He's in your father just as surely as he's in your mother.'

'You mean he looks like him?' I found it hard to reconcile what I'd heard of my grandfather – my double grandfather, as he now seemed to be – with the drab, uptight figure of my father.

'He did when he was younger. He had his colouring, his mannerisms. He was a very good-looking boy, your father. After all this happened, he changed. He faded. I saw less of Billy in him, more of our mother, as if he was trying to push the reality away.'

'You could be imagining it.'

'Helen, I don't think my mother was just causing mischief. She was quite sane, even at the end. She told me that it started in France, that Billy had been pestering her for weeks, ever since he came to my christening, and finally, when he got her alone in Nice she just couldn't hold out any more. She'd never stopped loving him; at least, she'd never stopped desiring him. It must have been very hard to say no to Billy. My father never could.'

'So he was screwing both of them? Edward and Geraldine?'

'Exactly. It must have been just like a Feydeau farce, hopping in and out of hotel rooms and beds and cupboards and so on. Don't forget, my parents were sleeping together as well.'

'Edward mentioned how desirable Geraldine had become. How keen she was.'

'Suddenly she had two men after her, and she just stopped resisting. Everybody had the best of both worlds, and they all thought they were keeping their secrets. But Geraldine made a big mistake – if it was a mistake, I'm not sure. She didn't use protection with Billy. She threw caution to the wind.'

'And with Edward?'

'She was careful with him. He had condoms, and when she remembered she slipped in her diaphragm. You can imagine how delighted I was to hear all these details from my own mother. Me, the dried-up old spinster.'

'So that's why she thinks David is Billy's.'

'I'm afraid there's really very little doubt about it.'

'And how did David find out?'

Valerie brushed ash from her skirt. 'I told him.'

'You ... what?'

'We were having a horrible argument. Mum was in her final days, she was slipping in and out of consciousness, and David was never there. He was avoiding the issue. So I got upset, and I had it out with him, I said he was irresponsible, he was a coward, all of that. And this secret was getting bigger and bigger inside me, like a tumour, I couldn't stand it any more. David said something stupid – "I don't notice Father exactly making much of an effort", or something like that. And I just snapped. I said, "Don't use him as an excuse, he's not even your father". Just madness, but I couldn't stop myself. When I realised what I had done he was staring at me, his face absolutely grey, and I thought he was going to have a heart attack.'

'Did he believe you?'

'Not at first. But then he wouldn't let it drop. He kept asking me and asking me and it all came out. I told him everything my mother told me. Then he ran off to the toilet and he was sick.'

'I'm not surprised.'

'And that, I'm afraid, is why this family has never really got on.'

'That's the understatement of the century.'

'I probably shouldn't have told you. I should have taken my mother's secret to the grave. But I can't bear seeing what's happening to you and David and Rosemary, hating each other, growing further apart every day. It's time everyone faced facts.'

'That's your opinion, is it?' My voice was cold, and I could not look at her, this woman I barely knew who had just smashed my world into pieces with her blundering good intentions. 'That's your pop psychology, let's all accept the truth and have a big group hug and move on. Closure. I love you Mom, I love you Dad, you guys are the greatest even if you are brother and sister. Roll credits.'

'Helen, please.'

I stopped myself from talking because I was getting hysterical. We sat in the quiet room for a while, feeling the past beating on our faces.

'Did Edward know?'

'I don't think he did. My mother says she never told him. Your parents certainly never discussed it with him. He was very fond of you when you were little, whereas Geraldine ... She could barely touch you.'

'I don't remember that.'

'I'm glad. Dad put it down to depression and illness. He persuaded himself that my mother was mentally ill; that was his saving lie. Perhaps he had his suspicions, but in the end he smothered them under layer upon layer of fiction.'

'He believed that Billy truly loved him.'

'And he believed that his wife was mad. And that way, he could remain quite happy in his own little universe where there was no one to challenge him. He was happy, don't you think?'

'Very.'

'Yes. In the end, it was fiction that saved Edward Barton.'

'He had his happy ending. But look at the mess he's left for the rest of us.'

Valerie sighed, and got up. 'The question is, are you going to clear it up?'

'I don't know if I can.' I felt very weak and tired, and desperately wanted to sleep. 'But I'll try.'

'Good girl,' said Valerie, as if I'd just taken some nasty medicine.

She left soon after that, driving away in her sensible little Peugeot, back to her sensible little life, glowing with the satisfaction of a job well done. She had told the truth and shamed the devil, and she must have believed, in that ordered mind of hers, that we could all move on. Yes, darling, you're the child of incest, your father married his sister, plenty of people know but they were far too nice to mention it, and then Billy, he who planted the bad seed, made sure that Edward would never suspect the truth by wrapping him in a cocoon of sentimental lies. For that's what it seemed to be now, Edward's 'happy ending' – the last attempt of a dying man to blind him to the truth. And before that? Before the bus hit? Those last two heavenly weeks in Manhattan, late-flowering love amid the hot dog stands of Central Park? Was that part of the same strategy?

A nasty little voice in my head said, 'No, stupid. It was all about money.'

Billy had worked his way through his dead wife's legacy, he couldn't touch the money that was in trust for Rosemary, and so he latched himself on to the only rich person he knew, Edward Barton, celebrity novelist and closet homosexual. A man he knew had always been in love with him, who would turn a blind eye to the most outrageous betrayals – like fucking his wife on holiday, while the child played nearby – and would pay for everything without question.

That was his plan, until a bus came along and changed it. And then, as he lay dying, all Billy could think about was covering his tracks. Blind the old fool with sentiment and he will never notice that the child he's raising as his own is the spitting image of its father.

And it worked. So well, in fact, that brother and sister married in all innocence, and had a child. Who knew what genetic time bombs they'd passed on to me – and, through me, to my children? Ben might start sprouting breasts at the age of twelve, like the pharaohs.

What should I do? Take them for tests? 'Oh hello doctor, I have reason to believe that my parents were related – well, brother and sister actually – so could you just cast your eye over my kids in case they're freaks?'

I was alone in the empty house with nobody to talk to. Valerie didn't stick around to pick up the pieces; she dropped her dirty bomb and fled. Was it conscience that prompted her, or malice? Did she hate David and Rosemary so much for stealing her parents' affection that she was visiting her revenge on the next generations? Was she even now cackling as she drove her Noddy car down the motorway?

The hopelessness of my situation crushed me. I'd ruined my marriage, smashed my family into pieces, and landed myself in shit of the worst kind. If only I could turn back time – forget Edward Barton, forget Harry Ross, become once again Mrs Helen Coleman. Hand back the inheritance – financial, literary, genetic, the lot – and be a wife and mother.

Just as I was steeling myself to pick up the phone and call Richard, and start what I hoped would be our journey to reconciliation, it rang.

Happy coincidence, I thought for a second – he's thinking of me too, we're both ready to put all this behind us.

But the name on the screen was not 'Richard' or 'Home'.

The name on the screen was 'Harry'.

Chapter Seventeen: Helen

I HAVE BECOME A calculating bitch, weighing up the pros and cons, assessing probabilities, spreading my bets like the most heartless banker. When did this reptilian part of my brain kick into action? Was it when I started cheating on my husband, or when I realised I was losing my children? Was it always there, part of my inheritance?

The moment I saw Harry's name on my telephone, I switched from 'poor little me, how can I save my marriage?' to 'right, let's find out if there's a viable Plan B'. Because if Richard and I get divorced and I am left with nothing but Stonefield and access visits, I need to consider my options.

'Hi, Harry.' Light and cool.

'Hey, Helen.' Strike One! I could never accept a Plan B that says 'Hey' as a form of greeting. 'How's it going?'

Assuming that 'it' was the great work, I said, 'Oh, it's at a very interesting stage. You know how you were always telling us that our characters should surprise us?' This was one of Harry's favourite creative writing clichés.

'Yeah.' He used his wise voice. 'Great.'

'Well, they've certainly been surprising me. The things they get up to behind one's back! Honestly!'

'That's exciting, Helen.'

Harry is not a great one for stating his business on the telephone. I let him stew for a bit. 'So, yeah,' he said after an awkward pause – I'd missed my cue, and he was prompting me – 'just wondering if you'd heard anything from the Barton estate.'

'I am the Barton estate, Harry.'

'Sure, sure.' An annoying calming tone in his voice, to be used with hysterical females. 'I mean, there's a lot of interest out there in this project ...'

'Is there? From whom?'

'And I really need to know that you're on side.'

On side? This man teaches writing for a living. Not a very good living, admittedly. 'Harry,' I said, 'there's something I have to tell you.'

'The thing is, I'm having lunch with this producer next week – well, she's going to be at a lunchtime thing that I'm going to, and ...'

'I'm getting a divorce.'

'You ... what?'

'My husband's having an affair with my best friend. How's that for a twist in the tale?'

'I don't ... I mean, I'm really sorry, but ...'

'So I wondered if you'd like to come round and talk about ...' Pause for effect. 'Us.' Just the sort of dialogue he'd put a red line through in his class. Romantic cliché! 'Harry? Are you there?'

'Sure, sure, I'd love to see you. The thing is, we've got to get all next year's course materials in by the beginning of next week, and I'm really behind.'

'Oh, I'm sorry. I had no idea you were so busy.'

'Hey, I'm not too busy for you, babe.'

'And what with your important lunch and stuff, I quite understand. Well,' I said, sounding cheery, 'just call me when you have a moment. If, that is, you're serious about me.' Pause; nothing. 'You are serious about me, aren't you Harry? I mean, this wasn't just a way of getting your hands on ... No. Of course it wasn't. Unworthy of me. Bye for now!'

'Helen ...'

I felt a moment's pang – the sudden memory of his hairy thighs, the muscles undulating on his back as he lay on top of me, the sensation of falling and floating and fullness – and it was over. The call was terminated, the window on my telephone blank. The thing that had given shape and purpose to my life for the last year had gone. Whatever the pains of withdrawal, I was glad to be clean.

I wanted desperately to speak to Richard, but I did not trust myself; I'd get upset, and we'd argue. So instead I did something I have not done for months – years, probably.

I took pen and paper, and I wrote a letter. *Dear Richard*, I wrote, *this is the hardest thing I have ever had to do*.

No: that sounded like I was begging. But that was exactly what I was doing, wasn't it? Begging for another chance. For forgiveness. I started again.

Dear Richard,

I'm sorry we didn't have a chance to talk properly at Ben's party, because there's so much I need to say. You and the children are the most important things in my life, the only important things, and I would do anything to save our marriage. I know I've made terrible mistakes – I was stupid and selfish and I let things get out of control. Nothing can undo the past or wipe out the pain I've caused you.

I had an affair with Harry Ross for ten months, and now it is over. It ended badly, as I always knew it would. I can't explain what made me do it. I can't excuse it as a moment of madness because that's not the kind of person I am. I think it was a mixture of selfishness, boredom and greed. Not very attractive qualities, are they, in a wife and mother?

I don't know how far things have gone between you and Annette, and for all I know I might be wasting my time. If you truly intend to start a new life with Annette, then I won't make any trouble. We'll work something out.

But if there's any chance that you haven't made your final decision, then I will fight with everything I've got to get you back. Please, Richard, give me that chance. I love you and the children more than my own life. When I started this letter I didn't want to sound as if I was begging but why beat about the bush? I am.

Please let me know what you think.

Helen

I read it over, walked away from the table, had a drink and a smoke (curse Valerie for introducing that to my repertoire), read it again and was satisfied. Not the most elegant thing I've ever written. Nothing interesting about the narrative voice, no twists in the tale. But it had the virtue of directness, and so I put it in an envelope, stuck on a first class stamp and walked down to the village to post it.

Samuel responded to my letter very cautiously. I invited him to lunch at Stonefield, but he was reluctant to accept – he hadn't been well, didn't feel he could make the journey and so on. I said I would visit him – he's living in Richmond now, in modest comfort, I imagine – but he didn't jump at that either. So I said I'd take him to the restaurant of his choice, all expenses paid by the Barton estate. This he could not politely decline.

Now that he is no longer a servant, Samuel is more of a puzzle than ever. He must be in his sixties, but his skin is smooth and he has a full head of hair, somewhat grizzled. There is no sign of a paunch, and he dresses in an ageless uniform of jeans and a shirt – just fitted enough to suggest a modicum of vanity about his figure. I arrived at the restaurant early, and had time to observe Samuel as he handed his jacket to the waiter and made his way to join me. It was a large, airy room with a glass roof, potted palms and a lot of rattan furniture; this, combined with a 'contemporary Asian' menu, gave an air of the dear old Raj. I stood, and we shook hands. He wore one thick gold band on his wedding finger that I did not remember seeing before.

'Thanks for coming,' I said. 'Would you like a drink?'

'Oh no, just coffee and water for me.'

On the defensive already? 'Good idea. Bit early in the day, isn't it?' This from a woman who's practically been putting gin on her cornflakes. We talked about my journey, the restaurant, the weather and so on, ordered food. I had about an hour to get what I wanted. We were in public – clever Samuel! – so we'd have to be discreet, but I'd commandeered a corner table well screened by foliage. If he bolted, he'd either smash through plate glass or blunder into an indoor jungle.

'Well,' I said, when my travel details ceased to fascinate, 'I've found some amazing material among Edward's papers.'

He scrutinised his squid, as if it might still be alive, and said nothing.

'Including a manuscript that he wrote in 1966.'

Further examination of tentacle.

'It's all about his time in New York.' No response. 'With Billy.'

'Mmm-hmm.'

'And you.'

'Ah.'

'Did you ever read it? It's called *The Happy Ending*.'

'I don't remember it.'

'I wondered whether Edward had asked you to put it up in the attic for him.'

'I was up and down that ladder a million times. I have no idea.'

'He didn't talk about trying to publish it? About being advised by his agent not to?'

Samuel shook his head, chewed thoughtfully, swallowed and smiled. 'You might not understand the nature of my relationship with Edward.'

'Why don't you enlighten me?'

He put his fork down and sipped his water. 'I was an employee,' he said at last.

'Of course. But you were also a companion and a carer.'

He thought this over. 'I suppose so.'

'And a secretary.'

'Mmm-hmm.'

'So surely you must have known ...'

'I did not read that manuscript,' he said, like an American president denying a scandal.

'Good. In that case you can verify certain things for me.'

'I doubt that.'

Was it my imagination, or did his eyes dart around, looking for an escape route? Better cut to the chase. 'Tell me about Billy. I never knew him.'

'What do you want to know?'

'He was my grandfather.' And how. 'I'd like to learn a bit more about him.'

'There's not much to tell ...'

'You lived with him in New York, I take it.'

'I ...'

'Didn't you? You were his "roommate"?'

Samuel gave a guarded, 'Yes'.

'You followed him from Los Angeles.'

'Mmm-hmm.'

'In what capacity?'

'I don't know quite what you're ...' He pushed his plate away, a few tentacles unchewed.

'I assume that you were lovers.'

'Ah.' Samuel sat back in his chair and folded his arms across his chest. 'I see.'

'I can't imagine why else you would move in with him.'

'I don't suppose you can.'

'None of my business, obviously. I'm only the poor granddaughter who inherited the estate.'

He nodded. 'Yes, you're that all right.'

Time for the knockout blow; any minute now waiters would be dishing up main courses, and I thought Samuel quite capable of terminally changing the subject.

'But am I, though?'

'Are you what?'

'Edward's granddaughter?' Our eyes met, and he did not look away. 'Or not,' I added.

He picked his outsize white linen napkin from his lap and carefully dabbed his lips. 'You know?'

'I do.'

'Who told you?'

'Valerie. Although if I had any kind of a brain I'd have guessed for myself.'

'Valerie. That figures.'

'You're not going to deny it, then.'

'It happened long before I came along.'

'You knew, though.'

'Oh, sure. I knew.'

I put down my knife and fork. 'Okay, Samuel. Let me make myself plain. We can sit here pussyfooting around, and I'll quite happily pay the bill and never bother you again. Alternatively, you can tell me what you know. It's entirely up to you.'

'That's true.'

'I'm sure you resent me for stealing your inheritance.'

'That's not true.'

His smooth, expressionless face was starting to irritate me. 'Have it your way. Let's sweep it all under the carpet, keep the closet door shut and pretend we're just two friends having lunch. I say, what a lovely ring you're wearing. Where did you get it – QVC? Or was it a gift from one of your many gentlemen friends?'

He took the ring off and placed it in the middle of the table. It sat there, fat and significant-looking.

'Billy gave it to me.'

'Ah.'

'In lieu of a wedding ring. He told me it belonged to his father.'

Now we were getting somewhere. 'I see.'

'I don't think you do, but never mind.' Plates were cleared, more food delivered. Samuel snatched up the ring and replaced it on his finger. For the rest of the meal he ate little, and turned the ring repeatedly, as if screwing the truth out of himself.

'I met Billy at a casting,' he said, looking over my shoulder at the comings and goings. 'I was young – I mean 18, really young. It was a bad movie about juvenile delinquents and I was up for the role of the black college kid who gets hassled by the bad guys. I had one line. "Hey, leave me alone, man!" Billy was trying to get supporting roles – he was up for a father or a neighbour or something. We got talking in the waiting room and after the audition we went for lunch down on Hollywood Boulevard. Well, neither of us got the job.'

'But you got something else, right?'

'He was living in a beautiful house up in Silver Lake at that time. I was amazed, not just because I was young and dumb but because I couldn't figure out why this guy who was living in a palace was trying out for bit parts in crummy movies. I mean, if he had that kind of money, right? But LA was full of things that didn't add up. Perhaps he was another one of those Walter Mitty types – borrowing a friend's house to impress the boys. You get a sense for these things when you're hustling for a living.'

'You were hustling?'

'I would have slapped your face if you said so at the time, but yeah, more of my income came from guys then ever came from acting jobs. I was cute, I was eager and there were plenty of men who wanted this sweet black ass.' He took a small forkful of chicken and watched my reaction.

'I'm sure it was a very popular ass.'

'You better believe it.' A sip of water, more dabbing of the lips. 'I thought Billy was just another trick – you know, a married man who likes to play. There were pictures of the wife and kid, and none of the usual gay stuff. No scatter cushions, no zebra-skin throws, no Judy Garland LPs or opera recordings. There were some weights out on the verandah, but that wasn't such a giveaway in those days.'

'What happened?'

'I was in no hurry to leave. I was living in a crappy little motel at the wrong end of Sunset, and I couldn't even afford that. I stayed for the weekend, still no sign of the wife or kid. We went driving in his car, we went out to bars, he paid for everything. And ... ' he whistled, and shook his hand, as if scorched, 'he was fun. Boy, was he fun.'

'So everyone says.'

'Yes indeed, your granddaddy was hot stuff.' He chuckled, and his eyes twinkled; the guard was finally down. 'I introduced Billy to a side of life that he'd never known before – the bars, the nightclubs, the gay party circuit. He was a big hit. And then, when the heat got too much in LA, we moved to New York.'

'What do you mean, the heat?'

'His father-in-law. Always making trouble. He contested the will to his dying day, you know. Spent more on lawyers than the whole of Billy's inheritance. Made trouble with the cops. Got to the point we couldn't step out of the house without getting a ticket for jaywalking. So we packed up and left.'

'And by that time you and Billy were ... serious?'

'As serious as we ever got. Neither of us was the faithful type. Never expected to settle down. Funny how things work out, isn't it?' He twisted the ring on his finger. 'He gave me this on the train, when we were finally getting out of LA for good. I told him I didn't want it, but he insisted.'

'You didn't wear it when I first met you.'

'Are you kidding? With Edward? He'd have cut my finger off to get it. No, this baby was well hid for a long time.'

'And what did you do in New York? What did you live on?'

'Good question. He got through his money so fast. I always told him to save a little, take the subway, cut down on clothes and limos, but he wouldn't hear of it. He wanted to live like a king. I picked up a few theatre jobs – it was easier on the East Coast, they weren't so scared of black faces – but he did nothing. Went drinking with his buddies. Screwed around.'

'Women?'

'Oh, no. His straight days were long gone by then.'

'So he was really gay?'

'Well, duh, I guess he might have been! Come on!'

'But Geraldine ... all the others.'

'Okay, he arrived a little late at the party. Billy was like a lot of guys back then, pretending he was straight. He didn't want to be queer. His Dad was gay, you know.'

'I guessed as much.'

'Billy hated camping and swishing. I had to watch myself with him. If he'd lived longer, he'd have been one of those butch queens with a big moustache and a Harley between his legs, fooling nobody.'

'Did Edward know this?'

'It suited Edward to go along with the masquerade. That generation ... ' He sighed. 'Well, it wasn't easy for any of us. Try being a gay black man in England in the 60s, baby.' He rolled his eyes. 'Kinda hard to explain.'

'Why did you come?'

'Follow the money, honey.' Samuel watched my reaction; if I'd shown any disapproval he would have clammed up again. But I nodded, and he went on. 'In the last months, Billy was broke. We were going to lose the apartment, everything. And then he heard that his old buddy Edward Barton was coming to town.'

'And the dollar signs appeared in his eyes.'

'Pretty much. I'd heard a lot about Billy's famous friend, and I never knew quite how much to believe. Billy said Edward was crazy about him, always had been, and all he had to do was make a move and' – he snapped his fingers – 'open sesame! And it worked! He borrowed the limo for the afternoon and put on a big show. Edward fell for it hook, line and sinker.'

'Did he know he was being taken for a ride?'

'Edward believed what he chose to believe. After a couple of weeks, I was getting seriously worried. It looked like I was out in the cold, and it was a long way down from our nice apartment to staying at the Y and peddling my ass for subway fare. We had some pretty nasty scenes.'

'And then all your problems were solved by a bus on Broadway.'

'I wouldn't put it quite like that, honey, but it sure simplified the picture. You won't believe me, but I was devastated when Billy died. I loved him.'

'I believe you.'

'But I had to think of myself as well.'

'So you moved in on Edward.'

'I made myself available, and he was grateful. I didn't force myself on him. He needed me.'

'Were you lovers?'

'Oh, girl, you and your lovers! Yes, there were a few nights when I comforted him in that way. Edward was grieving and drinking and that does not make for a hot time in the old town tonight. He appreciated the warmth of another body, but Edward's libido died with Billy.'

'But he brought you back to England.'

'A souvenir of New York.'

'What on earth did he tell his wife?'

Samuel laughed. 'A pile of horseshit.'

'And she believed it?'

'Baby, if there was one person in this world who was better at self-delusion than Edward Barton, it was Mrs Edward Barton. He told her that Billy was dead, and that I was a friend of Billy's who was coming to work as his secretary. And that was that, no further questions. She had her own interests.'

'And what were they?'

'The kids. Geraldine was a great homemaker. Good cook, loved the garden, got the house looking lovely. She had her friends and relations and her charity committees. She was busy, which is more than can be said for Edward. He spent a lot of time in his study, but there wasn't much to show for it. Obviously he did a bit of writing, but I never heard of any serious plans to publish again. There were little TV appearances and interviews, and he made a meal out of them. He read a lot. But really he just withdrew from the world. He was depressed for a long time, but he wouldn't admit it: that would have meant facing up to how he felt about Billy. I don't know what he was like before, but the Edward Barton I knew was a very detached kind of guy.'

'What about the children?'

'He liked being a father, it fitted in with his image of himself. He was no worse than most dads. I mean, my father ...' Samuel sighed. 'Anyway, the years rolled by. I had plenty to do – answering his correspondence, keeping his diary in order, dealing with the bank and so on. It was ridiculous him having a secretary really, he could have done it all himself, but he could afford me, and I was grateful.'

'Did you never get lonely?'

'I had a few *lovers*, as you would call them. And I had a nice home. I loved the kids too, you know. It was fun watching them grow up.' He put his knife and fork down. 'Until, of course ...'

'What?'

'You know.'

'David.'

'Yes.' He fiddled with his ring again. 'There came a point when it just couldn't be ignored any more. When he entered puberty, he started to look exactly like his father.'

'Was anything said?'

'Oh darling, you should know better than that! It was the elephant in the room, this mini-Billy in our midst and nobody saying a word. David didn't have a clue, and I guess Valerie was too young to figure it out ... But who knows with Valerie? A secretive little girl.'

'So they ignored it.'

'Not quite. You know who blew the whistle? Eleanora. Billy's mother.'

'They were still in touch?'

'Oh yeah. Geraldine didn't like it, but Eleanora used to come around quite a bit. First time I saw her, I thought she was a drag queen: she was in her seventies, showgirl make-up, huge red wig, the full works. She wangled an invitation to Sunday lunch, and she sat at the table chattering away like a parrot, all these far-fetched stories about her glorious theatrical career. The kids were sniggering behind her back. And then she said, clear as a bell, "Goodness gracious me, Geraldine, your son looks just like my poor Billy looked at his age!" I was clearing away some plates, but I stood out in the corridor listening to this deafening silence. Finally, after what seemed like ten minutes, Geraldine said something mean to Valerie, told her off for putting her elbows on the table or whatever, and then they all started talking at once. Later on, I saw Edward and Eleanora walking around the garden arm in arm, very slowly. And I just couldn't resist it.'

'What?'

'I eavesdropped. It was quite easy. There was an old potting shed in the garden in those days, and so I just snuck down there and waited. Eventually they sat on the bench against that big old copper beech.'

Samuel was enjoying himself. He took a sudden interest in his food, and made several appreciative remarks about the way the chicken had been marinated. He decided that he would have a drink after all, and after flirting with the waiter ordered nothing more than a glass of house white. He could see that I was burning with curiosity, and savoured it. 'I'll say one thing for the old woman,' he said at last, 'she had beautiful clear diction. A classical training, I guess. I heard every word.'

'And?'

'They were right in the middle of the big confession scene. Edward was mumbling away, every so often I heard the name "Billy", but you could piece it together from her responses. "Of course you did, darling, I always knew ... I understand. But he's gone, and nothing can bring him back. Those of us who loved him must keep his memory alive ... I'm so glad that you had some happiness before the end" and so on. Edward was finally telling someone how he really felt.'

'And did they discuss David?'

'They sure did. Edward just put his face in his hands and started sobbing. Oh God oh God, what have I done and so on. Of course it wasn't what *he'd* done that was the problem, was it? There was a lot of whispering which even I couldn't make out, and then I heard Eleanora give her big speech, as if she'd been rehearsing it for weeks. She said, "We all have a choice, Edward. We can make the best of things, or we can make the worst of things. I have always preferred the former. My marriage was not exactly a bed of roses, as you know, but I learned very quickly to turn a blind eye to the less palatable truths and to carry on. I suggest you do the same." And that was that. They sat for a while, she was rubbing his back, and eventually they tottered back to the house. This time he was leaning on her.'

'So he knew.'

'He knew all right.'

'And when David met Rosemary ...'

'Edward turned a blind eye, just as he had been told to.'

'My God, Samuel, that's horrible.'

'I suppose so. But it would have taken a very brave man to break it up. And there was no proof.'

'Other than what the eye could see.'

'I suppose they trained themselves not to see it.'

'Geraldine objected to the marriage, though.'

'She made a few bitchy noises, and that's as far as it went. She never put her foot down because that would have meant giving a reason. As far as I'm aware, Edward and Geraldine never had that conversation.'

'So they allowed my parents to get married and have me and they never said a word?'

'Pretty, isn't it.'

'And you, Samuel? Why didn't you say something?'

'Because I didn't want to get the sack.' He put his knife and fork down. 'Nobody comes out of this smelling of roses, Helen. The whole thing was rotten. But so many families are, aren't they? You peek behind the curtains and ... well, there you go. I can't say I feel better for getting it off my chest. I'd like to forget about it now.'

'Thank you, Samuel.'

'For nothing.'

'You've helped me realise something.'

'And what's that? Men were deceivers ever?'

'I've realised that throughout the whole of this story, nobody ever gave a thought to the welfare of the children. They took them for granted, as if they were just inconvenient by-products of their own all-important affairs. They made decisions without giving a second's thought to their responsibilities as parents, and even when disaster was staring them in the face all they could think about was themselves.'

'That's about it.' Samuel looked ashamed.

I signalled for the bill.

'Don't mind me,' I said. 'I'm just talking to myself.'

Chapter Eighteen: Helen

WHEN I WAS SIX years old, we went on a family holiday to Malta. One afternoon I was swimming in what was meant to be a safe three feet of water when suddenly, from around the headland, came a freakish wave that knocked me off my feet, turned me over, bashed and scraped me and filled my hair with grit and sucked me out into the open Mediterranean. I was saved by a nearby youth and handed back to my white-faced parents, shaken and grazed but otherwise intact. But I have never forgotten the feeling of powerless and disorientation that came as water and sky changed places, as bubbles and sand swirled past my open eyes. Who will pluck me out of danger now? Who will dry my tears?

I spend a lot of time staring at my lists. There are a few ticks and annotations, but they don't reassure me as they should. I've made progress, but in the wrong direction. Some of those questions would have been better left unasked. I drew thick black lines through the columns headed *Harry* and *Mum and Dad*. It is Richard I must focus on – Richard and the children. And even to one so wilfully blind as me, there is only one possible course of action.

I must face the music. I must see Richard and tell him the truth. If he's serious about Annette I will at least have the satisfaction of making a decent end of a bad beginning. If he has any kind of doubt about her, I'm in with a chance. After all, I am the children's mother – a fact that seems to have escaped me for the last year. Richard and I have loved each other truly and deeply for a long time.

The prospect of facing Richard, unshielded by lies, and of seeing my children, of returning to them as a penitent sinner, frightens me much as major surgery would frighten me.

So here we go. Pick up the phone, Helen. The game is on.

Everything at home was so normal – the sound of my key in the lock, which always sticks just a tiny bit so you have to wiggle and push slightly, I've done it so many times I never even think of it. The stains on the hall carpet, the scuff marks on the walls that always make me think in a dull automatic way 'we must get round to redecorating'. The smell of the air, the sound of traffic, the noisy freezer, the whoosh of the boiler, as familiar as my own face in the mirror but now strange, mutated, hostile.

Pull yourself together, Helen. This is not a nightmare. This is two adults, long married, who have hit a bad patch and are going to sort it out in a responsible way. This is not the final act of a drama, the denouement of an Edward Barton novel. This is not the Big Renunciation Scene. It's not the Happy Ending scene. No orchestra will play, no credits will roll, you will not snap the covers shut and put it back on the shelf. Life will go on, one way or another.

'Richard?'

'In here.'

The kitchen door opened. He was wearing an old brewer's apron of his father's, stained and faded from a thousand washes, and drying his hands on a tea towel – one from Ben's school, a few years old, printed with crude self-portraits of children and teachers.

He was halfway through washing up. The breakfast things but also, by the look of it, last night's dinner and possibly more.

He is not coping. He needs me.

'Kids out?' It was Saturday morning; I knew their routine. But were they with Annette?

'Yeah. Swimming and violin.' He looked at his watch; it was eleven. 'I'll have to go in an hour.'

Sixty minutes to save the world.

'It's okay. I can get them. You're busy.'

He put the wet tea towel over the radiator, untied his apron. 'That can wait.'

'Coffee?' I was already filling the kettle.

'Of course.'

The familiar rituals re-establishing themselves, like spring flowers pushing through bare earth after a long, hard winter.

Hope, in a hissing kettle and the smell of ground coffee.

'Well,' said Richard, sitting in his usual chair, 'here we are again.'

'Where's Annette?' It slipped out. Shit. Sounded bitchy.

'She's at home.'

'Right.'

The kettle boiled, clicked off. Steam filled the air, then cleared. We said nothing. I got up and made the coffee feeling very heavy and very old.

I filled the cafetière and placed it on the table between us. Cake. We should have cake. But I haven't been here to bake it, and it doesn't look as if Richard's had time. Annette? She's a great baker, but anything baked by her in my own kitchen would choke me.

'Richard ...' Where were those speeches I'd rehearsed in the car? My mind was blank, washed clean by thundering ocean waves.

'Yes?'

I wished he'd smile, or frown – anything to give me a clue. 'I'm so sorry.'

That was it, wasn't it? What I really wanted to say? What he needed to hear?

'Right.'

'I've made the worst mistake of my life and I'd do anything to take it back.'

'But you can't, can you?' He sighed, as tired as I was. 'You can't.'

Panic was starting to close my throat; it was going wrong. I stared at the coffee pot. A minute ago, it seemed to represent hope. I depressed the plunger, carefully, slowly, in control.

'No, you're right. I can't.'

We both stared at the same spot on the table, a pale mark where Lucy's experiments with a bottle of ink had been sanded away.

'Neither can I.'

I looked up, staring at his lowered eyelids. Please, Richard, see me now. Read my mind like you used to. Know that I love you.

His eyelids moved a little, up and down, undecided. And then they opened and his clear grey eyes met mine.

'Is it over, Helen?'

'Between me and Harry? Yes.'

'I mean ... all of it.'

'It's over. Everything is over.' And then it hit me like a truck, I gulped and swallowed. 'But not us, Richard.'

His face blurred and multiplied as my eyes filled with tears. *This could be the end.*

We said nothing.

And then: 'Is there anything you want to ask me?'

'Do I have the right?'

He almost smiled; oh God, one spark of light in the darkness. 'I think so.'

'There's so much I want to ask.' I started making a list in my head, bullet points forming in orderly lines. *Are you still seeing Annette? What do the children think? Are we getting divorced?*

'Fire away.'

'Is there any chance for us?'

He thought for a while before saying, 'I don't know, Helen. I don't know what's going to happen.'

No reaction shot, no theme tune, just two mugs of coffee, rapidly cooling.

'I can't take back the past, but I can promise you ...' God, this was so hollow. Promises? From me? What were they worth? As much as the steam rising from our coffee. 'That if you give me a chance ...' No, Helen, don't start crying now. Swallow it. Breathe. Complete the sentence. 'You'll never regret it.'

Richard tore a piece of kitchen roll from the wall-mounted dispenser, kept handy for the million spillages that happen in a family kitchen, and passed it to me.

'Helen.' He was looking at me, his expression inscrutable. My eyes were red, my nose running, my lips quivering. Not at my loveliest, but then again this man has seen me in childbirth.

'What?' I sounded like Lucy when she's about to be told off and is quite prepared to lie about everything.

'I have to tell you something.'

This is it. On this moment hinges my entire future.

'Annette and me ...'

'Yes?'

'I was wrong.'

What the bloody hell does that mean? You were wrong? Is it on or off? Tell me, deliver the blow, cut the cord.

'You ...'

'It's over between us.'

Us? Which us? Please God let it be them not us, her not me.

'I made a mistake.'

When I married a data analyst, I did at least hope that he'd be able to communicate clearly. Now I was stumbling in a fog of pronouns. My future depends on a point of syntax.

'Richard please!' I didn't expect my voice to sound so ragged. 'Tell me.'

He brushed a hand across his eyes, as if removing cobwebs. 'Me and Annette. We were stupid. It was just an idea that got out of control.'

'You mean you're not going to marry her?'

'No, Helen. I am most definitely not going to marry Annette. For one thing, she is married to Glyn.'

'Yes.'

'And for another thing, I am still married to you.' He touched the back of my hand. 'For better, for worse.'

I pulled his hand to my mouth and kissed it. And then I started crying so hard that I could not speak, the pain and sorrow of the last year leaving my body in spasms and salt water.

Acknowledgements

I would like to thank my agent, Sheila Crowley at Curtis Brown, and Claire Thompson and her team at Turnaround, for their support and faith in this book. The research phase encompassed too many titles to list here but I would like to make special mention of four particular books: Paul Cornwell's biography of Terence Gray, *Only by Failure* (Salt Books); *The Secret Lives of Somerset Maugham* by Selina Hastings (John Murray); Blake Bailey's biography of John Cheever, *Cheever: a Life* (Vintage); and Jane Sherman and Barton Mumaw's *Barton Mumaw, Dancer* (Wesleyan University Press).

Author Biography

Rupert Smith is the author of several novels including *Man's World*, which won him the Stonewall Writer of the Year Award and was shortlisted for the Green Carnation Award, and the acclaimed horror novel *Grim*. As James Lear, he has written a series of highly successful erotic novels including *The Back Passage*, *The Palace of Varieties* and *The Hardest Thing*.

A much-loved cultural commentator, he has written and spoken on everything from soaps to strippers, and was a journalist for over twenty years on the *Guardian*, *Radio Times* and many others. He is currently an agony uncle for *Metro* and has organised, presented and produced events celebrating LGBT history and culture all over the UK.

Rupert lives in London with his husband and their son.

BRITISH IMPERIAL POLICY AND
DECOLONIZATION, 1938–64

CAMBRIDGE COMMONWEALTH SERIES

Published by Macmillan in association with the Managers of the Cambridge University Smuts Memorial Fund for the Advancement of Commonwealth Studies
General Editors: E. T. Stokes (1972–81); D.A. Low (1983–   ), Both Smuts Professors of the History of the British Commonwealth, University of Cambridge

Series Standing Order

If you would like to receive future titles in this series as they are published, you can make use of our standing order facility. To place a standing order please contact your bookseller or, in case of difficulty, write to us at the address below with your name and address and the name of the series. Please state with which title you wish to begin your standing order. (If you live outside the UK we may not have the rights for your area, in which case we will forward your order to the publisher concerned.)

Standing Order Service, Macmillan Distribution Ltd, Houndmills, Basingstoke, Hampshire, RG21 2XS, England.